DRAGON MATES 2

THE FALK CLAN TALES BOOKS 5-7

C.D. GORRI

COPYRIGHT

Thank you for purchasing Dragon Mates 2.
This set features books 5-7 in my Falk Clan Tales.

Do you love complete series and anthologies?
Visit my website here for more boxed set and multi author
anthologies featuring me, C.D. Gorri, here!

A little intro to The Falk Clan Tales...

**After 500 years of servitude, these sexy Dragon males must find
and woo their modern mates. Read the Falk Clan Tales today and
discover unique Dragon Shifters and their journey to true love.**

This series began with four Falk brothers and their quests to
find their mates, but since its inception has evolved to include a
long lost brother, and a few other Dragons in need of true love!

Each of the Dragons in this series has a mark on his chest of his
rose. It is the magical link to his heart and his magic. A matching
gemstone goes with it and it can only be gifted to a true mate.

I hope you enjoy these fast paced, insta-love, happy ever after tales! Each one was written with a touch of humor and a pinch of sass.

Find out if they can keep the feisty females who steal their Dragons' hearts in the pages ahead.

Oh, and if you are interested in hearing about more, sign up for my newsletter here.

Happy reading!

Del mare alla stella,
C.D. Gorri

THE DRAGON'S TREASURE

A FALK CLAN TALE

C. D. GORRI

THE DRAGON'S TREASURE

A FALK CLAN TALE

THE DRAGON'S TREASURE
A FALK CLAN TALE

To Debbie Kummoung,
Thank you for entering my contest! Keep reading <3
Del mare all stella,
C.D. Gorri

BLURB

She doesn't believe in fairytales, until a Dragon comes knocking on her door.

Castor Falk escaped from the ruins of Castle Blackthorne on the Isle of Pain with one goal in mind, to find his half-brothers. If anyone deserved to hear tell of the end of Dragomir's reign of terror, it was them. Besides, what else did a dying Dragon have to do with the little time he had left?

Jozette Keeper was too old for story time. That didn't stop the curvy normal from indulging in the longtime tradition that filled the bookstore with local children every day at two o'clock. It was just something to pay the bills while she worked on her non-fiction book.

When a handsome stranger knocks on her door in the middle of the night, she finds herself in the middle of her very own fairytale. Is Jozette willing to take a leap of faith to save the dying Dragon at her door?

Castor needs help locating his brothers and winds up knocking on the door of the one person he never thought to find. His fated mate. Was Fate so cruel as to deliver his garnet rose, only to take her away again?

The Dragon must decide, either tell her who she is to him and bring her the pain of his imminent death, or simply fade away from memory.

PROLOGUE

"*The tyrant is dead!*"

"*FREEDOM!*"

"*Finally, we can leave this cursed rock!*"

Castor Falk tilted his head to better discern the voices coming from above. It had been three days of listening to the roars of the Dragons in the keep. The sounds of battle echoed down to the dungeons and rubble from the castle's falling walls fell in heaps through parts of the ceiling that had been weakened from the fight.

He was helpless to do naught but listen and smell the terror and chaos erupting above him. Castor struggled, but it was useless. He had been chained to the hard rock beneath Castle Blackthorne on the Isle of Pain for most of his adult life.

Chief Dragomir had been a most cruel and unjust tyrant. A right bastard of a Chief to one of the oldest Dragon Clans in the world. Weak and unjust, his claims on those who'd sworn fealty to the Blackthorne were by his blood alone. Yet, it seemed, that was not enough. The centuries had seen the number of Dragons in his thrall dwindle and lessen. Now it was clear they had finally had enough.

Castor snarled and roared. Anger coursed through him. He was forgotten! Doomed to die in the pit that bastard had thrown him in.

Before madness born of despair could take him in its icy grip, he pulled on his heavy bindings one last time. Still, it was no use. Castor could not break free. Darkness shrouded him and he cried out into the ether.

Weak from hunger and lack of sunlight, the Dragon Shifter roared his last ounce of hope that someone, anyone, would hear and come to the bowels of the keep.

Maybe to free him. Maybe to end his suffering. Either was welcome at this point.

"Is anyone down here?"

"Too much light," Castor gasped, blinking rapidly against the torches the men held.

"Look," one said, lowering his lantern. "It's the

slave I'd often heard that black-hearted tyrant speak of!"

"No! Can it be?"

Two young Dragon Shifters spoke mostly in English. A word or two was said in *Dracan*, the ancient language of their people. Castor understood some, but not all. His deliberate ignorance another one of Dragomir's punishments.

"What is your name?" one man asked.

Both wore robes splattered with all matter of blood and gore, reeking of the battle that had finally come to an end. As they came into view, hope welled up inside Castor. If they freed him, he could flee. Perhaps even find the half-brothers Dragomir had taunted him with so very often.

Using every bit of strength he had, he rose to his feet, squinting once more at the glare coming off their torches. He'd been in the darkness so very long. The two strangers waited, a good sign for sure.

"I am the son of Castor Falk and the Lady Igraine, named for my father. I have been chained here since my first shift, but it is true that I spent my life a prisoner to the tyrant Dragomir—"

.   .   .

His voice was gravelly with weariness and muted rage. The beast inside him too long stifled and forced into hibernation was only now poking its long serpentine snout into his mind's eye. Castor shuddered at the invasion, unused to it as he was.

Rrrrr.

"No longer, brother! Call me Nicholas," one of the two men said.

"Aye, and I am Devine. We shall release you from your chains if you swear not to harm us."

"Of course," Castor replied.

"There is no treasure left, for the rest of the Clan fought and divided the remnants. Running off with what they could before the rest of us could rally, but there is food and drink," Nicholas offered.

He was older with silver hair and shorter stature than Devine, though they had the same nose and chin. Castor could only imagine they were related.

"We are brothers," Nicholas said, guessing Castor's thoughts and hefting a large axe in his hands.

"Should we do this?" Devine asked.

"We know nothing of this beast. Perhaps he is chained for a reason."

The two men glanced at each other, then they

looked at Castor. He could understand their wariness. But he could not risk losing his chance for freedom.

"I swear I mean you no harm. If you free me, I only mean to leave this forsaken place and search for my kin."

"Alright." Nicholas nodded.

"We will free you, then. And perhaps later, you will repay the debt," Devine added with a grin.

Castor nodded. He might be a prisoner, but he was a Dragon of his word. He knew they were trusting him, a stranger who appeared like a common criminal. Dragons must be wary when dealing with each other. Though lies were easily discerned among their kind, Castor had not been in the company of others all that much.

He trusted they did not want to harm him. After all, it would be much easier to kill him chained then loose.

"You certain?" Devine asked his brother.

"Aye, none of us shall live or die under the poser Dragomir's rule any longer. Are you ready, Castor?"

He nodded at the two strange Dragons, trusting that when they raised their axes, they would not aim for his head.

"Release me from these bonds and you will have my thanks," he said.

"Good enough for me," Nicholas growled, and swung.

Castor braced himself as the first blow from the heavy axe came down on the metal chains that bound him. They took turns working in tandem to free him. It took dozens of whacks to break through the links twice tempered in Dragon fire.

"I doubt 'twas Dragomir's weak flame that made these," Devine men remarked.

"Definitely not," the other said, grunting as he continued his work.

"It was my own," Castor confessed.

"He forced my own flame against me before he made it impossible for me to shift."

"How have you survived?"

"Long periods of hibernation between bouts of neglect and torture. Dragomir used to parade his lovers down here to catch a glimpse of me," he added uncomfortably, but Castor figured he owed them the truth.

"Hold on a bit longer, lad," Nicholas grunted before returning to swing his axe on the chains.

Castor gritted his teeth against the pain that lanced through his body at each of their whacks.

Smoke poured from his nostrils as his inner beast began to wake, and that alone was a feat. It had been so long since his Dragon had truly been roused.

Used to the torture of his bindings, each strike brought a fresh wave of pain that only served to temper his determination. Castor would be freed. He would finally be able to leave this hellhole. He closed his eyes and waited until, finally; the chains began to loosen.

The rose over his chest, faint and wilted, seemed to burn as the last chain fell. And when the final link clanged on the cobblestone flooring, Castor joined it. Knees hit the hard floor as he clutched his chest.

"It burns," he growled as pain ripped through his body.

"Fuck! Is he alright?" Devine asked, backing away.

"I'm not sure," Nicholas said.

"Can you stand?"

"Nay, do not touch him," Devine yelled above the sudden wind whipping around inside the dungeon.

"Look, his skin glows with his beast!"

Castor heard his words, but his head was ringing, and with blurred vision and dry mouth he could neither speak nor pay attention. Something was happening inside of him. He felt his muscles stretch and bones snap.

Anger and rage clouded his mind, had him seeing red. But before he could explode in a rush of fury, that was replaced by relief. Joy shot through his blood.

CHAPTER I

Frrrreeeeeeeeeeeedddddoooooooommmm!

That part of him he'd been denied so long roared inside his mind's eye. Castor had been denied so much of what life really was to a Dragon Shifter. At first, Dragomir had granted him some freedoms. He was confined to his cell, but he was given books, paper, and coal to learn to read, write, and draw.

The second he'd begun to show signs of his beast, the ruthless and evil Chief had iron chains forged to hold him at bay. The stronger he became, the more chains were added. Only once in five centuries had Castor ever successfully shifted into his Dragon.

He'd never forgotten the feeling. And it was the same as he felt now. Older, angrier, but powerful and hungry. The great beast with his diamond shaped scales, dark blue and edged in red and purple, burst free from his mind and skin.

Those same scales seemed incandescent as he watched inside his mind's eye. Castor tossed his head from side to side, unsure of the terrible strength that seemed to fill him. The Dragon inside him charged forward, suffering from no such trepidation. The creature took shape inside his mind until it stretched outward, transforming his very person.

Castor struggled against the pain that filled him as he fought his shift. He was too weak, too far gone to hold the beast back. The shouts of the men who'd come to the dungeons and freed him reached his ears as if he were underwater.

"He's shifting, but fuck, what is he?"

"It is not right! Look how his scales glow blue and red both! Fucking hell. Back up, now!"

"Tis a Demon!"

"Worse. He is a Change dragon!"

"No, it can't be!"

"He should have been killed at birth."

"Death is his only future."

"Let us end him before he leaves," Devine snarled.

His voice was trembling with either fear or rage, Castor could not tell for certain. He was too busy trying to stem the pain coursing through him to give it much thought.

"Nay! We are not murderers. Pray he finds his kin, the Falk brothers, so they can end this blight on their names!"

Molten lava replaced his blood, or so it seemed. Was he dying? Castor sure felt like he was. As if he were being burned on the stake like the Witches of old in tales heard from the servants who sometimes came down to his cell.

And what of his brothers? Was it possible his kin, four half-brothers Dragomir had taunted him with, were alive? He'd heard the older two were warriors. The younger brothers had other talents. They worked with modern day computers and science. Things Castor had no inkling of other than the words.

Were they alive? He did not know, but had always dared to hope. It gave him solace in times when he was very low to think of them living outside of this terrible place?

An idea began to take shape in his mind even as he lay prone and huddled against the flames inside of him that were trying to burn him alive. The two Dragons bickered about what to do, but neither came any closer. Good. he would not like having to fight the men who freed him.

Maybe he could find them. Maybe his Dragon would know the way.

Without any other recourse, Castor stopped fighting his shift. He relinquished full control to his beast. His human side was far too weak to endure much longer. His Dragon trumpeted into the night air, opening his maw he sent a stream of blue and red flames shooting out into the sky.

Fuck! That felt good. He'd never had a chance to revel in his other form, and though weak and tired, he took stock of his new physique as he shed his human skin like water off a duck's back. Strong, leathery wings protruded from his back. His arms and legs were no more, having shifted into the thick, powerful quarters of his Dragon.

He was enormous, towering over the two males still in human form, but he paid them no mind. He was almost free of his torment. Castor growled and turned, using the spade at the end of his tail to bust through the brick and mortar of that terrible dungeon.

The icy air surrounding the Isle of Pain felt good along his fiery blue scales. He took in the raging sea with its ice floes and the wild storm brewing over the still burning castle. He needed to leave before his saviors turned enemy.

But Castor stood for a moment, looking out at the abyss that was the sky above him. He'd never flown before, had never had the chance. Would he freeze up there? Would he be lost?

Nay.

His Dragon seemed to reassure him, and Castor realized his fire would keep him warm from the inside out.

"He's leaving! This is our last chance to end the monster!"

The shouts of Devine reached his ears, but his beast merely turned using his tail to knock down the rest of the wall. He did not mean to harm the men, merely slow them down.

"We don't have to kill him. A ChangeDragon's fate is death! He will be gone sooner than he knows it," Nicholas shouted back to his brother.

Was Castor's Dragon really such a terrible thing? He wondered. Was he the demonic being that Dragomir had claimed? Born of the traitorous love affair between his parents. But if death was to be his fate, he wanted to at least see his brothers once in life.

Rooooaaaarrrr!

His Dragon spat fire into the night air once more, the beast none too thrilled with any talk of death.

But if those men were right, then he was dying. The pain he'd felt had surely been great. And if a *Change-Dragon's* fate was death, there really was nothing he could do.

Yes, there is, he thought. Castor had a journey to begin. A clear mission began to take shape in his Dragon's mind and heart. He had to find his kin, the four brothers Falk. He had to meet them, to let them know he existed, and to express how very sorry he was to be the cause of their misery for so very long.

He knew the tale from a servant, untainted by the evil Chief's lies. His mother was to be Dragomir's prize, but his father had fallen in love first. The two mated and wed in secret, and she was swollen with him by the time they were discovered.

Dragomir had taunted him with the way his father and mother's sins had caused not only his unfortunate birth and their immediate death. But also the imprisonment of his kin. The four brothers had suffered 500 years of servitude to that monster.

It was almost too terrible to think of. Just as terrible perhaps as 500 years of being chained to his dungeons. Sorrow and hope warred within Castor as he took to the white gray skies above the Isle of Pain.

Plumes of black smoke from the still burning

Castle Blackthorne filled the air, but Castor could only celebrate its demise. His beast roared, the sound splitting the sky like lightning.

The words of Nicholas and Devine, the Dragons who'd freed him, echoed in his mind. He might be a demon doomed to die, a *ChangeDragon* they'd said, but he was free.

Finally, I am free. And I will die free.

Pity he would never get the chance to live free. Castor did not know what good, if any, could come of his new and brief freedom. But maybe there was this one thing. Maybe he could find his brothers. And maybe, just maybe, they could offer him forgiveness before his death.

As if on cue, a sharp pain struck him over his chest, a sharp tug from beneath the symbol of his rose. Each Dragon had his own rose and Castor's was called his *garnet rose*. It was his Dragon's true and only treasure, or so one kind guard had told him when he was very young.

If his rose was burning so, he must be dying indeed. Accepting it was hard, but maybe once he found his kin, they could send him off to the next world with their blessings. He could not tell whether they would truly forgive him or not, he could only hope.

But how was he to find them? He flapped his great wings, battling against the stormy skies and searched his mind for any bit of information from the rare tomes Castor had read or anything he might have overheard during his imprisonment.

He recalled hearing of *bonds*, those ties that connected one Dragon to another. If that bond was strong, they could seek one another out over vast distances. If there was a blood tie, that created a particularly strong bond.

His brothers might not know of him, but he knew of them. The bond had been forged with his birth. So, he decided to take a chance and searched deep within himself. It seemed far easier now to do so, unencumbered by chains and the hate that smothered him in that dungeon.

No more of that, he told himself.

He had no time to revel in his newfound freedom. Time was too precious for such a selfish endeavor. Instead, Castor searched for that spark, that inkling that would lead him to his kin.

Castor took to the open skies, flying higher and higher, soaring with the wind instead of against it. Once he began to glide, Castor looked hard within his own mind's eye, searching that magical, metaphysical plane where he waited for his beast to swap scales for skin.

Then, as if on demand, he found it. In that mystical place, he found a faint glowing thread. Small and thin, but there. Could this really be it? The bond between him and his kin? Ignoring his physical pain and bone deep hunger, Castor dug deep inside himself for the answer.

Yes.

He roared his triumph, opening his Dragon's eyes and, like a homing pigeon, he set course for his final destination. His blood was being called from very far away. Without hesitation, Castor sped off in that direction.

I am coming, my brothers, and may the creator allow you to forgive my trespasses, he thought.

Castor Falk might be dying, but he would see them first. His brothers. The only beings he could lay claim to in the entire world.

Yes, he thought.

I will taste home and family before my end.

Rooooaaaarrrrr!

CHAPTER 2

Jozette opened the front door and stepped aside before the whirlwind that was her BFF could knock her on her ass. Again. Unfortunately, Marissa was not only strong for someone so petite. She was also as graceful as an elephant in a china shop most of the time.

"OMG, Jozette! Your parent's new house is so big! And right on the water!"

"Come on in," Jozette said.

She shook her head and closed the door while Marissa zipped from room to room like a fly on crack.

"*OHMYGAWD!* Look at that view! Super nice."

"Hmm?" Jozi turned toward the woman who had been her best friend since she was seven.

Marissa was pointing at the view of the intracoastal behind the house. That was the waterway that ran parallel to the ocean and stretched from Manasquan to Maccon City, Caster's Corner, and all the way down to Cape May.

It was pretty. She had to give her parents that. Even in winter. Jozette nodded as she padded across the kitchen floor to start a pot of tea.

"Yeah, it's great. Got the intracoastal right back there. Perfect place for me to sit and write," she replied.

"How is your *History of Maccon City* book coming, anyway?"

"Well, I mean it's odd really," she hesitated. "Do you know we have a history around here of strange sightings and unexplained phenomena? I'm fascinated, truly, but I just can't seem to narrow things down. I think maybe I should just scratch the whole thing—"

"No way! You always wanted to write, Jozi. But maybe it's the topic?"

Jozi shrugged, taking in her words. Marissa was not mean, just blunt. She sat down at the breakfast nook while Jozette grabbed the small wooden box holding a variety of teas and the honey from the shelf.

Every Saturday, like clockwork, no matter where Jozette was living at the time, the pair of them got together and shared a pot of tea. There was nothing better! Tea paired with whatever goodies Marissa had whipped up, and a good dose of honest conversation with someone Jozette respected and cared about.

"If only you were a man," Jozi murmured.

"You couldn't handle me," Marissa replied with a wink.

It was a running joke since college. Marissa had kissed a girl once. She liked it too. But alas, she was still attracted to men. Usually, men who started out okay. But somehow, they all seemed to turn into lazy asshats who wanted her to wait on them hand and foot while they complained about the size of her ass.

"We sure were smart kiddies starting this little tradition," Jozi remarked, as she gathered some napkins.

They had started this routine as kids after Jozette had a minor crisis over needing to wear reading glasses at the age of ten. At the time, getting glasses was devastating. She'd had several dozen pairs since, often losing or breaking them, until she eventually had corrective laser surgery.

"Okay, truth?" Marissa asked, choosing lavender

citrus tea to go with the almond biscotti she'd brought.

"Always," Jozette replied, choosing a plain English breakfast tea for herself.

"I think you should write whatever the fuck you want. Stories you want to read. Not some history your parents said would be a 'cute project' for you. *And*," Marissa continued.

She was not going to hold anything back. Going for broke, as always, Jozi figured.

"I think you need to start dating again, Jozi. Like now."

"What?" she asked, almost spilling the hot water onto her hand. "No way. It's too soon."

"No, it's not. It's been three months, almost four, since that loser dumped you and ran off with that exotic dancer he met in Manhattan."

"Must we go over that again?" Jozette moaned.

She lifted her steaming cup of tea. If anything could soothe her battered soul, it was this. Time with her bestie and some top notch noshing.

"These are really good," she said, crunching on another excellent cookie.

Jozette did not want to talk about her jerk of an ex. The truth was, her ego had been badly wounded by the awful cliché that was the way her last relationship had ended.

Heck.

Not only had that cheating moron kicked her out of their shared apartment, but now she was here! Living in her parents' new house, which they'd bought only six months after she'd officially moved all of her things out of her childhood home.

It was like they couldn't wait to get rid of any evidence they'd once had a child. Not the most loving of parents, Henry and Darla Keeper, were currently on an ornithology expedition in Europe.

"Thanks," Marissa replied. "Seriously, Jozi, why not go out on a date?"

"Um, my parents, for one," she replied.

Both retired Math teachers from the local high school and junior colleges respectively, they were also avid bird watchers. They'd gone on this extended trip for two reasons. One, because it was a good excuse to do something they both had in common. And two, to avoid having to live with their adult daughter.

"What do they have to do with this?"

"Marissa, do I even need to say it again? Mom and Dad are more than disappointed in me after this fiasco. If I date someone new, they will really freak out!"

This was just another one of a series of choices she'd made that they did not approve of. They blamed her for the failure of her relationship and her current living situation. Never considering her boyfriend had not only lost his job one month after she'd moved in, but he also cheated on her. According to them, that was her fault, too.

But that wasn't all. Jozette's desire to be a writer, and not a teacher, after she'd 'wasted time and their money' by getting her degree in English Literature was another point of contention between Jozi and her parents.

So, to hear them tell it, Jozette was a total failure who couldn't keep her man interested. They also acted as if it had been her plan all along to get thrown out of the apartment she'd shared with her ex and move back home.

How humiliating!

Her current temporary home might be a new house on the water with a dynamite view, but it would never be cozy and warm like Marissa's family's home. But hey, at least the water was always pretty to watch.

"I think it is safe to say I am not made for relationships," Jozette replied confidently.

"You don't need a relationship to have sex—"

"Mar! You know how I feel about that," she replied with a faux shocked expression.

Marissa could be bawdy as hell when she wanted to be. Sometimes it was for shock value. Other times, she didn't think the woman even realized it. Sex always was easy for her best friend, but for Jozette, not so much.

"Jozi, you're thirty-one years old. Sex is not taboo anymore. It's a part of life!"

"Easy for you to say. Look at you," she nodded at her stacked blonde hottie bestie.

Not that Jozette was a dog. But, reality check, thirty-one was looking a little plumper on her hips, and less chipper in the boob department than twenty-one. Of course, Marissa still looked toned as fuck.

Beyotch.

"Oh, shut up! Look, it's time to move on. You don't need to find Mr. Right to enjoy a little sucking and fucking," Marissa insisted.

"Ew, Mar. What next? Are you going to say the *m* word?" she asked, shivering noticeably.

There was nothing more disgusting than

listening to Marissa go into gory detail about sex. She'd heard it all over the years. The cum stains on her prom dress.

The bulging veins on the underside of her jock boyfriend's cock. How she thought spraying rosewater on her pussy made it more appealing.

Jozi could go on, but this particular trip down memory lane was too much for breakfast. Make that forever. She never, ever wanted to talk about these things. But did that stop Marissa? Nope.

"Yes, I am going to say it. When was the last time a man got you—"

Marissa's eyes glinted in the sunlight like gold coins as she slapped her hands on the table and leaned close to Jozi's face and yelled the word she had been dreading.

"Moist!" Marissa yelled, with a satisfied smile on her face.

"Ugh! Why? Why would you say that?"

CHAPTER 3

Utterly grossed out, Jozette got up and dumped the remnants of her tea down the drain, rinsing and washing the cup dutifully. Marissa was gasping for air and wiping her eyes because she was laughing so hard.

Super beyotch.

"Okay, okay. I am sorry for using the *m* word. Do you wanna talk about what happened with Larry? You never told me the whole story."

"I don't think so, Mar. I mean, it's not them. It's me!"

"Jozette! That is not true."

"Of course it is," she said, grabbing another biscotti.

She deserved it. *Heaven*, she thought, and moaned

around her mouthful of yummy goodness.

"These are really great, by the way," she mumbled, so as not to drop any.

"Thanks," Marissa replied, looking pleased with herself.

"So, me and Larry—"

"The unemployed loser who looked a little like Ernest Borgnine after he ate too much," Marissa chimed in unhelpfully.

"Anyway," Jozi said, rolling her eyes.

"*Larry* announced his leaving with a text that said, *'found someone else, get your things out by noon'.*"

"Oooh, ouch."

"Yes, ouch. Add that to the fact I've worked in the same bookstore since college, and had to return to my parents' house, it doesn't exactly amount to hey check me out I am quite the catch."

"Jozi—"

"No, no, look, I am being a realist here, Mar. I am not cut out for men or sex. I mean, men find me boring. Just look at me," she indicated her thermal Henley and baggy jeans.

"You could use new clothes," Marissa replied.

Her best friend's stylish apparel was always up to date and perfect whatever the occasion. She currently wore a pair of tailored brown pants with a sage colored blouse and an ivory scarf. Her blonde curls were piled on top of her head in a seemingly careless bun, but Jozi knew differently.

Her bestie had taken at least thirty minutes to create that just rolled off a hot guy look. Her sun kissed cheeks, despite the snow on the ground, and pouty pink lips were perfect as always. Marissa looked beautiful. And Jozette, well, she looked clean at least.

"I don't care about clothes, Mar. Besides, I am going to use this time while my parents are away to work on my book. I just can't seem to get anywhere with it."

"It has been years, you know. Maybe time to give up on the whole history thing—"

"OUCH! That hurts, you know," she grumbled.

"I'm sorry! Look, I just mean write something not so, you know, blah."

"Really?"

"If you can't get anywhere with it, maybe you should switch genres or something. Just cause your parents think nonfiction is the only thing worth writing—"

"I know, I know. I must have some serious writers' block or something," she said, frowning.

"I just want you to be happy, Jozi. I promise I

won't say another word about dating, okay? Come on, forgive me?"

"There is nothing to forgive. I'll figure it out," she murmured.

Marissa worried her lower lip, but Jozette stuck her tongue out and soon both women were smiling. She took another bite of biscotti, then cleared the table and refilled the electric kettle. Of course, she was not insulted. Marissa was like family, for Pete's sake.

Despite being friends, they were as opposite as any pair of women could be. Marissa was tiny and petite. Every man's dream of a woman with her size two waist, natural blonde hair, and an excellent job as a financial analyst for *Eat Well Live Proud*. The international company was renowned as one of the world's largest meat and fish importers and exporters.

"Enough about me. How are things at work?" Jozette pretended an interest while Marissa jumped into a detailed account of her office interactions with Hector, the hottie, and Stella, the bitch.

An hour and a potful of tea later, Marissa left her bestie with air kisses and a hug.

"Don't give up on love yet, Jozi. You never can tell."

"Yeah, yeah. Stop by the store later if you have time."

"Are you doing the story hour today?"

"Yep. As long as my boss has morning sickness, it is all up to me to keep the kids of Maccon City entertained," she joked.

"Alright, maybe I will stop by. I told Hector I could assist him in shopping for a birthday gift for his nephew. Books might be a great place to start," she said, wagging her perfectly tweezed eyebrows up and down.

Jozette laughed and shook her head. The woman was incorrigible, but she loved her like a sister. Not having any would do that, Marissa had informed her. She had three herself and assured Jozette sibling rivalry simply was not worth it.

Being an only child was terribly lonely at times. It was why she'd become such an avid reader. Of course, both her parents were older when they'd had her. Her mother had turned forty and her father was forty-eight when she'd been born.

Both were professors at a nearby private college and had never planned on marriage, let alone children. The problem with being an only child to older parents who worked in education was they felt the need to explain everything.

So, from the time she was very young, Jozette understood she was unplanned, therefore, had no right to infringe on their life plans. Oh, they loved her. At least, she was assured they did. But they were not openly affectionate. There was no hugging, kissing, and petting as a child. She was given gold stars on a calendar when she did something right, and told with unerring accuracy to the detail when and why she was wrong.

Okay, for a college student, maybe. Not so much for a preschooler. One particular memory was the time she had come home from school after losing her first tooth with a picture she had drawn of the tooth fairy.

Three year old Jozette had been so proud of the purple and blue drawing. She'd made it in the school nurse's office while waiting for her babysitter to come get her.

When her parents had come home that evening, they did not place it on the fridge like the other kids had talked about. Instead, they sat her down and told her there was no such thing as the tooth fairy.

Or the Easter bunny. Or Santa.

Yep. Her parents had effectively murdered all fairytale and fantastic creatures for Jozette when she was still tender aged.

"And I wonder why I'm fucked up," she muttered and went to dress for work.

Heck.

Her parents hadn't even planned for her to stay in their new house at all. There was only one spare bedroom which her mother had made into a bird lovers' library. Pictures of sparrows, seagulls, and other feathered critters crowded the walls. Jozi wasn't exactly fond of them with their pointy beaks and sharp looking talons. In fact, she was kind of afraid of birds. Blame it on that old movie, or whatever. It was just another thing for her parents to dislike about her.

Sigh.

The good news was there were tons of books on the hand-carved shelves inside the room she was sleeping in. The bad news was that only left room for a very small pull out couch. Uncomfortable was the word that immediately came to mind. The mattress was thin and lumpy, and she felt every spring as if it were digging into her spine.

Jozette had a mattress. A nice double firm queen sized one, but like everything else she owned, it was currently in storage. Her job was steady, but it did not pay very much, and rent was sky high in this part of the state. But she did not know how much longer she could take all this.

In a few weeks, her parents would be back, and Jozette had some serious thinking to do. She couldn't go on like this. It was unfair to them and not so fun for her.

"One day at a time," she murmured and headed out to work.

Story time at *Crescent Moon Books* was her favorite part of the day. Ever since her bosses Clara and Delia Crescent had hired her, she'd been enthralled by the daily tradition.

Recently, Jozette convinced the sisters to let her add another story hour to their workday. They already had ten and eleven covered, so Jozette had asked to try one at two in the afternoon. With a special emphasis on dragons and myths, her story time hour had become a fast favorite of some of the local children.

Once a month, Jozette brought in crayons and paper and had the kids draw their favorite characters. Afterwards, she would hang them on the community bulletin board at the front of the shop. A way for the kids to show off their work to their parents and nannies who brought them.

Usually, those happy parents turned into paying

customers. Something most small bookstores needed more of. As long as the kids and her bosses were happy, Jozette was happy. It was a win-win.

If only the position was full time. Maybe then she could move out of her parents' home and sleep on something other than a sofa bed. And if she was a very good girl, maybe she wouldn't have to sleep in her new bed alone.

Hmmm. That would be very nice.

She stopped her silliness with a shrug. No more men. She was through with them. Not like they were banging down her door, anyway. Not the way she looked with her difficult to tame, curly dark hair pulled back in a ponytail, a bomber jacket covering her plain thermal, and her baggy jeans tucked into her snow boots.

Jozette was ready to battle the elements, but not the dating scene. Nope. Not now. Maybe not ever.

One day at a time, she reminded herself as she got inside the same small used compact car she'd had for years. It still ran and sure beat walking in this weather, and that was all that really mattered to her.

One day, when her book was finished, and she wasn't living in her parents' house, then she would revisit the dating thing. When she had a few successes under her belt and didn't feel like a complete and utter failure at life. Someday in the future she would consider looking for a partner to traverse through life with.

Someday, she thought.

Just not now.

CHAPTER 4

Castor did not know how long he traversed the skies after fleeing the Isle of Pain. The two Dragons who'd freed him had not followed, and that was good. He did not want to fight them.

Truth was, he did not know if he could fight, let alone win. His strength was waning as he flexed his wings, using the air currents to propel him farther towards the place his Dragon's heart felt the call of his kin.

I am coming, brothers.

Hope was the only thing that kept him moving against the bleak night sky. It was dark and gray. The kind of sky that told of coming storms. How much longer would he have to go?

He wondered, but then finally, he felt the answer

inside of him. It was in the sudden burning in his chest, over his rose. Yes, Castor was getting close.

Using his inherent magic and darkened scales to hide among the stars, Castor pushed himself harder. He flew and flew until suddenly he felt as if a magnet was pulling him towards the earth. Stronger than any force he had ever felt. His blood raced through his veins and his Dragon roared loudly, shooting flames into the heavens before he began his descent.

Castor had had very little time as a Dragon. Being chained had stunted his communion with his beast, and he did not quite yet understand what the creature was telling him. So many emotions roiled through him, they were hard to discern. He had no time to react or get used to the sudden zeal that swept through him.

The beast turned and nosedived, aiming for the water to cushion his fall. The eagerness of his Dragon was palpable, and though the beast seemed to know what it was doing, Castor doubted the rough water would be any more welcoming than the surface, which appeared sandy and strewn with rocks and shells. Figured his kin would reside near a seashore.

The air was bitter cold, but he hardly felt it compared to the freezing depths of the deep blue that engulfed his two ton form. Castor's Dragon receded and scales turned to skin as he pushed up past the freezing depths to break the water's surface.

When he finally rose to the top, he was exhausted and fully human. It was a mile to shore, and though the water was frigid and the waves plenty, he could manage it. He had to.

Finally, dragging himself out of the cold wet depths, Castor crawled, sucking in air as the water on his hair, brows, and eyelashes froze the second they came into contact with the wind. He stood up, gritting his teeth against the sharp pain in his limbs. Naked and barefoot, he crept along the rocks and sandy path. He had no idea where he was, but he knew he had to be close to finding his brothers. He still had hope. His Dragon had brought him here for that very reason.

Yet, there was no obvious sign of any Dragons. He closed his eyes to find that beacon that had led him there, but no more did he feel his brothers calling to him. There was something, though.

Indeed, Castor was sure of it. He felt something else, something sharp and hard. Like a hot knife slicing through skin, muscle, and marrow, hooking him deep inside and pulling him forward.

Bloody hell!

What was that pain? He was no stranger to physical hurt, but this was beyond that. Far worse than any of the petty tortures he had endured in his lifetime. In Castor's mind, it could only mean one thing.

Nicholas and Devine, those two Dragons who'd freed him, were right. He was a demon, a *Change-Dragon*. And worse, he was dying. Why else would he suffer from this piercing, relentless pain?

Whatever had brought him crashing down from the skies, that same force was right then pulling him towards some sort of dwelling. The building was very unlike the castle that housed the dungeon he'd spent his entire life in. It was frightfully small, yet pleasant. A two-story structure with several glass windows that fascinated him, and white wood planks on the outside.

Not a castle. But a hut, perhaps? Would Dragons live in a hut?

Shivering, he continued to look as he slowly crept up the stairs to the back door. This was the moment he'd both longed for and dreaded. The few contents of his stomach threatened to make a reappearance with each step he took closer to the abode.

What did he expect from swallowing a few seagulls while in his Dragon form? The stringy tiny birds were hardly food, but it was just to keep up his strength. He hated the things. They'd often flown in his cell and shat upon the stone walls from the one rectangular hole in the walls.

Those foul fowl were infuriatingly scrawny, and he'd thought it fitting he swallowed down a few after all the shit he had to live with for centuries. Alas, he was mistaken. The gulls did not agree in the least with his digestive system. *Dragon or human.*

You're wasting time, he thought to himself as his inner Dragon puffed out a smoke circle.

Castor shook his head. After centuries of his beast being bound and locked away from him, to have him suddenly inside his mind at all times was a little unnerving. Fantastic, to be certain, but it would take getting used to.

But time was the one thing he had in short supply. It made him unbearably sad to think how short lived his freedom would be. It was tragic. He was dying before he ever had the chance to really soar.

He growled, annoyed at his own weakness. Castor would not lament his own wasted life. There would be no point. After all, meeting his brothers and apologizing for their suffering, as his mother bade him before she'd been escorted to her death, was the least he could do for both his parents.

Perhaps it would bring some closure to his kin. And maybe, just maybe, he could taste happiness before he perished.

He approached the gleaming white door with caution. This was it. Terror and excitement welled inside of him. The first was a common enough feeling, but the latter, well, that was new.

Castor shivered, sending icy droplets of sea water dripping down his face. His breath came out in white puffs of vapor, and though temperatures were low, it was nowhere near the freezing of his old dungeon room.

Stop dawdling.

Castor cursed himself for his own hesitation. He squared his shoulders, trying to prepare himself for their hatred and rejection, things he was sure they would feel.

Of course, there was a tiny sliver of hope that his half-brothers would accept him. That they would rejoice in him finding them, however, short the reunion. But how likely was that, really?

Doubts assailed him, but he was no coward. Reaching out with a closed fist, Castor Falk braced himself for disappointment, and finally knocked on the small wooden door. It was the longest thirty seconds of his life, but he counted them away one by one.

"Coming!"

A voice cried, and his stomach did that thing again. Castor's heart began pounding inside his chest. What was this? A female? Perhaps one of his brothers' mates? Lucky Dragons!

He waited impatiently, with trepidation at the sudden dampening of his palms and racing of his pulse. Fuck! Whatever disease his being a *Change-Dragon* meant for his own life, it seemed to speed up.

Castor was going to die. There was no doubt about it. But maybe, if he were luckier than the past would have proved, fortune would smile on him this one time so that he may meet his end, knowing his brothers were well and happy with families of their own!

"Hello?" A voice like a siren's song reached his starved ears like manna from the heavens.

"Oh my GAWD!"

That accent! Unlike any he had ever heard. Cute, though, but still a tad shrill when she screamed thusly.

"You're naked!"

The female continued, her enormous brown eyes bulging as they traversed his male parts. And he understood why. His organ was suddenly pulsing. A feeling he had never felt.

Castor could not move an inch. Not even to cover himself. He was frozen to the spot. Aside from breathing, he remained a statue. He gawked at the dark, chestnut haired beauty, mouth open like a fish out of water.

Never in all his decades in the dungeons of the castle had he ever seen hide nor hair of the likes of her. He had seen women, yes. Dragomir did love showing off his prizes.

The son of a traitor to the throne was of much interest to his concubines over the years. But those painted women were hardhearted and cold like the man they gave their bodies to.

Not her. He thought, staring at the beautiful creature before him.

She was all things soft and round and perfect. Her full figure commanded his gaze, beckoned his fingers, and struck his heart like a blow from a hammer.

Bam!

A surge of energy struck him right in the gut. His very blood seemed to burn. And his skin, too. Castor growled as he felt his stomach churn and squeeze with electrifying heat.

What sorcery was this? What curse has struck me low?

The flesh under his wilting garnet rose, sizzled and burned like an iron fresh from the fire. The female gasped, her dark brown eyes went from shocked to concerned as he fell to his knees on the snow covered porch. Small hands reached out to touch him and the result was like lightning searing his skin.

"You're freezing!" she shouted, yanking her hands back.

"Quick! Come inside. Hurry!"

The female was the most glorious thing Castor had ever seen. Emotions never felt before threatened to drown him. An inferno of desire, need, lust and something more raged inside.

Castor wanted to speak. To bid the fair lady not to trouble herself with the lowly likes of him, but he was actually struck dumb.

Speak? No. He could not utter a single word. He'd never had much physical contact in his life, especially not anything so kind as a caress or embrace. But that was what he wanted. With her. The feeling so strong he had to fight to keep himself from reaching out and pressing her flesh to his.

All of his blood seemed to be rushing and running through him like a raging river. He felt it all the way down to his balls. The two orbs squeezed and tightened, tucking against his body.

Was this it? Was this to be his end?

Maybe she was indeed an angel come down from the heavens to send him off to the unknown. Dragons had many gods, many stories of the afterlife and the Underworld. Even a lowly prisoner such as he heard the tales. Time and again, some servants managed to smuggle books to his cell.

Who knew which one was the right one? Maybe none. Maybe all.

Muscles twitching and shaking, he fought against the pain of death. For that was surely what this was. Castor had to fight it, just so he might speak to the fair creature. If his course had been correct, then he'd arrived at the home of the Falk brothers, and she was mated to one of them. A beauty such as she undoubtedly belonged to one of his kin.

He'd formerly thought them lucky Dragons, but now knew they were infinitely more than that. If she belonged to them, they were the luckiest damn creatures on the whole fucking planet.

He felt her hands wrap around his bicep and the sting was damn near unbearable. Heat threatened to consume him, and for a moment, he feared he would harm the fair creature.

Never.

His Dragon seemed to push the word inside his brain. Followed by another, something he did not quite comprehend. Not at first, anyway.

Es Meus.

The enormous beast inside of him growled the word in *Dracan*. Castor was not all that familiar with the ancient language. But it meant something, this phrase. Something profound.

He closed his eyes on the pain that followed. No! It couldn't be. Castor could never be so low as to covet his brother's wife. Whichever one of them she belonged to, he would do the honorable thing.

Castor would give the man his head on a silver platter for his own dishonorable thoughts. And what thoughts! It was worth it, just to think them.

His Dragon's fire churned as passion flared for the beautiful creature. He imagined their naked bodies touching, writhing, joining. Visions of which he had never felt, only ever heard whispers of, flooded his brain.

Fuck, yes, please.

He'd had 500 years to wonder about sex, but he'd never felt anything like this. If this was desire, no wonder men died of it. And he too would die of it. Gladly.

"You have to help me, pal," the angel grunted as she tried to pull him inside.

He saw her shivering in her thin night clothes and, as if to punish him for his carnal thoughts, Castor felt pain anew. It sprang upright between his legs. A tension so hard it made his staff rigid and his balls near to bursting apart.

Dying really sucked, he thought before he blacked out.

CHAPTER 5

*W*hat *do you do when a drop dead gorgeous, and very naked, man knocked on your door then proceeded to almost drop dead? Call your BFF.*

At least, that was what Jozette did.

"What?!" Marissa shrieked over the phone, and Jozette had to pull the thing away from her ear.

Her gaze went back to the huge, and naked, *did she mention naked,* guy who was covered in melting ice all over his hair and body, and dripping all over her parents' floor. Jozette had tugged him, barely able to move the giant, until he was on the area rug near the fireplace.

Luckily, she had been able to make a small fire that night and the embers were still glowing and warm. The mystery man was well over six feet tall, and so handsome she could not stop looking. But he was hurt, or something, and she was trying hard not to be a total creep with her thoughts.

After a few seconds of acting like an idiot, she'd grabbed the blankets nearest her and tossed them on his shivering frame. Blue eyes so deep she'd swear they were purple looked at her once, before he passed out.

Gulp.

"Um, so, yeah, a totally butt naked man knocked on my door. He was freezing, and I dragged him inside and now he is sprawled out on my parents' rug."

"The one with the birds on it?"

"Yep."

"Good. I hate that rug." Marissa snorted.

"Be serious!" Jozi growled into the receiver.

"Well, who is he?"

"I don't know. He just showed up, Mar! I mean, I just had the longest day at the bookstore ever, right? So I was having a glass of wine—"

"Or three," Marissa inserted.

"Fine. Or three," she admitted. "Anyway, then someone started knocking on the door and when I went to answer it, there was this naked dude standing there. Then he fell, and like, passed out or something."

"Did you call the police?"

"Uh—"

"Yeah, you didn't. Okay, first, take a picture for posterity's sake," Marissa said.

"What? You pervert. I am not taking a picture of some naked man—"

"Didn't you cover him up yet?"

"Yes. Of course, I did. I'm not the pervert here," Jozi hissed at her friend.

Her pulse had been racing ever since she opened the door and met the stranger's intense blue-eyed stare. Yes, he was drop dead gorgeous. More beautiful than any man she'd ever seen.

That he was naked hadn't even registered at first. But it was hard not to notice. He looked like he was carved from marble. The perfect man.

Then he'd started convulsing. Jozette had just reacted. She might not be a lot of things, but she was human, and she had a heart. It wasn't like she could just let him die out in the cold.

"Is he on drugs?"

"How would I know?" Jozette asked, gnawing her lower lip worriedly.

"Well, is he skinny and does he have bags under his eyes? It could be heroin or meth? Is he acting crazy? Like on steroids or it could be PCP? Jozette, he could be a serial killer!" Marissa gasped.

"What the fuck, Marissa? Are you trying to scare the shit out of me?"

"No! But, well—"

"He is not on drugs, and he is not a serial killer," she hissed.

"Well, I mean, I hope he's not," Jozette corrected herself. After all, she didn't know the guy. But for some reason, her gut was okay with it. In fact, she felt almost compelled to help him.

"Look, if you are worried, come over."

"I can't. I, uh, might be in the city right now," Marissa admitted, biting her lower lip.

"In Manhattan? With whom? OMG! You did it, and by it, I mean *him*. You're in your boss' apartment, aren't you? You are such a slut," Jozette whispered and snorted at Marissa's grunt of shame.

"Shut up, and it's not my boss' apartment! It is for the executives to use," Marissa growled.

"Fine. If I am dead in the morning—"

"Sheesh. Don't even kid around, Jozi! Alright,

when he wakes up, make sure you dial my number so I can call the police if I need to."

"What?"

"You heard me. Now, go sleep in your room with the doors locked."

"You are worse than a mother hen," Jozi muttered, walking away from the beautiful man.

She didn't know why she trusted he would not harm her, but for some reason, she did. Besides, it was a bitterly cold and stormy night. She couldn't leave him outside in the cold to die.

What a waste that would be!

After a few more minutes on the phone with Marissa, she locked her bedroom door and slid the small dresser she was allowed to use in front of it. Then, she activated the nanny camera, the one her parents still used to spy on their maid in the living room, and set her laptop up to monitor the sleeping stranger.

"Still out cold," she whispered, zooming in on his face.

He really was beautiful. Even in slumber, she sighed as she brushed a finger across the screen. Hopefully, she would get the truth out of him in the morning. Then, they could call whoever they needed to in order to get him some real help. Meanwhile, she could dream.

And dream, Jozette did. It wasn't often she woke up near climax, but holy cow, there was something about the stranger in her parent's living room that sent her libido into overdrive.

Getting an eyeful of the *full on boner* the dude was sporting before he collapsed might have had something to do with it. At least a dozen *x* rated dreams had flipped through her brain during the night, and she was so riled up by the time she woke, Jozette needed a shower. A cold one.

Yowza.

The man was seriously packing. And fuck, she just could not help but imagine him in all sorts of sexy situations.

Eeek! She was a dirty little lecher, wasn't she?

Gross, Jozi, she scolded herself before checking the monitor.

His sleeping hotness was still out cold. Maybe she did have enough time to jump in the shower, and definitely brush her teeth, before she woke him up.

Ten minutes later, dressed in a pair of cozy leggings with an oversized button-down shirt, Jozi padded into the living room in her slippers. Her hair was still damp, but she was clean and minty fresh.

That was about all she could manage under the circumstances.

After all, it would be super creepy of her to dress up and pretend this was some sort of date. The man was naked, and either lost or on the run. Neither of which spelled fun times ahead.

She kept walking, headed straight for the kitchen. Another ten minutes of sleep might be the difference between waking *prince charming* or the *beast*. And she was so hoping for the former.

Not that she expected him to fall at her feet spouting poetry, she just didn't want him to murder her.

Low standards much?

Yeppers.

Despite working in a bookstore, Jozette was a realist. Her parents hadn't tolerated any fantasy in her childhood at all unless it was to dissect the old tales down to their true horror roots.

She never played with princesses or read books about fairies and elves. She did have a killer set of Legos and a subscription to *National Geographic* though. Those were fun at least.

Was her childhood terrible? Not really. But it wasn't the same as her peers,

Marissa included. Her BFF had worshipped

every fairytale remake ever made by certain mouse owned and operated conglomerate. Jozette had sometimes snuck along to see the flicks, but she never really understood them. Even the later, more feminist version seemed off.

Did princes really love the nerdy girls, or the outcasts? She doubted it.

Either way, she could at the very least wake up her strange guest with some hot tea. *And pants.* She should really grab the guy some warm pants.

Turning the electric kettle on, she grabbed a couple of mugs and bags of English breakfast tea, then turned toward the small laundry room that sat right off the kitchen.

Jozette found a clean pair of sweats and a tee shirt from the pile, figuring he would just have to make do. On second thought, she also grabbed some socks. Jozette hated cold feet and imagined anyone would appreciate a pair of warm and fuzzies after being stuck in the cold.

She loaded a tray with some biscotti Marissa had made, and the two large mugs of tea. Adding a small jar of creamer, honey, and sugar to the lot, she also grabbed a few napkins. Jozette tucked the clothes under one arm, then lifted the tray in her hands.

He was tossing and turning restlessly until she

entered, then he seemed to still. As if having her near to him somehow gave him peace.

Now you're being fanciful, she mused.

The quilted blanket she'd covered him in last night rode low on his waist and she meant to avert her gaze, truly she did. But it wasn't every day Jozette had almost seven feet, *she did a quick calculation and corrected herself from the night before*, of naked man lying in her parents' living room. And what a man he was. He could've been sculpted from marble.

His shoulders were impossibly wide, and his arms roped with muscle, though, in truth, he was a tad thin. His chest tapered into a narrow waist, with slim hips and long, powerful legs. The ripples of muscle across his abs had her mouth watering, and she cleared her throat in an effort not to drool.

Thick black curls brushed against his forehead, and Jozette exhaled as she imagined running her fingers through them. Would his luscious locks be soft as they were glossy, or would it feel dry and coarse like some curly hair felt? Would he moan and lean into her touch, crave it the way she craved touching him?

Eeeek!

Her cheeks heated, and she squeezed her legs

together to ease the sudden throb, feeling her blush intensify at the moisture she felt there.

OMFG!

This was bad. Like really bad. Like *welcome to super-slutdom bad.* Jozi should be ashamed of herself, ogling the poor man when he was hurt or lost. What was she thinking?

She might not know what she was thinking, but she knew what she was thinking with. Certain pink bits that had been ignored for much longer than the last few months it had been since she'd moved out of her ex's place.

When was the last time she'd had sex, anyway?

"Stop it," she growled to herself.

"This is ridiculous," Jozi muttered, and stood up.

Her phone buzzed, but she ignored it. Whoever was calling to sell her solar panels could wait, for Pete's sake. She leaned over with one of the spoons from the tray and did the only thing she could think of. She jabbed him. Right on his chest.

Of course, Jozette wasn't expecting him to wake up wild eyed with the strength of a water buffalo. The seemingly sweet stranger had her flat on her back on the rug and was looming over her before she could even blink, an inhuman growl sounding from his lips.

"Grrrrr!"

"OH MY GAWD!!" Jozette squealed, as the naked stranger pinned her to the area rug beside the couch.

"Milady, 'tis you," he muttered before his eyes smoldered with undeniable heat, then proceeded to roll back inside his skull and he slumped on top of her.

"Are you serious?" Jozette mumbled beneath his enormous body.

She'd always been a big girl. A solid one hundred seventy-seven pounds since high school. Along with her not very tall, five foot six-ish frame, she had always thought of herself as sturdy.

But this guy weighed a ton. And he was cutting off her oxygen supply. What's more, his skin was on fire. *Shit.* Did that mean he had a fever?

Using all her strength, *which she got from lifting book after book at her day job, thank you very much,* Jozi finally managed to slide out from under him. Chest heaving, she stilled a moment, trying to catch her breath before sitting all the way up.

Of course, once she did that, she saw the blanket had slipped, and the guy was rocking some serious glutes. *Great.* Now she had the image of his perfect backside burned into her brain.

Was nothing ugly about this man?

Looking back, she realized he was not trying to hurt her. In fact, the second his blue eyes had focused, he seemed shocked, then docile as a kitten.

"Milady, 'tis you," he'd said.

Like some knight in tales of old. And he spoke as if he knew her or something. Looking at him, she had the strangest feeling she did too.

Crazy? yes. She would have remembered meeting a man with his incredible looks, but she decided to trust herself. Next time, instead of using a spoon to poke him, Jozette went with her instincts.

She tossed the discarded afghan over his hips, doing her best not to check out his ass again. Then she brushed her own hair behind her ears with her fingers and knelt beside him. Her phone buzzed once more, but she ignored the stupid thing. No one of consequence would be calling her at this hour.

Her hands trembled, but she ignored that, chalking it up to real fear, which was pretty understandable considering what happened last time she tried this.

"Mister? Hey, Mister, you have to wake up," she whispered, pushing his hair back from his forehead.

Damn. He was even more beautiful this close. The dark circles under his eyes seemed to lessen with each passing minute. For some reason, Jozette smiled as she continued to touch his hair.

"Who are you?"

She wondered aloud, giving his face a soft caress. He had chiseled features and thick, lush lips. His eyelashes were impossibly dark, but she didn't believe for a second the man sported guyliner or any other cosmetic. His was a natural beauty, and Jozette was certainly old enough to appreciate it.

Once he began to stir, she backed away, not getting very far as his hand snaked out and wrapped around her wrist. He wasn't hurting her. Not by a mile. In fact, that small touch sent flickers of awareness racing through her.

This was insane! She should not be feeling this way. Okay, so maybe she browsed the romance section of *Crescent Moon Books* now and then. And yes, she might have stopped and read a few pages from *Claimed by the Demon* and *Bearly Breathing*, but for Pete's sake, things like that didn't happen in real life!

"Wait. Please. Do not leave me, milady," he said.

His voice was husky and thick like gravel as he slowly came awake. Beautiful blue eyes blinked up at her, and Jozi found herself captivated by them. She'd never seen eyes like that.

So blue they were like ink. Twin pools of deep indigo. They widened, suddenly rimmed in reddish flames, but when she blinked, it was gone.

A figment of her imagination? Perhaps. But she doubted it.

"Forgive me, lady fair. Is your husband home?"

"My husband?"

"Yes. Pray tell which of my brothers is lucky to call you mate, milady?"

"What? I don't have a—"

"I have come from very far to speak to my kin, fair lady. Please, do not deny me, I beg you."

"I wouldn't deny you," she replied softly, swallowing the lump that rose in her throat.

It was like he was stuck in some sort of time warp, she thought. His words, while clear, were old fashioned and out of place. Sexy, but not modern.

Like Jozette had stepped into some time travel fantasy romance. *Maccon City's own little version of Outlander*, she mused near to hysterics.

His hand moved from her wrist up her arm to her elbow, and she could see fascination and something else flare to life in his inky blue depths.

"Lady, you are beautiful," he murmured.

"Who are you?" she asked again.

"I am Castor Falk, and I know I am low to beg such a thing, but a kiss, milady, please?"

"What?"

"'Tis bold and foolish. I know this and I cannot help myself. I have never longed for anything like I yearn for your lips," he whispered, and to her surprise, she found herself leaning down.

Close, so close to meeting his mouth with hers, Jozette could not believe it. A mere hair's breadth away from total slutdom. But how often did chances like this really emerge, she wondered?

"Okay," she said, or maybe it was more like she breathed the word and swore she saw his eyes flare in the morning light streaming in through the curtains.

But before their lips could meet, the front door slammed open with a loud thud. The lock flew apart, busting under the force of some hard blow or other. Jozette almost screamed, but then she saw who was there and frowned hard.

It was Marissa, with Hector close behind her. Her bestie looked frenzied and angry, and fuck, were those fangs? Jozette blinked and jumped up, but *Mr. Tall Dark and Naked* was faster on his feet. He leapt in front of her, crouching low and growling menacingly.

"Get the fuck away from my friend," snarled Marissa.

"'Tis you must back away, she-Cat!" The stranger sneered.

"What are you? A lizard?" Marissa asked, head cocked.

"Lizard? I am a Dragon, she-beast, and I will end you before you touch a single hair on my fair one's head!"

Hector snarled then, clothes tearing from his body as he turned into something big and golden. Fuck. Was that fur?

The stranger growled. A warning, perhaps? And a stream of smoke escaped his lips. His eyes glowed, and Marissa crouched threateningly.

What the actual fuck was going on?

"Time out! Time out," Jozette shook her head and stepped between the three, whatever the fuck they were. In truth, she didn't know what to call them.

"Jozi! Are you okay?"

"I'm fine, Mar, but what the fuck is with your teeth? And nails? And is Hector a Lion?"

"Jozi, I can explain—"

"Milady, please, I only wish to protect yo—"

"You know what, never mind," she said, and turned, gesturing to the naked man.

"Milady?"

"Do you mind—"

That was all she got out before she fainted dead away. With any luck, he caught her before she hit the ground.

Fuck me.

CHAPTER 6

Jozette blinked against the cacophony of voices knocking against her already messed up head. What the heck happened? Oh yeah.

First, she'd been about to make out with a naked guy who spoke like he was from another time.

Second, her BFF had busted through her door, *pussy-blocking* Jozette, and sporting three inch fangs and claws, and her very own Lion man.

Third, she was pretty sure she heard some shit about shifters and dragons.

Not to be confused with that roleplaying game

whatever and dragons, she was certain. Maybe this was like that time she and her buddies stayed up late playing *WolfMoon* and accidentally drank some of her father's Sambuca. The dreams she'd had that night, boyo!

"Jozi? Wake up!" Marissa shook her hard, and Jozi slapped her hands away.

"What the heck, Mar? You broke my parents' door!" She seethed.

"Milady, are you alright? Please, imbibe some refreshment, I insist," her naked guest was sitting there in the pants and shirt she'd gotten out for him.

He looked freshly showered, too. She leaned in and sniffed. Oh yeah, he smelled good, too. Like that coconut body wash she'd recently splurged on. His indigo eyes narrowed in concern, and she damn near swooned.

OMG! She was being ridiculous.

"Easy, Romeo." Marissa snorted and crossed her arms over her chest.

A move that drew Hector's dark gaze like a moth to a flame she noted for her friend for when they chatted later.

Sans men.

"My name is Castor Falk. I have told you twice, female—"

Hector turned and snarled at her guest. *Castor,* she repeated inside her head, testing his name. It was unusual, but nice. She laid a hand on his arm, and he dropped his responding growl to kneel at her side.

"Okay, easy with the grabby hands, dude!" Marissa snapped.

"Jozi, there's some stuff we need to go over," Marissa interrupted, but Jozi squeezed when Castor tried to move aside.

"I shall remain here till the fair Jozette sends me away," he said sternly.

Jozette sat up, hands raised. Her head was pounding, rare for her, but even more bizarre was how good it felt holding on to Castor's hand. He stood beside her, like her own personal bodyguard. Near seven feet of muscled, handsome man, and she absolutely loved having him there.

Dangerous? Maybe. But she was totally prepared to indulge herself for the time being.

"Okay, explain," she snapped at Marissa. "And do not leave anything out."

"This is going to sound strange, but you see, Jozi, I'm a Shifter. A Lioness, to be exact."

After ten minutes of listening to her best friend talk about the supernatural world, a huge secret from the human or *normal* world, Jozette had had enough.

"What do you take me for? An idiot! Did she put you up to this?" Jozette asked Castor, and yes, she might have stomped her feet a little.

"Milady?"

"Don't you *milady* me, buster! Did my so-called best friend set this whole thing up?"

"Jozi! I would never!" Marissa snarled.

And yes, she really snarled. Like a cat or, er, *Lioness*.

"I'm not some idiot," she began, but Hector was already taking off his shirt.

"OMG! What are you doing? Mar? What is he doing?"

"Showing you proof, slowly this time so you don't think it's a trick," Marissa said, lounging on the side arm of the sofa.

Castor tensed when Hector went for his pants. His lip curled, and he loosed an angry sounding growl. Jozette gasped at the animalistic sounds, but Marissa just rolled her eyes.

"Will you calm down, lizard boy," Mari grunted. "If we don't show her, she won't believe us."

"Fine," Castor relented. "But I insist he move behind the chaise for that part."

"What?" Jozette said, turning to stare at him.

"He wants to protect the innocence of your eyes," Marissa said between giggles. "Hector?"

The big man moved behind the couch with a shrug, and though she couldn't see him exactly, Jozette knew when he'd finished undressing. She wasn't sure how he did it, some trick of the light or whatever, but one second Hector was standing there on two legs, the next he was down on four. Four golden furred legs. For the second time in the last few minutes, her BFF's boytoy had turned into a fucking Lion.

Then, a few things happened. Jozette gulped. The Lion roared, shaking his head with his dark gold mane. Marissa laughed and called him a showoff. And dark blue smoke started streaming from Castor's mouth.

Jozi covered her mouth with her hand, and Castor snarled once before cutting off his stream of smoke. He dismissed the animal as if he was no more than a house cat, turning his attention back to Jozette.

"Easy, Scales," Marissa snapped at Castor.

"He need not make such a display," Castor replied.

"He's just being himself!"

But Jozette had had enough. Her BFF was arguing with her *not naked anymore* guest and there was a fucking Lion in her parents' living room.

"WHAT THE FUCKING WHAT IS GOING ON!"

All the humans in the room turned to look at her. Both with concern filling their gazes. She knew she screamed loudly, but Jozi had to get their attention somehow. They'd been far too busy bickering to notice her.

"You, explain now," she demanded, pointing a finger at Marissa. "And he better not pee on my mom's new throw rug, or you are cleaning it!"

"Relax, Jozi. He's housebroken," Marissa said, smiling widely.

Funny, Jozette had never noticed how very much like her predator her best friend looked when she grinned like that. All this time she'd joked about the blonde being a maneater and she really was! Who'd have thunk it?

Forty minutes and three dozen bagels later...

"Okay, from the top once more—"

"Sorry, is this really salmon?" Castor interrupted.

He was on his eighth sesame bagel loaded with herbed cream cheese, sliced tomatoes, capers, olive oil, and smoked salmon. Jozette nodded, impressed by his ability to keep all that down. A big girl herself, one bagel, was quite enough to satisfy her hunger.

"Fascinating. I never did like the taste of salmon head soup, but this is extraordinary."

"Salmon head what?" Hector asked, making a moue of distaste.

"Yes, well, when one is jailed for several lifetimes, there is not much choice menu wise," Castor offered.

"Cool, but use a fork, dude," Hector said lowly, and proceeded to show Castor how to use utensils.

"Remarkable! Tools for eating! Not that I was complaining, but I had nothing so fine in the dungeon. I am grateful now that Dragomir had kept me alive when he did not have to," Castor said, gazing at Jozette with a look that made her feel warm all over.

"Why did he?" Hector asked.

"I believe it was simply to torture my father and mother's souls even in the beyond."

"We should kill that fucker," Hector said, and Jozette had to agree with the sentiment.

"Too late, my friend. He met his end badly, and rightly so at that," Castor said, popping an entire half a bagel loaded with more salmon and cream cheese into his mouth.

"Uh, okay then," Jozette said, opening and closing her open mouth like a fish out of water.

"So," she began, trying to wrap her head around everything.

"You guys are Shifters. You can turn into animals and have their traits. It's a big secret. And this guy is really a 500 year old Dragon who doesn't know much about modern life because he was kept in a dungeon by some other Dragon tyrant who is now dead, and he is here to search for his family? Do I have that right?"

"Perfectly," Marissa said, heavy in the *purr*.

"So, how did you end up here?" Jozette asked Castor.

The gorgeous man's cheeks went ruddy as he looked away. He seemed nervous, embarrassed, and unsure all at once. Also, he seemed sad.

"I am not sure, milady. I felt a pull to this place, like a magnetic force was guiding me here. I thought for certain this was the dwelling of my brothers."

"Oh," she said, a tad disappointed. "Well, it's not. I mean, I sure as shit am not hiding a bunch of Dragons under my bed."

"You are now," Marissa chimed in.

"What?"

"Well, it's obvious. You have to help him find his way, Jozi. He didn't seek you out for no reason. This is Fate."

"Fate?" Castor's eyes snapped to Marissa, Then to Jozette.

"What does that mean?" Jozi asked.

"You'll find out. Well, Hector and I better run—"

"But I have work!" Jozette said in a harsh whisper, nodding her head at Castor, who was back to sitting at the table, eating, and watching TV with a myriad of expressions crossing his face.

"'Tis sorcery, this is!"

"Nah, man, it's reality TV," Hector explained, showing Castor the remote.

The big, sexy man gasped and laughed, a good loud sounding expression. It made Jozette's belly warm, and a smile spread across her face. Of course, Marissa caught that, and she gently elbowed her bestie.

"So what? You work in a bookstore, Jozi. Take him with you. Grab him some history books and bring an iPad. Plug him in. He should be caught up in no time," she said with a wink.

Marissa gestured to Hector who stood up and shook hands with Castor. But Jozette just followed her BFF to the door. Nervous and a little more than anxious to boot, she had no idea what to do next.

"Marissa, you can't just go! What am I supposed to do with a Dragon?"

"Just look at him, Jozi. And if you can't figure it out, I know a few websites that can show you."

CHAPTER 7

"Hey Jozi," Clara Crescent greeted her from behind the counter.

From the time Jozette had first met her, Clara had walked with a slight limp and had been rather introverted. But over the last few months, the woman seemed to completely change. She was radiant. Ever since she announced her recent engagement and pregnancy, and Jozette could not be happier for her.

"Oh, um, who's your friend, Jozi?"

She turned and tugged Castor towards her boss, smiling nervously. She hoped he didn't do anything to give away his secret. Eeek! Nerves made her palms sweat, but she tried to play it off.

"This is Castor. He's, um, just visiting. You don't mind if he hangs out today?"

Clara stilled and her eyes seemed to look through her Dragony guest. *Crap.* Could she tell there was something unusual about him? Jozi bit her lip a little nervously, but eventually her boss just nodded.

"Not at all," Clara responded to her question, a little belatedly. "I'm off to meet Kurt for lunch, but Delia should be in to lock up."

"Have a good time," Jozette said, placing her things behind the counter and showing Castor to the break room.

"You can hang out here," she began, and he was already looking around, eyes filled with wonder.

"A TV? At work. It is amazing you get anything accomplished, but I suppose I should thank your Wolf boss for being good to you," he said with a tiny smile playing at the corner of his mouth.

"My what?"

"The female is a she-Wolf," he replied matter-of-factly.

"No shit?"

"Shit?" Castor frowned looking about the floor. "I see no defecation indoors. Surely, modern Wolves are housebroken?"

"What? Oh, sorry, it's just an expression," Jozette

said, shaking her head. Her bosses were Wolves? How many supernatural things existed out there?

"Several, milady. But have I worried you?" Castor stood, taking her hands, concern glowing in his indigo gaze.

"Did you just read my mind?"

"I do not know. Did I?" he asked, not breaking his stare.

Jozette felt heat seep into her from where he lightly joined their hands. She'd never felt so much attraction and was uncertain if it was all hers or coming from him as well.

"You must work," he muttered, letting go of her hands and stepping back. The space between them seemed to clear her mind, and Jozette blinked slowly.

"Um, yeah, I do."

"I am grateful you allowed me to accompany you, and I vow not to disturb you whilst you are busy," Castor said, making a small bow.

Jozette shrugged, taken aback by his chivalrous display. It was difficult not to feel guilty about the things she'd taken for granted when he approached everything with such gratitude and humility.

"Go ahead and have a seat. I'll be right back."

Jozette went to grab some magazines, newspapers, and a couple of world history books while she was at it. When she returned, Castor was exactly where she'd left him. Standing at ease, hands behind his back, just waiting for her.

"Oh, you could sit down," she said, gesturing to the couch behind him.

"Thank you, milady—"

"Call me Jozette or Jozi," she replied, and handed him the pile she'd collected for him.

"Here. These are so you can try to get acclimated to current events and stuff."

Castor frowned and took the books from her, then Jozi felt like an idiot. Could he even read? OMG. She was so thoughtless.

"Look, if you can't read, um, I'd be happy to—"

"No, no! I am sorry, thank you. Yes, I can read, milad-, I mean Jozette. I just never saw such fine printed materials before. The servants at the Castle would bring me whatever old books and scrolls they managed to smuggle out from under the Chief's nose. I was simply surprised, is all. Thank you," he said, placing his hand over his heart and bowing slightly.

Again, the old world gesture left Jozette feeling warm and tingly. Her cheeks heated, and she found herself drawn to him. In fact, she'd moved unconsciously closer. His blue-eyed stare so poignant she would swear he could read her thoughts.

Jozi wondered if it would shock him to know right then she was thinking of kissing him. Of pressing her body against his and melting into his rock hard body. A bell rang in the background, and she jumped, breaking the spell.

"I have to work," she whispered. "Will you be alright?"

"Of course, Jozette. Thank you."

She greeted the elderly couple who'd just walked in from the cold, noting it had started snowing again.

"Hello Mr. and Mrs. Fredericks, how are you?"

"Very well, thanks," the pair replied.

Day by day, for a dull week, Jozi and the Dragon went to her job at *Crescent Moon Books* together. The long winter hours ticked by minute by minute. Each second dragging out longer than ever before.

February could be dreary in the Jersey Shore town, but Jozette had never felt such angst. Not since high school, at any rate. Her parents had decided to increase their vacation for another month, which was good considering she was living with a stranger in their house.

"Ugh," she grunted after dropping a pile of the store's mail onto the floor.

"Allow me," Castor jumped up from around the desk and picked up the pile, tidying it deftly.

He was a great help. But she only admitted that when she was feeling generous. The jeans and tees she'd grabbed for him at the local Walmart with Marissa and Hector seemed to fit him well enough. Though she was pretty sure Marissa had gotten everything a size small just to torture Jozi.

He hadn't liked the idea of her paying for them, but it wasn't like there were any other options. Besides, he couldn't keep walking around naked.

"You're just sexually frustrated," Marissa had said over the phone that very morning when she called to check in on Jozi and her new roommate.

Now that her friend had let that cat out of the bag, pun intended, Jozi couldn't seem to put it back in. Castor was busy researching the White Pages for any sign of his brothers in between bouts of heavy reading. The man devoured books. But that wasn't the issue. The problem was, even though he currently sat in the back room with her laptop and any number of tomes on the table beside it, Jozi could still smell him.

Oh my, could she smell him.

His scent reminded her of a burning bonfire on a summer night down on the beach, with a salty sea breeze wafting through it. The Dragon smelled good, warm, enticing, and so damn sexy she was liable to lose her mind any second now.

Dammit. Marissa was right. Jozi was feeling mighty frustrated. She tried to concentrate on work, splitting her time between helping customers and stocking shelves. She soon learned her mysterious guest could not only read, but he was incredibly fast at it.

By the time four o'clock rolled around, Castor had gone through a quarter of the new books she'd handed him that morning concerning the last hundred years of warfare and other atrocities that plagued the humans on their planet. Maybe it was different for Shifters, but since they all shared the same space, she figured he should know.

"Jozette?" Castor asked, walking into the room with his hands in his pockets. The gesture made the white cotton tee he wore stretch across his pecs.

A week of eating regular meals meant the man had filled out in all the right places. There was no more hollowness in his face or stomach. He was hot before, but now he was drop dead gorgeous. She looked down at her leggings and sweater and scowled.

Oh well. Why should she even make the effort? He was way out of her league. Besides, this was what she liked to wear. She was comfy and covered. And that was as good as it was going to get.

"Yes?"

"I am not interrupting you, am I?"

Castor asked, his indigo eyes gazing down at her from his incredible height.

"Not at all," she replied. "Actually, I was just coming to get you. The snow is really coming down now, and Clara called to tell me to lock up early."

"Ah, that is good news then. Do you require help?"

He stood there larger than life, his blue eyes searching, and Jozette's pulse raced in response. She wished she had the right to walk up to him and drop a kiss on his full lips. To have the right to wrap her arms around his waist and just rest her head on his chest.

Eeek! When had she become one of those women whose innermost longings stirred at the mere sight of a man? She supposed it was ever since a Dragon had knocked on her door.

Too fast? Maybe. But sometimes she felt like her

heart was going to beat her to death just from looking at him.

Silly. And for more reasons than one. Heck, she even made a list.

First, she was a realist, and just accepting the reality of him was asking a lot.

Second, he was way out of her league. Like light years.

Third, what kind of person would take advantage of a man who was completely out of his element and only just finding his way?

She would not prey on his gratitude by forcing him into anything he was not ready for. Yes, she'd caught his stares, but maybe that was a proximity thing. And even if she were modern enough to fall into bed with him, she wasn't so sure she could do that and not fall in love.

There it was. The dreaded L word. No way. She had to stop looking at Castor like he was chocolate. The Dragon was officially off limits!

"Sure, you can help," she replied to his earlier question. "Please turn off the lights and lock the back door while I get the alarm system ready."

CHAPTER 8

Castor had been helping the last few days and knew what to do. She felt guilty for not being able to dedicate more time to finding his family, but even in a place the size of Maccon City, it was slow going.

Once they were in her car, she turned to him, having forgotten he'd asked a question just a while ago. The engine started quickly, but visibility was low. She used every precaution before turning onto the street. Her parents' house was a bit farther away than she'd have liked in this weather, but Jozi had grown up in Maccon City. She knew a few back roads that might prove better than the bumper to bumper traffic on Main.

"What was it you were going to say?"

"Oh," Castor continued, hands braced in front of him. "I was going to ask if there was a more current listing of residents than the one you gave me?"

"I'm not sure. The phone book comes out pretty regularly and not everyone is in it anymore. We can log onto the internet when we get back home and try to request something from the town, maybe? Is that alright? I am so sorry for being thoughtless," she said, pushing her hair back from her face as she squinted to see through the snow covered windshield.

"You have been kinder and more generous than anyone I have ever met, Jozette Keeper. Never call yourself thoughtless again," he said, frowning at her.

She couldn't help but smile and shake her head. It was a wonder he remained so gallant and considerate in spite of all the book reading and TV show watching he'd done in the past few days.

"It is dangerous to drive in this, no? Should we perhaps walk?" Castor asked.

"Uh, it's fine," she murmured, trying her best to maneuver the vehicle down the slush slicked streets.

They drove in silence for the first few minutes, and Jozi was glad for that. It was hell on her nerves these last few days, being so near to this virile strange man who seemed to bring out her innermost secret wishes. She'd never been all that hung up on sex before, and with good reason. It was oftentimes a messy, short disappointment followed by uncomfortable conversation.

She'd blamed that on herself in the past, but just lately, ever since a certain Dragon had knocked on her door, Jozi had been having the strangest dreams. Vivid naughty ones involving much less clothing than either of them was wearing at present.

"Are you alright?"

"What? Oh, yeah," she murmured, ignoring the sudden flare of embarrassment.

"You seem upset," Castor noted, his head cocked to the side in that way he had about him that told her she had his full attention.

That was different, too. No one else had ever given Jozi their full attention before. But she didn't question it. Not yet anyway.

"Just driving," she replied.

The steady swoosh of the wipers sounded nice in the din of the vehicle. The snow fell harder, and the wind really started blowing.

"The storm is getting worse," she murmured.

Castor's hands were stretched outward, touching the dashboard, and both of hers were gripping on the wheel.

"Hold on!" Castor yelled, just as Jozette gasped and squeezed the wheel tighter.

Dammit!

Of course, the second she was about to say it was all good, her car began to slide and fishtail down the ice covered street and straight into a ditch. With two more miles to go, she did not know how they were going to get out of this mess.

"Jozette!"

His rumbling growl echoed inside the small car. Somehow, it got through to her rattled brain, and Jozi blinked rapidly. She was whole. Sound. Not hurt, but definitely shook up.

"Castor! Are you hurt? Jeez. I am so sorry. Are you okay?"

Jozette turned towards the big man, frantic to know if he was alright. She would never forgive herself if she did anything to hurt him. Her heart squeezed inside her chest as her hands grabbed onto his.

"I am well, sweet lady. 'Tis you I am worried about," he said, cupping her face in his large hands, gazing into her eyes before running his fingers across her shoulders, arms, and legs, checking for injury.

"I'm good," she said, nodding.

He lifted a warm palm to her cheek again, and she closed her eyes for a brief moment, simply glad they were both okay. Ever since he'd knocked on her door, Jozette felt a compulsive need to take care of the big, sexy man.

She opened her eyes again and saw him staring down at her. Face so serious, those twin indigo pools seemed to glow as he watched her. Like he was studying her, she thought idly. Castor nodded once, growling softly, and she felt the sound reverberate through her body until she shivered with it.

"Um, my door is stuck," she murmured, turning away to break the strange spell that had settled over them.

Jozette shook the handle before banging on the steering wheel. Frustration and embarrassment took over and she couldn't remember a time she'd felt so useless. How could she drive them into a ditch like that?

"Blame the weather, not your driving," he instructed wisely.

"I should've been more careful."

"You are not at fault. Now, I mean no offense to your vehicle, but I am afraid I have to break the glass to free us. Shield your eyes, please."

Jozette thanked God once more that neither of

them was injured. Still, she hated to think of having to explain to her parents what happened to their dependable little sedan. Closing her eyes and turning her head, as he suggested, she knew the second Castor's fist slammed through the windshield. Aside from the sound of breaking glass, the car, which was almost completely turned on one side, rocked against the force of the blow.

Whoa.

The man was seriously strong. Inhumanely so, she supposed. When she turned back to face front, Jozette noted that Castor did not only break the windshield, he tore the thing clear off. She could barely get a handle on that one profound truth when he leapt out of the vehicle.

One moment he was beside her, the next he was standing on the car. Then, as if he did this every day, Castor leaned over, broke her seat belt, gripped her under the arms, and proceeded to lift her out of the mangled car and into his arms. His warm, unsurprisingly strong arms.

Was it bad that it felt so good to be held by him? Probably.

"Now what do we do?" She asked, blinking against the rapidly falling snow and freezing gusts of wind.

"Do you trust me?"

Jozette was momentarily struck dumb by the sight of Castor's deep blue eyes glowing against the whited out sky. His inky black hair was tossed carelessly about by the strong winds, but Jozette had never seen a more gorgeous being in her life.

Maccon City had more than its fair share of handsome men and beautiful women. A truth that kept the tourists coming back to the Jersey Shore town the year long. But she had never seen anyone more handsome or virile in her life.

He might be light years out of her league, but that didn't stop Jozette from wishing. Maybe her mother and father hadn't destroyed her desire for a fairytale ending of her own, after all? With their rigid reading lists and lack of open affection for their only child, it was highly unlikely. But still, a girl could dream.

"Yes," she said, answering his question honestly.

Truly, it was the only way she knew how to be. Jozette was not made for games. When she felt something, she said it. And yeah, she trusted him. How could she not? He looked like some sort of god standing in a blizzard with her chubby ass in his arms.

"Not a god, milady, a Dragon," he grinned, and

one minute she was in his arms, the next, she was being cradled inside one massive claw.

Josette yelped when he took off for the skies. She could not believe it. She was flying! Really flying! And in the arms of an enormous Dragon right out of a fairytale!

Exhilarating! Phenomenal! Better than any roller-coaster!

She was at a loss for words when it came to the sensations that went through her as Castor zoomed through the whited-out skies. Her eyes studied the large dark blue shape, and she realized his scales were like his eyes. More indigo than blue, with hints of red and purple. Diamond shaped, hard, and smooth as glass, she ran her fingers over them remarking at their heat.

He was beautiful. Majestic. Mystical. And fucking real.

That was the part she couldn't believe. He was real. A few minutes later, she peaked over the edge of his massive claw and saw the ground coming up fast. Jozette had to work not to scream, but she managed it, letting out one large exhale when he touched ground.

His shift back to human was quick, only his clothes were gone. Jozi squeaked a little when her hands came into contact with his bare chest, as she was still in his arms.

"Let's get you inside," he murmured beneath fiercely blowing winds.

Jozi simply nodded as he carried her up the dune to her parents' back door. Good thing there were few houses nearby. It would be difficult to explain what she was doing with a giant Dragon. Or with a naked man, for that matter. Marissa's words came flitting back through her mind.

"Just look at him, Jozi. And if you can't figure it out, I know a few websites that can show you."

Jozette knew what to do with a man alright. The sudden swelling of her breasts, hardening of her nipples, and a flood of wetness pooling between her thighs left no doubt about that. The question was, did he know what to do with a woman? And if he did, would he be game?

Gulp.

CHAPTER 9

ear gods in the heavens.

Castor growled and paced while the beautiful female was inside, taking a warm shower. He'd already had one in the guest bathroom. Now, he was anxiously awaiting the woman he was indebted to for everything he had since arriving on her doorstep.

How could he ever repay the beautiful female for all she had given him? It worried Castor that she might think him a beggar or worse, the lowly prisoner Dragomir had made him.

No! The beast within him refused to accept such drivel. It was nonsense. He was imprisoned through no fault of his own. Still, he would need to do much to improve his circumstance to be worthy of even her notice.

Was it fair of him? To continue on this path when he knew he was not long for the world. The words of Nicholas and Devine still echoed in his mind. Castor was not meant to live life as a free man or beast. His *ChangeDragon* was not right. He felt it in the pain that sometimes burned him on his chest and in his blood.

Castor should tell the sweet lady Jozette about his impending doom. Before the attraction he knew she felt, for he felt it too during those odd times he could read her mind, got any stronger. Even now, he struggled to control his desires. It did not help him to think of Jozette in the shower, under the spray of water that flowed like magic, thanks to the wonder that was indoor plumbing.

What he wouldn't have given for warm water and a shower stall over the past five centuries! Having spent the better part of the last several days reading and catching up on modern times. The Isle of Pain was grossly out of step with the modern world, a fact which had contributed to Dragomir's downfall.

A growl crept up his throat, his mind wandering to the sounds of what was going on inside the master bathroom.

She was in there. Beneath the warm water. Gloriously naked. Sliding her hands over her slippery skin. Touching that which he coveted.

Es Meus.

His beast growled the unfamiliar phrase, and Castor hissed with smoke puffing from his nostrils. Suddenly, pain lanced through his body from his chest to his stomach. So powerful was the feeling, Castor fell to his knees.

Bloody hell.

He'd almost forgotten the one terrible truth that had sent him halfway across the earth to find his half-brothers. Castor had little time left. He was dying.

Whatever he felt for the amazingly kind and beautiful human, Castor should not give the false impression that he had forever. It was both cruel and untruthful.

Hadn't he spent enough hours thumbing through the pages of the books in the section marked *Romance* at Crescent Books to know better? Sweet Jozette had grinned the day she found him thumbing through a novel with a bare chested man on the front. She hadn't said a word, but he could tell it amused her. After that, he'd read dozens of the things, paying close attention to the sections on coupling with a female.

500 years in a dungeon left Castor void of any sex education, and the one thing he wanted above all was to experience that. With her. But how? And was it unfair of him?

You must not insult the only being to ever show us kindness. Do not touch her. She is not ours.

He repeated the phrases in his mind. Giving every argument for why he should not go near the female, his Dragon grunted and growled unhappily, but Castor was determined to treat Jozette with respect.

Then she came into the room, and he couldn't remember a single word of his promises to remain unaffected by her presence. Castor's mouth went dry. His palms started to sweat. His cock grew hard inside the soft fleece he wore.

Es meus, his Dragon insisted, growling softly inside his mind's eye.

Castor could not blame the beast for wanting her. She was, in a word, exquisite. Her pale skin held a pink glow from her warm bath, and her hair was thick and glossy, hanging down her back. Big brown eyes blinked at him through dark lashes, and her small bow of a mouth held the promise of a smile in just one corner.

Fuck. He would give anything to have the right to touch her. To be worthy of such a prize, but Castor had to remain firm.

Not a problem, his inner Dragon mused, and his cock throbbed, echoing the sentiment.

After the first dozen romance novels, he now recognized that as a sign of carnal lust. It was like a fever burning inside him, making him want to kiss every inch of her flesh, to touch and feel and claim her as his own. There would be no other prize in the world worth having. Knowing her physically would be the culmination of his wildest dreams, and yet, how could he taste her pleasure knowing it would only be short lived as he?

"Hungry?" Jozette's husky voice reached his ears and there was only one word to suffice.

"Yes."

"Let's see what's in the fridge," she murmured.

The nightly meal prep was something Castor usually looked forward to. It was strange, the modern world with its packaged meat and abundance of fresh vegetables. Blessings indeed. And common too. Though, from what he'd read and seen on television, many still did not enjoy them. Something he felt the world was not working hard enough to correct.

Usually, he enjoyed helping Jozette and learning from her. Tonight was different. Awareness seemed to hang in the air, like smoke, as the two of them worked side by side.

Yes, he enjoyed cooking. Found he had quite the knack for grilled meats and chopped vegetables. He worked at slicing peppers, onions, and broccolini while Jozette cut thin strips of sirloin and turned the rice cooker on. In thirty minutes, they each had bowls of what she told him was beef stir-fry over brown sushi rice.

"This is amazing," Castor said, moaning over a sumptuous bite.

"Thanks. You did most of the hard work," she returned.

"Nonsense. 'Tis your know how made it possible. I thank you."

She blushed under the faint praise, and he shook his head. If it were up to him, Castor would ensure she grow used to that kind of thing. Jozette should be properly complimented and on the daily. He only wished he were the man destined to ensure it.

Determined to enjoy his time, however short, Castor turned his attention to the meal and the company. The meat was tender, the vegetables crisp, and the sweet and tangy garlic soy sauce glaze she'd taught him to make was fantastic. Castor had thirds.

"How are you? Nothing hurts after the accident, right?" he asked once the dishes had been washed and put away.

"I'm fine. You?"

"Yes. Fine."

Usually, they would read companionably or watch something on the flat screen television set. But Castor was wound so tight, he thought for sure, he'd break if tested.

"Um, I think I will turn in early," Jozette said, racing from the room.

"Fuck," he growled softly, turning to watch the snow falling in front of the large living room window.

His mettle had never been tested before. Not like this, at any rate. Sure, he'd lived through long bouts of hibernation when Dragomir had forgotten him. Had survived even longer times when beatings and lashings were dished out twice daily. Castor was no stranger to discomfiture.

He sat on the floor in front of the fireplace. Jozette had allowed him to light one every night since he'd arrived. Every flick and flare of flame soothed him and his beast.

He closed his eyes, wondering when and if he would find what he came for. His brothers. Closure. And how would he reconcile that with the wondrous creature who'd come to mean so much to him?

Castor was uncertain how long he sat in that quasi meditative state before the crash sounded outside. That was followed by a sharp buzz, then silence. Utter and complete silence.

It took mere moments for the house to begin to lose heat. Though he worried about such a transgression, Castor went into Jozette's bedroom, fearing the tiny human would freeze to death if he did not wake her.

Her fragrance seemed to permeate the air as he pushed the door open. Her scent was a heady mixture of sweet coconut and sea foam. Castor licked his lips as he approached her bed, taking in her sleeping form.

She looked so peaceful, so innocent. Completely relaxed and unburdened for the first time since he'd met her. Reaching out with shaking hands, he touched her face, brushing back her long, dark hair.

The room was cold, and soon it would wake her. Better he get on with it now, he figured.

"Jozette? Wake up, my treasure," he murmured the endearment before he even realized it, smiling sadly as he realized how true the sentiment was.

CHAPTER 10

Chills ran through him that had nothing to do with the temperature as he stood gazing down at Jozette's beloved face. Castor had never seen anything more beautiful than her. Everything about her radiated warmth and light from her hair that was a glorious deep mahogany with chestnut highlights, to her big brown eyes, small pert lips, and stubborn little chin.

She stole his breath every time he looked at her. And when he was near enough to catch her scent, hell, his Dragon purred inside of him. The beast was completely besotted.

A Dragon purring! Who'd have thought that possible? Well, his was. Like a great big house cat.

But Castor could not feel anything other than pride in his response to her nearness.

In the span of a week, this woman had become more important than his one goal after leaving the Isle of Pain, and that was finding his brothers. Right then, he did not care if he ever found them. If it meant he got to spend the rest of his days with her, he would gladly forfeit his quest.

Once cemented in his mind, he took in her sleeping face, noted the puffs of breath, and determined her room had already started growing far too cold for her comfort. Castor didn't need to wake her up, he realized. He could simply carry her to the other room by the fireside.

"Mm? Castor?" Jozette slowly came to, the whisper of his name on her lips sent shivers of anticipation racing through him as he cradled her in his arms.

"I'm sorry to wake you," he whispered, still holding her close.

His Dragon stirred as she pressed closer to him, nuzzling his chest with her face. Her coconut and sea foam scent filled his nostrils, and it was all he could do to not press his nose to her skin and breathe her in like a bloodhound.

"What's going on?" she questioned softly.

"The power has gone out. Your room is ice cold. I thought you would be more comfortable by the fire."

Her body was soft and pliable in his arms, and Castor worked hard to ignore his raging arousal as he walked down the hall with his precious bundle. The fact he now knew his hardened cock was a sign of lust didn't make it any easier to bear, it was simply an explanation.

"There you are," he whispered, placing her down on the mattress he'd dragged in front of the fire.

"Oh, wow," she said, sitting up to face him. "When did the power go out? How did you light the fire without the electrical switch?"

"It went out about an hour ago now, and I am a Dragon," he said without adding that he thought she was exceedingly beautiful in her repose, and that he would give anything for the privilege of watching her sleep for as long as he had left on the earth.

"I wanted to let you rest, but I was afraid you would become ill with the temperature dropping," he explained.

He had stood and stared at her as long as he could without disturbing her slumber. Up until the temperature dropped. Then he'd worried about her health and weighed the risks.

"This was all I could do to ensure your safety," he finished.

"It's good. Thank you," she replied and shivered.

"Is it okay if I join you? I mean, I am warmer, naturally. I can help—"

He indicated her covers, and Jozette nodded, making room for him beside her. Castor could see her shivering, hated that she was cold. And since he could not get the electricity up and running, the least he could do was to share his warmth.

Jozette eased closer to him, and finally, he wrapped his arms around her. The second he did, she snuggled right into his side and exhaled.

"I'm so sorry. This is probably awful for you," she said, and he could taste her embarrassment on the air.

Castor frowned.

"Why would it be awful for me?"

"Well, I mean, um," she said, shivering against him. "You know what I mean."

"No, I am afraid I don't. What is it you think I am doing against my will?" he asked, genuinely confused.

"I meant you having to get into bed with me. I know that's not something you probably thought about or want and I—"

"Are you mad?" he scoffed, cutting her off.

"what?"

"Lady Jozette, there is nothing I have wanted in my life more. And if you need the proof, as much as my warmth, here you are then," he growled, and lifting her, placed her directly on his lap. On top of the blatant evidence of his desire.

"Oh, um, wow," she murmured, rocking her hips involuntarily and causing shivers of desire to race through him.

"Are you embarrassed for me now?" Castor asked, shaking his head on a laugh. When she looked up, he saw mirth in her own mahogany depths.

"I just didn't want to assume anything," she primly replied.

Castor scented her desire, reveled in it. She wanted him! Would wonders never cease in this modern age? In the few times he had felt or read her emotions, Castor had not been certain that she returned his desire. But now, he was. And his Dragon roared thunderously in his mind's eye, proud and insistent.

Es meus!

"Assume away," he said, thoroughly enjoying her reactions.

The woman was a wonder. She seemed both elated and confused. As if she disbelieved he could find her attractive. Was she truly mad? He had to wonder. How could someone like her not know her true beauty and appeal?

Even if Castor had not been chained in a dungeon for most of his entire lifetime, he would see her worth. And by the gods, was she worthy. A treasure of a being. One his Dragon wanted right down to the marrow.

"Listen to me, fair maiden, days ago I would not have known what desire meant. I have never had the chance to experience it."

"Never?" she asked, and swallowed nervously.

"Never. I was never free around women."

"And now that you are free and have been around them?"

He tasted her nervousness in the air and frowned. Did she need him to say it? Couldn't she tell this was only for her? Either way, he would let her know beyond a doubt that he was a one woman Dragon. And she was his one woman.

"Now, it makes no difference if I am around ten thousand women. I only ever feel this when I am with you."

"Oh, wow. That's just, wow," she said, head tilting back, face raised to his.

She looked like an offering. One made up of sweet promises and whisper soft dreams, and he gladly wanted to indulge both of them. But how when he was not long for this earth?

"Castor," she said his name, linking her arms around his neck.

"Milady?"

"Do something for me?"

"Anything you want," Castor growled the words.

He was like a bow tightly wound, ready to strike at a breath's notice. Her scent invaded his nostrils, and he breathed her in, drunk on her essence.

"Kiss me." Jozette's lips parted, and her eyelids lowered until they were half-closed.

Fuck.

With her softly whispered plea, Castor could do nothing else but obey. Supporting her soft body on his lap, he closed his hands over her waist and leaned in, his entire focus on her. Slowly, as if he were approaching a small child or animal, Castor moved. With great care and precision, he zeroed in on her parted pink lips.

"Are you certain, milady?"

"Oh, yes," she replied.

Then he moved, pressing his mouth to hers. In that moment, there was no past, no future, only the present. Only her. With that kiss, Castor's entire world changed.

Es Meus.

CHAPTER 11

She was really doing this. Jozette was really kissing him.

Castor wrapped his arms around her, and Jozette wiggled slightly, still straddling his thighs. Heat seeped through her from the firelight or him.

It's him. Definitely him, she thought.

It was like a dream come true. His taste was smoky and sweet as his lips moved over hers. Like he was born to do just that. The heat from his body was more than enough to warm her.

She pressed her core against him, never breaking their kiss, and moaning into his mouth when the hard bar of his cock stroked her through their clothing.

He had on a pair of black boxers while she wore a

long flannel nightgown and cotton panties. Not the least bit erotic, and yet, she felt like a sex goddess when his hands squeezed her waist.

"Jozette," he growled her name, sending lightning bolts of pleasure striking throughout her body, hitting every nerve ending.

Oh, dear lord.

The man growled, and her panties were suddenly flooded. Jozette had never thought herself capable of this, but she was a total slut for him. Turned on beyond measure as they kissed and petted one another in the common pursuit of pleasure.

One night, right? She could do this for one night. She could have raunchy hot AF wild smexy times with a man who looked like a god and was also a fiery Dragon, right?

What about disease? Pregnancy? Or her poor broken heart when he realized he could do better than her pudgy ass and walked away?

Ugh.

Her and her darn puritanical hang ups. Jozette moaned, rocking her hips against him as she slid her tongue into his mouth. Castor really seemed to enjoy that if his growl and the tightening of his fingers on her waist were anything to go by.

Get the condoms already and maybe ask him about Dragony diseases...

Shhhh!

She wanted to yell at her conventional side. Was it too much to ask that she just take a risk? Sigh. Yep. It was.

"Mmm, Castor?"

Grrrrr.

Fuck. He's growling. OMG. That was so fucking hot.

"Castor!"

"Yesssss," he said, hissing and trying to recapture her lips.

"Um, have you, um, you know, had many partners before?"

"Partners?"

"Yeah, sexual partners, I mean."

Easy girl. You can do this. Talking about sex is easy. Natural. Besides, what did her mom always say 'if you can't talk about it you shouldn't be doing it'!

OMG. Please don't think about Mom and Dad right now!

"I have never had sex," he replied, staring at her mouth like it held the secrets to the universe.

Jozette stopped.

"You've really never ever with anyone?"

"I thought I explained I had not been free with a woman—"

"Oh, I thought you meant like to have a relationship with one."

"No, sweet, I was a prisoner for 500 years. Not a lot of women wanted to have sex with the son of a traitor chained in the dungeons on the Isle of Pain," he grunted, one eyebrow raised.

"Uh," she said, licking her lips and trying to wrap her head around that bombshell.

Wait, a sec. Did he just? Holy fuck. He's a virgin!

Her panties were ruined at this point. She knew it. But she didn't care. Need and desire pumped through her veins, and she kissed him again, wrapping her tongue around his and running her hands up and down his muscular body.

"Does that bother you? Jozette?"

"What?"

"Did you want me to stop? I know I am not worthy—"

"Shut up," she moaned, kissing him again.

"Lady Jozette," he growled softly.

"Hmm?" She said, drunk on his taste and on the feel of his long-fingered hands kneading her ass as she ground herself on top of him.

Close. So close.

"Are we going to have sex?" He growled, hips flexing up against her, and she moaned helplessly against him.

"Yes," she said.

If she had anything to say about it. Maybe she should have yelled it? Nah. Better not scare him with her raunchy ass thoughts.

Yes, fuck yes, absolutely, I'll explode if your cock is not inside me in two seconds kind of yes. Yes yes yes. Let's do it.

Instead, she said.

"Yes, Castor. If you want to, I mean."

"Yes. I want to. So much, my sweet treasure. I want to pleasure you," he growled. "Show me how."

Jozette's entire body lit up like the Fourth of July at his hotly whispered words. She moaned and whimpered as his hands slid under her nightgown, ripping the thing off her head.

Whatever the Dragon thought, he did not need lessons. He already knew what to do to please her. The sexy way he'd ripped her gown off was one thing, but when Castor held her away from him, eyes wild as he stared at her naked breasts, well, Jozette had no words.

Her sex swelled and dampened her panties under his hot, appraising gaze. She felt warm and needy. So very needy, as her Dragon simply looked and looked some more.

"So beautiful," he murmured, looking at her for permission before reaching out to touch her skin.

Jozette moaned as his hands cupped and tested both plump mounds. His growl rippled through her as he teased and caressed, learning the shape and weight of each one. He laid her back on the mattress, careful of the fire. Hovering over her with his naked torso highlighted by the flames.

"I want to kiss you there," Castor grunted, finger-tips skimming over her nipples.

The erotic dance of his bronzed hands on her pale skin was mesmerizing. She couldn't help but watch as he touched her, and fuck, she felt it, ten times over. His own amazement shone in his eyes, the indigo pools glittering with heat as he waited for her reply.

"Yes, please, kiss me," she said, arching off the mattress when he did, settling his mouth on one tight nipple.

Jozette moaned as Castor explored her skin with his mouth, teeth, and hands. She'd never felt so treasured in her entire life. The way he murmured words of praise, kissing, and sampling her skin like he was committing the taste and texture to memory, had her already damp panties growing wetter with every passing swipe of his talented tongue.

"More," he growled after releasing her tight bud with a loud pop.

Jozette nodded, more sounded good to her. Castor's nostrils flared, indigo eyes glowing as he nuzzled and kissed his way down her soft belly. She didn't even mind her rolls as his hands reached for her panties, tearing them clean off her skin. The Dragon seemed impatient to get at her, and she couldn't fault him for that. Not when she needed him there so desperately.

Jozette leaned up on her elbows, watching him kiss his way down her pale flesh. Some areas were pink from his attentions, others needy and wanting more. Hell, make that all of her. Knowing what he was about to do made her breathing race and her heart pound.

Castor parted her legs, a low growl rumbling deep in his chest. He breathed in her scent, eyes closing as if in ecstasy, before pinning her with his stare.

"Tell me what to do, sweet," Castor said, eyes blazing with hunger.

Jozette licked her lips. She knew what she wanted. But she'd always been too shy to tell her few and far between lovers what it was she needed to feel good.

It was plain that he wanted her, but it was also very clear her sexy virginal Dragon needed the words.

Fuck it.

She thought, owning her own sexuality for the first time in her life. Embarrassment had no place here on this mattress between the two of them. So with a boldness she'd never had before, Jozi met his indigo stare.

"Tell me how to please you," he said again, growling with his beast.

The rumbling sound sent lightning strikes of pleasure shooting through her body. Jozi was already so turned on, what did she have to lose?

Only my pride, she thought. But it was a price she was willing to pay for the pleasure promised in his unwavering stare.

"When two people want each other, anything goes," she began, stroking his broad chest with her hands.

"I want to do everything, anything, to make you feel good," he growled.

"I want that too," she said, and her body heated. "I

want you to touch me, Castor. Everywhere. I want you to kiss me—"

"Can I kiss you anywhere?" he asked, eyes glowing and accent thickening with his beast.

"Yeah, you can. Kiss me here," she said, pointing to her lips.

"Or here," she moaned, and her hands cupped her breasts.

"Or even here," she said, indicating her sex.

"I can kiss you here?" Castor's eyes opened wide, heat filling them as he stared at her sex.

"Oh yeah. In fact, I'd like for you to kiss me there."

"You would?"

"Yes. I want you to kiss me, to lick my pussy, Castor. I want to feel you push your fingers deep inside. To tease me until I come apart. Then I want you to replace your fingers with that thick cock of yours. I want you inside me, Castor."

"You do?"

"Yes. I do. Only you."

Castor swallowed hard. Chest heaving, he looked ready to burst. But Jozette wasn't finished yet. She had to know how he felt about all this.

"What about you, Castor? Do you want that too?"

CHAPTER 12

"Yessssss," he hissed the word, drawing it out and rolling the *s* in a way she hadn't thought possible.

Then Jozi couldn't talk anymore. At least, not coherently. Suddenly, he was everywhere. Hands, lips, tongue, and teeth. He explored her with his mouth and body.

His smooth, muscled body slid up and down hers, making her feel things she'd never experienced. Castor had admittedly never had sex before, but he was a fast learner.

His skilled, *and did she mention forked when he wanted it to be,* tongue slid down her body, suckling her breasts. He kissed her soft belly, spreading her thighs once more, and settling between them.

Then, as if he knew it was going to torture her, Castor dropped whisper soft kisses on her thighs and her labia. He watched her as he opened his mouth and sucked on her nether lips, kissing her pussy and moaning as if she were something delicious and sweet.

"You are sweet," he growled, then spread her wide and lapped at her from her forbidden hole to her clit, curling his skilled appendage around the tight bud with every single swipe.

Castor moaned as he ate her, dipping one thick digit inside her heated channel. Next there was two, then a third. Jozette was overwhelmed by sensation and pulled on his hair. She moaned and whimpered with every stroke, swipe, plunge, and withdraw. Arching up to meet him, she bucked her hips, wildly seeking her pleasure. Demanding it even.

The man really was a fucking god. Whether it was intuition, instinct, or pure joy leading him, she did not know or care. Hands tangled in his hair, Jozette let go of every inhibition. Castor's free hand cupped her breasts and skimmed her thighs until she felt him everywhere. Like he was in every cell and pore.

The first spiral of pleasure began soft and low, and like an apex predator chasing prey, Castor seemed aware of it. He hunted it, chasing down her orgasm until it crashed into her like a hurricane wind, and Jozette screamed with it.

"Es meus!" Castor roared, sliding up her body and sinking into her with one hard thrust.

———

Castor was holding onto his scales by a thread. This was a moment to be forever etched in his mind. Dead or alive, he would never forget the feeling of sliding into her heat and joining with the only woman he'd ever loved.

He had no past, no pain, no emptiness, not with her. Castor had never felt this way before. So in tune with his beast. Both parts of him seeking to bring his mate the ultimate release. The dragon urged him on, wanting to give her everything he had inside.

Barely hanging on to his self-control, he thrust his hips, spearing her on his engorged cock. They were so close he felt her heart beating as if it were his own. And it was glorious.

The sounds their bodies made in the darkness were symphonic to his Dragon's ears. Her gasps and moans increased his attentions, adding to the building pleasure, so much so he thought he would expire from it.

Castor increased his pace, developing a rhythm old as time and yet new as the dawn. He wanted her to know how much she meant to him, wondered if she could feel his love through every thrust and grind.

"Jozette," he growled her name before closing his mouth over the honey sweet skin on her neck.

Her body cradled him like she was born for him, and Castor wanted to stamp himself all over her. Jozette was eager and earnest, hips rising to meet his downward thrusts as if she, too, could not get enough of him.

It was a heady thing being wanted, needed in such a manner. And Castor loved her all the more for it. If he could spend the rest of his days kissing her, balls deep in her heated channel, he would die a happy Dragon.

Fuck, he didn't want to think of that.

Death and sadness had no place here. This was joy. This was communion. And he had never felt so complete and full of purpose.

His sweet Jozette moaned, her tiny nails scoring his back as he shifted, delving deeper into her sopping heat. Every inch of him was coated in her slick heat. It felt so good and so very hot, Castor never wanted to leave her.

Her sex squeezed him, and he damn near went cross eyed at the shock of pleasure that zipped through him. She moaned and bucked, scratching him with her nails.

How could anything feel this good? Fuck if he knew. His body tensed, and he felt Jozette in every cell of his being. The Dragon inside him watched closely, his instinct to give her all the pleasure she could take and then some.

The gorgeous female panted and moaned. At first, he was afraid he'd hurt her, but she was neither weak nor faint of heart. Jozette's thick thighs squeezed his hips and her heels dug into his buttocks, urging him on.

Her shouts of *faster, harder,* and *more* echoed in his ears. That was when Castor's beast truly took over. The Dragon was breathing down his neck, and he was helpless to do anything other than feel as the beast urged his movements on.

"Please," Jozette begged, her small hands clinging to his sweat damped shoulders.

"Anything, my treasure," he grunted, grabbing her hips, and tilting her for an even deeper, harder penetration.

"Yes, more," she demanded.

And he obliged. How could he not? It felt too damn good to resist. If Castor was going to die anyway, he was damn sure going to give this first coming together with Jozette everything he had.

The beast in him was starving for her. He pulled his cock nearly all the way out, then pushed in hard and swiftly. She liked that, *fuck yes*, she did if her moans and cries were anything to go by.

With every withdraw and plunge, he brought her closer to imminent pleasure. Hot on the heels of pure ecstasy, Castor growled her name.

He wanted her to climax. Craved it. Needed it. For her to feel the very thing he'd been denied till now. Pure, unadulterated bliss.

Yes, that was what he worked for, it was in his every move. Like a man possessed, or a Dragon he supposed, he moved in perfect precision with her piercing little cries.

"Castor," she moaned his name, her body moving jerkily as her pleasure peaked.

"Es meus," he growled.

Her sweet sex massaged his cock, milking his thick shaft with every plunge. Her brown eyes were glazed with passion as she leaned up to kiss his mouth. Castor went crazy then. He kissed her hard and deep, his tongue mimicking his cock thrusting into her heated depths.

He trailed more kisses down her chin to her neck, beneath her ear, as she squeezed her legs around him and he swiveled and circled inside of her. Watching her every move and response, he paid close attention and learned what pleased his sweet, beautiful female.

His?

Yes.

Fuck, yes.

Es meus, the Dragon inside him agreed.

He would not let her go. Not ever. However long, *or short*, a time he had left on this Earth, Castor was going to spend it with Jozette. He loved her. The realization rose inside him like the tide, and he increased his efforts. Rotating his hips and increasing his pace.

Her pussy squeezed, and the sounds of her passion filled the air. Before he knew what he was doing, Castor had opened his mouth wide, then he clamped down, biting her flesh with his shifted fangs until he drew blood.

Pure pleasure seemed to explode from everywhere as Castor swallowed down the coppery sweet liquid, lapping twice at the wound, before tossing his head back and shouting his own culmination.

Castor's mouth opened and his mighty roar shook the room, sparks of bluish fire lit the room and waves of magical energy encapsulated them both as he came inside Jozette's heavenly body.

Words in the ancient tongue of the Dragons, *Dracan*, escaped his lips as he came, and came, and came.

Promises and vows he whispered to her and into the night, pledging his loyalty, honor, and heart. He ended the litany in one phrase, the same one that had been on repeat in his brain since he'd first knocked upon her door.

"Es meus," he repeated.

That possessive phrase roared inside his mind as he came and spilled his seed inside her womb, marking her with his bite and scent.

As a prisoner, Castor had never learned the ways of his Clan, especially not when it came to matings. But some things were instinct. His Dragon was certain she was meant to be his.

For days he'd been reading about love and mates in the romance section of her bookstore. But this was better than any book. This was his destiny, he realized as he finally came down from the high that was loving on her. And it was love. Of that, he was certain.

Castor loved Jozette with everything he had inside of him.

"Can I have you?"

The question slipped from his lips without hesitation as Castor cupped her blushing face in his hands.

"What? You have had me," she replied, biting her lower lip in a way that made him growl with need.

Still buried inside her, he was careful not to crush the beauty as he rested between her thighs, waiting for her to respond. The question was impromptu, but he wanted an answer. Needed it.

Jozette turned her brown gaze to him. Her breathing was still shaky as she came down from the same heaven he'd just visited inside her arms. It filled him with pride to know he'd satisfied her, brought her pleasure. Even sated, his body responded to the truth of their passion immediately. Swelling with need, he hissed as her sheath squeezed his shaft so perfectly.

Fuck me. Yes, Castor wanted her. Hell, he found himself wanting to bring her even higher this time. To see her erupt with pleasure, like a volcano from his touch.

Es meus.

"How is that possible?" She murmured, seemingly astounded by his ability to perform again.

"I am Dragon," he growled as her eyes rolled back inside her head when he circled his hips, sliding his hardened cock in and out of her soft, wet sheath.

"You feel so good, my treasure," he growled, kissing her lips. "Can I have you? Sweet Josette, can I? I must."

"Yes," she replied. "God, yes."

CHAPTER 13

Jozette woke up with Castor's arms wrapped around her, and she'd never felt so safe and cherished in all her life.

"You are my treasure," he murmured, kissing the top of her head.

"Did I say that out loud?" she wondered.

"Yes," he replied, and she felt him smile against her head.

"Are you hungry, sweet?"

"Mm mm," she shook her head, wiggling happily against him and loving the recognizable swell of a certain something against her backside.

"Stop that, minx, or I'll have to have you again," he teased, kissing her shoulder and neck.

His hand cupped her breast, and he teased her

nipples as he spread her legs. With one slow and unerring stroke, he filled her from behind. Castor's magnificently thick cock felt so good inside her, stretching her just right, and stroking that secret place no one else had ever managed to touch.

"Yes," she murmured, already wet and ready, seconds from coming.

With him buried deep, how could she not? Yes, she was going to explode again in passion, for him, with him, only him. Her Dragon lover.

"God, it gets better each time," she whispered, still panting some long minutes or hours after.

"Indeed," he agreed with her. "Making love with you has no comparison, my treasure. Your body is a wonderland, a feast for my eyes, mouth, and hands, and I am always starving for you," he said with a playful growl in his voice as he turned her over to kiss her lips.

"Mmm. I need a toothbrush and a shower."

"Yes? Can I join you?"

"I think that can be arranged."

"Hey, what is that?" Castor frowned, pulling the blanket away from her chest.

Jozette laughed, then looked at her body. What the what?

"How did that—"

"I don't understand," he muttered, looking down at his chest than at hers.

True, the first time Castor made love to Jozette, she'd been too overwhelmed by passion and pleasure to notice the burning sensation on her chest. But now, in the light of morning, with the return of the electricity, she recalled feeling a stinging sensation there.

"Oh my God!" Jozette yelped as she stood up and ran to the bathroom mirror.

There had been a sort of electrical buzz on her body, but she'd assumed that was just from the friction. Of course, turning her head, she noticed the sharp pain she had felt on her neck was not what she'd assumed, a hickey gone wild, and was in fact, a bite.

"You bit me!"

"Um, well," he hedged, brushing his hands over his mussed hair.

"And you tattooed me!"

"What? No I did not," he said, then frowned, looking at the matching image on his chest.

"My garnet rose," he whispered, touching it.

"'Tis not possible."

"Yes, it fucking 'tis! I am looking at it, Castor!" Jozette yelled.

And it was there, plain to see in front of their eyes. She recalled his tattoo being a small wilted looking bud of a thing, but now it was a rose in full bloom etched in indigo and red ink. On her chest was the exact same image, smaller, but there.

Jozette gasped and skimmed the flower with her fingertips, noting that same buzz of electricity.

"Oh my God! Did you see that?" she asked.

Jozette repeated the movement and noting the blue and red flickers of light glowing from the rose.

"It is a legend," he whispered, clearly shocked.

"What legend? What does this mean?"

"I am a Dragon Shifter, Jozette. A *ChangeDragon*, though I know not what that means entirely as I was imprisoned since birth."

"I know, and I am sorry, but what does this mean?"

"I should have told you last night. You see, I am dying, Jozette. And in my selfish greed I wanted to have you, even if only for a short while—"

Tears sprang to her eyes at his words, and she covered her mouth in horror. Dying? No! He could not be dying. He looked healthy. And he was magic, for fuck's sake.

"Please do not cry, my treasure," he whispered, gathering her in his arms. "I am sorry. I did not know making love to you would produce a mark on your skin. I will find a way to fix it—"

"I don't care about that. What do you mean by dying? Castor, you can't be dying!"

"I am afraid I am. The Dragons who freed me after Castle Blackthorne fell said it. They called me *ChangeDragon* and told me death was all I could hope for from my kind—"

"This was why I hate fairytales," she said and sat down heavily on the closed toilet, sobbing.

"The endings are always fucked up."

"Sweet, please do not cry," he said, kneeling in front of her and taking her face in his hands.

That act of compassion only had her crying harder.

"I am so sorry, my love."

"I am the one who is sorry, Castor. You are dying. Why? How? Can we fix it?"

"I do not know. As for the rose, there were rumors in the castle of fated mates. Two souls destined for one another who shared a bond unlike any other. It is that which every Dragon aspires to, but I do not know all of what it means. All I know is I would never give my *garnet rose* to another."

"Garnet rose?"

"Yes, my treasure. All Dragons have a stone and a

rose. My rose has always been that of the blue garnet. Not at all common. Sort of like my *ChangeDragon*."

"Okay. Look, I am not mad. And I don't think you are dying—"

"Jozette, I do not wish you to lie to yourself—"

"No, listen. I am going to help you find your brothers, and we are going to get to the bottom of this."

Then several things happened.

One, after Castor dropped the bomb about his garnet rose and possible death, the sexual haze that had filled the long night had already cleared. It was replaced by something deeper, calmer, but no less emotional.

Naked, and standing once more. Jozette cupped his cheek, resolved to help the man she'd shared her home, work, and body with. And she had the sneaking suspicion, also, her heart.

Two, the front door opened and Jozette froze instantly at the sound of her mother's shrill yell, and her father nervously clearing his throat.

"Jozette! What on earth is going on here?"

Henry and Darla Keeper stood in their living room with pinched expressions on their pale faces.

Their time away certainly had not improved their dispositions. Jozette grimaced.

She hadn't been caught in the buff with a guy since she was seventeen and that had been prom weekend. Poor Mom and Dad had had *the talk* with her, but they were not at all happy with show and tell. A lesson she'd learned the hard way.

Eeek!

"Mom! Dad!" She slapped her hands over her mouth while Castor thoughtfully grabbed a towel and draped it in front of her.

"Who is that man? And is that the guest room mattress?"

"Mr. and Mrs. Keeper," Castor said, wrapping a smaller towel around his waist. "I am Castor Falk."

Oh shit.

Jozette shook her head and spoke up. As lovely as her parents' new house was, they lacked the same charm and warmth that made the structure appealing. Something she hadn't really thought about until right then.

CHAPTER 14

"When and where did you come from?" her mother asked.

"What are you two doing back? You said you were extending your stay," Jozette interrupted. stepping in front of Castor to deflect her mother's questions.

"Our plans changed, Jozette. This is our home, not a motel. I am shocked and appalled by your behavior. Is this why your last boyfriend left? This kind of reckless behavior—"

"The heat went out, and we had to sleep by the fire last night—"

"And what? You had to have sex to stay warm?" her mother asked nastily.

"Wow, Mom! I'll clean the living room. I just

wasn't expecting you back so soon."

"It's a good thing we came back in time to catch you making a fool of yourself. Where is the car, anyway?" her father asked, muttering.

"What?" Jozette asked. She might be used to her mother's dismissal, but hearing derision in her father's voice was new and entirely unwelcomed.

"Jozi, honey, you just got out of one bad relationship and here you are—"

"Okay, you know what? We are not having this discussion and I am a full-grown adult—"

"Really? You still live at home, sweetheart. You have no prospects," her mother said.

"I have a job. And you said I could stay at home while I work on—"

"Yeah, yeah, honey. We know you say you are writing a book, but is that actually viable? And lord knows you can't make enough at the store to afford rent."

Her parents looked at each other and then back at her. The condescension was just too much. All her life, whenever she'd had a dream, they'd been there to point out the irrationality and unlikelihood of it. She wanted to tell them then and there that they were wrong. That she had a bright future. But before she could say another word, Castor stepped out from behind her.

"Enough! What foolishness is this? My parents were both killed before I could know them, but I swear they would have had none of this nonsense you call love!"

He glared at the two of them, and Jozette couldn't stop her mouth from hanging open at his brazen approach. The Keepers were renowned for their ability to make even the most learned of people feel small and start to doubt themselves. It was just who they were.

"Your daughter is a treasure! So full of warmth and generosity, a kindness of spirit I see she must have found elsewhere, for it was not from the likes of you."

"How dare you call yourself father when you dismiss her ideas and hopes? How dare you call yourself mother when you deny her affection? I say again, Jozette is a treasure on this dark and cold earth. She is the best of us, and you are lucky to have her in your life. The gods know I am."

"Jozette," her mother said, frowning so hard her lips had become a straight line. "Just who is this person?"

"Never mind, Mom. Castor, get dressed. We're leaving."

Usually, when she'd been berated by her parents, Jozette was moody and quiet for days. This time, she was angry. Castor was right. Her parents were not supportive of her at all. Never had been.

But the thing of it was, Jozi was not a child anymore. She did not need their permission or approval. But she also could not live with them, or as they saw it, off them, any longer.

It was time to stop looking for love where it did not exist. Time for her to take her Dragon and learn to trust her own instincts.

"Are you alright?" Castor asked as they gathered their few things.

"I will be," she said, and kissed him on the mouth.

And for the first time, Jozette Keeper truly believed that.

Later that day...

"Thanks for the ride, Mar," Jozette said to her bestie.

She was watching amusedly as Hector tried to teach her Dragon how to play table tennis. Amazing how a silly game could get so heated between two men, *er*, Shifters.

In fact, it wasn't long before they'd resorted to

wrestling. Honestly, if they weren't both so good looking, it would have been laughable. And where Hector was built and handsome, she only had eyes for her Dragon.

"Should we break that up?" Jozi asked.

"Who? Them? Nah," Marissa shook her head and handed Jozette a mug full of spiked hot chocolate and a tin of homemade fudge.

"So good," she sighed, and took her first sip.

Marissa was always a great friend, and the second Jozi had texted, she was on her way. Good thing Maccon City took care of plowing and salting the roads earlier that morning. It was after the snowstorm had suddenly stopped, of course, and the temperature rose to a balmy thirty-seven degrees. February at the Jersey Shore was temperamental at best.

"Shifter males are like perpetual teenagers," Marissa continued.

"Yeah, I can see that," Jozette said, shaking her head.

"It was my point," Castor growled, flipping Hector over.

The Dragon was winning for a moment, but the Lion was strong too, and more used to playing with others.

"No, it wasn't. It was my serve!"

He flipped the Dragon once more, leading to more tumbling through the main living room of the other male's Maccon City home.

"Can I ask you a question?" Jozette asked seriously.

"Sure, fire away."

Marissa was blowing on her own mug of the hot cocoa and vodka infusion when Jozette dropped the little bomb her lover of the previous night had shared with her.

"He's what?"

"He says he is dying," she whispered, hoping the music in the background and their wrestling was enough to keep the guys from overhearing.

"Oh, Jozi," Marissa replied, leaning forward to touch her friend's leg.

"Is it true, do you think? Cause I don't know if I can take that," she said hating the crack that sounded in her voice.

She turned her head to wipe her eyes, and Marissa grabbed the tissue box and handed it to her, joining her on the sofa. Her BFF wrapped her arms around her and hugged her tightly. Then she stopped, sniffed, and pushed her back.

"Holy fuck! You're mated!"

"What?"

"What?"

Hector and Castor stopped rolling round on the floor, the Dragon had the Lion in a headlock. Castor tilted his head to the side and looked at Marissa, then Jozette, and back.

"Mated?"

"You bit her!" Marissa accused.

"Yes, well, I, um, got carried away, but I did not harm the lady," Castor said.

He stood up with his arm still wrapped around Hector's neck. The Lion was turning red, but no one really seemed to notice. Except for Hector, who started slapping at the Dragon's beefy arms.

"Sorry," he murmured, dropping the other man.

"What does that mean, we're mated?" Jozette asked, blinking rapidly.

"Well, I am assuming you had sex," Marissa said.

"Yes, well, we—"

The Lioness closed her hands over her ears, shook her head, and started yelling before Jozette could finish.

"Don't wanna know details. *La La LA!*"

"Okay, already."

"Look who got all slut-tastic last night!"

"OMG. Look who's talking. We only—"

"La La LA!"

"OMG! Shut up already with that! Sheesh Mar, grow up!" Jozette said, slapping Marissa with the pillow.

"Alright," the Lioness replied, giggling. "Seriously though, he bit you, right?"

"Yes."

"Then you're mates."

"We're mates? Like friends?" Jozette asked.

"No. It is like being married, but more," Marissa explained.

"Pardon, but what does that mean?" Castor asked, interrupting their banter.

"What it means, lizard breath, is you are truly fucked," Hector answered.

The Lion was patting Castor's shoulder and shaking his own leonine head when Jozette stood too suddenly. Maybe Marissa was too heavy handed with the vodka.

Or it could have been the shock of being told she was essentially married to Castor that caused Jozette to faint. She could not be entirely sure as the room began to spin and tilt dangerously.

The latter, she thought as her body hit the floor. *Definitely the latter.*

CHAPTER 15

"Jozette? Wake, my sweet treasure," Castor whispered to his mate as he gathered her up off the cold floor.

"Here, bring her in here," Marissa held the door open to the guest room where they would be spending the night.

Once more, he found himself indebted to someone for his rescue. He was eternally grateful for the kindness Marissa and Hector had shown to both him and Jozette. One day, he would repay them. That, he swore.

He placed his precious bundle on the bed, hovering near as her eyelids started to flutter. Thank the gods! Her big brown eyes started to focus, and he never thought anything so beautiful as she.

"Hey," she whispered, sitting up.

"Do you need anything, Jozi?" Marissa asked from across the room.

"No, um, can you give us the room?"

"Sure, hon. Hector and I will be inside."

"Okay." Jozette nodded, and Castor was glad when the two Lions left.

His inner beast wanted them gone. He wanted Jozette all to himself. Especially after her collapse. The need to make certain she was right and well burned inside of him.

"You gave me a fright, love," he murmured.

His eyes roamed over her sweet shape, from the top of her dark head to the bottoms of her pink stockinged feet.

Socks, he recalled with a grin. She called them socks.

"What?"

"Nothing. I like your socks," he murmured, tucking her hand in his.

Castor lifted her palm to his mouth and pressed his lips there. His heart filled with joy when she did not pull away.

"I did not know, Jozette."

"That you were marking me as your mate when you bit me," she said in a low voice.

"Is there a way to undo it?" Jozette asked.

Castor's heart thundered and squeezed. It felt as though his soul was being ripped through his chest. Did she not want him? Was that it?

"Jozette," he said, mouth dry. "I know I am not long for this world, and that I have nothing to offer you. No worldly goods. No castle. No money. No kin. But I love you Jozette. With everything I am, I love you."

"You want to be mated to me?"

Her eyes met his, and he thought he saw wonder in them. And joy.

Could it be?

Es meus.

"Want you? With all my heart, for all my life, however long or short. I swear I will never want another. Only you, Jozette Keeper. *Es meus.*"

Castor tugged her towards him and wrapped his arms around her. Happiness spread through him like lightning when she clung to him, saying back the words he'd never thought to hear.

"I love you too, Castor," she mumbled against his shoulder, sniffling against him.

"We will make it work. Somehow, we will," she said, laughing and crying at the same time. His heart squeezed inside of him, he would do anything to keep her happy and safe. He would work till his fingers bled for her.

"I will do anything, Jozette. Anything to keep you safe, warm, happy, loved. Gods, you are so very loved," he growled.

Castor took her face in his hands, her hair got tangled in his fingers, but he didn't stop. He tugged her gently, till she could press her mouth to his. And press, she did. Crashing into him like waves on the shore.

"I'm sorry that I am poor. That I cannot give you more than my heart," he growled as he disrobed.

Castor pulled off his clothing roughly, while never parting their lips for too long. He eased her down on the mattress, savoring her unique flavors as they danced across his tastebuds.

"Your heart is the only thing I want from you," she replied, and bucked against him.

"The only thing?" he teased.

"Well, that and your very sexy body," she said, grinning wickedly.

"I'm glad you think I am sexy, mate. But you should know, you are better than anything I have ever dreamed. I love you, my treasure," he growled.

Her coconut and sea foam kisses undid him. He was putty in her hands. Determined to bring her nothing but pleasure, Castor unwrapped his mate like a present. Like a treasure.

"*Es meus*," he growled and freed her bountiful breasts from their confines.

"Yours," she confirmed. "I want every day we have together, Castor. I don't ever want to be apart."

"Good. I want that too," he moaned the words as he licked a trail from nipple to nipple.

Castor suckled each berry ripe bud, lavishing attention on one, then the other. Meanwhile, his hands found her thighs and parted them. He spread her heated lips apart, using her own wetness to ease his passage.

"Please," she moaned, bucking up against his hands, searching for more.

"Anything. I will give you anything you want," he murmured.

"You," she gasped as he pressed the head of his cock into her sheath. "I want you."

After that, there was no more talking. Only feeling. Castor could not get enough of her. Never would. And when she took control, pushing him till he rolled them over, fuck, he thought he died right then.

Jozette straddled him, the change of position sent his cock deeper inside her slick heat. His sweet treasure moaned.

Scratch that.

She purred. Like she had a beast of her own inside, and fuck if that didn't make his dick even harder. The little vixen started riding him in earnest. Her breasts bounced with each move, and Castor could hardly contain his beast.

He sat up, hands kneading her plump buttocks as he sucked one hardened nipple into his mouth. The sounds of their pleasure, hopefully muted to the rest of the house as Hector's earlier words came back to him "don't worry, the rooms have all been sound proofed", were like an erotic symphony to his sensitive ears.

Up, down, swirl, grind.

Castor could hardly breathe for the pleasure sizzling along his skin and deep in his blood. Like a goddess she moved with her hair floating around her like a dark cloud.

"Jozette," he growled her name.

Castor whispered words of encouragement and praise to her as she made love to him. No one had ever made him feel these things. She was his first, his only, and would remain so forever. However short or long their forever was, was up to the gods, but Castor would not waste a moment of it on regret.

"I love you," she moaned as her sex clamped down on his.

"I love you," he growled back.

His lips travelled to her neck, teeth skating across the bitemark he'd given her. Castor felt her orgasm rip through her, speeding him on the same path, and if possible, her sex squeezed even tighter.

They collapsed in a tangle of arms and legs atop the bed, and Castor vowed to do right by her. Always.

"Es meus, my sweet treasure." He murmured as they slipped into sleep.

Days later...

"Jozette will have my ass if I let you wander around by yourself," Marissa growled, trying to catch up with Castor.

"Fuck man, it's cold here," Hector complained.

The two Lions had become his constant companions on days when Jozette worked at *Crescent Moon Books*. He still went to the store with her, but she really needed to work on her manuscript during the lulls in customers. And he was a distraction.

He was man enough to know this. Dragon

enough not to care. The beast was more than happy to distract her. And with what interesting ways!

Indeed, there was no sex education in the dungeons of Castle Blackthorne, but he'd done some very interesting reading in that little store. When no one was looking, of course.

Still, the fact they lived in the home of another, while kind, did not sit well with him. He reminded himself he could not simply do nothing. In fact, he *would not* remain idle while she worked to support them. His Dragon understood this, and the beast quickly relented his former position.

"I must try something," Castor explained to the two shivering Cats. "If you are cold, pray leave me here. I will be fine."

"Aren't you cold?" Marissa yelled over the wind.

"Not at all. I am a Dragon," he said, and let out a bark of laughter.

"Are you sure this part of the beach is isolated?"

"Yeah," Hector said, nodding and wrapping an arm around Marissa.

"There's a private home about half a mile down that way, but they can't see anything from here."

"Good," Castor nodded. "Did you bring the bag I asked for? And Marissa, did you call your contacts?"

"Got it here," Hector said, showing Castor the large backpack he carried with him.

"Yeah, I called my uncle. He works in the diamond district in Manhattan. He is expecting us in an hour. But what is this about?" Marissa asked.

"I need a moment. Just make sure you stand back," Castor instructed them.

There was a sort of sea stack that went all the way out to sea for a quarter of a mile or so and began on the shore, blocking them from view. Or so he hoped. What he was about to try was based on some scientific reading he'd done earlier that week. He had to do something.

"What are you going to do?" Marissa asked.

Castor did not answer. He was too busy seeing what he'd dreamt only the night before in his mind. But was it a dream? Or just his Dragon trying to show him the path that would lead to a fruitful future for his mate?

As a prisoner, Castor had been helpless. But he was free now, and beyond all expectations, he had found his mate. The two who had freed him did so before they knew what he was, before he knew what he was—a *ChangeDragon*.

Whatever the fuck that meant.

Rrrrr.

His inner beast objected to the idea it meant anything other than greatness. A Dragon trait, he thought, but how was he to know? Maybe he really was fucked since birth, as Dragomir had said.

No!

This time, it was the man who rejected that notion. Chief Blackthorne had been the worst kind of tyrant. Weak. Ignorant. Miserable. And ruled by jealousy and greed. Nothing he said should be taken to heart by anyone, least of all Castor.

Still, if death was his only recourse, he would not go quietly. Certainly not without providing for the woman who meant so much to him.

"Shouldn't we be looking for signs of your family?" Marissa shouted above the roar of waves and whipping wind, interrupting his thought process.

"Mar, he's busy," Hector replied for him.

Castor approved of the other male. He was a good, strong man. A stouthearted Lion, indeed. Why the pair were not mated, he had no idea. It was not his business either. But he could not understand it. After all, the thought of touching Jozette and not claiming her was beyond his own abilities.

After taking a few more steps away from the

bickering couple, he set his gaze on a pile of small rocks mixed in with the sand some feet from where the waves were crashing into the shore. Castor allowed his beast to surge forward. Slowly. Carefully. And not completely. He needed to remain a man in case anyone happened by.

He closed his eyes and reimagined his dream from the night before. Gemstones aplenty and in all hues, with his blue-red Dragon guarding the lot. The beast growled approvingly at the hordes of treasure in his mind's eye.

He saw the stones. Weighed and measured them carefully in his dreamscape vision. Now, to make them reality. He shook off the nerves assailing him. There was no room for self-doubt. Not where Jozette was concerned, or her care. No, Castor could never be anything other than certain when it came to his mate.

He opened his eyes, pulling on his Dragon's power. It filled him until he felt it in every cell. Raw and pulsing, a wild and powerful thing, but it was not evil as he'd feared. And it was not reckless so long as he was not.

His beast scratched at his skin, but Castor held on to the reins. He shook himself once, then released his power in a shock of blue flames etched in red.

The laser like beam of his *ChangeDragon's* fire shot from his lips with unerring accuracy.

There was little smoke, but he knew it was hot enough to sever even a Dragon's limb clean off through scale, sinew, and bone. But his own fire would never hurt him, that much he knew. Once the flames died down, he huffed out a cloud of smoke from his lungs, surprised at the sight that greeted him. First, the mountain of stones appeared white hot, still glowing from the heat of his fire.

Once the February wind hit them, they started to cool, revealing an array of gemstones in every hue and size imaginable. Some were so big, he wondered if they were larger than even his fist.

"Holy shit!" Marissa exclaimed.

"Dude!" Hector gasped.

The pair whooped and patted him on the back. Castor exhaled softly. The pile of gems was surely valuable. He could only hope they would provide his mate with a worthy home.

"Will this be enough?"

"Yes, absolutely," Marissa said.

"Good. Let us go meet your uncle, so that we may share the news with my Jozette."

Just thinking about his dark haired treasure caused his Dragon to prowl within him. The creature was proprietary, to say the least. And why shouldn't he be? Castor was one lucky bastard to have Jozette in his life. And he was going to show her, guaranteed.

Es meus.

CHAPTER 16

Jozette looked down at her laptop and frowned. She'd been trying to work on her *History of Maccon City*, but for some reason the only words that came to her were utterly ridiculous.

Or were they?

She wondered as she opened a new document. There'd been a lull in customers after the morning rush, and *Crescent Moon Books* was blissfully quiet just then. She had an hour till story time, so why not sit down and write?

Mind made up, Jozette did something she'd never thought possible. She trusted herself and let her imagination run wild. A smile played on the corner of her mouth as she wrote page after page of a fantastical romantic adventure.

Her parents would be horrified, she thought with a laugh that soon had her frowning. Dammit. She did not want to think of them. It had been days since she'd last seen them. Jozette had no choice but to go back to their house to gather her clothes and the few things she'd not placed in storage.

It had been uncomfortable as hell, but necessary. She did not want to have to explain to her parents her sudden attachment to Castor. It should be enough for them that she was happy. But it never was.

They obviously would not understand, even if she was allowed to tell them about his circumstances. One of the first things Marissa had explained was the Shifter world was a secret world. They existed apart from humans by necessity.

No wonder, Jozette thought with a shake of her head. After all, what would society do to people like her BFF and her boyfriend? They'd put them in a lab and dissect them most likely. Just before they rounded up a crazy mob to attack them.

Yeah. No. Humans were not the best at dealing with things that were *different*. Just thinking about it gave her chills. And not the good ones.

"Hello?"

Jozette closed her laptop after clicking save and ran to the front of the shop.

"Hey there," she greeted a woman with a gaggle of small children with her.

The woman was beautiful with long blonde hair and Jozette recognized her as a frequent customer and story time attendee. She crouched and said hello to the kids.

"How are you all doing today?"

"Well," the woman said, grinning, with a toddler snug in her arms. "We could not wait for the plows to come through so we could get over here for story hour. Are we too early?"

"Not at all. Come on and let's find some cushions for you guys," Jozette said, leading the way.

"Alright, now what are we going to do today?" she asked.

"*Story! Story!*" The older children chanted, giggling as they sat down *criss cross applesauce* on the various cushions on the story time rug.

"Is it okay if I stay for this one?"

"Sure. And I apologize, I forgot your name, I'm Jozette," she said and held out her hand.

The stunning blonde smiled and shook her hand in return. She was tall and rather strong, but maybe that was mommy muscles or something. The glint in her eyes reminded Jozi of Marissa, and she started getting a rather strange sensation just over her chest.

"My name's Fred. This is little Eddie, my nephew, and my daughter Calla, niece Nicky, my son Castor— "

"I'm sorry," Jozette said, interrupting the woman. "Did you say *Castor*?"

"Yes," she replied warily. "It's a family name."

"You're last name?" Jozi asked, pulse racing as she dared hope.

"Falk, my husband, is Callius Falk. Are you okay, Jozette?"

Before she could stop herself, Jozette was in tears and hugging the poor woman in what could only be described as a death grip. She couldn't believe it. She found them. Castor's family! He was going to be so happy.

"Oh! Okay, there there," Fred said, obviously humoring her.

Jozette couldn't help but notice when the other woman sniffed her. Then she stilled, and Jozette pushed back. Wiping her tears, she shook her head.

"You smell familiar," Fred said hesitantly.

"Yes, and with good reason," Jozette began.

"We want our story!" Little Castor exclaimed grumpily.

"Um, let me read for the kids first, okay? But in the meantime, maybe text your husband and his brothers, too."

"How do you know he has brothers?"

"It's a good thing. I promise," Jozette said.

"I think you should tell me first," Fred replied cautiously.

"I will."

Jozette nodded at her. She could not blame her. After all, Jozette was only a human. Would have smelled human too, especially to the woman who was obviously a Shifter. It was in her height and strength, and that special glow to her eyes. Now that Jozi got a good look at her, it was a wonder she did not see it before.

Fred would be a fool to trust *a normal*, except for the fact that Castor's scent was all over her. Only that morning, Marissa had said that Jozette's mate's scent clung to her skin like perfume. Apparently, it would forevermore now that they were mated.

She loved the smoky richness of Castor's natural scent and loved even more that she would carry it. The rose tattoo above her heart warmed whenever she thought of him, and she placed her hand there now. Jozette sat down in front of the children, her eyes went to Fred's as she started to tell them a story.

"Once upon a winter's night, a maiden sat alone and watched the snow fall on the seashore from the window seat inside her warm cottage," she began telling the tale, embellishing here and there, and leaving much out for the children's sake.

"Oh my," Fred gasped.

The toddler she'd been carrying was now cuddled on his cousin's lap, leaving Fred free to grab her cell phone. Jozette nodded, but didn't stop spinning her story to the children gathered around. Since the weather was bad, the Falk children were the only ones there.

They clapped and roared when asked, participating in Jozette's tale about a maiden who helped a Dragon make his way through the modern world. The boys loved it when he learned to play ping pong and wrestled with a Lion. The girls giggled when she told them how the maiden gave the Dragon his first kiss.

"Who wants to draw a picture of the maiden and the Dragon?"

"Me!"

"Me! I do! I do!"

Jozette laughed and handed out crayons and paper to the kids. Then she turned to Fred, who was smiling at her nervously.

"Well?"

"My husband is on a trip, due back this afternoon," she began. "But he is very excited to meet Castor and to hear his story. Will you bring him to our home tonight, around eight?"

"Yes. Of course," Jozette said, taking down the address.

"They won't be cruel though? I won't have anyone hurt him—"

"Of course not," Fred said, immediately alleviating Jozi's sudden fears. "The Falk brothers are as close and protective as anyone, believe me. But they would never harm anyone unless they were attacked, or their families threatened. They never knew your mate existed. I think this is quite a shock, but a good one," Fred replied.

Jozette paused a moment and thought about the incredulity of it all. Fred seemed honest and trustworthy. The woman obviously loved her mate and her family. Of course, she would be cautious. Jozi would too.

"Okay. We will come by later."

"Great!"

An hour later, Fred and all the children were gone, and Jozi was gathering her things. Delia came by to finish the afternoon and close the store.

"How was business today? Anyone come round for story hour?"

"Okay. Slow at first, but yeah, story hour was fun," Jozette said, smiling.

She waited for Castor and Marissa and Hector to swing by to pick her up, but they were a little late. Tapping her hands on the counter, she thought about the story she told the children and how she'd plotted it out on her laptop afterwards.

She was going to do it. Jozette was going to write a series of books based on it. The first one was going to be *The Maiden Meets Her Dragon,* and it would be the tale she told today. Of course, she wanted to run it by Castor to get his approval.

Her stomach tensed. She was nervous as hell, but excited, too. Her sweet Dragon had come so far to find his half-brothers. Men he had never even met who did not know he existed before today. She only prayed they were as kind and welcoming as he deserved.

Jozette hadn't really considered that they might not want to meet him. From what she understood, he was the son of their father and another woman he'd met after their own mother had died. She didn't really understand the particulars nor the context. It was mindboggling to imagine. After all, it had happened over 500 years ago. The world was very different than in some respects.

Did I do the right thing?

She bit her lip, her brows creased pensively. So lost in thought, Jozette hardly responded to the sound of a horn beeping outside. When she looked up, she gasped. Castor was standing beside a stretched limo with a bouquet of roses in his hand.

"Hubba hubba! Isn't that yours?" Delia asked, her boss laughed and waved at the man she'd met several times.

"Oh yeah. He's mine all right," Jozi grinned and said her goodbyes before running outside to meet him.

Struck by how gorgeous he was, she stopped a foot away and looked him up and down. He wore a simple pair of jeans and a black shirt, but he was spectacular. Jozette realized she was more in love with each passing minute. And those were so precious, she realized she couldn't keep him waiting.

"Castor!" She exclaimed, jumping into his arms.

"My treasure," he murmured into her hair, spinning her around.

"What is all this?"

"For you, my love," he said, placing her back on

her feet and handing her the bouquet of slightly smashed roses.

"Sorry."

She giggled, sniffing the pretty flowers. The only times Jozette had ridden in a limo were for her prom, her cousin's wedding, and her grandfather's funeral. She'd never been picked up from work in one, and it was an unexpected treat.

"Champagne?" he asked, offering her a flute, which she accepted.

"Thank you," she murmured.

"I have news," Castor began.

"Me too," she said, excitement bubbling within.

He was still smiling and nodded for her to proceed him. Jozette shook her head.

"No, no. This was your surprise first, tell me what's going on."

"I insist," he said, nibbling her ear and skating his teeth over her mate mark.

Shivers and chills spread throughout her body at even the slightest contact, and Jozette wondered if it would always be that way. She loved him so much, her heart nearly strangled her to death when she thought about the little time they had.

She could not accept that he was dying. Hated that she didn't know enough about his kind to do anything about it. But how did a human save a Dragon? She couldn't possibly know, though she would give everything she had to do just that.

But Jozette could not save Castor. It was a hard truth to face, but one she had to accept. Only maybe his brothers could? All she knew was however long he had left on the earth, Jozette intended to spend it with him. Laughing with him. Cherishing him. Loving him. So, yes, going to meet the brothers Falk was risky, but she had to try.

"Castor," she began.

"Yes, my love," he said.

"I found them. Or, actually, they found me."

"Who?"

"Your brothers."

CHAPTER 17

Castor had been quite pleased at the outcome of his meeting in the city of Manhattan with Marissa's uncle. But that town! So busy and crawling with people. He hated everything about it.

"It grows on you," Marissa had said.

"So do warts," was his snarled reply.

He did not like the place, but he was well received by the businesses there. The gems he'd created had proved quite valuable. About a hundred million times more valuable than they'd been sitting on the sand in their previous states. Made sense since they were but rocks and shells before his Dragon's fire had touched them.

The older Lion Shifter had practically danced when he'd tested the largest of the stones. The blue garnet was a rare gem indeed. His Dragon's own rose was named for the gem, so it made sense to him.

Of course, Castor had learned something new every day since he'd attained his freedom. The world was a lot larger than the dungeon from whence he'd come. Now that he'd solved the issue of his wealth, he had only to share the news with the one person on the planet who mattered most to him.

"You have brought me a real treasure trove, son," the Lion had exclaimed before he departed.

"Nay, my real treasure waits for me at work. Hector has sent you the information to wire the finds to my accounts, yes?"

"Yes, Mr. Falk. Everything has been handled, you have my word."

"Thank you, Mr. Leopold."

And with that, he'd left the jeweler with a case full of gems and a signed contract.

"What now?" Hector asked.

"I want to do something for Jozette. A surprise."

"I know!" Marissa jumped up and down excitedly.

The two Lions had been instrumental in what followed. They took Castor to a few Shifter friendly banks and businesses to grab a set of specially tailored clothes, a few odds and ends, and means of transportation.

He was surprised to see these places were more than happy to set a Dragon Shifter up with credit cards aplenty. After making some rather splendid purchases, Castor was ready to get his mate.

It seemed his kind had quite the reputation and wasn't that handy! Flowers in hand, he did not want to think about anything but getting back to her. His sweet mate was the only thing his Dragon wanted in this world.

Money and material things were hardly consequential to a man who'd spent five long centuries in chains. But he understood the importance. Knew they meant he could and would provide for his real treasure. His sweet mate. His Jozette.

Es meus.

Once he arrived at the bookstore, he waited for her to look up. Had the driver honk the horn, actually. She was so surprised!

Her face lit up when she saw him and came rushing out. He could hardly wait to spin her around and kiss her sweet coconut and sea foam scented skin.

"I have news," he'd started to say.

"Me too," she replied.

Castor would never interrupt his love when she had something to say. Her excitement was his own, but while he waited for her to continue, she shook her head.

"No, no. This was your surprise first, tell me what's going on."

"I insist."

Tenderly, he kissed her neck, nibbling the mark he'd given her. Like a beacon, it drew him, and he wondered if the partition separating them from their driver was really soundproofed. Modern wonders never did cease, he thought amusedly.

Castor," Jozette said, leaning into him as he continued to lick and nibble.

"Yes, my love," he said.

She pulled herself away from him, taking his hands in hers, and meeting his stare with her big, luminous eyes. Fuck, he loved her eyes. So warm and so deep a brown, so big, they could swallow him whole. And he would go willingly.

In fact, there was little in this world that sounded better to him than losing himself in Jozette's eyes. Unless it was, of course, losing himself in her body. Or her heart. Yes. That.

"I found them. Or, actually, they found me," she said, but he was confused.

"Who?" he asked, baffled.

"Your brothers."

The words sat there, plain as the day. And yet, he could not comprehend them.

"What?"

"I said," she explained, grinning up at him. "Your brothers are waiting for us."

"They are? You did? How?"

"Let me give the driver the address, then I'll explain."

Castor held Jozette's hand as she told him about her encounter with a tall blonde female who claimed to be married to one Callius Falk. Castor's mouth went dry, and he felt her small hand squeeze his.

"Are you alright?" she asked.

"Yes," he replied, pressing his forehead to hers.

"I'm a little overwhelmed."

"Of course," she murmured. "I'm sorry if I was thoughtless. I was just so excited for you to meet your real family, but if you don't want to go, I can call—"

"No! Jozette, my love, do you have any idea what you've done?"

Castor took her face in his hands and kissed her head and her lips.

"Castor? What?"

"You've already given me a family. You are family, my love."

"Oh," she gasped, tears welling in her beautiful eyes.

"No! Don't cry. You see, that's what this all was. This was me asking you to marry me, to be my family in every way. However long I have here, I want to be with you. Will you, please?"

"Yes," she said, laughing, and pressed her mouth to his in a kiss full of promise and hope.

Just then, the car slowed, and the driver got out and opened their door. Castor exited first, offering Jozette his hand. Before them was an enormous home, a castle, really. Beautiful and looming from its perch on the shore.

The winter wind had Castor tucking Jozette closer to his side as they walked to the front door. She was his anchor, his strength, and his peace. The calm before the storm, he thought as he raised his hand to rap on the thing.

"Oh," Jozette gasped when the door opened before Castor's knuckles ever made contact.

"I am Callius Falk," a tall, dark-haired man said in a deep, gruff voice. Behind him stood three other adult males, all large, all strong looking, and all smelling of Dragon.

Castor stood his ground, gently easing himself in front of his mate. Head tilted back, he dared any of the four before him to do anything in front of her at their own peril.

"OMG! Guys, will you back the hell up? Hi! I'm Joss, come on in!"

A short woman with a rounded frame and head full of curls pushed and shoved the males, handing a squirming toddler to one, until she was standing by the door and holding it wide.

"Castor," he said, and nodded to his mate. "This is Jozette."

"Wonderful! You work in the bookstore, right? My little Eddie loves your stories," she said, smiling at his mate, and Castor nodded approvingly.

Once inside, the other females welcomed them warmly even as their males stood, frowning and sizing him up. What did he expect?

Castor smiled as Jozette, obviously already acquainted, knelt down and greeted the children. They were beautiful young dragonlings, and his heart swelled with both pride and sadness. Would he live long enough to see her carry their young? He hoped the gods granted him that.

"You say your name is Castor Falk?" Callius asked.

He turned to face the four men and replied in a low voice so as not to upset either the females or the young ones. He took a breath and met each of their stares as he did so.

"I am Castor Falk, named for my father. My mother was the Lady Igraine. She was killed after birthing me, and the heinous Chief Dragomir had me locked in the bowels of his keep below the regular dungeons for the last 500 years."

"What?"

"How can it be so?"

"I only know it is so, for I am here," Castor replied.

"Our father fell on his sword after Igraine was beheaded—" Callius growled.

"Yes, but that happened after my birth. She was already pregnant when our father left the castle to wage battle for Dragomir," Castor said, telling the story as he knew it.

"It rings true, Cal," Edric replied. "Father was gone many months that time."

"And Igraine was kept hidden, and we thrust in irons," Nikolai said.

"What else do you know? What news of Dragomir now?" Aleksander asked.

"Well," Castor said, clearing his throat. "You

should also know the Blackthorne Clan has been vanquished by a band of his own Dragons. They were tired of his lies and tyranny. His castle is burnt to the ground."

"Fucking hell."

"Good riddance!"

"About bloody time."

The chorus of answers coming from the other Dragons met Castor's approving ears, and he nodded. Callius was the only one who did not reply, but he could see the older man was deep in thought.

"Brother?" Callius asked, gold eyes boring into Castor's.

"I believe him," Edric said.

"He has father's chin," Aleksander murmured.

"And his mother's hair," Nikolai agreed.

The four Falk brothers made a circle around Callius, then, as if as one, they each placed a hand on him. At first, he flinched, and Jozette yelled at them to get off him.

"Just wait," Joselyn told his mate, and he met her worried gaze, nodding before he was seized by a rush of power.

Inside his mind's eye, Castor saw his Dragon surrounded by his kin. The four Dragons were enormous, especially the black and gold which belonged to Callius. They were red, white, and green next.

Callius the *FireDragon,* Edric the *ThunderDragon,* Aleksander the *IceDragon,* and Nikolai the *Energy-Dragon.* Each with their own powers and roses. Each transmitting memories to him and shared pasts. It was unbelievable and his own *ChangeDragon* roared with happiness when the multitude of memories stopped assailing him.

"That was," Castor gasped, falling to his knees.

"Are you okay?" Jozette joined him, and he looked at her and smiled.

"Yes, I am well, love. Very well."

He saw a hand in front of him and took it, grinning as his brother helped him stand. In turn, Castor helped Jozette.

"Welcome home, brother," Callius said, grinning widely at Castor.

CHAPTER 18

"Are you sure you two have had enough to eat?" Melody, Nikolai's mate, asked as Castor and Jozette made their way to the front door.

"Yes, I couldn't eat another bite."

A flock of dragonlings were trailing their feet, and Castor grinned at how much the young ones seemed to love his mate. That was good, he thought, especially since he guessed she was carrying his young already.

Something he would have to tell her later. Right after he discussed the other thing he'd learned when his brothers were sharing information with him through their Dragons.

"Alright, well, make sure you come back soon.

We want to go over plans for the fifth wing," Fred said with a wink.

"Yes, we shall discuss that," Castor said, shaking his head.

"What was that about?" Jozette asked as she pulled on her hat and gloves.

It was cold near the water, but Castor did not think he could wait another second to talk to her.

"Will you walk with me a moment?" he asked when she would have gone straight for the waiting limousine.

"Sure."

Jozette smiled and took his hand, following him down the path to the beach.

"Have I told you how much I love you?" he asked, turning her to face him once they reached the shoreline.

"I think I can stand to hear it again," She grinned and nuzzled his nose with her cold one.

"I'd love to stay here with you, but I am freezing. Let's get back."

"Stop there!"

"Brother, I have found the demon!"

Castor spun around, wind whipping his hair as he faced the two Dragons who were responsible for his very freedom.

"Who are they?" Jozette asked, her fear palpable.

"Nicholas and Devine, the Dragons who freed me," Castor explained.

"Silence wench! You will not speak," Devine pointed his sword towards Castor's throat.

"We have hunted you here *ChangeDragon,* and watched from the shadows while you consorted with this human filth. We have come to do what your brothers have not," growled Nicholas.

"You will not speak thus of my mate," Castor growled.

"Ha! You have left us no recourse," Devine sneered.

"Meet us as man or beast, you will not leave alive!"

"Jozette, run back to the castle. I will not have you hurt," Castor instructed, but his mate was too stubborn for her own good.

"No! I won't leave you!"

Castor's beast snarled in fury as Devine switched tactics and pointed the sword at Jozette instead. He was already warding off Nicholas' attacks, but without a weapon of his own, it was hardly a fair fight.

Castor snarled as the other dragon's blade cut through his clothing, scoring his forearm. Blood splattered onto the sand and Jozette cried out in alarm.

"Silence," Devine sneered and moved his sword to shove Castor's mate.

"Hey!" Jozette yelled.

"YOU WILL NOT TOUCH HER!" Castor roared.

He was still not as fast or powerful as he would have liked. True, Hector had been practicing with him, but in that moment, pure fury overrode reason and Castor's change was swift.

He stomped on the sand, blocking his mate from the two attackers, loosing a mighty roar as they tried to hit him with their swords. Devine was faster than his brother, changing shape to a muddy colored Dragon who was smaller than Castor, but covered in spikes.

Spikes that apparently shot free of his body at will. Castor bellowed as one hit him in the ribs, bruising though not piercing his tough hide.

"Ouch!"

He turned as Jozette yelped, the bastard Nicholas had her by the hair. Castor was through fucking around. He used his spade-like tail to pummel the *SpikeDragon*. He hit the beast with one accurate shot to his chest, sending him careening back into the waves of the Atlantic.

"You killed my brother, you scum," Nicholas growled.

I merely pushed him to sea, Castor's beast thought the words to the other Dragon.

"*SpikeDragons* can't swim, can they? He sunk to the bottom and is now drowned and dead!"

Smoke puffed from Castor's mouth. He had not wanted that. Did not want to battle the two men who'd set him free. But what could he say or do to make up for it?

With his sword pressed against Jozette's throat, Castor wanted to annihilate the bastard. But he couldn't do so without hurting his mate. What was he going to do now? He could not risk his treasure's life. Swapping scales for skin, he opened his arms to show he had no weapons.

"I am unarmed. Let her go, and you can have me."

"No!" Jozette yelled, whimpering when the Dragon pulled her hair.

"Fine, come then. Your life for hers, you bloody bastard."

"Castor!" Jozette cried.

"Shut up, wench! He is a low bastard, he is. Alone and unworthy," Nicholas said, raising his sword as

Castor knelt at his feet on the cold sand. "And this is a mercy—"

Jozette nearly died as the stranger held his sword up high, ready to strike down her mate with one blow. Her sweet Dragon had told her about his impending demise, but she thought they would have some time still at least. Not this. This was too soon.

Before she could move or react, the man's sword was ripped from his hands. Jozette spun around. It was his brothers! Callius, Edric, Aleksander, and Nikolai! All four of them surrounded Castor. Her mate stood and ran to her while the others growled and barked questions at the asshole who'd almost killed them both.

"Are you okay, my love?"

"Yes, are you?"

They held each other for a moment. Hardly moving as Edric dove beneath the waves and came back moments later with a naked but still alive, Devine. Nicholas shouted in joy at his brother's return though he was being held roughly by Callius.

"You two heathens thought to trespass on Falk

Clan lands and wage war against one of our own!" Callius snarled.

"But, but he is a demon! A *ChangeDragon!*"

"And just what does that mean to you? Castor, did you not tell these men what you are?" Nikolai asked, head cocked to the side.

"I don't know what I am. They said I was a *ChangeDragon* and called me demon," Castor replied, quickly wrapping the towel Fred handed him around his hips.

"You two dolts believe that, do you? Idjits!" Callius growled.

"It was you then," Aleksander said, grinning and pointing to Castor. "I told you, my little Maggie said she saw a wizard making sparkles in the sand. Ha!"

"Oh, I did not realize anyone saw me," Castor said, mussing his hair and grinning sheepishly.

"Can we finish this inside? Um, not all of us are Dragons," Jozette said, dying to know what the hell was going on but freezing to death on the wintry shores.

Some minutes and several shots of whiskey later...

"Here," Callius said, handing Castor a rock. "Show your mate what it means to be a *ChangeDragon.*"

Two brothers grinned and stood nearby while the other two guarded their unwanted guests. Jozette was wary. She didn't understand what was happening, but one look from her mate and she decided to trust him. After all, her gut hadn't been wrong so far.

Dressed in borrowed sweats, Castor took the rock and placed it inside the fireplace in the large living room inside the castle. He looked at her one more time, and she nodded encouragingly.

Despite being one of seven Dragons in the room, in her eyes, he outshone them all. Her drop dead gorgeous mate concentrated on the stone, eyes flashing dark blue rimmed in purple and red, then he opened his mouth and the same colored flames shot out, heating the stone.

The heat was so intense, Jozette had to move back a step. But in the a blink of an eye, it was over. The brothers clapped, the women too. The two men who'd come to hurt them seemed dumbstruck, and Castor just reached into the fireplace and took out the white hot stone.

"Here, let me."

Aleksander stepped forward, and where Castor blew hot, his breath was cold. He leaned over and blew across the stone, cooling it rapidly until she saw the rock was no longer a rock. It was a gemstone.

"*Ohmygawd!*" Jozette said, covering her mouth.

"It's a blue garnet, my love," Castor explained, handing it to her.

"Earlier today I went to the beach and found a pile of rocks and turned them to gems. Marissa took me to her uncle, who is a jeweler in the city. I have amassed a small fortune, to take care of you," he explained while she just stood and stared.

"You see," Callius said, turning to the two intruders.

"A *ChangeDragon* is no demon. He can change stones to gems!" Callius said with a bark of laughter.

"The legends are true?" Edric asked him.

"Just look, our brother is the proof," Nikolai said.

"But the legends said they were evil," Devine said, confused.

"Yes, but you see, I uncovered the truth behind those tales back when I still worked for Dragomir," Nikolai explained.

"The truth is the Dragons who started that lie simply did not want anyone in their Clans to amass fortunes greater than their own. Because people then feared *ChangeDragons* many were unfortunately killed. I imagine Dragomir had no idea what you were, did he?"

"He did not witness my first change. Only had me help forge the irons that bound me," Castor said.

"Unbelievable," Fred murmured.

"Hey are you okay?" The tall blonde turned to Jozette.

"I think so. It is all a little overwhelming."

"I'm sorry, love. We better go," Castor said.

"Alright, we will take care of these two. See you soon, brother," Callius waved.

After their goodbyes, the limo took them home. Jozette hugged the older man goodbye once she discovered he was not only a Shifter too, but he was responsible for alerting the Falk brothers about what was happening on the beach.

"Aww shucks, ma'am. I would've stepped in, but us sloths are no match for Dragons," he explained with an embarrassed grin.

"Thank you, truly. What you did was plenty!"

"Where are Hector and Marissa?" Castor asked as they walked into the Lion's house.

"I texted them and asked if they wouldn't mind giving us the place for the night," Jozette murmured.

"Did you now?"

Jozi nodded, leading him by the hand until they

were inside their bedroom. She turned and looked into his eyes. So much light and love inside of them! It hurt to think their time was so limited!

"What is it, my love?"

"Nothing. I want you," she whispered and pulled off her clothes.

Castor stood mesmerized as Jozette stripped. She'd never been the type of woman who wore her heart on her sleeve, but there was no hiding from this man. Her man. Her Dragon.

Jozette was truly, madly, deeply in love for the first time in her life, and she wanted each moment to be worth it. To live entirely for the present, to hide nothing, shed her misgivings, and simply bask in the love she knew he held for her in his heart.

"Now I get to undress you," she said with a sly smile, stopping his hands when he went to grab for her.

She was having way too much fun unwrapping her present. His shirt removed, revealed his deliciously golden and well-muscled arms and pecs. Jozette kissed each one and then his abs, as she undid his belt buckle and tugged on his pants.

"Not yet. I told you, it's my turn," she said, removing his hands from her and dropping to her knees in front of him.

"What are you—"

"Mine," she said, grinning.

"Fuuucckk!"

Castor's head hit the wall when she opened her mouth and took his long, thick, swollen head inside. Jozette moaned, humming in her throat as she swallowed down as much of his incredible length as she could. With one hand, she cupped his balls, massaging and stroking the tight orbs while using her other hand to squeeze the base of his cock.

"My love, my love, love, love. Jozette," he growled, flexing his hips, and fucking her mouth so good she felt heat and liquid pool between her legs.

"Stop, love, please," he said. "Stop or I will spill myself."

But she shook her head and kept right on sucking and bobbing, squeezing, and licking. Yes, she wanted him inside her sex, but Jozette was going to have this first.

"Es meus!" Castor roared, hips moving jerkily as his orgasm surged forward, filling her mouth.

"Mine," she replied, kissing his still hard cock one more time right on the head before turning to stride to the bed.

Castor slammed into her from behind, hands so

good and a little rough on her breast as he kneaded and squeezed the flesh.

"Want you, mate," he snarled, closing his mouth over the bitemark he'd given her.

A fresh wave of heat coated her pussy and Jozette had never felt so fucking turned on in her life. Her Dragon seemed to know exactly where she wanted him. One hand slid down her soft belly, parting her soaked lips. He toyed with her clit while positioning his cock. Jozette leaned forward, using the bed to hold her up while he knelt behind her, fitting himself at her soaked entrance.

"Is this okay, mate?" he asked, voice thick with his Dragon.

"Yes, please," she moaned, pushing back, and taking him into her heat, inch by glorious, thick inch.

They both moaned when he pressed forward, finally joining them. Tension built steadily as he pounded into her, filling her so good, and stroking that secret place she'd only ever felt with him.

Before she knew it, she was halfway to her first orgasm, screaming when it hit her. Her Dragon knew exactly what she needed, stopping his thrusts to kiss her neck, and nibbling her skin in just the right spot.

He started moving again, slowly at first. He withdrew completely, flipping her over and stroking his hands over her breasts and belly, spreading her legs wide, then he filled her again. With long, hard, stroke after stroke, Castor's face loomed overhead. So gorgeous. So hers.

Inside her mind, she saw him and his Dragon, images of them together, spread over the years. She wanted to weep at the visions she knew could only be coming from him. But then he took her by the hips and lifted her, grinding his pubis in a slow swirl that made her see nothing at all but white hot lights.

"Castor!" she yelled as her next orgasm eclipsed the first.

He allowed her to calm down, kissing her lips, catching her breath, but only for a moment. Then he was stretching her again, filling her once more. And touching her everywhere.

Jozette felt him on top of and inside every inch of her. His hands clasped hers, chest pressed tightly to her breasts, lips locked onto her mouth, and cock filling her so completely. She had no idea where she ended, and he began.

"Castor," she moaned his name, whispering unintelligibly.

But he knew. He understood. This was more

profound than any words in any language. They were one. Joined. Unified.

Pleasure so intense, she could have died from it, filled her blood as Castor brought her to unchartered heights. Then they came together. She gasped, and he roared her name into the ether. It was like the world exploded into a thousand million multifaceted gems, then reknit itself back together in that one perfect moment.

Mine.

EPILOGUE

Castor stroked Jozette's back as they held onto each other through the night. Words seemed superfluous in the face of such passion, but she had to speak. Needed him to hear the words she felt to her very soul.

"Castor?"

"Yes, love?" he murmured.

"I wanted you to know that no matter what, you are the only man I will ever love in my entire life."

"I better be, darling," he said, sounding amused. "Otherwise, I shall have to read more law books to keep myself out of jail for murder," he joked.

"Ha ha. Very funny. But I am serious, I mean, after *you know*," she said, eyes filling with tears at the thought of him not being there.

"Oh, fuck!" Castor sat up, taking her with him, and scaring the shit out of her in the process.

"What?"

"I forgot to tell you. I am not dying!"

"What? You're not?!" She yelled, jumping on him, and sending them both crashing to the ground.

"Are you okay?" Castor asked, pushing her hair out of her face.

"Jozette, answer me? Are you hurt?"

"No! I am not hurt," she said, only realizing then that she was sobbing.

"I am so happy," she climbed on top of him, hugging him tightly.

"Thank goodness. You startled me," he growled against her head, squeezing her waist, and crushing her to him.

"Well, what happened? How do you know you aren't dying?"

"From my brothers. When they each laid a hand on me in their castle, they were performing a sort of *mindsharing*. It is a Dragon thing, but only kin can do it. It seems all that pain I felt, even the tug on my heart strings that brought me to your door, was all my Dragon attempting to unite me with my fated mate. With you, Jozette," he explained, grinning widely.

"For real?"

"Yes, my love. And what I told you about those gems is real, too. I got a text from Marissa's uncle. It seems we are very wealthy. We do not have to mooch off your friends anymore. Though my brothers' offer to build a new wing in Castle Falk is real," he said.

"Do you want that?"

"I want *you*," he replied. "You are my beacon, my guiding light, my only real treasure. I will live anywhere you want to live, as long as you are there, I am home."

His words had an amazing effect on Jozette. Her heart, once shy and scarred, seemed to blossom and shine. For the first time in her life, she felt the true meaning of family and love in her Dragon's arms.

"Let's do it," she said, trusting her gut. It hadn't let her down so far.

"Good. Our dragonling will enjoy being raised with his cousins," Castor said, kissing her with intent.

"What? You got me pregnant!" She yelled.

Her Dragon's smile dropped, concern marring his gorgeous face. But the second the words were out, she realized she could not be happier. Jozette had a Dragon and a baby on the way. What more could she want?

"I know it is fast—" He began, but she stopped him with a kiss.

"It's perfect."

"Really?"

"Yes! I'm going to write the kind of books we can read to our baby from my desk in our very own wing of a castle. What could be more perfect?"

"If you'll marry me," he said.

Castor leaned over and grabbed his pants, pulling something from the pocket. He handed it to Jozette, keeping his hand closed for a moment until she raised her eyes to his.

"I thought we could have this made into a ring," he whispered, revealing the most beautiful blue garnet she had ever seen.

"Yes," Jozette replied. "I will marry you."

"My treasure," Castor murmured before claiming her mouth with a fervent kiss.

And they lived happily ever after...

The end.

Did you enjoy this Paranormal Romance? Awesome! You can read the other Falk Clan Tales here! & Guess what? The Dragon's Surprise: A Falk Clan Tale 6 is coming in 2022!

THE DRAGON'S SURPRISE

A FALK CLAN TALE

USA TODAY BESTSELLING AUTHOR
C.D. GORRI
THE DRAGON'S SURPRISE
A FALK CLAN TALE

THE DRAGON'S SURPRISE
A FALK CLAN TALE

Dear readers,

This story was an unexpected surprise that popped in my brain one day, when I was writing The Dragon's Treasure. You might recall Dev and his brother Nick from that tale. Anyway, this is Devine's story and I hope to enjoy it!

Del mare all stella,

C.D. Gorri

Don't forget to sign up for my newsletter here:
https://www.cdgorri.com/newsletter

BLURB

Nothing can surprise this six hundred-year-old Dragon, except maybe her.

After the fall of the Blackthorne Clan, Devine and his brother, Nicholas, find themselves in Falk Clan territory. Once they'd cleared up the little—*okay, more like huge*—misunderstanding, the two brothers are invited to stay with the Falk Clan to adjust to the modern world.

What choice do they have? Vulnerable and without a home, Devine Graystone still had his brother. As the last of their line, they had a duty to carry on. But finding a mate in today's world seemed an impossible task.

Would loneliness be this *QuartzDragon's* fate?

Sunny Daye was as bright and perky as her name. But when a girl had hippie Werewolves for parents, she had little choice in the matter—uber cheerful was her norm.

Always looking for the next adventure, she's stunned when it comes walking through her shop door in the shape of a seven foot tall Dragon.

Can this curvy Werewolf tame a cranky Dragon and change his outlook on life?

PROLOGUE

Devine Graystone froze in place. His heart hammered inside his chest as he waited in the darkness for the signal.

He heard the seagulls crying and waves crashing against the icy black rock that held the ruins of Castle Blackthorne aloft and the QuartzDragon shuddered. The Isle of Pain was about to explode. He'd heard the rumors and had done nothing to stop them.

Why would he? This was not the Clan of his youth, and the castle was not home. It should have been a place of warmth and safety. A place where the Dragons could store their hoards, take mates, and raise young. But it was not that. Hadn't been for many lifetimes now.

Anger filled his veins as he waited. The revolution was coming, and for his brother's sake, Devine would be a part *of it. He would break the shackles binding the Graystone brothers to that monster, Chief Dragomir. The fleshy beast stalked him down the hallways. Devine could hear him now shouting, at his ruthless minions with him. He was looking for his blade to take out the opposition. He was looking for Devine.*

His Dragon snarled, the beast hated the sorry excuse for a leader. It had been this way for a long time now. Dragomir had bound him to the Clan using blood magic, but those bonds had grown thin. Devine could barely feel the pull, and the moment Nicholas was safe, he would join the attack.

They used to have a sacred duty. Dragons had been created to fight the Demons who tried to break into this plane of existence from their hellish homes. That had been a noble cause and the reason they lived in that harsh climate. So close to the hellmouth.

Dragomir had forgotten that sacred duty and other supernaturals had stepped in. Devine felt the dishonor in that down to his bones. All the old Chief cared about was growing his hoard and bringing pain to his people. The coffers had grown thin, and he'd been squeezing his people for taxes. The Clan was falling apart, and the old Dragon Chief was madder than a hatter.

Devine had heard of those who'd escaped the Isle. Released from servitude, these brothers had been bound to the old bastard for their father's trespass. No one knew what happened to the brothers Falk, but rumors had spread. Some said Dragomir still held one in secret. Others claimed the brothers were killed by the Chief's blade.

The latter was not true. Devine had not gone after any of them. Living far away from the world, supposition was all the Dragons knew. Dragomir ruled with fear mongering. It was the only smart thing the man did, though evil. Always evil.

Fear of the unknown was the most powerful tool the Chief could wield against his people. It would keep them in line and serving a wicked master. Devine knew that, even if Dragomir was too shortsighted to see it.

But he would not tell the Chief that. No fucking way. The Dragons needed to escape this place. To leave the rock that stunted their growth.

Devine needed to leave. He should go now. He should flee. Spread his wings, see the world, find a maiden, build a hoard. But he couldn't abandon his brother. The sacred oath he'd made to his father had been to stay with his brother. To protect him.

Though older, Nicholas was stubborn and set in his ways. He would not leave the Chief. Not while the cretin was still breathing. Devine huddled deeper into the shadows. They were close now.

"We go to see my favorite plaything. Then we shall remind these cretins to whom they serve!"

Fuck. It was true. The Chief was on his way to torture the prisoner. He who had been kept secret for centuries. Forgotten by most, but the Graystone brothers had heard the whispers.

Nicholas tiptoed down the hall from the other end and sided up next to his brother. He held his hand out when Dev would have startled, a reflex from his time in battle. He looked at Nick and nodded his head.

Finally, things were falling in place. He wanted to speak, but Nicholas shook his head slightly. Good thing too, Dragomir had stopped and sniffed the air. The sounds of screams and claws clashing as the few Dragons left began to fight sounded loudly from the floors above.

"Bloody hell! Come, we will leave off the prisoner and see what this shit is," Dragomir hissed, and sped the other way.

Holy fuck.

It was happening. Too late to stop it. Devine and Nicholas had hoped for this revolution and relished the chance to join in the battle, but it was not wise. Many hated Devine Graystone, as they well should. Dragomir had pushed them all too far. Now they would have to fight to survive.

"We have to get you out of here, Dev. You were his blade. They will be looking for you," Nicholas whispered.

It was true. How many orders had he carried out on the wicked Chief's command? How many Dragons had he cut down with his spikes? Devine was a QuartzDragon, keeper of the galaxy stone, but he was known as Spike-Dragon. A Weapon. A murderer.

"There he is!" someone screamed.

"Fuck, they are coming for us, Dev. Let's go!"

The sound of roars and snarls that had filled the halls of the castle still echoed in Devine's brain. Blood, gore, smoke, and death filled his sensitive nostrils. Those could be washed away—but gods, the screams. Would they never end?

CHAPTER I

Devine jumped up in his bed. For one, long, drawn out moment, he could still hear them screaming—the sounds of his Clan folk as they hunted him and his brother in the halls, fighting for freedom from a tyrant.

Didn't they know he was following orders? Didn't they know he was only trying to keep his brother alive? So much pain, regret, and death— countless Dragons had died that day, and the others had fled never to be heard of again.

Screams of ghosts from the revolution that had freed him and his brother from that monstrous rock still stuck there in the middle of the frozen sea made up the song that woke Devine every single morning he still breathed.

He supposed he should be grateful, but just like everything else in his life, each day was another sad disappointment. As usual, it took him a moment to realize where he was—*safe, I am safe.* It was the truth. Devine was safe, his brother too.

Why am I still here when so many aren't? Do I deserve to be here?

He could not answer those questions, but facts were facts. Devine was still breathing. Warm, fed, and safe in their new home on the shores of the Atlantic, with the Falk brothers castle a couple of hundred feet down the lane. He had found those legendary brothers in a roundabout sort of way.

The property technically belonged to the Falk Clan, but those good brothers had granted Devine and Nicholas a small parcel for themselves, making them members without all the pomp and circumstance of traditional Dragon Clans.

Theirs was a modern group. The Falk brothers, Castor in particular, had taken Nicholas and Dev under their wings—made them a part of what they were trying to build on the shores of the Atlantic.

They were the only Dragon Shifter Clan to settle in the new world, and it was so much different from the one they'd been raised in. He still could not believe it.

Devine did not deserve their forgiveness and trust, but he took it—for his brother's sake. Devine had no other choice. Dragons were territorial creatures, but the modern world was so close now.

They could not afford to wage wars against one another. When Dragons formed a Clan, it was best if all dwelled close by. Sometimes, in the same castle, *er*, house, if possible. And if not possible then as close as they could get without drawing eyes.

Devine and Nicholas had both agreed trying to add to Castle Falk was not ideal with five wings already, it would be a monstrosity on the Jersey Shore. So, they'd opted for their own dwelling, carving two distinct homes out of the one structure.

Together and separate.

The distinct wings of their home were necessary so he and his brother could have some privacy. It was still not a castle, but it would serve them well. Really, it should have been perfect. But as Devine looked out at the stormy seas from his large bedroom window, he felt that familiar hollow nothingness he'd brought with him unintentionally from the Isle of Pain expand inside his chest.

That feeling of distance between himself and his Dragon was growing daily. A Dragon needed his maiden fair, and his brother was pushing him to find one. But how? And who? Devine was not made for a mate. He would see Nicholas settled, and then, he would fade away.

That was his destiny, though the knowledge was little comfort as he stood up and paced his bedroom discontentedly. The actual room was fine. Builders before they'd been warriors, he and his brother had spent the better part of the last year constructing the perfect modern beach house with every luxury they could afford.

Having a nice little hoard of treasures had helped, of course. Dragons were very good at gathering riches, it was part of their nature. Money seemed to flow towards them. In just a year, he and Nicholas had quadrupled their net worth with little help from the Falk brothers. They had enough to live very comfortably without having to work for, *well*, forever.

But idle claws were tempted to do the devil's work, or so his father had always said.

So, they'd designed and built their home, and Nicholas was making plans for another on the next lot. Pushy Dragon, he had taken it upon himself to incorporate their business, calling it *Graystone Builders Inc*. He was taking meetings all week to get the necessary permits. Until then, Devine was on his own.

Having just finished construction in the last week, Devine was proud of their accomplishments. Materials were new now, and building was not the same as it had been. Learning about modern advances had been educational and had kept their Dragon's busy. Fast learners, skilled workers, the two of them.

It was not conceit if it was true. Reasonable? Yes. The Graystone brothers' were very good at building and their four story home was a testament to that—two separate wings with their own entrances and private garages gave them the opportunity for privacy while the common dining room, kitchen, and large siting room were all shared.

Done in neutral colors—lots of bone and beige, the house boasted warm hardwood floors, the best modern appliances, heating and cooling amenities, and every floor cabinet had stone countertops, matching the dining tables and kitchen islands, quartz of course.

Each wing had a master bedroom and bath, several smaller bedrooms with two full bathrooms on every floor, designated home office spaces, theater rooms, game rooms, and parlors with fireplaces. There were small kitchenettes in each wing, and one enormous kitchen on the ground floor where there was also a formal dining room for large parties.

King-sized beds, sleek furniture, and large, comfortable sofas and chairs were placed thoughtfully throughout bedrooms and sitting rooms. Beach access was private of course, as was the entire strip where they lived with the Atlantic at their door and the intracoastal across the street, behind them.

All in all, the house was really quite striking.

Nicholas had insisted on a two level wraparound porch encompassing the entire structure. Devine had not objected to that, or to the large pool and patio off the side of the house. He'd enjoyed swimming after work when the days had grown so warm, he thought his scales would burn. New jersey had the strangest weather patterns of any place he'd seen. It was damn near tropical in the summer, and cold as the tundra in winter. Strange, but also awesome.

The pool had been a stroke of brilliance on his brother's part. The Falk dragonlings had certainly enjoyed breaking in the water slide and diving board for them. It was growing colder now, with the approach of winter, and Devine wondered if they would see the young as often.

Of all the things he had ever wanted, his own young had been topmost on his Dragon's list. Of course, that was not in the cards for him. He would never find his mate, simply did not deserve one.

Rubbing a hand over his face, Devine walked to the large floor to ceiling window that faced the ocean and watched the waves battering against the shore. Winter would soon be here, and he had to prepare. Nicholas was busy working on the new project, and it was up to Dev to winterize the house.

All the patio furniture was wrapped up and stored in the shed, the pool had been covered, and the filters all shut off. The gutters still needed cleaning, and securing, and he wanted to recheck the weatherstripping around every window and door. But really, Devine was anxious about one thing and that was his own private sanctuary. His rooftop greenhouse.

Pride filled him when he thought of the structure as he planned his day. Growing things was not necessarily part of a Dragon's nature, but one of the Falk brothers' mates had suggested it as a hobby, and after chatting with Nicholas, Devine had agreed.

A greenhouse would be perfect. It had been challenging to design the proper roof with the harsh winters and scorching summers New Jersey was prone to. But it was called the Garden State for a reason, and Nicholas had been optimistic they could make something of it.

Besides, Devine needed a hobby. Ever since they'd fled the Isle of Pain, making one bad decision after the next, his Dragon had not felt right. It was like the beast was broken. Even now the creature stirred weakly, his growl a faint echo of what it used to be. It was a bad sign.

Devine grunted and watched the waves solemnly. Nicholas had not understood why he had been eager to accept the Falk Clan's offer to stay. It made no sense to his brother that he would want to live on the same shores of the waters that had almost killed him. No, Nick didn't understand, but Devine did.

His Dragon needed a reason, and his human side liked the reminder of what he had done to anchor him in reality. Before the madness that claimed single Dragons came for him too, Devine needed to create a safe place for Nicholas to carry on their name. Maybe then he could salvage it, remove the taint he'd brought the Graystone crest for serving that ripe bastard for so long.

Dragomir is dead, he reminded himself. *He can't hurt you any longer.*

The daily reminder was enough to make him grateful he was still breathing. Devine had to face his truth every day, then maybe he could hang on a bit longer, see that Nick was alright. Too often did Dragons think themselves immortal, but that was not the truth. His *QuartzDragon—nicknamed Spike-Dragon because of his unique ability to loose bony spines from his tail and back during battle—*was all too mortal, as his time beneath the salty cold waters could attest.

Devine and his brother had fled the castle after the revolt, only to find the secret prisoner Dragomir had kept from his people. After freeing him, they discovered what he was—a *ChangeDragon,* and stupidly believing the old rumors, they had tried to kill him. Good thing Castor Falk was strong as fuck and had found his brothers to aid him, otherwise Devine might have done the unthinkable and killed an innocent.

They'd come to New Jersey, hunting the *Change-Dragon* they had freed because of a stupid age old misunderstanding. Castor Falk had not been dealt a good hand, but he'd found his brothers, the legendary Falks. Against all odds, Castor tracked his kin and even claimed a mate. But Devine and Nicholas found him, and it was the worst and best thing that ever happened to them.

The Graystone brothers attacked Castor and he had tossed Devine's Dragon into the cold sea which had almost drowned him. His Dragon was too heavy to swim, the stones in his spine sinking him to the sandy bottom. It had been enlightening, and humbling, and made him more determined than ever to see to Nicholas' future.

He still did not know why Castor had saved him or why he'd stood up for Devine's brother afterwards. They were the ones who had hunted him, for fuck's sake. And yet, he granted them mercy.

The Falk Dragons could have killed Nicholas and Devine, but they did not. Instead, they welcomed them into their territory and made them part of their Clan—*even if they called it a family.*

It was all very confusing. But Devine could see that Nicholas was grateful, and his brother had even seemed to settle into a routine. Who was he to question anything? He just had to keep going for Nick's sake.

There was no chance for a happy one for himself. Too much blood on his hands But until the day his

Dragon was no more, Devine had a job and today that was prepping the greenhouse for winter.

"The day has dawned, and I am already weary," he murmured, stepping into the shower to wash the sleep from his eyes.

Nick had been grumbling lately about their lineage and their duty to carry on their name. The constant whining an annoying buzz in Dev's ear.

"We must see about having our own young, Dev. Yes, that is the key to this life, as the Falk brothers have done. We need mates," he'd said after one particularly long night—*and several cases of whiskey.* Ever since then, neither one had mentioned it again, but it was heavy on Devine's mind.

Mate, his Dragon whispered.

Devine felt his beast's soul-deep longing keenly. But how was he going to find a mate in this too big modern world?

CHAPTER 2

"Sunny, I've got a customer with a question over here?" Mom called from the front of the shop.

There was nothing wrong with her ears—a Wolf could hear perfectly fine without all the yelling—but in order to pass in front of normals things like shouting were necessary—*horrible, screechy, and possibly deafening, but still, necessary.*

Sigh.

Sunny rolled her neck and shoulders, trying to relieve the tension that seemed permanently stuck there. She knew what her best friend would say.

Minerva Lykos was a renowned artist, and a bit of a dog, even for a Werewolf. Whenever anyone had a physical ailment or complaint, the she-Wolf always found a way to blame it on sex, or the lack of.

"Sunny, you need to get laid."

It was her favorite sentence whenever they talked, and that had been rather infrequently these last few months. Minnie was on tour, and there was no one to give her any of those fabulous pep talks about her dull social life.

Double sigh.

Even Sunny's Wolf was antsy. The beast was scratching at her insides, impatient to be let out. It was just another fall morning, before the Thanksgiving rush, and Sunny had a ton of work to do in the office for the organic produce and garden center she ran with her parents' help. This store had been her dream, her baby, and it was finally turning a profit.

"Sunny?" Mom yelled again.

"Just a sec," she called back.

Sunny adjusted her apron and patted her hair to try to minimize the fly-aways that were the bane of her existence. That's what happened when you had a head full of frizzy curls that refused to be tamed.

Come on, hair, behave. Grrr. Damn. Oh well.

She frowned at her reflection and rolled her eyes. This was as good as it was going to get thanks to her parents, Moonbeam and Leaf Daye. The pair had been hippies in the sixties, as their names suggested. They still wore tie-dye clothes, worn out jeans, hemp headbands, and woven bracelets—like they'd never gone out of style.

Truth was, her parents were the most open, free, honest, and madly in love Werewolves she had ever met. They cared for each other with a fierceness and romance that spanned the ages, and secretly, Sunny aspired to be them when she was finally ready to grow up and find a mate of her own.

Smiling, she skipped down the aisle and tried to locate her mother and the customer who needed her help. It would have been easier had she been able to sniff them out, but with all the scents in the shop, it was harder for her to differentiate fragrances than she'd liked to admit. That didn't get her down though, nothing hardly ever did.

Sunny was luckier than most of the Macconwood Wolves she had grown up around. The Curse of Natalis that had bound them all to the moon had really done a number on Wolf Shifter-kind, but her folks had shared their love with all three of their three pups. It was difficult when she'd had her first Change back in junior high.

She still remembered the terrible feeling that

lurked in the pit of her stomach from being separated from her Wolf during the weeks between full moons. It had hurt like hell.

Still, she was lucky. Her parents and siblings, Crystal, the older sister, and River, the younger brother, had been there for her, and for each other. They were the ones talking her down from the ledge every single time she thought it got to be just too much for her.

Moonbeam and Leaf had raised their pups right, teaching them to be confident, compassionate, well-mannered, and true to each other and themselves. Sunny could not have asked for a better family. In the years since the Curse of Natalis had been broken, their kind had to figure out how to handle the sudden reality that they were Werewolves all the time, and not just once a month.

Even Minnie had some difficulty. Lucky for Sunny, she had her siblings and parents to help. They'd learned to relish their new closeness with their Wolfy selves a lot faster than many of the Wolf Shifters in their large Pack.

The Macconwood Wolves covered almost the entirety of North America. How Rafe Maccon managed all those creatures from his home base in Maccon City, she had no idea. But he was an awesome leader, and she could not ask for a better Alpha.

His mate, Charley, frequented *One Daye at a Time* for their organic produce, and she brought her adorable pups with her whenever she went shopping. Imagine triplet Werewolves rumored to have special problems, and another on the way—she was so happy for the Alpha pair.

It was a new dawn for the Werewolves of the world, and she was just so happy to be part of it. Truthfully, Sunny loved children. Someday, she wanted a whole gaggle of them. Boys girls, ten of each—*snort, JK*. Not ten, maybe two of each.

Sigh.

It was a nice dream. She even had it on her vision board in her bedroom. A house, four point five kids, a big sexy man waiting for her. Oh yeah. That sounded good. Sunny just had so much love inside of her, she was ready to burst. But she was saving it, waiting for the right mate.

"Sunny, you need to get laid."

Minnie's favorite refrain echoed in her head, but Sunny was not listening. Aches or not, Sunny was on a dick boycott. In other words, she wasn't up for any kind of tomfoolery unless the male had the words "mate me" tattooed on his privates. She'd played the fool too long to waste anymore of her time.

The clock was ticking, as her older sister—*a CPA obsessed with numbers*—liked to point out. Crystal had always hated their lifestyle growing up. The years when they'd had to scrimp and save were hard on Sunny's sister. But it was what drove her in her studies. Crystal had wanted to distance herself from their hippie upbringing the second she'd landed her first accounting job.

Sunny was proud of her. Even if she did not agree with a damn thing she said or did. Nothing wrong with growing up in a trailer in the middle of a field on the outskirts of town. Hell, it was full of nothing but fond memories for Sunny. That lot had seemed so big when she was a pup, always overrun with dandelions and daffodils in the spring.

It was poor and cheap, but she never remembered feeling ashamed or wanting for more back then. That came as she got older, not the shame, but the wanting. That was when Sunny had understood her sister a little better.

She'd even moved in with Crystal after high school, while she'd commuted to college, and her parents had understood. They loved and supported her decision, and when she'd come to them with a business plan, they'd jumped right in to help.

Armed with her degree and a solid proposal, Sunny had gone to the *Maccon City First National Bank* seeking a loan. After they'd turned her down, she went to see their Pack Alpha.

Rafe Maccon had approved of her plan after giving it a quick perusal. The man had looked at her with ice-blue eyes and then, he'd asked one question, *"Is this truly what you want, Sunny Daye?"*

She had only one answer for him, and that was *yes*. The Wolf had stared at her a moment longer before he nodded, then the big dark -haired Alpha had signed off on a hundred and fifty thousand dollar loan.

It was a huge amount, and he was taking quite the gamble. Sunny's mother had always grown things, and her dad had a way with people his inner beast should not have allowed but did. He was a smooth talker. Friendly and handsome, and he could set people at ease with just a smile. That little bit of charm had worked wonders on customers when they'd started out.

Her parents hadn't wanted a partnership, but she'd insisted. Werewolves lived a long time, and even if money was not important to them, Sunny wanted them to have it.

So, they'd opened *One Daye At A Time Produce & Garden Center*, and a couple of years later, it was doing even better than she could have imagined. A lot of blood, sweat, and tears had gone into it, but now—*that very morning*—Sonny was mailing the last payment to her Alpha.

A sense of profound accomplishment filled her as she patted the envelope in the pocket of her apron, finally tracking down the customer her mother had sent to see her. Sunny paused a moment, almost tripping over her own feet. Grace was part of a Werewolf's makeup, but not hers.

Sunny was a certified klutz. Something she'd proved time and again as she landed in a heap at a pair of enormous, work boot clad feet.

"Oof," she muttered, as the wind got knocked out of her.

Sunny's gaze traveled up, and up, and up, until she was staring into the stormy eyes of the agitated man—no, not man. Sunny gulped. Could it be? She had heard of them, knew there were a couple in town, but she had never seen *him* before.

"Are you always so elegant?" the male muttered,

his eyes glittering angrily as he grabbed her arm and pulled her back to her feet.

Sunny would have been put off by his rudeness, only she was too tickled to meet him. A mate. Her mate. He was her mate. Christ, he was good looking, but she sincerely hoped he was interesting too. Sunny appreciated beauty, but she was a realist. She needed interaction, honest conversation, laughter, and affection to be happy. Was that too tall an order? She hoped not. Because if this male was really hers, she might just have the happily ever after she had always wanted.

Please be real. Be mine. Mate.

"I need help with this," he growled, rolling his eyes as he held a half-dead potted plant in his hand.

She really should answer him, but Sunny was too caught up in wondering what he looked like when he shifted, and why he smelled so good like sandalwood smoke and marshmallow cream, and what was he doing in her shop? Today of all days!

Christ, he was good-looking. He had short dark hair and stormy blue eyes, so dark they could have been black. He was easily eight or ten inches over six feet tall, and she wondered if that would be a problem cause she was only five foot three.

That was Sunny for you, short, curvy, and she

had a mind that could run away with a thought faster than a runaway train. She could not believe he was standing in front of her. Her pulse was racing and the Wolf inside her whined and growled.

"Do you speak?" he asked a little too loudly for her sensitive Wolf's ears.

She winced at his volume but nodded. Of course she spoke. Sunny was even considered a good conversationalist by some members of her acquaintance—and not all of them were family members.

She wanted to regale him with her wit, to prove she was intelligent—contrary to the opinion he seemed to be forming. Christ, she was making a jackass of herself. Steeling her nerves, Sunny prepared to say something charming.

Unfortunately, the only thing that came out of her mouth when she opened her lips was one word, and she probably should have kept it to herself.

"Mate."

CHAPTER 3

"Wait! Please, just hang on a sec." The she-Wolf's voice was husky and melodic —*sexy*, his Dragon added. That had him stopping short in his tracks. Since when did his beast have an opinion on women? He growled and walked faster.

"No fair! Your legs are twice as long as mine, buddy," she said. Closer now than before.

Now, why did that make him all tingly? Dragons did not get tingly. It was unseemly. He snorted and shook his head. Devine did not give a fuck if her voice was scratchy and cute, not at all screechy, and annoying like he found so many females. And so what if his Dragon was taking notice? He was not the boss of him.

Am too. Snarrrrlllll. Stay.

His legs froze in place, the Dragon exerting his will. What the actual fuck? No, he was not doing this. He wrestled his beast down, forcing his body to obey him. This was what happened when a Dragon like him indulged in a hobby that did not involve maiming anyone.

Grrr.

Now he had to deal with clumsy little she-Wolves following him around, for fuck's sake. Devine Graystone stomped out of the ridiculously named garden center, ignoring the lunatic Werewolf who seemed to work there. What was she thinking? Was it play a trick on a Dragon day? He did not believe his ears.

Mate. Ha!

The crazy canine had called him her mate. What kind of game was she playing? Devine snarled and almost tore off the door to his custom Ford F-150 pickup truck. The vehicle was perfect for work and play with its brand new lift kit, wheels, and tire package, giving it that little bit of an extra boost a man his size needed.

He'd had them work on the interior, as well. Devine had a thing for design and when he wanted something, it was his way or no way. True, he liked all the modern toys and gadgets he and his brother had been learning ever since they'd left the Isle of Pain.

When he ordered his truck, he had a computer console upgrade, woodgrain additions, custom luxury leather seats with hand stitching, and those high endurance weatherproof mats on the floor. It was a good thing he was a fast learner.

Computers seemed to run the modern world, and the things he'd seen on the internet were both awesome and terrible. Humankind were miles away from being civilized despite calling themselves a civilization.

The atrocities they afforded on one another reminded him of his old Chief. Terrible, wasteful, and lacking all trace of compassion. He'd grown up hard, like every other Dragon he knew. Devine had spent most of his youth fighting the Demons that spilled from the hellmouth not far from his former home.

It was a Dragon's duty to protect the world from the evil wanting to take over. A small band of supernaturals called the Wardens of Terra were doing that job now and he could finally retire. But how did a Dragon like him learn to live without bloodlust and war raging through his veins?

"Easy," Callius Falk had told him. "You find something else to take up your time."

Devine had discovered the F-150 quite by accident. He'd spent months designing his perfect vehicle, and yeah, he enjoyed that truck. One might even say, he loved it—but just then, this she-Wolf had his inner beast two seconds away from ripping the door clean off.

He turned around, holding his arms out lest she crash into him one more time. Gods forbid he touch that curvy, soft, utterly feminine form again.

Grrr. Good idea. Touch.

Frowning, Devine pushed his beast down once more. This was lunacy. He was not looking for his mate. he could not possibly have one. And even if he did, who would have picked this female for him? Dragons were old-fashioned with strict tastes and ideas on how their females looked and behaved.

This utterly modern she-Wolf was not for him. He scoffed and took in her messy hair and completely inappropriate work clothes. Her eyes were bright and her grin wide, honest. She smelled fucking delicious like woods, Wolf, and woman.

Fuck.

"What do you want?" he growled.

She wore skintight leggings—*almost see through in*

some places—that molded to her curvy legs and plump bottom. She was petite and yet buxom, short enough for him to tower over her, but she appeared hearty. She was a Wolf, after all. But the woman was entirely too damn soft for a rough monster like him.

Her cropped shirt showed a strip of pale soft skin at the hem of her ruffled top. The short sleeves fluttered in the breeze like butterflies' wings and had the most intriguing effect on his Dragon. The beast could not stop staring at her.

She was not wearing a bra, that much was obvious from the way her tip-tilted breasts showed off her cherry-ripe nipples through the thin material of her shirt. A small red apron was tied around her waist, making him glance once more at that teasing strip of bare skin, and it was almost as distracting as her mess of multicolored curls that circled her head in a frizzy halo.

Her skin was pale, and she had a smattering of freckles across her nose, plump lips, and a cute little upturned nose. Wait—*cute?* No. She was a disaster. And she was mistaken. Devine was not her mate. He was no one's mate.

"Whew! Thanks for stopping," she said and expelled a breath. "Wow, you are fast."

She wore an enormous smile, showing off her

straight white teeth, and for some reason his Dragon approved of that grin. It was ridiculous. He looked down at her feet and frowned. The woman had on the ugliest pair of shoes he had ever seen.

Were they tie-dyed? How the fuck did you tie dye rubber?

"What are those?" he asked before he could stop himself. Damn his curiosity.

"These? Oh, they're Crocs. They are like my favorite shoe ever. Not these in particular, though I do like the colors they went with," she said pointing her toes in the huge, rounded boat things she called Crocs. *Ridiculous.*

"You must be joking," he grumbled, shaking his head.

"I'm not," she said, smiling even wider. "Seriously, I stopped wearing all other shoes like fifteen years ago. I have over fifty pairs on account of I wear them so much, I have actually put holes through the soles of them, but I can't bring myself to throw them away. They are just so cute. Don't you think so?" she asked after her explanation, sucking in a breath before continuing with her rambling nonsense.

"No, I don't," he growled, closing his eyes when the Dragon snarled at him.

Be nice.

"Oh, well, some people are put off by their appearance, but really if you haven't tried them, you should save your opinion," she said with just as much enthusiasm as before.

Devine was aware he'd been rude and insulting, but the she-Wolf did not seem put off at all. IN fact, she turned her foot this way and that, studying her shoes with a silly grin on her face, *and fuck*, she was really cute. But she was not his.

"I keep hoping they will offer some kind of sole repair where they can, I don't know, glue new bottoms on or something—*oooh!* Maybe I should write to them and see if they can be recycled within the company! That's a great idea. Thanks," the woman—*not woman, she-Wolf, meus lupus*—finished.

Meus lupus. What? No. Not mine.

Devine had enough of his meddling beast and was ready to tell this female to leave him alone when she turned her wide, brown eyes on him and smiled. Fucking hell. He'd be lying if Dev said he did not feel something stirring deep within himself at that rapt gaze.

She had thanked him—this crazy, strange she-Wolf and Devine had warmed under the praise she gave so freely, even though it was without cause. He had nothing to do with how she got from point A to point B—which had to be via the world's largest fucking loopdeloop ever because this female was nuttier than a fruitcake. They stood there, her with a soft, expectant smile on her face, and him with a confused grimace.

"So," she began, biting her lip nervously.

She was practically glowing under his angry stare, and he felt like a total undeserving shit. She was strange, but good—wholesome even. Too good for him.

"Look, Miss, there has been a mistake. I am no one's mate," Devine explained gently as he could.

Of course, he wasn't. If he had a mate, she would likely be some giant warrior like himself. A mean, hard-eyed female who did not take crap from anyone. Not this soft, sweet smelling she-Wolf.

What would he do with a creature such as she? Standing there, staring at him with her warm, guileless brown eyes, and ready grin, showcasing straight white teeth and plump pink lips. She exuded happiness—seemed to radiate it, but if she knew the horrors of what he'd done, she would run screaming from him. That didn't bear thinking, and Devine frowned at the image and the sudden pain in his chest.

"You know, you can fight it, but it's true. You are

my mate. At least, my Wolf is pretty damn sure you are," she returned easily.

"I suggest you speak firmly to her, little Wolf. I am not mate material. Truth is, I only came here to ask about this plant," he muttered, looking around uncomfortably for someone to rescue him from this nightmarish conversation.

"Oh, right," she murmured, her attention flitting to the small potted plant he still held.

Now, why did it rankle with his beast that she was no longer focusing on him? Shit, Devine grumbled. He was not going to indulge that question for even a moment.

"It's from my rooftop greenhouse. I am in the process of winterizing it, but something is wrong. Some of the plants have started dying," he mumbled, concern in his voice.

He did not know why it bothered him so, but the sight of the poor wilting plants had struck a chord inside of him. Devine rubbed the back of his neck, avoiding the pained glance she gave him before she turned her attention to the plant. Someone soft and sweet—someone like her—would be better for the plants, he knew.

For the briefest of moments, Dev wished he was different. Wished he was kind and good and deserving, but what was the point in that? He could not change his past. And regardless of her suppositions, the she-Wolf was not his future.

"May I?" the female asked. Whether she was excusing, or simply ignoring his rudeness, he could not be sure.

She lifted the small potted plant, and he noticed her fingernails were short and clean, and she had small scars on her hands probably from work or play. Werewolves were tough, he knew, and that meant strength. She had strength, but not enough to take him on.

Devine frowned as she handled the fragile stem. He did not know why he'd brought it. It was sick and delicate, but whatever was going on with that one orchid, was happening to all of them and he would be damned if he lost any of his plants.

He had needed something to do when he was finishing building. He hated computers and making money was easy. When Winifred Falk had suggested a greenhouse, he had no idea what he would fill it with, but after much research he'd settled on growing orchids.

Horticulturists around the world agreed growing orchids was a taxing hobby, but Devine was a Dragon. He had laser-like focus and ample time to spare. He needed a project, something to do to fill the long hours of the day.

For the first few months it had seemed fine, but as he started winterizing the greenhouse, things had turned to shit. He had somehow thrown off the balance of the environment or maybe it was the food. Really, he could not say.

So, he'd come here and waited as the she-Wolf pursed her full, naturally pink lips. She turned the pot around, studying it carefully before meeting his gaze.

"Arethusa bulbosa, commonly known as Dragon's Mouth," she murmured, smiling as if she knew his secret. Maybe she did. He could not be sure how many Wolves were aware of the Dragons in their midst.

"Yes," he replied, and he was pleased she had guessed correctly.

"Do you have more of them? It seems like this one was separated recently, and I wonder if any of the others are suffering the same."

"How did you know?" he asked, surprised by her intuition.

"I own this place, it's my business to know plants."

"I see," he murmured. "Well, if you can just give

me some tips, maybe point me to a new kind of fertilizer or something so I can fix whatever this is—"

"Actually," she said, stepping into his personal space, bringing with her the scents of sage and clean earth. "I think I need to see your setup in order to properly diagnose the problem."

Clever Wolf.

His Dragon preened inside his mind's eye, happy that she wanted to see his den, *er*, house. Devine had his doubts, but one more glance at the wilting flower and he knew he had no choice.

"Fine. Here is my address," he snapped, thrusting a card into her hand. "Come in the morning."

"I have work—"

"Come in the morning or not at all, little Wolf. I have other things to do with my time," he said, not entirely truthful.

"Okay," she replied with a sharp nod. "You make coffee, and I will bring the bagels."

"I don't eat bagels," he lied. "Look, we're not having breakfast. You are just looking at my plants and giving me a solution."

"Don't worry, *Hot Stuff*. I'll fix what's wrong."

She gave him a cute wave then jogged back across the parking lot, and fool that he was, Devine could only stare. Her parting statement played over and over again in his mind, and he growled, getting into his truck, and slamming the door.

I'll fix what's wrong.

"You can't," he whispered hoarsely.

Devine placed the potted orchid back inside the small cardboard box he'd brought for it on the floor of the passenger seat. He glanced in the direction she'd run in one more time before peeling out of the parking lot. Emotions the likes of which he'd never felt crashed into him, and fuck, it hurt like hell. His Dragon was scratching at his skin, begging to be loosed.

He needed to change. Now.

Grrr.

CHAPTER 4

Sunny hopped out of her old, beat up, little Jeep Wrangler, patting the faded yellow door as she hefted the three dozen bagels, and a bag of other goodies she'd brought, along with some things from the garden center, in her capable hands. She'd always wished her hands were dainty and pretty, with long fingers and painted nails, but that wasn't in the works for a gal who liked to dig in dirt all day.

Her feminine affinities had to be satisfied with pedicures when she had the time. Painted toes and colorful crocs were her go to when she needed an ego boost, which was why she'd been up half the night carefully applying hot pink polish to her ten little piggies.

Nerves assailed her as she walked down the

newly paved driveway, admiring the stones and the image they made on the ground. The picture was like a heraldic crest—a Dragon soaring above a jagged rock with a giant wave behind them. She could not believe it. Her fated mate was a legendary creature of magic and mystery.

Sunny had a Dragon. Her very own flying, fire-breathing Dragon. Wow. Just wow.

She'd called just about everyone she knew to get information on Devine Graystone, Dragon Shifter, Falk Clan member, new construction business owner—and her fated mate. Luckily, her mother was friends with Winifred Falk.

The Werewolf was a former bartender and was mated to Callius Falk, the Alpha of the Dragon Clan that had settled in Maccon City, with the permission of Rafe Maccon, Werewolf Alpha, of course, a few years ago. She'd seen them infrequently at the store and in town, and they were good, honest people.

But Sunny always looked for the best in folks. It was part of the curse of her name. She snorted and climbed the stairs, admiring the wraparound patio of the extravagant beach mansion her mate not only lived in, but had designed as well. *Graystone Builders Inc.* was fairly new, but already they had plans to further develop some vacant lots right along the pine barrens and close to the ocean.

Prime real estate indeed, but Sunny did not care about that stuff. She was not at all materialistic, but she admired beauty, and this house and its view was beautiful. She'd turned to stare at the crashing waves, a small smile of contentment teasing at the corner of her lips. The Atlantic was wild and beauti-ful, and she'd loved it ever since she was a little girl.

How it must be wonderful to go to sleep at night listening to Mother Nature's lullaby, she mused fancifully.

"You're late," an angry voice sounded behind her, and Sunny startled. She did not hear him approach or open the door, and when she turned, he stole her breath.

The man was dressed in a pair of sweats and nothing else. His muscled torso glistened with sweat, as if he'd been working out. or, *sniff*, was back from a change. She smelled the faint scent of smoke, scales, and the woods clinging to his skin.

"Did you just get back? I wish I would have known, I would have run with you—"

"Dragons don't run. We fly," he growled and turned back inside, leaving her to follow.

Okay, so he was rude, she thought, shrugging as

she carried the bags inside. Sunny would just have to nice it out of him—*you'll catch more flies with honey,* she recalled the saying and moved to follow the big, ornery beast.

But before she took more than one step, he was already turning and taking the bags from her hands, careful not to touch her though. Warmth surged through her at the gesture, and she knew it was silly, but his showing even the slightest manners was a good sign.

"Thank you."

He didn't answer, his stormy gaze rested on her for a millisecond before he turned his back and stomped towards an enormous kitchen that looked as though no one ever used it. She ran her fingertips along the stainless-steel appliances and the stone countertops.

"Beautiful. What is this? It's not marble," she remarked, liking the feel of the cold, strong rock.

The color was fascinating—a deep midnight black with blue with black accents, highly glossed, and somehow, it went perfectly with the warm wood cabinets and high-end appliances.

"Quartz, or as my kind call it, galaxy stone," he muttered, and she noticed then that his eyes were the same stormy combination of colors as the stone she'd just admired.

A blend of sapphire and onyx. Looking at his eyes was like looking through a telescope at a galaxy far, far away. It was aptly named, indeed.

Breathtaking.

"I brought bagels," she said, grinning as he set the bags on the counter.

"I told you not to," he replied, crossing his arms over his chest. "This is not a social call, Wolf."

"My name is Sunny, and, come on, you gotta eat. I mean, I don't know much about Dragons," Sunny replied, moving past him to unload the groceries she'd brought.

"But I figure, you are bigger than Wolves, and we eat a lot, so you must eat more. I got eggs, bacon, veggies, bagels, butter, three kinds of cream cheese," she rambled on, chatting away while she moved about the kitchen with more confidence than she felt.

"Sunny," he warned, but she ignored him.

"Great frying pans. And this stove, wow. I love a good kitchen setup. I mean, I grew up in an RV, so this is like wow."

And just like that, she told him all about her upbringing. This was her mate. She knew it down to her marrow, even if he needed convincing. Devine watched her a moment, then started helping.

He washed and sliced the veggies. Grabbing plates and utensils, he set them on the counter. She talked about her siblings and parents, and he muttered his responses, but he was talking to her, and that was a plus.

There was something broken about this man, this Dragon, and until she knew what it was, she could not make it right. A fixer by nature, Sunny could not help herself. Fated mates were tricky. A blessing, most would say, but in some ways, she thought it unfair.

They might be fated, but Sunny believed in personal choices. This could be great—they could be great together. Or not. It would all depend on what each was willing to put into it.

Her Wolf whined and scratched, the animal needing to be closer to him. She could not understand why he was not mounting her, marking her already. Heat rushed to her cheeks as she placed bagels in an empty basket and took out a skillet to start some bacon. As if he knew she was not going to relent, her ornery Dragon hissed out an annoyed breath and walked to the coffeemaker. Good. She loved coffee. In fact, Sunny was useless without it.

"How do you like your eggs?" she asked brightly, hoping for the best as was her nature.

"I don't like eggs," he grumbled, crossing his arms over his chest.

"Everybody likes eggs. I know, I'll surprise you," she said, challenge accepted.

"I don't like surprises either," he muttered, glaring at her before sitting down at the counter. She hid her grin when he started poking through the bagels until he found a half burnt salt one.

Score one for me.

Sunny had asked the girl at the bagel store to give her every well done bagel they had. Something told her Dragons preferred their food extra toasty, and she was not wrong. He ate six while she finished up the bacon and cracked two dozen eggs into a bowl.

Ten minutes later, she had a fluffy platter of perfectly scrambled eggs with shredded cheese, diced jalapeno peppers, scallions, and a little fresh dill smattered across the top, along with bacon, sausage, and two ham steaks.

"Well, what are you waiting for?" she asked. "Dig in before I eat it all."

"A tiny thing like you? Yeah, right," he grumbled.

"Do not even throw that gauntlet down," she said, chewing a bite of the fruit salad she'd made a side.

"Don't let this body fool you, I can eat." Sunny snorted, waiting for him to laugh, but he just looked at her curiously.

"That was a joke," she told him. "Cause I'm what my mom calls pleasantly plump. And no, that is not a criticism. I am very pleasant, and I am plump. I love food. That Werewolf gene that makes us have super metabolism must have skipped me, or mine is just broken—"

"You are pleasant, I will give you that, but your body looks fine to me, Sunny Daye," he murmured.

Sunny's smile went into eclipse at that compliment, and she felt her cheeks burn with joy. He thought she looked fine. Well, well, wasn't that nice?

"Eat," he growled, and she nodded, dutifully scooping food into her plate.

Devine huffed out a breath she could only categorize as annoyed, but it didn't last. Sunny was fairly certain she hit the nail on the head when he moaned after the first bite. Maybe food was the way to this grumpy Dragon's heart?

Score two for the she-Wolf.

"Like it?" she asked, worrying her lip between her teeth.

"It's okay," he replied, not giving an inch.

She smirked, returning to her food, knowing full

well it was a good breakfast. Though, she wished he didn't dress while she'd been cooking. Sunny was looking forward to a pleasant view with her meal, but *Mr. CrankyPants* had ruined her plans.

Sigh.

He ate quietly, and clothed, having already pulled on a hoodie over his massive muscles. Sunny was just about to say something when the door opened.

"Hey Dev, did you cook? Something smells fantasti—oh, wow, you have a guest," a giant of a man walked in. He resembled Devine, same chin, slightly bigger nose, and his hair was different. He had dark roots and silver-tipped tresses, and his eyes glittered like the stainless-steel knife she'd used to slice her bagel in half.

With eyes and hair that color, Sunny could only imagine what his beast looked like. He stood there, looking curiously, and Sunny smiled politely. It was simply her nature to be kind to strangers. She extended a hand and introduced herself, having no other choice as Dev had not said a word.

"Hi, I'm Sunny."

"Yes, you are," the male replied, shaking her hand eagerly. "Like a ray of sunshine, aren't you, little Wolf? Ha ha. I'm Nicholas, this lump's more charming, better looking, and slightly older brother," he informed her with a saucy waggle of his eyebrows.

"I see," she replied, laughing with him. "Won't you join us?"

"There's not enough," Devine interrupted.

"Oh, come on, brother, there's plenty," Nicholas said, sitting right next to Sunny.

"So, have you known Dev long?"

"Not long. Just a day," she replied, shrugging her shoulders, and still waiting for him to say something—*anything*.

Disappointed that Dev did not join the conversation, Sunny and Nick bantered easily. Truth was, she had a good time, even if she was slightly hurt by Dev ignoring her. Still, she made the most of it. That was just her way.

Breakfast turned out to be entertaining as hell. At least from Sunny's perspective it did, but Devine had been correct. There was not enough food for two Dragons and a Wolf Shifter, but that was okay. She'd taken the day off of work. That meant she could eat again earlier than her usual lunchtime.

"Don't you have to get to work? We should look at the greenhouse so you can get back," Devine murmured. he'd grown quieter since his brother had arrived—if that were even possible.

"Actually, I am not going in today," she told him, bumping shoulders as they worked side by side to clean the counter and load the dishwasher. "I asked my brother, River, to fill in for me. He just got his MBA but hasn't found the right job yet. I know it is different for males, but he is almost thirty and still living with our parents in their RV, and he refuses to let me hire him full time."

"Your parents reside in an RV?" Nicholas asked. He sat perched on one of the stools as he refilled his coffee mug.

"Yeah, they love it. They're parked in the old Von Holland lot near Baker Street," she told both brothers.

"That is where you grew up, correct? In an RV right here in Maccon City. What was it like?" Dev inquired, and his questions warmed her inside.

She liked that he was curious, and she nodded her response. Devine looked as if he was going to add something, but then his brother was there, shoving him aside lightly. Nick turned a megawatt smile on her. Unfortunately, it did not have the same effect as one of Dev's rarer, smaller grins.

"So, you are ours for the day, are you?"

"Yours? Ha! Are you flirting with me, Nicholas Graystone?" Sunny asked, half-teasing because she liked the Dragon, but her real interest was for her mate. If only his brother was in the teasing mood.

"A little, but who can blame me with a maiden fair such as you in our midst?" Nick admitted and winked.

"Maiden fair? Okay, I see. Well, you are a shameless flirt, sir," she teased, turning her focus back on Dev.

"Anyway, to answer your question, yes, I grew up here, in an RV, with my parents who love the RV life. This is their fourth one and believe me when I say I had to twist their arms to buy it."

"You mean, they choose to live in one?" Nicholas asked, seemingly shocked.

"Yep. Have you never been inside an RV, Nick, Dev? It's not that bad. In fact, the one they are in now is probably the same price as the average three bedroom home in Maccon City. It's not this," she said, gesturing to the grandeur surrounding them. "But it's super nice. I mean, I grew up in a much older one, but I think I turned out okay."

"More than okay, little Wolf," Dev replied softly, and closed the dishwasher with a sharp slap, leaving the kitchen and Sunny just standing there.

"Hmm, my brother seems affected by something," Nicholas said.

"I rub him the wrong way," she replied and shrugged, worrying her lower lip between her teeth. "I told him the truth about us, and he's been growling ever since."

"How do you mean?" Nick inquired. Sunny waited a beat, deciding whether to tell him. Oh well. She never was any good at hiding things.

"He's my fated mate. I felt it the second I saw him, but he says I'm wrong," she murmured, sadness filling her gaze. "My Wolf is not wrong. She knows what he is. I know what he is. And I think he knows too," she continued on a deep exhale. "But he doesn't want to know it. Or maybe he just doesn't want me. Either way, it will be a choice."

"A choice?"

"Yeah, mates might be fated, but it's our choice to make it something good and strong, If he doesn't want me, I will go away. Simple as that."

"Simple?" Nick scoffed.

"No, I guess I should say difficult as that. But what can a girl do? I can't force him to want me."

Sunny's heart wrenched at that small confession, as she stared after Devine. He'd left the room and already she felt the loss keenly. She was getting attached, and fast. If he did not want her, she had to distance herself soon. She turned her attention back to the big man with silver-tipped hair who was still standing next to her.

She saw Nicholas' Dragon peeking through his eyes, as if weighing her, and she stilled. The way she saw it, this man was her mate's brother. Let him evaluate her, and if she was found lacking, maybe he could tell her, and she could fix it.

"I know I'm not the kind of mate he expected. I'm not rich or refined I'm clumsy, and I talk without thinking, but I am honest. I'm loyal. And I'm kind. I don't know why I am explaining myself at all, Nicholas, but here I am," she said and shook her head sadly.

"Do you love him already?" he asked, and Sunny sighed. She thought about it and formed her answer immediately.

"The seed is there, the bond already formed, but it needs to be tended to grow. The Fates can only pair us up, but we have to decide to nurture or deny our relationship. I am willing to try, Nicholas. Your brother does something to me I never hoped to feel," she confessed, looking down and exhaling the breath she'd been holding.

"You know something, Sunny Daye? I think my brother is one lucky bastard. Don't give up on him yet, okay?"

Nicholas forced her to lift her gaze with his forefinger and thumb against her chin. They were standing kind of close to keep their conversation secret, but the Dragon who'd returned to see if she was ready to look at his orchids did not know that. The sound of his growl reverberated in the room and Sunny jumped back as Devine launched himself at Nicholas from the doorway.

Thank fuck for Werewolf reflexes! Stunned, she watched as Nicholas barked a laugh just before Devine's fist smashed in his face. They tumbled across the tiled floor, and Sunny ran to open the sliding door to the patio facing their yard before they crashed through it.

She yelped, avoiding their claws as they snarled and snapped, and beat the living piss out of one another. Footsteps sounded, and she turned to see three hulking males racing across the sand. One of them had a small child on his shoulders. She smelled of Wolf and Dragon—*must be Callius and Fred's young.*

"What is going on?" roared the black-haired man holding the tiny girl. But she was not frightened, being raised Shifter was a lot different from human. Fights were natural even among kin.

"Uh, I'm not sure," she said, watching as the two

brothers continued their fight throwing each other off the patio and onto the sand. "We were having breakfast and Devine left and Nicholas and I were chatting—"

"Who are you?"

"I'm Sunny, Sunny Daye. I met Devine at my garden center. He needed help with some orchids, and well, my Wolf says he's mine. I came over today to get to know him and to help—"

"Ah, I see. This is fine then," he laughed. "I am Callius. These are my brothers Castor and Sander. And this is my little princess," he said proudly.

"Nice to meet you. But, um, why aren't you stopping this?" she asked, clearly confused by Dragon politics.

"They will be fine. Sometimes, it is good to clear the air. You say your Wolf identified him as yours, but Devine has not yet claimed you. Nicholas has the right to challenge him for your hand—"

Thunder roared in her ears as the two males backed up and half-shifted. Holy fuck—was it terrifying! Enormous bat-like wings protruded from Nicholas' back and curling silver horn sprouted from his head.

Devine, on the other hand, seemed to grow

gigantic stone spikes from his back, shredding his clothes with his half-shift. His tail was thick and enormous, the beast a muddy brown color at first glance, but she soon realized his scales glittered with dark blues and blacks, offsetting the dark brown tones.

He was magnificent, and she could not stop staring. But this was wrong. All wrong. He hardly acknowledged her claim. Why would he fight for her? Shit. Did Callius say Nicholas was challenging Devine for her?

No! her inner Wolf snarled. The big gray and brown brindled beast inside her was not happy with that idea at all.

"Wait a minute—Stop!"

"Sunny, you should not interfere," Callius said, but she was so not doing this.

"Oh, yes, I should. I am not a freaking carnival prize, for fuck's sake," she growled and stomped her feet towards the two battling half-changed Dragons. "I said STOP!"

She vaulted over the patio, landing on her ass between the two warring brothers. A scream hovered on her lips as Nicholas charged, but Devine, seeing her directly in his path, turned around to shield her and, using his tail, propelled his brother some twenty feet away where two of the Falk brothers wrestled him down.

Thank. Fuck.

"Sunny! Are you crazy, woman? Jumping between two fighting Dragons! Do you have a death wish?" Devine snarled at her, raking his hands through his hair, and pacing in front of her.

His chest was heaving, and *dayum*, he was hot—if a little bloody. Sunny frowned. He was really going to have to stop yelling at her.

"First, help me up," she snapped, and he turned, offering his hand. Sunny pulled herself to standing and crossed her arms. They had a lot of things to say to each other, but first things first.

"Second, what the hell was that all about?"

"What was what about?" he asked, chest heaving with exertion.

"The fight. You and Nicholas. What happened?"

"He was touching you," he whispered, and his face turned bright red.

The whole world seemed to disappear as his words sank into Sunny's brain.

Touching her? Nicholas touched her—when? Ohhhhh.

Realization dawned, and Sunny could hardly stop herself from whooping with joy. Devine was jealous, and that meant, he cared.

Holy shit.

Her mate was trembling with fury, but Sunny, she was grinning like a lunatic. He stopped and turned and walked right into her space.

"What, that makes you happy? Having my brother's hands on you?" he snarled.

"No. His hands don't make me happy. You do," she said, surprising him into silence.

The energy around them became charged with another emotion, and she felt her Wolf staring into the eyes of his Dragon. Something was happening here. Something big.

Score three for Sunny.

CHAPTER 5

Devine was a total moron. He had to be. Why else would he have started a battle with his own brother for touching the chin of some stranger who meant nothing to him?

The rosebud marking on his chest burned with her touch. It tingled and moved, and she gasped as her fingertips ran across it. Every Dragon of their Clan carried a rose on his skin, symbolizing that mate bond each strived for.

It was a Dragon's hope to find his mate, for without one, he would die. That was the sad reality of powerful, immortal beasts. Oh, dying would take long, a millennium perhaps, but Devine could not be sure about that.

He only knew this was a complete shock to his

system. He had never expected to find his maiden and was determined to live his days trying to repay the Falks for the wrong he did them in hunting their brother.

But everything was different now. Sunny had claimed her Wolf knew he was her mate the second she had seen him. That had to mean something, right?

Fuck fuck fuck.

Devine knew what that meant, even if she didn't. Fuck, he would ruin her. But there might still be time to stop this. To save her from binding herself to him any further. Devine was no good for a kind, outgoing person like Sunny. She ran her hands closer to the edge of his rose again, and he growled.

"Don't touch me there. It hurts."

Liar liar.

The Dragon's mocking words made his growl worse, and the female currently cleaning the wounds his brother made across his skin flicked her molten gaze to his. She had deep, dark brown eyes that lightened to honey when her Wolf was peeking through, as the beast was now.

"You know, you are a loud thinker," she remarked, her gentle touch soothing his still pissed off beast. "I admit, I'm a bit confused, Dev. For someone who is *no one's mate*, you sure seemed a little jealous, overprotective to me."

Devine grunted. There were no words to explain what had just happened. Fine, that wasn't true. She had described it perfectly. He was jealous—of his own fucking brother. Shit. This was bad.

"I mean, he is your brother—"

"He touched you. Nicholas had his hands on your skin and I, fuck—he should not have done that," Devine growled, unable to stop the flow of words.

"What's the difference, Dev. You don't want me. You said it yourself, I'm not yours—"

Thunder roared in his ears at her words, and Devine could not help himself. Anger and hurt poured from her and those harsh words describing his actions, his treatment of her rankled with his beast. They seemed to propel him into action faster than anything else could have.

One moment, Sunny was sitting on a chair applying gauze and ointment to his wounds, caring for him in a way no one ever had. The next, Devine had her wrapped in his arms, his mouth crushing hers under the force of his kiss.

Fucking hell. He was not slow or gentle or kind. He was brutal and hungry. Monster. But he could not slow down. Sunny tasted like heaven, and he was a Dragon starving for a bit of warmth. He expected her to hit him, or pull away, but she gave him no sign she wanted him to stop or slow down.

Thank fuck.

Devine could not do that if he'd tried. He was not there to savor. Devine was there to claim. This kiss was hard, angry, and demanding. But Sunny was no weakling to cow beneath him.

She was a Werewolf. And fuck, she was beautiful in her ready response and her submission to him. His female was a powerful being in her own right, and she gave as good as she got. Her lips were eager, her tongue tangled his in a duel worthy of the most stout-hearted warrior.

"Mine," he snarled, opening his eyes, finally.

His stormy gaze raked over the beautiful, the messy-haired Wolf in his arms. Her pink bow of a mouth was bleeding where he'd been too rough, and he leaned forward, lapping the bruise, tending the hurt and begging her forgiveness with his actions instead of words. Her eyes went wide, and then she did something he was not prepared for.

Sunny smiled at him, and damn, the woman was radiant.

Fuck, but that reaction was stronger, deadlier, and more accurate than any arrow to his heart. The she-Wolf growled, melting into him with her plump breasts pressing firmly against his chest, the tight buds biting into him.

Fuck, he knew she was wearing next to nothing beneath the calf-length dress she wore. His beast scented her need, and he salivated just thinking about coming inside her sweet, tight, hot little slit.

Devine growled, wrapping her up closer. He lifted her clear off the floor, nodding his approval when she wrapped her legs around his waist kicking those awful gator shoes off her feet.

Her heated center pressed against the thick bar of his cock, and he groaned, hating the clothes between them. No. This was not a good idea, but Devine couldn't stop it any more than he could turn the tide.

"Devine," she moaned his name, egging him on further.

His cock was so fucking hard he could hammer nails with it, but that was nothing to what happened to him when she scratched her claws against his skin and called him *mate*. Her tongue snaked out to lap at his lips, begging entry. And who was he to deny it?

Still running on adrenaline from fighting his own brother, Devine took her face with one hand and stroked the tender skin there before moving to grip her by the back of her neck. His other hand moved beneath her dress, squeezing the firm globe of her ass, and grinding her against his cloth-covered cock.

He pulled her closer to him, kissing her deeply, thoroughly, leaving no inch untouched. Pure animalistic need drove him as he deepened their kiss. He wanted her so fucking bad, he would die to have her.

This strange attraction was addicting. Was this what was meant by Fated Mates then? He wondered, groaning as she squeezed her thighs and rubbed her sex against his cock. Sexy little she-Wolf felt so fucking good, his Dragon reared up.

Es meus.

Fuck, that was all the confirmation he needed. Cock throbbing, heart racing, and rose burning, Devine pressed Sunny up against the wall. If she wanted the Dragon, she was going to get him. No rose-colored version, either. He would confront her with the real beast and let her decide. Sunny moaned and pushed her pelvis into his, her eyes a blazing gold with the Wolf as he leaned back and tore the clothes from her body.

She was even more perfect in the nude. Her skin so soft, so place, luminous in the light filtering in from the window of his kitchenette. No, he did not take her back to the communal kitchen. He did not want her anywhere that Nicholas—or anyone, for that matter—had access to.

So warm, so responsive, nothing he did frightened or turned her off. His sexy little Wolf met him move for move, using her own clawed hands to shred the waistband of his pants as she opened her legs and took his cock inside her.

"Fuck," he growled, giving her no time to adjust.

"Harder," was her only reply as he started pounding into her.

They came together like an avalanche. His need, her desire, their pleasure slammed into him, into her, in relentless succession. And still, it wasn't enough. Devine carried her to the bedroom, placing biting kisses along her neck and chest.

"Oh that feels so good," she moaned as he slid down her body, taking one plump nipple into his mouth.

He sucked and squeezed, sliding two thick fingers into her pussy. So tight, so hot. He fucked her with his hand, loving the way she squeezed him.

"I'm gonna come," she whimpered, arching her back against the sensual onslaught.

Devine growled against her breast as the first wave of her orgasm gripped his fingers, then he bit down, slicing through skin, and swallowing the coppery essence that was her life's force. Sunny howled. Her climax ripping through her as he slid up her body and filled her with one hard thrust. Her pleasure clenched around him, squeezing his dick so fucking good he went cross-eyed.

Fuck fuck fuck.

He did not know what was happening to him. She was undoing everything he thought he'd built to survive with her breathy sighs, and her smoldering kisses, not to mention, her sweet, honeyed sex. The female was perfect in every way. A beautiful disaster that was made just for him. Fuck, he loved her frizzy, curly hair, those warm brown eyes that glowed gold with her Wolf. She had the perfect body, made for a Dragon.

Whatever he dished out, she could take it. She could take him. A small part of him held back, even as he relentlessly chased pleasure, his and hers. Pounding into her sex, Devine growled, returning to her mouth. Fuck, he just could not seem to get enough of those drugging kisses of hers.

Es meus, his Dragon grunted.

Then she struck, her mouth closed over his shoulder, fangs buried in his skin. His rose burned with the force of her claim, and his gaze found hers glowing gold with her Wolf. His pleasure exploded inside of her, coating her womb with his cum, marking her with bite, scent, and rose.

Her silky sheath tightened, closing around him like a vise, and fuck if he did not feel like this was exactly where he was supposed to be.

"Es Meus."

CHAPTER 6

A Dragon. She'd claimed him. And he'd claimed her too. Sunny Daye was mated to a real live Dragon. Holy. Fucking. Amazeballs.

Sunny sighed and stretched. She rolled over in the enormous bed, frowning when she found she was alone. Her body was deliciously sore from the carnal workout she'd gotten. Hell, it had been a long dry spell between lovers, not that anyone compared to her sexy as sin Dragon.

The moon was high in the sky, and she smiled thinking of how they'd spent the day in bed. There had been no conversation. She should be worried, but she felt too damn good just then to indulge in those kinds of pesky and destructive doubts. Besides, he'd given her his bite.

Rising from the bed she looked in the mirror, and her eyes widened. Dev had given her something beside his bite.

"Wow," she murmured, tracing the shape of the mystical tattoo now marking her skin.

On her chest, in the same place as his, Sunny now had an amber outlined blue-black rose. It was a faint rendering. The small bud still tight, not yet mature, but she had hope. This hippie raised she-Wolf was nothing if not optimistic.

She could still feel his hands on her body as she stepped into his shower and turned the water on warm. Sunny had not felt that good in a very long time. In fact, never with another person. Oh, she'd had boyfriends. A Wolf and a couple of humans, but they all treated her like glass. Sunny was not fragile, and Devine knew it. In fact, he seemed to relish it.

She glanced at the love bites that marred her skin. They were already healing thanks to her she-Wolf, All except for the mating mark on her breast. That would scar over and remain there for life. She couldn't wait.

Her body warmed, thinking of her mate, and Sunny ran her sudsy hands along her belly, hips, and ass. She felt so loose, so good. Thinking about Devine, she opened her thighs and teased the edges of her sex. Biting her lip at what she was about to do, Sunny moaned with the first swipe of her fingers against her slit.

Devine's image filled her mind as she stroked along her needy clit. His chiseled jawline, stormy eyes, firm lips, and callused hands had traveled across, mesmerizing, and tantalizing every inch of her flesh, and fuck, if she didn't love it.

The door to the bathroom opened and there he stood, ducking his head slightly to walk inside. His eyes glowed with his beast as his stare traveled down her body to where she was still touching herself. Her pussy clenched around her fingers, and she moaned, panting now.

"Stop," he growled, and her hand stilled.

Fuck, what was she doing? Sunny was this close to coming, and this bastard wanted her to stop? She wiggled and moaned, hurting with the need to continue.

"Please," she begged, but he held his finger to his lips and made a shushing noise. The sexy bastard.

"Put your hands on the showerhead," he commanded in a tone that brokered no arguments.

"What are you—" Sunny's eyes widened as Devine strode into the shower, not caring about the fact he wore shorts and a t-shirt.

He kissed her hard, and her head slammed back against the tile. Not enough to hurt, but enough to show her Wolf who was in charge. The beast whined and panted, desperate for her mate to dominate her. Sunny never expected to feel this way, to want his possession, but she did. There was something so freeing about being with a powerful creature such as Devine. She trusted she was safe and protected when she was in his arms.

"You are always safe with me, *meus lupus*. Nothing shall harm you when I am here."

Then he was kneeling at her feet, the water from the showerhead beating on his shoulders, plastering his clothes to his body. Devine did not seem to notice as he pressed her thighs open, his big, callused hands practically wrapping around each one. She whimpered, her sex throbbing. But he would not be rushed.

Damn the man.

"Look at you," he growled. "Pink and pretty, and mine."

Then, he was on her. Sunny gasped as he swiped his tongue against her heated core, lapping at her in long, rough strokes. One, two, three, four times and he added two thick fingers to the mix, pressing them deep inside her. He fucked her with them, flicking his tongue against her clit, harder, faster, and fuck, she was coming.

"Dev, Dev, DEV!" she called out his name before falling into his arms, a boneless mass of well-fucked flesh.

That night they had each other countless times, and the food he had apparently gone to get when she woke the first time had been consumed and forgotten on the floor of the bedroom. It was morning before she woke again. The sound of the shower loud in the silence of the bedroom.

When he returned to the room, his face was hard, closed off, and she knew something was wrong. Her chest ached with it.

"Morning," she whispered, smiling, and waiting for him to come to her.

Devine nodded, grabbing some underwear before opening the large walking closet. *Okayyyy,* so they were doing that then? Shy even after all they did.

"I have work today," his deep voice shattered the silence, and she nodded before realizing he could not see her.

"Oh, okay. Me too. Can I borrow some clothes? Mine got, *er,* a little shredded," she said, still trying to smile.

He avoided her gaze as he stepped out of the closet, fully dressed in jeans and a tight black long sleeve. He looked good, and her heart thudded at the sight.

She was not all that impressive when she first woke up, and she knew it. Her hair was likely frizzier than usual and sticking up every which way. She hadn't had a chance to brush her teeth yet and her body smelled like sex, and a mix of Dragon and Wolf. She liked that part though.

"Here, I have to go," he mumbled dropping a pair of sweats and a t-shirt on the bed.

"Dev?"

He stopped with his hand on the doorknob, and Sunny felt her heart sticking in her throat. Was he really just going to leave like that? As if last night had meant nothing to him at all. She wouldn't be able to stand it if he did.

"I have to go, Sunny. I will talk to you again later."

"Okay Dev. I will let you go. I will let you run for now. But only for now."

The sound of the door slamming shut resounded in the room, and Sunny went to the shower. There were only two choices for someone like her at this point. She could quit now and fall apart, or she could fight back and weather the storm.

"I've never been much of a quitter," she murmured as she dressed in Dev's oversized sweatpants and shirt.

Being curvy did not mean she was Dragon sized, and extra fluff or not, Sunny still found she had to roll the waistband twice and tie the shirt beneath her boobs to make any kind of outfit from her borrowed clothes. She liked them though. Her Wolf approved of the Dragon scented garments.

Walking around Dev's section of the enormous, two-family house, she finally found her carelessly discarded Crocs. She slid her feet into the comfortable clogs, made a quick cup of coffee, and wandered around a bit. River was at the store with her parents, so there was no need to rush.

It was a fine time to get to know her mate a bit better, even if he wasn't technically around to show her himself. But patience was never her strong suit, and no one was there for her to apologize to for that itty bitty flaw.

Grrr.

Her inner she-Wolf was of the mind she had no flaws, but Sunny was not so sure the animal wasn't a bit biased. Everyone had flaws, even her.

Agree to disagree. The she-Wolf barked, circling

around in her mind's eye, eager to get on with the tour.

Devine and his brother had built a truly superb mansion with their own hands. She was impressed by the detail, never mind the quality of the materials used. Quartz was used on every countertop and tile trim. The wood floors were highly polished and buffed to a glossy shine. He was a creature of comfort. She guessed by the thick, expensive carpets that sat elegantly in his living rooms and bedroom.

The windows were made of one way glass, and Roman shades were hung, currently opened all the way to let in the late fall light. She followed the winding staircase to every level, noting with pride the carved bookcases and plush couches. All the furniture was custom, sturdily built for Dragons —*and Wolves*. Sunny had silently added the latter with a soft growl and a satisfied smile.

Her body still ached in all the best places, and her beast was content to wear his mark, though the she-Wolf wondered where he had run off to. Sunny's heart squeezed inside her chest. They had time. Oodles of it. And she would be sure to let him know she was not going anywhere.

He'd been alone a very long time and needed to adjust to her presence. Sure, it stung, but she wasn't an overly emotional person. Their bond was thin and light, but it was there. She could see it, tethered to her gray Wolf in that metaphysical realm where she waited to be called. The animal was eager to run with her mate, and that too would come with time.

Patience.

It would be difficult, but she would try. For him, she would try anything at least once. Sunny sipped her coffee and entered the greenhouse, and this was when she really fell in love with the complex man the Fates had chosen as her mate.

I choose him too, the Wolf said.

And yes, she supposed she did. The Fates tied people together, but their dual natured hearts really did the choosing. Sunny grinned as she passed the rows of blooming orchids. He must have had over two hundred ripe with fat, colorful blossoms.

Clever Dragon must have crossbred the rarer blue blooms with some of the white and pinks, creating lavender shades so delicate they brought tears to her eyes. Past the healthy stock were several rows of wilted looking plants. The blossoms had fallen, and the stems were turning brown. This was why he had come to her, she thought, and frowned.

Sunny took some soil samples and walked over to the large stainless-steel worktable. He had a very modern set up with carefully labelled crates housing soil, moss, sand, fertilizer, rocks, and other fillers for the pots. There were tools and tests, microscopes, and chemical analysis kits, but she did not need any of that to do her job.

Sunny closed her eyes and lifted the first sample to her nose. She breathed in the soil, sifting through the elements there. Everything seemed on point, she frowned and started the process over with the next sample, and so on.

She didn't know how long she stood there, but suddenly, the hairs on the back of her neck stood up, and Sunny opened her eyes, spinning around to find him watching her from the doorway.

"Thought you left," he murmured.

"Oh, um, no, not yet. Thought I would see what was troubling your orchids. After all, that is why you came to find me yesterday," she whispered her reply, feeling naked and bare despite wearing his clothes.

Just the sight of him had her pulse racing and her Wolf pressing her to get closer. He smelled good, like pine trees and frosty air and scales. Fuck, she loved that smell. The scent of his Dragon was an intoxicating combination of smoke, spice, and raw power that made her inner Wolf want to howl and yip at his heels.

She was completely submissive to his dominance, but not in a bad way. The guy was a walking, talking anthropomorphism of testosterone. Her she-Wolf was all about that primal beastly urge to find the biggest, baddest, sexiest male to be her main squeeze, and she had succeeded.

Oh boy, had she ever. Hubba hubba. Awooooo!

CHAPTER 7

"What are you doing here, Dev?" Nicholas asked from the trailer they had used as their office when they were building their house.

His brother looked like hell. He seemed exhausted—haunted, as the telltale bags under his eyes portrayed. Devine walked inside the trailer where he'd tracked him down through the bond that connected the brothers. It was so odd now. Used to be just the two of them, but now he had ties to the Falk Clan, and to her.

Fuck.

How could he have behaved so recklessly? Tying that sweet Wolf to a monster like him? Devine took a moment to gather his thoughts, feeling his beast settle at being nearer to his brother. The Dragon had been pissed when he'd walked away from his slumbering mate.

Mate. No.

Devine could not keep her despite what the beast wanted. His arrogant lizard had grown selfish, possessive the second he'd seen her. But Sunny was too good to be tied to the likes of him forever. He stole a glance at Nicholas.

His big brother was still pissed about their fight, not that he'd blamed him. The male had only been teasing Sunny, and Devine had gone and blown it all out of proportion. He just could not stop fucking things up.

He exhaled a deep, long breath and allowed himself one moment of pride. Nicholas had really done it. His big bro had gone ahead and moved their office trailer to the parcel of land he'd been eying for months. He must have gotten the Falk brothers to lease it to them, after all. Judging from the stack of yellow parchment on his desk—permits to build, Nick had also gotten approval from City Hall to build the four-unit development he'd proposed to Devine a few months back.

It was a good idea. The property was a mile and a half away from their home and further still from Castle Falk. Located across a somewhat private street from the ocean, with the intracoastal at the rear, the units would be perfect for anyone looking to rent a private, secluded bit of paradise.

New Jersey winters could be harsh, but summer was magical, sometimes not ending until late October. Nick's plans were to include a small yard behind each unit and a dock in the back for fishing and smallish boats. The big draw was, of course, the beach right across the street.

Yes, they would definitely see interest from renters. But it was not the money that made his brother want to start working on the project immediately. Devine was all too familiar with the emptiness driving Nick.

It was a deep-seated, gnawing, almost constant craving—a need to do something, *anything*, to try to stop the memories from rushing into his overcrowded brain. Devine shared his brother's history and was haunted by the same ghosts. How many nights had they both taken up arms for Dragomir? How many battles had they bled fighting against whatever and whoever the old Chief had decided earned his wrath?

Too many—that was the only real answer. He'd started to think they would end their existence as mad wrecks long before they were freed of that terrible island. But look at them now, he growled and ran a hand through his newly shortened hair.

"Well? I have work to do, Dev. Say what you want to say, or get the fuck out."

"You order the concrete yet for the foundation?" he asked, stalling.

"Yes—and the lumber, and the nails, the bricks, and roofing too. Why are you here, Dev?" he repeated.

Nicholas raised his face to look at his brother, his eyes bleeding to the orange-red color of his Dragon. He'd been doing so very well here in Maccon City, fitting in with the town and the local Wolves, and the Falk brothers. Suddenly, Devine realized he missed him. Used to be just the two of them until, suddenly, it wasn't anymore.

It was silly, and stupid, and he knew they were better off here with this Clan—but a small part of himself felt left out with his brother always joking with Niko Falk, or grumbling at Edric, laughing with Callius, or giving his opinion to Sander about his latest artistic creations.

Fuck.

He was so broken. Nick was light and carefree in a way Dev could never hope to be. Always working to fit in, to do what was best for both of them after they'd accidentally started a war with Castor Falk. Luckily, the *ChangeDragon* had forgiven them both. But Dev had been a selfish asshole.

Broken. I am so fucking broken.

Devine was not good like his brother. The atrocities he'd committed were too great to wash away. He'd been Dragomir's knife, but even with the bastard Chief's death, he was still unclean. Devine was no good for his brother, no good for the Clan, and no good for *her*.

The realization had his stomach bottoming out and heart feeling heavy inside his chest. For the first time, Devine truly saw Nicholas' struggle to keep him sane and alive. A Dragon needed his maiden, or he would perish, that was the legend. Sunny was his mate, but he did not deserve her. Maybe he could give his bond to Nick. Maybe then they could both be happy?

His soul ached, and his beast rebelled. The Dragon roared and burned him from the inside out with his flames filling the mystical place he waited till called. Fuck, he did not like that idea at all. But what else could Devine do?

"I fucked up, Nick," he said, not quite knowing how to start.

"Do tell, brother. How did you fuck up? You

lucky bastard! I have been searching for months to find a mate and here one falls into your lap, and you can't even see her for the gift she is—" Nick snarled and shoved his papers right off his desk, facing off with Dev.

"I won't fight you again, brother. Look, I am no good, Nick. You know what I was. My past haunts me, and I acted too rashly."

"How?" his brother demanded.

"I claimed her, but maybe I can change it, though. Maybe I can transfer my bond to you," Devine growled, running his hands over his face to try to stop the Dragon from charging through his skin.

"What the fuck are you talking about?"

"I'm talking about Sunny. I did it. I fucked her, and I bit her, but we both know I can't keep her. I will destroy her," he whispered the last so low he barely heard himself.

"You finally claim your maiden fair, the one who can save your Dragon from a fate worse than death, and you want to throw her away?" Nicholas raged.

"No! I thought maybe you can—" Devine's Dragon snarled. The creature was tearing him apart from the inside, and he could not stop the pain. Fuck, he deserved to feel every inch of it tearing through him as he stupidly tried to suffocate the only good thing about him. His connection to *her*.

"You really want to give away your mate, Devine? Listen to you, for fuck's sake! Don't you have a heart at all beneath your stone spikes? You were given a gift, Dev. How could you think to pass her off to me like some loose wench? What the fuck?"

Though apt, given what he'd said, Nicholas' description of Sunny enraged Devine's beast to the point of no return.

Loose wench? Motherfucker.

Dev stalked his brother across the trailer and slammed him into the wall. Nicholas snarled back, grabbing his brother's wrists, and stopping his assault.

"Sunny is no wench," he grunted.

"No? Then why offer her to me like a fucking slice of pizza, Dev? What is wrong with you?"

"You know what's wrong! I was his fucking sword, Nick. I killed, not just the Demons we were charged with stopping, but other Dragons. Anyone he saw was a threat. Anyone who had something he wanted—"

"I know, Dev, fuck, I know, alright? But that wasn't your fault," Nicholas answered. "None of it was your fault, and it sure as fuck was not your choice. I was your older brother. I should have protected you—"

"Bullshit. That is not on you," Devine said, releasing his brother and stepping back.

His chest felt heavy. Too fucking heavy, and he had no idea what he was going to do next. *Sunny*, his Dragon supplied the answer and images of her filled his mind.

Sweet, beautiful Sunny with her curly hair and free smiles, her ugly Crocs, and her bountiful laughter. And her gorgeous, curvy body that made his mouth water and his dick hard as a rail just thinking about it. Sinking into her tight sheath was the best feeling Devine had ever known in all his very long life. It felt like heaven.

It felt like coming home.

"Dev, look, you and me, we're good with each other. The past is done. We were not to blame, brother. Dragomir abused our ties and bonds to suit his desires. He was not a good Alpha. Callius is different. This place is different. Can't you feel it? Won't you give up this morbid existence and trust us? Trust in your Clan, Dev, and they can make you whole," Nick said in earnest.

Dev sat down heavily in one of the folding chairs and leaned over with his elbows on his knees. He held his head in his hands and tried to make sense of all of this. How could he be a good mate with so many stains on his soul? What could he offer the beautiful Werewolf who'd brought him more pleasure than he'd ever felt? And it wasn't just her body that was healing him. It was her heart. She was too good, his sweet mate.

Es meus, the Dragon seconded, approving of Devine's description of Sunny at last.

"Look, Castor and I had a meeting this morning. He knows we are having some difficulty adjusting, and he wants us to come to Thanksgiving dinner at castle Falk," Nicholas explained, and Devine went rigid.

"What did you say? You know I don't do dinner parties—" he began, but his Dragon seemed to take hold of his vocal chords, and he could not get another word out.

"Not usually, no, but don't you think you should try, Dev? For you, for me. For *her*. Invite your mate to Thanksgiving and show her the Clan. Let her decide if you are truly her fate, then you can claim her—"

"I have already claimed her. But what if she learns what I have done? What if she hates it? If Sunny finds out the truth, and leaves me as I deserve, my Dragon won't survive, Nick. I need to know you will watch out for her," he whispered.

It took a lot for him to admit that which scared him the most. But if Nicholas promised to look after Sunny, then Devine would willingly accept his Fate. He just needed her safe and cared for. Yes, he'd been fighting this mating and arguing against it, but he was already too attached for his own good.

Shit.

Devine was in love, and it just might kill him.

"Minnie, slow down," Sunny whispered into the phone, listening to her bestie go off the rails about her manager during her latest art tour.

"That rat bastard has been stealing half the profits, overcharging clients and not reporting it," Minerva screeched.

"Wow. What a dick! Look, call Macconwood Law and get the Lowell brothers to give you some advice. They're the Pack attorneys and will have a solution," Sunny replied.

She listened a few more minutes, Sent Minerva her best, and hung up the cell phone. Poor Minnie. It must be terrible, being such an important artist only to have the one person you trust make a fool of you like that. Sunny shook her head, hurting for her friend, but she could not give Minnie the attention she deserved.

Not when her head was still spinning and her heart still reeling from the last forty-eight hours. She'd left Devine's home after the encounter in his greenhouse just yesterday, but the Dragon had not called or come to see her since. Her Wolf was scratching against her skin, wanting to go and check on their mate, but she just couldn't bring herself to do it.

Desperate much?

Dang it. Sunny hated feeling this way. She rolled her shoulders and tugged on the hem of her tie-dyed crop top she wore with wide legged linen pants that hung low on her hips, revealing a smooth strip of skin from her soft belly. Most Werewolves were muscular and trim, but Sunny was one of those blessed, or cursed depending on her mood, with ample curves and a fuller figure.

That never stopped her from wearing what she wanted or enjoying herself. She was a big girl with tons of energy and was as happy in her own skin as she was in her fur. She and Minerva, another Werewolf, had met in high school when the latter moved to Maccon City. They'd bonded over being fluffy she-Wolves and had stayed besties ever since.

And yet, for some reason, Sunny had not confided in her about her newly mated status. She hadn't even mentioned him. But what could she say? Everything she knew about him read like a really lame dating profile.

Devine Graystone, QuartzDragon, dark hair, stormy blue eyes, terrific body—*meaning hot as fuck and packing*—great in bed and growly out of it. Oh, and he grows orchids.

Wait—that was it! The flowers were her in. She'd been checking up on why his beauties were not doing well, and Sunny might have stumbled on an answer. Simple really, and so typically male, it was laughable. That was it. She was going to stop by with new food and a couple of books for him that very night.

"You can run, but you can't hide," she muttered.

"Sis, you are getting weirder and weirder—wait, what the fuck? Who bit you?" her brother snarled, his eyes glowing with his Wolf.

"Shhh! River, there are humans all over here," she whispered, grabbing him by his shirt collar and flinging him into the nearest supply closet.

"Hey, Sunny girl—"

Her father's smile stopped as he leaned forward and—*sniff.* "Where is he? I'll kill him," he growled.

So much for being a pacifist Wolf, Sigh.

"Hey guys, Crystal's here. Say, are we having a family meeting or something?" Mom walked in with Sunny's older sister, and the shit had officially hit the fan.

"Okay, before you all start snarling, and sniffing me—*for fuck's sake, River, back off*—I have an announcement," Sunny said, facing her family. "I have a mate."

She'd tried to smile after that declaration, but what happened was a sniffle, a gasp, and a sob. Sunny was suddenly in the middle of a Daye family group hug—the most embarrassing and oddly comforting of all the Daye family group hugs. Her siblings used to fight when her parents forced them to do these kinds of things. Yes, Werewolves needed physical contact for reassurance and to reinforce familial bonds. But sometimes, too much was just too much, and that was never a good thing.

"Who is it?"

"I'll kill him!"

"Dad, you don't believe in violence—"

"Shut up, River. This is your sister."

"Shut up, everyone," Mom said, pushing them all

to break up their stranglehold hug. "Sunny? Are you okay? Wanna tell us about it?"

"Not really. Look, I'm sorry I got emotional, we're just starting, and he's, well, he's not a Wolf, he's a—"

"He's a fucking Cat, isn't he? I hate those bastards," River growled.

"No! And don't hate anyone, idiot," she replied sternly.

She closed her eyes and shook her head. Dammit. This was why she should have stayed home that morning. Of course, they would be able to tell the change in her scent. Mated Wolves took on some of the aspects of their mates' essence, and Sunny's was now infused with the smokey spice and fire of her Dragon.

A fact that would have made her proud any other day. If only Devine had been with her to make this announcement to her family. But she was alone, confused, and in a supply closet at her place of business.

"Shoot, I can hear Mrs. O'Neill ringing the bell at cashier 2. Let me go check on that, hon, but look, you come find me when you are done here, and if some young buck needs his ass kicked, I am your guy, kiddo," Dad said, giving her a kiss on the cheek.

"Thank you, Daddy. He's just different from us, and we have some things to talk about. I'll be fine. Promise."

"Okay, baby," Mom added, kissing her other cheek and ruffling her already frizzy hair.

Her parents left, leaving her with *Tweedle-Dum* and *Tweedle-Dummer*, and Sunny shook her head. River and Crystal glanced at each other, and she knew what they were up to.

"No. I can see it in your eyes. Stop right there," she said, lips twitching as she started to back up.

Rule number one in Werewolf pup horseplay— never turn your back on a predator, especially small ones with tiny, sharp puppy teeth. Sunny could not hold back her grin as she made a dash for the door, but she was just so damn clumsy. She got tangled in her feet and fell backwards as her siblings attacked, tickling her till she almost peed herself.

"Stoppp! Ahhh!" she screamed.

Suddenly, the door was torn open and an enormous male trembling with rage barreled into the small closet and roared. Yep. He actually fucking roared as he grabbed Crystal and River by their shirts and lifted them off Sunny.

"Dev! Stop. No, no! Put them down!" Sunny scrambled to her feet but moved too fast and she started pitching forward—fuck, that was gonna hurt, but then Dev was there. He'd dropped her siblings and caught her mid-fall, whisking her up in his arms like some hero from a romance novel.

Fuck, was he hot. Sexy, romantic Dragon. Good mate.

"Um, Sunny?"

"Oh shit. Put me down, Dev. It's okay," she said, wiggling to get down, and he allowed it, barely. The big man had his arms wrapped around her waist and pulled her back to his chest while she tried to check on her siblings.

"Are you guys alright?"

"What is the meaning of this attack?" he growled.

"They weren't attacking me—"

"Technically, we were," Crystal replied, giggling as she stood and rubbed her butt.

Her sister was so beautiful, and for a moment, Sunny felt old self-doubts creeping up, but she refused to indulge them. Crystal had been born with honey gold locks and bright cerulean eyes. No freckles. She'd lucked out in the gene pool, for sure, but Sunny was nothing but proud of her.

"Tickle attack. A Daye family tradition whenever one of us is down," River explained. Her goofy younger brother grinned, offering his hand to Devine, who looked likely to snap it off.

"Dev, this is my sister Crystal, and my brother River," she said, and Devine took the younger male's hand in a tight, but brief shake.

"Why were you down?" he asked.

Clever Dragon, getting right to the heart of the matter.

"I'd say that was your fault, hotshot," Crystal said, smoothing her hands over her hair. "You good, sis?"

Sunny nodded.

"Okay then, looks like you both have some talking to do. I'll keep Dad busy," River said, which was probably a good thing.

Sunny waved them off and stepped out of Devine's warm embrace. Her skin felt the loss of his warmth keenly in the unheated room. November weather was fickle at best, and today it had stayed under fifty degrees. Normally, she wouldn't care, but Sunny had gotten used to being near his Dragon's inner fire. If Werewolves ran hotter than normals, then it was safe to say Dragons walked around in a permanent fever state.

Focus, Sunny. Ask him what he wants.

"What are you doing here?"

"I missed you," he replied, and she could scent his honesty.

"It's only been a day," she said, trying to play off her hurt.

"And it felt like a year," he whispered, so low she wasn't sure she heard it.

"I was going to stop by with some books for you on orchid care. I think I know the problem."

"Really?"

"Yeah. It's just the change in the temperature and humidity in the room. It's off balance. I think adding more moisture to the air will help, and less fertilizer." Sunny was rambling, but she could not seem to stop.

She turned around, giving him her back while she straightened bottles and boxes, turning their labels to face front. Stuff like that did not usually bother her. Sunny wasn't particularly neat or anal about stuff like that, but she was clean, and she needed to do something with her hands or else she'd end up tackling the poor guy.

Get a grip, girl.

"Will you go out with me?" he asked suddenly, and she stopped her fiddling with the bottles on the shelf, turning slowly to face him.

"Why?" she asked.

"Because I want to get to know you, and I want you to get to know me," he mumbled, ruffling the hair on the back of his head with one big hand, elbow pointed towards the ceiling, like he was nervous or something.

She found the gesture endearing and smirked as she pretended to mull over his offer. He wanted to take her out—like on a real date. Hot damn! Typically, when supernaturals found their fated mates, that was it. It was like *wham bam let's getcha pregnant ma'am*—the biological imperative to procreate overpowering all others.

Some believed the Fates blessed supernaturals with this, knowing when they met their mates to make life easier on them to have fulfilling relationships, and yes, that also meant propagating the species. But it was a burden too, wasn't it? Brokering no choice for the supes involved. Sunny felt that truth keenly as she looked at her mate. Devine had not been given a choice. The Fates had taken that away and here he was, trying to make the most of it. After all, it was not the big, sexy, dumb Dragon's fault she'd gone and fallen for him.

"Okay," she replied, trying to stem the heavy beating of her heart. "I'll go out with you. When?"

"Now."

"But I'm not dressed—"

"Look fine to me," he grumbled, and she warmed

at the way his heated gaze raked over her body like hands.

The man was so damn sexy. Too sexy for his own good. They'd set fires in bed, *and out of it,* together already, and Sunny knew he liked her body just fine. But Devine was right. She did not know him, and the Wolf was as curious as her human side.

"Alright. Let me tell my family," she said, untying the work apron she wore around her waist.

The entire room seemed to reverberate with the sound of the powerful growl coming from Devine's throat. She met his blazing blue-black eyes and swallowed the moan that immediately tried to escape her lips. Helplessly attracted to the man, that's what she was. Sunny moved closer to him and rested her head against his chest, allowing him to soothe her frazzled nerves with a tender hug.

"Will you let me meet them?"

"Who?"

"Your family," he replied, and she heard the smile in his voice without having to raise her head.

Duh, Sunny. Lol.

She stepped back reluctantly and nodded as she led the way from the supply room. Once they were in the aisle, Dev took her hand in his and immediately her Wolf stilled as feelings of care, comfort, and protection filled her.

"Mom, Dad?" she called, approaching the service counter where her parents were chatting over a flat of fall mums.

Both Werewolves looked up, her father growling at the sight of her mate holding her hand. Devine stilled, and she felt him purposely tamping down on his natural dominance. Werewolves were snarly as fuck, but he was a Dragon. A *motherfucking badassed Dragon,* and she preferred her parents alive and breathing.

"Dad, this is Devine Graystone of the Falk Clan," she whispered, knowing her parents would hear and understand. "My mate."

"I see," her father said, still not bothering to hide his Wolf from the larger predator. "I'm Leaf and this is my mate Moonbeam, Sunny's mom. Now, I'm a pacifist and you might be a Dragoon, but if you make my little girl cry again, there's not a fucking thing in this world that will stop me coming after you," her father stated, and damn, if she didn't love the man a little more for it.

"Leaf, hush," Mom said, elbowing him with a wink at Sunny.

"Daddy, I'm fine," Sunny said, stepping away

from Devine to give her old man a hug.

"You cried?" Devine asked, and his expression was almost comical if he did not look entirely devastated.

"It's no big deal, Dev. I was just being emotional—"

"I understand if you should like to seek revenge, sir. Lashes, perhaps or something else—"

"Eek! What? No," Sunny said, shaking her head. "Not necessary. Dad, tell him," she growled at her father, who seemed as taken aback as she.

"Um, no, we are all good. This time," Dad added, earning him another elbow from Mom.

Thank you, she mouthed at her mother as she hurried Devine out the door, barely missing an angry old man with a shopping cart.

"Whoops," she said as Dev pulled her into the safety of his arms once more.

"You really have no sense of self-preservation at all, do you, Sunny Daye?"

Nope. Apparently not, she thought as she gave another chunk of her heart to the sexy Dragon.

"Where are you taking me?" she asked, pulling out of his arms and tucking a few curls behind her ears.

"It's a surprise."

CHAPTER 9

"OHMYGAWD!" Sunny shrieked as she clung to Devine's back, nestled between two enormous spikes as he flapped his huge, bat-like wings through the frosty air above the pine barrens.

He'd wanted her to get to know him, and the first thing that involved was a formal introduction to his Dragon. At first, they'd changed together, and Dev was astounded by the beauty of his mate's brindled she-Wolf. Her golden eyes had followed him as he slipped into his scales, and both beasts seemed to understand and recognize each other on a level their human sides had yet to catch up with.

Afterwards, Sunny had shifted back into her skin and asked him for a ride. How could he resist when she was so enthusiastic and tempting as she slid her clothes back on—*sans panties?*

Fuck, this woman's disregard for underthings was going to be his complete undoing. He felt her heated core pressed against his back, and even on his scales, he wanted her. She whooped and hollered, held him tight with her Werewolf strength as he twirled and dipped high and low, giving her a flight to remember.

He'd learned how to cloak himself when he'd been very young, and using those skills and that Dragon magic, Devine shielded both himself and her from the normal world. He felt her shiver and the beast inside him became concerned, slowing his speed, he aimed for a good landing spot near the small cabin the Falks used to teach their offspring how to control their Dragons.

"What is this place?" Sunny asked, sliding off his back easily.

"This belongs to the Falk brothers," he explained. Devine had been quick with his change but did not want to appear too eager with his hard on swinging out all over the damn place.

She was so tempting, so gorgeous, but he was trying to take this day to get to know her without jumping her bones. A task that was easier said than done. Walking into the cabin, Devine opened the closet for one of the extra pairs of sweats the brothers always had on hand.

"Look at all these books and toys," Sunny said, and grinned, walking over to admire the playroom.

"They have young. Six total and more on the way. Eddie is Edric's dragonling," he said, pointing to a large family picture that hung in the center of the main wall. "These two are Calla and Castor, the offspring of Fred and Callius, the Alpha of the Falk Clan. This here is Nicky, he is Melody and Niko's son. They also have a daughter now, Cherie. And Castor and Jozette welcomed their son not too long ago," he murmured.

"Oh, what's his name?"

He exhaled, sitting down on the sofa and tugged Sunny by the hand to join him. This was only one story of how wrong he was for her, and he had to tell it. It was the only way she would know the real him, and scared as he might be, Devine knew Sunny deserved nothing but the truth from him.

"Before I tell you that, I must tell you how we came to be here, Nicholas and I," he started.

"Okay," Sunny murmured, tucking her feet beneath her while she sat beside him as if readying herself for his story.

Smart, sexy, pretty Wolf with a big heart.

"I was born with a sword in my hand," he started, figuring honesty was best. "Not literally, of course, what I mean is I was born to serve my Chief as his blade. I was sent to battle the Demons that tried to escape into our realm as has been the mission of dragons on this planet since the dawn of time—"

"Wait—what? Demons are real? Like really real?" she asked, her brown eyes wide with wonder and maybe a little fear. His Dragon did not like that. Not one bit.

"You are safe, *meus lupus*," he murmured, touching her cheek with one long stroke of his finger.

"No, I know, but Demons? Wow. I had no idea—"

"Wait—you're a Werewolf, and I am a Dragon, but you never heard of and did not believe in Demons?"

"I mean, it's not like it's common around the Jersey Shore to see a Demon walking by," she muttered, and fuck, she was so cute.

"Fair enough." Dev relented, grabbing her hand.

He kissed her fingertips before replacing it on her own knee. It was not fair to touch her yet. Not until she knew it all. Then she could decide for herself. Devine sucked in a fortifying breath before continuing with his tale.

"I wish I did not have to tell you this, but it's only fair you hear all of my truth. My only regret is I claimed you before I told you, but I promise Sunny, whatever you decide, I will abide by it," he said, body trembling with his beast as he tore open the scars that held his old life at bay and forced them through his frozen lips.

"Fighting Demons was easy. It was why the Universe and the gods had created Dragons with our tough, fireproof hides, our wings, and our fierceness. But it was not the Demons that blackened my soul," he said, voice barely above a whisper. "It was the others."

"What others?" Sunny asked, her voice low, full of heartbreak and compassion.

Fuck, he could not stand to see himself reflected in her eyes. Not like this, when he was so exposed, so wounded and raw from the truth. Devine was a monster.

"Chief Dragomir forged a weapon in me. *Spike-Dragon* was my name," he growled.

"I thought you were a QuartzDragon?"

"I am," he told her and nodded. "Or I was, before my scales rusted over with the blood of my kills, and my soul darkened with the sins of my transgressions. You see, those spikes you sat between on my back are my fiercest weapons. For some Dragons, it is their fire, but for me it is those spiny thorns that I loose like bullets upon my targets. I can shoot them from my spine at will and with unerring accuracy. The result is death, even for a Dragon."

The silence that fell between them deafened him, and Devine hazarded a glance at the always happy she-Wolf. Only Sunny was not smiling. Her optimism was nowhere to be found as she sat in suspense, waiting for him to go on. So he did.

"Dragomir was a greedy male. He coveted the hoards—*the accumulated wealth*—of other Dragons. Sometimes, their mates too. He would fill me with lies, tell me of their treasonous plots, then send me to kill them. And I did, gods help me, I did," he murmured, confessing his greatest sins to the one woman in the world he should have hidden them from. "I am no good, Sunny Daye. Not good enough for you. You deserve a better mate. I am broken, tarnished, and undeserving of a mate."

Devine finished speaking, and the silence stretched. He waited, looking up, when she remained quiet. He had been expecting her anger and rage, not this muted Wolf before him. What was she thinking? He pulled on their bond, hoping to get an inkling of her feelings, but it was too thin yet for such things.

"So," Sunny began. She stood up and started pacing, her bright green Crocs moved silently across the hardwood floor of the cabin. "What you are saying is because you were at the mercy of some gods-damned madman, you think you don't deserve a mate. Is that right?"

"Er. Um. Well—"

Devine was at a loss for words. Fuck, this felt like a trap. He was too smart to fall into one, or so he'd thought. But it was already too late. The little she-Wolf was already on a roll.

"You think me so shallow and weak that I could not see through the hurt and pain you endured to the warrior you truly are, Devine Graystone? Is that what you think of me? That I would somehow blame you for carrying out the wars you were told to by your Alpha, your Chief? What kind of Wolf do you think I am?" she asked, and then he saw the spark of anger he'd been waiting for, only it was for the wrong reason.

Fuck. Fuck. FUCK.

"I think you're perfect, Sunny. Not weak. Not shallow. I only meant—"

"You only meant you're too much a big bad dragon for a little puppy like me, right? You think cause my parents are hippies, I am some airhead who can't know the real you? Well, fuck you, Dev! The Fates paired us up, but that doesn't mean we don't have a choice. Now, from the first second I saw you, I chose you. I believed in you, in us, but I guess you don't feel the same way," she growled, and walked away from him.

"What? Wait a second, dammit. I am trying to spare you the heartache of having someone as fucked up as me for a mate. I am trying to save you, to salvage your chance at a future, Sunny. I can't break the bond, but maybe I can transfer it to someone better. Nicholas, or someone of your choosing," he began, grabbing at her arm, but the she-Wolf was ready.

With surprising agility, Sunny dodged his seeking hands and turned on him, her eyes blazing with hurt and some other unnamed emotion. Fuck, his own beast was tearing him apart from the inside out and he felt ten times a shit heel. What was he doing?

"You don't get to make decisions about what I need or want. You want to break our matebond,

Dev? Then that's on you, but fuck you, if you try to say it's for my sake."

"Sunny," he whispered, moving towards her. Her raised arm stopped him.

"I mean it, Dev. Fuck. You."

Then she was gone. Her clothes burst apart as her she-Wolf tore through her skin. The enormous brindled beast did not turn to look at him as she raced through the woods, as far as her furred legs could take her. Devine sank to his knees and watched her go. What else could he do?

Monster. Broken. Weak.

His hands grabbed at his chest, trying to stop the pain that overwhelmed him. His quartz rose was burning, aching so fucking badly. He looked down and saw the tiny bud that had always been there had doubled in size. But right then, it was wilting, bent over, and dying like his orchids back in the greenhouse. Devine had fucked up again. But this time, it just might cost him everything. Maybe Nicholas was right. Maybe it was time he started looking to his Clan for help.

He walked outside, locking the cabin before calling his Dragon forth. Yes, Nicholas was right. It was time to trust in his Clan.

CHAPTER 10

"Sunny? Did you send that huge order of mums to *Flowers by Jill* over in Barvale?" Mom asked, her voice carrying over to where Sunny sat hunched over her desk.

"Yes, Mom."

"Good. The weather forecast is calling for some bad storms tonight. Looks like we are getting the tail end of some tropical hurricane, late for the season," her mom informed her. "Anyway, I wanted to make sure they had everything they needed," the older she-Wolf continued, mentioning something about impending accumulation of snow and strong winds.

Whatever.

Sunny was only half paying attention. It was the Tuesday before Thanksgiving, and everyone was just about finished winterizing their gardens. The produce section of the store was doing fabulously, and she had just finished sorting the tags for the delivery of Christmas trees they were expecting to arrive any minute now.

The lot had been cleared out, thanks to River, but the truck was late. She'd already set a few of their employees to stocking the new shelves with ornaments, lights, and other decorations she'd ordered for the holiday season.

One Daye At A Time Produce & Garden Center was growing by leaps and bounds. Sunny should have been thrilled. She had worked so hard to lift herself up, to help her family succeed financially, and to provide for the community in a way she felt they could all benefit with good for the environment, and for people, products.

Hell, I should have been a lot of things.

Of course, *happily mated* was the first that came to mind. Blasted Dragon! How dare he? Huge, growly beast with a bad attitude, walking into her life, and turning it upside down. Who did he think he was?

Stupid, big, sexy, perfect man.

Why couldn't he have just gone to *Home Depot* or *Walmart* instead? Oh no. He just had to walk into her store. Without even trying, he had changed her life. Sunny had never felt such an intense, immediate attraction and connection with anyone before. Then he had to ruin it by going off and making idiotic statements like he was not good enough for her, and hey, since he could not do the job, maybe she could have his brother instead.

What. The. Actual. Fuck.

Anger and sorrow rose like the tide inside her, and her Wolf tossed her lupine head back, loosing a howl that shook the metaphysical plane where her beast dwelled, just waiting for Sunny to call on her.

Okay, Devine had a chip on his shoulder, and maybe it was for a good reason. She had heard the stories. Knew what he had done, but didn't the silly man see that was not his fault? He was compelled to listen to his Alpha. That was how Clans and Packs worked. Sure, he'd had to do bad shit for a really bad guy, but he was different now. Better. Stronger. And he had a different purpose. She could be his purpose. If only he loved her, too.

She could forgive him anything, if he just loved her. If he just chose to be with her. Hell, Sunny was a fixer by nature. Her Wolf was built to be leaned on, and she would have been so fucking proud if he'd have chosen to lean on her, and not just shit all over their mating.

Devine thought he was a worthless monster cause he had blood on his hands. Well, Sunny had no problem taking those hands in hers and washing them clean through patience and love. But no. The stupid scaly jerk had to go and offer to sever their bond—no, *transfer it.*

He wanted to give their still new and fragile matebond to his brother or someone else she might want. Pain lanced through her, and she closed her eyes to catch her breath.

Fuck oh fuck—why?

It was not a half bad offer, really. Who wanted to be mated to someone who valued her so little? And let's face it, he could not think that much of her if he wanted to give her to someone else within days of her claiming. If only she had viable options, but the stupid, stubborn Wolf inside her only wanted him.

That two-ton, fire-breathing jerk.

"Sunny? I closed down the registers, and Dad and I were going to go for a quick run before the weather turns, then go home for the night. Why don't you get going?" Mom interrupted, leaning against the doorjamb with a sad smile on her face.

"I'm fine, Mom. I'm just going to give the truck

another twenty minutes. We need those trees stocked before the big rush on Friday," she reminded her mother needlessly.

The woman knew as well as she did the *Black Friday* rush of shoppers was an annual necessary evil. Her mom nodded her head and leaned in close for a hug. So pretty, just like Crystal, with blonde wavy hair that never seemed out of place, and a ready smile that charmed every man, woman, and child for miles around.

Sunny had not inherited her looks from her mother. Instead, she got her father's big feet, frizzy hair, and freckles. They worked on a man, but on her, well, she'd always felt a little different. Not ugly. She did not have low self-esteem, but sometimes she wondered if she'd been born more classically pretty if things would not have been easier on her.

Maybe her Dragon would have forgiven his supposed shortcomings if she'd been a damsel who'd inspired him. Not a clumsy, big-boned she-Wolf who could probably out eat him in a chicken wing contest.

"You sure you're fine, honey?"

"Yep. Go run with Dad. I'm good."

It was the first time in her life she'd lied to her mother, and even though the older Wolf knew it, she let it slide. The Daye's were not always known for allowing their kids to have personal space, but Sunny needed it. And she appreciated her mom so much right then for giving it to her.

Alone in the store now, she checked her phone. It was almost eight o'clock and the wind was picking up. Of course, one minute it had been endless Autumn days with soaring temperatures in the seventies, and now they were getting snow.

Sigh.

She walked through the back of the store to the semi-covered tree lot her father and brother had just finished building. The open lot was behind the store and closed in with a high, chain-link fence. She usually reserved this space for annuals and seedlings folks liked to plant in the spring. In the summer, it was usually full of pool and lawn care and products.

Last month, she had it converted to a Christmas tree lot, and would use it to store palettes afterwards. In fact, the truck coming with her trees was also supposed to hall away the three stacks of palettes she had already waiting. They were over fifteen feet high, left over from deliveries throughout the year. She hated to waste fuel and refused to throw them out. This way they would be recycled, maybe turned into mulch or something useful.

Sunny sighed, tucking her sweatshirt tighter around her body. Good thing she grabbed the hoodie off the back of her chair before heading out. She did not usually bother with outerwear, but her mom was right. It was cold as hell, and the wind had really picked up. The roof was supposed to be temporary, only slightly sturdier than a tent which—after their fourth of July rain disaster—Sunny was vehemently opposed to.

She'd seen this kind of quick solution in other lots and figured it was only a little plywood and some roofing tiles, what was the big deal? This way they could serve organic hot cocoa and fresh baked gingerbread cookies to the little ones while their families shopped for the perfect Christmas tree.

She'd tried it last year, but they'd had too much rain. The customers could not enjoy the treats and they were not at all thrilled with having to traipse through the wet lot to bring a soaked tree. She couldn't really blame them.

So, this year, she'd had Dad and River construct this temporary shelter over the lot, and once the trees were delivered, and the palettes taken away, it would look great. The sound of wood creaking as the wind picked up and lightning cracked across the sky had Sunny biting her lower lip.

Where was the truck? Rain and hail were coming down hard, and she was scrolling through the emails on her phone until she found the one containing the phone number and name for her driver. Sunny dialed and waited.

"Hello? This is Sunny Daye from One Daye At A Time—" Sunny paused while the driver shouted over her.

"So sorry Miss Daye, weather turned fast, had to pull off at a weigh station—" Static was breaking up his voice, and Sunny blinked against the wind and rain that was pelting against her. "I can probably get there tomorrow afternoon—Miss? What was that sound? Miss!"

Sunny looked up. Thunder boomed, and the sky lit up with lightning as hail and rain battered against the roof. But that wasn't the noise that had her dropping the phone and screaming for all she was worth. Somehow the wind had moved the palettes, and as they toppled onto the top of the roof and the poor, temporary structure could not handle the weight.

The door was too far away, and even as she tried to run. She knew she would never make it. Why did she have to be the only clumsy Werewolf in the whole damn world? The thought screamed inside her mind as she slid on hail and rain just as the roof came crashing down on her head.

Sunny had been taught to live her life with the least possible regrets, and yet right before the blackness took her, Sunny's heart swelled with pain as her only regret rose above all her other thoughts.

She shouldn't have walked away after their fight. She should have made him see there was no one else for her. Only him. Devine had been hurting. Her sexy, growly mate had been trying to explain his reticence, but she'd been so angry at him for what she saw as giving up on them. She'd wanted to punch him in the nose for assuming he knew what was best for her. Mad, scared, and hurt, but ultimately, she was the one who gave up on them before they had even started.

She. Her. Bright eyed and ever-optimistic Sunny Daye.

She'd let him just sit there while she'd forced a Change and tore out of that cabin in the woods, leaving him behind.

Dev, I am sorry. Sorry, love. So sorry.

CHAPTER 11

"How long do I wait, Nick? Fuck, I feel like I'm dying," Devine growled, pacing their living room while a storm raged around their house.

Normally, he liked them. There was something beautiful about the raw, elemental power of a winter storm in South Jersey. Waves crashed angrily against the shore and lightning broke the cloudy gray black sky apart into tiny ethereal fragments every time it struck. Winter was coming in quickly.

"I am not the one who's mated, brother," Nicholas reminded him. "But if I had to guess, I would give her time to heal. I mean, you fucked up big time. Asking her to mate me, for one thing, which would be the best idea for any female since I am better looking, funnier, smarter, and my dick is bigger—what? Why are you wearing that expression?"

Dev, I am sorry. Sorry, love. So sorry.

"Did you hear that?" Devine asked—ignoring the whole bigger dick comment, which was a total lie, and turning to face Nicholas.

"Hear what?"

"Hello! Are you guys home?" Castor Falk came in without knocking, but since they had given him leave to do so, it was not all that unusual.

"Everyone is gathering together at Castle Falk for the storm, and we wanted to extend the invitation— hey, what's going on?" Castor said, using the towel Nicholas had tossed at him to dry his hair.

"I don't know. Something is wrong with Sunny," Devine grumbled.

"Sunny? Who's Sunny?"

"Sunny is his mate," Nicholas explained, a frown marring his face.

"Mate? That's good news, my friend, but what do you mean something is wrong? How do you know?"

"I felt it here a moment ago. Like I could hear her in my head saying goodbye, but now there is nothing. It's all black," he growled and slammed his hand on his head.

"Shit. Okay, look Devine can you look within yourself and find the matebond?"

"Fuck, it's so small, like a thread," he murmured and felt his own heartbreak damn near swallow him.

This was his fault. He did this. The phone rang and Nicholas rushed to answer. He heard someone talking on the other end, a female, hysterical.

"Dev, it's Sunny's mother. She says her daughter was waiting for a delivery when she called the trucker. The line went dead after the driver heard a crash and he contacted the company he was working for to reach out to the client—"

"Give me the phone," he said, taking the receiver from Nick. "Hello? Mrs. Daye? Yes—I'm on my way."

"Hurry!" Sunny's mother yelled.

"Sunny isn't picking up her phone. I have to go," he growled, yanking off his shirt and barely opening the door in time before his Dragon took him.

"Fuck. Don't forget to cloak yourself. My brothers and I will be behind you!" screamed Castor as Nicholas took off right behind him.

Later, when Sunny was alive and safe in his arms, he would think back on how good it felt to have Clan at his back. But that was for after. After he found her. After he apologized for his idiocy and made up for all the mistakes he made. And after he re-claimed her, fortifying the bond between them that he'd almost killed with his self-doubts.

Devine flapped his wings hard against the raging storm. Lightning damn near hit him, but he was quicker than he looked. His spikes had grown double their size in his agitation, as they had a tendency too when he made ready for war.

This was not the typical battle. This was a fight to save his mate's life and to win her love. No matter what else happened, Devine had to fix the hurt he'd caused. He just needed time.

Please be alright, Sunny, mate of mine. Stay strong for me. I am almost to you. Es meus.

When he landed at the rear of the building because that was where he felt her strongest, Devine saw the problem right away. Someone had built a temporary roof to cover the back lot without using the necessary frame to hold it against heavy burdens. It should have been fine against the rain, but with the added weight of what looked like more than three dozen heavy wooden pallets, the thing collapsed and fell apart under the onslaught of the storm.

Someone had already tossed the things off to the side, but it was too large a structure for any one person to lift alone. Even two people could not do it without risking the integrity of the structure. He spied two gray and brown Wolves circling the collapsed thing, trying to dig their way through.

Her father and brother, he thought, recognizing them despite having never seen their Wolves before. Devine landed quickly, his claws raking through the gravel. His brother was beside him in a matter of seconds and the two Wolves came racing over. They swapped their fur for skin and Devine and Nick did the same, so they could communicate.

"I scented her strongest this way," her father yelled over the howling wind. "I just can't get to her—"

"Don't worry, Mr. Daye. I will get her," he promised, looking into the Wolf's eyes.

"The easiest way is to lift the structure entirely, Dev. I have an idea, but you need to change into your Dragon," his brother shouted as two more Dragons joined them from the air, and another two drove up in enormous SUVs.

Devine felt torn. He did not want to give up his skin. He wanted to be the first to get to her, but knowing Sunny was in danger, he Shifted to his immediately. Never before was he so damn glad to be a *SpikeDragon.*

QuartzDragon brother, his brother pushed the

thought into his brain, and Devine growled softly. *These are your pillars, and this is what they are truly for. For protecting your mate, your Clan. Now, prepare five of them. The Falk brothers will lift the structure from the corners, and you will use your spikes to hold them up. I will hold it up from the center. The Wolves will get Sunny. Ready on three?*

Devine snarled his acquiescence, and his brother called the other Dragons and two Wolves to shift back to human.

"Ready on three!" Nicholas roared. "1, 2, 3!"

Everyone moved at once and Devine raced from corner to corner, concentrating on his aim as he shot one spike into the ground, acting as a stone column to hold the roof. Luckily, he was able to level one each time, creating a nice foundation for the roof.

Nicholas was able to let go as Devine changed to his skin and hauled the last spine with him to drive it into the ground at the center. Leaf and River, Sunny's father and brother, were sifting through the shelves and empty display cases that had fallen when the roof crashed down, for any sign of her.

"I swear I scented her here," Leaf growled angrily, and Devine saw why.

"Her shoe!" he yelled, racing over to lift the neon

purple Croc from the wet rubble. It only took him a moment then to find the rest of her covered in mud and hidden beneath at least two dozen giant spools of twine that would undoubtedly be used to tie Christmas trees to the customers' cars.

"Sunny. Sunny, wake up. SUNNY!" he yelled, lifting her none-too-gently from the rubble. Anguish washed over him like a tidal wave and Devine was fucking drowning in it. She was unconscious, pale, and wan looking.

"Sunny, please, please, please wake up," he sat down hard on the ground, uncaring about his nudity as he wiped at her fast, rocking back and forth and pressed her closer to him murmuring all sorts of nonsense.

"Devine, maybe we should—" but he snarled and snapped at whoever the fuck was trying to get near them.

No. he would not let them. Sunny was his mate. His quartz rose. His maiden fair, and there was nothing he would not do for her.

"Please, meus lupus. Come back to me. I promise not to run again. I swear I will be the mate you deserve," he whispered, kissing her eyes, her head, her cheeks, and fuck, he was sobbing, blabbering all over her, tears raining down his cheeks as he promised to be better for her.

That was the way this should be. He felt his Clan surrounding him, accepted the blanket her father offered, and wrapped her up in it. His Sunny, his sweet mate. So brave, so happy all the time. Fuck, she'd come into his life and disturbed everything, but in a good way. He had to tell her. She deserved to hear the words from his lips.

"Sunny, I didn't think this would ever happen for me. I did not believe I was destined for a mate, and then I met you and my Dragon knew. You said mate first, and I scoffed. For the first time in centuries, I was afraid," he said, laughing through his tears, and confessing to everyone exactly how much of a loser he was. "I was afraid of a pretty little Werewolf with a halo of curls and a wide grin, who wore no makeup, and no bra, and the ugliest damn shoes I have ever seen in my whole life on her pretty, and yes, really big feet."

"You had to say big, didn't you," she whispered, her big brown eyes glazed with pain and something else.

Was it emotion? Maybe love? Please let it be love.

Hope flared to life and Devine pressed his head to hers, letting his tears fall unabashedly when she reached up to hold him back. This was the best fucking night of his life.

"Welcome to the Clan," a booming voice said from behind him, and he recognized his Alpha.

"That's Callius," he told Sunny, who was trying to sit up slowly. "These are the Falk brothers, and you know my brother, Nicholas—"

"Nice to meet you, all, uh, damn, my head hurts. Do I have a concussion?"

"What? Why do you think that, love?" Devine asked.

"Well, I think I'm hallucinating. Did I just get rescued by the *Thunder Down Under* or something?"

"Gross sis. And inaccurate. How can you compare us to a measly human male review?" River asked, shaking his head and pulling on a pair of sweats. The young Wolf was handing them out as realization dawned.

Devine snarled, and everyone jumped, pulling their pants on a little bit faster. He felt Sunny's giggle before he heard it, and damn, had he missed that sound. She was still cradled in his arms like the perfect precious mate that she was, and even better, it did not appear as if she wanted to leave. Devine just held her, praying she understood what he was saying without words.

"A male review?" he asked, had to since she was the one who said it.

"What? I wasn't a nun before we met," she admitted.

"Sweetheart, didn't I ask you, as your father, to not talk about those godawful shows you and Minnie used to go to in front of me?"

"Sorry, Daddy," she said and turned her head to grin at her dad.

"How are you, baby girl?"

"Perfect. You rescued me," she replied, and let him kiss her head, without leaving Dev's embrace.

"Actually, I almost killed you. Me, River, and this shoddy roof job we did," the man said, his face burning with too many emotions to name.

"It was my fault, Dad. I'm the one who designed it," River said, claiming the blame, and Devine smelled the acrid stench of his embarrassment and regret fill the space.

He frowned. As much as he would have liked to beat the piss out of anyone who dared hurt his mate, the truth was these men would have never willingly done so. What happened was an accident. A perfect storm of missteps that all led to this near disaster.

Fuck, he was so grateful she was okay.

"That is not exactly true, gentlemen," Nicholas

said before Devine could. "The roof is sound. The real fault is with the foundation, or lack thereof. This is a temporary structure and should have been fine if not for the extreme weather and the palettes crashing onto it. Some tweaks, and it would have been perfect."

"Really?" River's eyes sparked with interest, and Nicholas pulled the Wolf over to show him what he meant, and Leaf followed.

"We'll be off, Devine. Hope to see you all at Thanksgiving dinner," Callius Falk said, before tossing a set of keys at Devine, and leaving with his brothers.

With Nicholas showing the Wolves what they did wrong, and where to improve, that left Devine alone with Sunny. He picked her up in his arms, taking her to the SUV.

"I will fly home, brother, and I will see the Wolves safe. You take care of your mate," Nicholas called out, and Devine nodded his thanks.

"Let's get you home," he told her, tucking her against his body as he ran into the storm towards the vehicle.

Once seated, Devine turned to her. This was it. The moment of truth.

"Sunny, I—"

"Home first, Dev. Aspirin. Warm clothes. And food. I really need some food," she whispered—and, sure enough, her stomach growled. "Then we will talk, okay?"

Devine nodded. It was hailing, but he had super-human reflexes and would see them home safely. His mate needed tending, and nothing in the world was going to stop him from taking care of her.

Poor beautiful mate. She'd suffered an ordeal, and after he made sure she was whole and fed, he was going to give her hell for scaring the shit out of him. Who was he kidding? He would never harm a single hair on her head.

All he wanted to do was get her home and make up for lost time. He wanted to kiss every inch of her. To let her know exactly where she stood with him. To explain with superb clarity precisely what she meant to him. His Dragon scratched and snapped, the enormous creature very on board with his plan.

Es meus.

CHAPTER 12

Sunny rinsed herself off and patted her skin dry with one of the fluffiest damn towels she had ever used in her life. Dragons really did have a thing about luxury.

Everything in Devine's house was top quality, designer labelled, and name brand. Some stuff was so damn fancy, it did not even have a label. She was a simple girl at heart, having grown up hippie in the wilds of New Jersey.

She did not know Gucci from Prada to Nevada. Labels meant nothing to her, and she worried her lower lips as she went through his closet and found a silky button-down shirt to wear. The material was so light against her healing, but still-bruised skin, Sunny did not want to take it off. So she wore it and walked down to the small kitchenette in his wing of the property he shared with his brother.

Devine had explained about the design of the house, and why he lived with his kin and a stone's throw from Castle Falk. Dragon Clans were a lot like Wolf Packs. Of course, the Macconwood Pack was the largest, covering almost the entirety of North America, so it was harder to get that close-knit feel, but was why her own family unit was so strong.

The Daye family was like a Pack unto themselves, with her best friend Minerva Lykos taking up permanent residency in their hearts ever since she'd lost her parents. Speaking of Minnie, Sunny should probably call her to let her know her cell was busted. But not just then.

Something heavenly scented was wafting through the house, and Sunny followed her nose down the stairs to the kitchen. Devine's back was towards her, and she noticed he had taken a shower too and was wearing only a pair of boxer briefs as he stood making grilled cheese sandwiches over the stove.

"Smells good," she said, startling him.

Devine turned around so quickly the sandwiches almost went flying out of the dish he'd been stacking them in. He righted them, then stared. Didn't move, didn't speak, only looked with his head cocked to the side.

His mouth was open as he raked his gaze from the still wet curls on top of her head to her pink polished toenails, and though she was decently covered, Sunny felt like every single inch of her was on display. Not in a bad way, on the contrary. She liked how he made her feel—all soft, feminine, and desirable.

Only Devine had that power with her. He was the only man who'd really looked past the frizzy hair, and the clumsiness, the Crocs, and the close-knit family who kept tabs on her and liked to drive her nuts. Goddamn, was he beautiful. His stormy blue-black gaze glittered at her, and she thought about his Dragon. The beast had come for her. He'd used his spiny quartz stones to form columns, holding the roof that had tried to crush her under the weather.

Brave Dragon, you saved my life. Good mate.

"Hi," she whispered nervously.

"Hi. Um, food. You're hungry," he said, growling that last but in a way that sent little electric pulses of lust surging straight through her core.

Sunny nodded, not trusting herself to speak. She sat down at the small kitchen island and picked up a warm sandwich.

"Mmm, sour dough and cheddar, and *omg*, what is that?" Sunny gasped and moaned as she chewed the gooey goodness that had been laced with something cinnamon and spicy. It was like apple pie and grilled cheese had a perfectly delicious little baby, and she wanted to eat it all.

"That is New York Sharp Cheddar from Organic Valley Farms and fresh baked sourdough bread with a teaspoon of Noelle's special holiday apple butter."

"Who is Noelle? Seriously, so I can decide to scratch her eyes out or send her a thank you note."

"Oh," he said and laughed. "No, it's not like that. She is Sander's mate. A good female who is a great chef."

"Ooh," Sunny replied, and picked up another half. "Good. Glad you told me. I would hate to get all murder-y on your friends."

"I see," Dev replied, inching closer to her, and holding up part of his sandwich for her to bite. "Does this mean you would like this mating, *our mating*, to continue?"

Sunny chewed slowly, thoughtfully, before swallowing the rest of her bite. She'd eaten two sandwiches and a hefty chomp of his, and though she could have kept going, that was more than enough to satisfy her hunger for now.

"That depends," she told him, honesty ringing in her voice. "I want a mate who wants me back, Dev. I know we are fated, and that is fantastic, but I believe we have choices. I want to be with you. I choose you. The only real question is, what do you choose?"

She waited with bated breath for what felt like an eternity before he moved. He took their plates and returned them to the sink, then he stalked her—what else could she call that slow, predatory walk as he came to stand directly in front of her?

He did not touch her, not with his body, but he leaned forward and grazed her lips with his own. Once, twice, three times before delving his tongue into her mouth. He was so hot. Completely ruining her with his lips. Her pussy ached, moisture dripping down her thighs and her nipples beaded so tight they hurt.

"Please, Dev," she murmured against his mouth, and with a snarl, he gripped the back of her neck and pulled her into his body.

So. Fucking. Hot.

She moaned, clutching at his shoulders, and breaking skin with her extended claws. Fuck, she didn't mean to do that, but he did not seem to care. Devine kept on kissing her, and kissing her, until she was kissed so thoroughly, she thought she would come from his mouth on hers alone.

He kept that maddening hand on the back of her neck, lifting her up with his other arm wrapped around her ass. His lips still touching hers, licking, nibbling, placing biting little kisses of possession all over her neck and chin.

"I like you in my clothes," he growled, backing her into the floor as he made it to the first landing. "But this has to come off."

Sunny was panting. Her legs were open. The hard bar of his cock was nestled against her wet folds, but the fucker still wore his boxer briefs, and the torture was exquisite.

"Let me," he said, moving her trembling fingers out of the way while he slowly opened her borrowed shirt, undoing button by button.

"Dev," she whined, head lolling back as he finally parted the material, sliding it down her shoulders.

"Don't rush, sweetheart. We have all night, *meus lupus*, and I want to take my time with you."

"Want you."

"You've got me, Sunny. And I have you. I never thought I would have a mate of my own, and you turned out to be the best damn surprise I have ever had in my whole life. Let me show you what you mean to me. Let me have you, Sunny," he growled, closing his mouth over one distended nipple.

"Yessss," she hissed, moaning as pleasure built deep within her.

"That's a good girl," he growled, pushing her breasts together and lapping at the valley between them before sucking the other one into the hot cavern of his mouth. "Fuck, you taste like heaven. Was that a yes, love? Can I have you?" Devine repeated his question.

Of course, it was a yes, how could he think it was anything else? But he stopped sucking, moving back to stand, tugging her hand until she stood to. She was shaky, but he steadied her, his strong fingers clasping her hips as he walked her backwards, up the stairs, to his bed.

"I need the words," he said, teasing her with light, feathery swipes of his tongue. "Can I have you?" he repeated, and every time he did, her clit throbbed, and her pussy readied for his imminent invasion.

This was big, she realized suddenly, and taking his face in her hands, Sunny looked into the stormy eyes of her Dragon and gave him her answer.

"Yes, Devine Graystone. You can have every inch of me, body, heart, mind, soul, and Wolf. I choose you, mate. I love you."

The air was pregnant with power as the force of their matebond hummed and flared to life. Sunny gasped as the mark over her breast, her quartz rose burned and glowed, Devine was trembling, his eyes burning a glittering shade of blue-black she had never seen.

"Es meus," he growled, shredding his boxers off his body. His Dragon was right there, in that stormy gaze as Devine grabbed her thighs in his hands and penetrated her with one swift thrust of his hips.

Sunny's mouth opened in a silent scream as Devine wrecked her body, bringing her to heights never felt before. He was relentless in his mission, branding her with his touch, kindling fires in her soul as he kissed, licked, caressed, bit, and fucked her to within an inch of her life.

Holy. Motherfucking. Claiming.

If Sunny had thought the first time Devine claimed her as his mate, the Dragon had rocked her world—then *this* was something else. This coming together was a whole new level of sexing Sunny had not believed possible, never mind experienced. Sunny wanted to let go of herself, to feel nothing but the pleasure he could bring, but Devine commanded her attention.

"Watch me, *meus lupus*," he growled, his dick

stroking deep inside her, touching secret, hidden places and filling her so good. She wanted more. She wanted all of him.

The thin smattering of hair against his chest felt delicious rubbing against her nipples, and Sunny growled, arching her back to meet his thrusts with her hips. She begged him to move faster, harder, but he would not budge. The bastard was grinning as he slid his big, thick cock deeper, shortening his strokes and grinding his pubis right into her needy clit. Sunny went cross-eyed from the pleasure. Fuck, it was so good. She was so close.

Just. Needed. More.

Closing her mouth over his neck, she bit down, her canines sliding from her mouth, teasing his neck, she did not pierce his skin this time, just reminded him of her claim, and it was all he seemed to need to lose that carefully maintained control. Devine withdrew from her almost completely, then he slammed back home.

"Fuck, yes," she moaned with every thrust and retreat.

His fingers bruised her thighs as he pushed her open wider. Devine was insatiable as he drove himself into her, and she loved it. Sunny clung to his arms as her pussy tightened.

So wet, so hot, so good.

Her orgasm hovered just there. So close, so fucking close. As if he could hear her, Devine snarled, his Dragon glowing in his stormy blue gaze. He leaned down, clamped one tight bud between his teeth, and he bit her. Hard.

"Oh fuck Dev, I'm coming!"

And she was coming. Like really coming. Holy fucking hell. The man was unstoppable, hellbent on making her lose her mind, and she was, she had. Her mind, heart, body, soul was his. Devine was everywhere now. She felt him inside her, and not just her body. He was inside her heart.

Sunny spiraled from the pleasure. Her orgasm was so big, so long, it went on and on—better than any she had ever had. Pleasure filled every cell. Her neurons were sparking, short-circuiting from the fire he'd created in her veins. She never knew love like this was possible. Yes, love. Fate may have matched them, but love made them choose each other. She knew he loved her now. Felt it in his touch. Heard it in her brain, like he was whispering it through their *matebond*.

Devine was still pumping into her as his litany whispered through her very soul.

Es meus. In aeternum. Mine, for always. Meus lupus. Love you. Love you. Love you. Love you.

Tears pricked her eyes, and the pleasure built again. Devine rolled them over and she was on top of him. Fuck, if he didn't slide even deeper in this position. She leaned back, loving his hands seemed everywhere, touching everything as she rocked her body in time with his thrusts. She wanted him crazy for her, needed him to lose control. And she worked for it, swiveling her hips and raking her claws against his skin.

"So beautiful, mate," he growled, his hands digging into her hips.

Devine sat up, sucking her nipples, and kissing her skin. She worked him harder, faster, rocking her hips and gripping him tighter with her pussy. His cock pulsed, and she knew he was close.

"I love you, Dev. Do you hear me? I pick you. Always," she cried out and bit down, marking him once more.

Devine stiffened with his release. He roared as he coated her insides with his cum and fuck, she howled her pleasure as another orgasm took her by surprise.

"This, this is how matings are supposed to be," she whispered as she collapsed against him.

"Messy?" he teased, and she laughed, pinching his ass.

"No, perfect. I choose you, Dev," she whispered, loving the glow of his Dragon as the beast joined them.

"And I choose you, Sunny. Forever, I choose you," he whispered and kissed her softly.

Mine.

EPILOGUE

Devine spent the next day with Nicholas, helping Sunny, and her family put the store to rights. They'd brought in one of their smaller crews to help with remodeling the outdoor roof, though Sunny opted to keep the enormous quartz columns.

"They'll remind me of you when you're not here," she whispered and nipped his lip.

He would have to get used to her PDAs, but that wasn't so bad. Hell. Who was he kidding? Devine could not keep his hands off her and he loved the fact that it seemed reciprocal.

Christ, she was perfect for him. Here he'd thought the modern age had ruined his chances at finding happiness, but Sunny with her charming curls in wild, radiant disarray, her tight black leggings hugging her gorgeous ass, topped with a flowing, green blouse that she wore without a bra, and yellow Crocs on her feet, with little turkey charms stuck to them, could not have existed in any other time.

His surprise mate was—*in a word*—breathtaking, and Devine could not have anyone better. Throughout the day, she'd caught him staring, and this delightful pink blush would creep up her neck and spread to her cheeks.

Irresistible woman. Meus lupus.

"Hey, they got this. Do you want to go for a run?"

"Oh, um, think it's safe with the storm and all?"

"If there are any downed trees, I will move them out of your way. We can spare an hour," he cajoled until she agreed.

"Mom, Dad, I'm going out with Dev," Sunny called out to her parents who simply waved them off.

Devine had spoken to her father earlier and had told the male of his intentions. The Wolf was not exactly happy, but who could blame him? His daughter was a fucking gem, and she was getting him for a mate.

"Do you love her?" Leaf had asked.

"Yes, sir. I love her more than my life and I will keep her safe as long as there is breath in my body."

"You better," was his only reply.

Fine words from a father, and Devine looked forward to asking his advice should he and his beautiful mate be blessed with young. But, children or not, Sunny was his real surprise. She had given him more than she could ever know.

These moments with her were precious, and he was not going to waste another one. Stupid. He'd been stupid for waiting, for dragging his feet. Thank fuck, she was smarter and more patient than he was . Sunny was his all. She was his everything and he would spend his entire life being worthy of her.

She chatted as they drove to their house, parking the truck and walking towards the woods behind Castle Falk. He took her hand, making sure she did not trip or fall on the downed branches and slippery chunks of ice that dotted the landscape. He guided her to the shed the others used to hide their Change from outsiders. This area was secluded, protected, and privately owned, so the chance of having any unwanted onlookers was pretty nil. But even so, Devine had something to share. Sunny took off her clothes, not shy or embarrassed in front of him, and he thanked the gods for that.

There was nothing sexier than his mate as she prepared for her shift. She turned her head, frowning when he just stood there.

"Aren't you going to change with me?"

"Yes, but first I wanted to tell you something."

"Oh, I see," she said on a laugh, and walked into his arms only in her leggings, breasts bouncing beautifully in their bareness as she moved. "You just want me naked while you talk."

"Well, I hadn't thought of that at first. But now that you mention it," he replied with a wicked grin. "Seems like a great plan to me, love."

"I bet," she returned and nuzzled his face with hers. "Tell me already, my Wolf wants out."

"I love you, Sunny," he said, unable to help himself as he dropped a kiss on her open mouth.

"I love you too, Dev."

"I know. I feel it in here, and that is why I am giving you this," Devine said, taking the small thing out of his pocket.

He held out his handiwork, worrying over the simplicity of the design. A dozen black diamonds circled the chunk of galaxy quartz he'd pulled from the earth. He'd used Castor's connections to set and polish the stone. To make it worthy of her.

"Dev?"

"I am new to this world, but I understand you grew up beside the humans here. I know not all supernaturals do this, but my Clan practices human tradition with so many of their mates doing so as well," he rambled, clearing his throat. "Anyway, um, I want you to wear this, Sunny. It has been imbued with magic to stretch and shrink as you change shape. It is unbreakable and a symbol of my devotion to you, my love. Will you wear it, Sunny?"

"Oh Dev," she whispered, tears flowing freely now.

"Will you be my mate? My bride? Can I keep you?" he whispered the last, his voice thick with emotion.

"Yes. Yes. My answer is yes," she said, launching herself at him.

But Devine was ready. He caught her. Always would. Holding her tight to him, he crashed his mouth to hers and kissed the hell out of her. She was glorious like that. Happiness radiated from her as she clung to him, bare-breasted and moaning, inside the changing shed on the edge of the woods his Clan used, but with no one else there to witness except themselves.

Devine never believed in luck before he met her. But his Sunny was a pleasant surprise, gifted by the

Fates, and claimed by him. His choice. And he would pick her again, and again. For always.

———

Castle Falk was simply the most luxurious place she had ever dined in. Everything from the floor to the furniture to the glass she sipped from was expensive.

But the people, they were the real treasure and here on Thanksgiving Day, Sunny felt truly blessed. She had her family, her mate, and her new Clan around her. What could be better?

Callius and Fred sat with their two youngest children on their laps and fed them bites of the pumpkin and pecan pies Sunny's mother had made to contribute to the meal. Sander and Noelle were laughing at something Castor said, while his mate Jozette just sighed and rocked their baby in her arms.

Edric and Joselyn were in the living room, setting up a custom set of wooden train tracks for the other children to play with while the grownups enjoyed some coffee, wine, and desserts.

Thanksgiving with Devine's Clan had been quite

the affair, but most surprising was how simple and good it felt to belong to something as wondrous as this. Crystal had dropped by, but she hadn't stayed very long, and River was deep in discussions with Nicholas over his new job proposal. The youngest Daye was changing his life's plans, and that was alright with Sunny, as long as he worked hard and didn't mooch.

"He'll work hard," Devine whispered, dropping a lingering kiss on her cheek.

She loved when he did that—*read her mind*. It was just another facet of their growing matebond that she had come to love. Every day she was surprised with something new from her formerly grouchy Dragon mate, and she could not wait for what tomorrow would bring.

"Sorry everyone, I have to go," Nicholas said, standing up and straightening the jacket of his tux.

The man was gorgeous, even after cutting his long silver-tipped hair down to just the inky dark roots. He resembled his younger brother quite a lot, but Sunny was inclined to find Dev the more handsome of the two.

"Oh, but you'll miss meeting Minnie," she said, and he gave her an apologetic smile.

"No worries. I'm sure I will meet your friend

some other time," he said, leaving without a backwards glance.

"Where is he off to in such a rush?" Fred asked, popping a bite of Sunny's mom's famous cream cheese pie crust into her mouth.

"He is looking for a mate," Devine said and shocked everyone.

"What? How?"

"Dating apps. I believe he has lined one up for every night this month," Devine informed them sadly.

"I wonder if the Fates work like that," Sander remarked.

"Well, I just hope he is safe," Sunny said, concerned for her brother-in-law.

"He is a Dragon, love. He will be fine," Devine reassured her.

Later that night, Devine wrapped his arms around his mate, and Sunny sighed contentedly. Her body was deliciously sated, and she inhaled the heady fragrance that was her scent mingled with his.

"Feel the bond now, love? It grows stronger," he whispered, kissing her head, making her feel cherished.

"Mm, yeah. Like our roses," she murmured,

lifting her hand to trace the mark he'd given her—his quartz rose with her fingertips.

"Have I told you how much I love you today, mate?" Devine growled, and her body heated as that rumbly sound moved through his chest and into her.

Sunny pushed her body back into his, loving the feel of his hardening shaft against her buttocks. His body was incredible, his appetite for her insatiable, and she could hardly believe this was happening. Joy like this was too precious for words.

So instead of talking, she turned her head, catching his lips and pouring all her emotions into that one breathtaking kiss. Her body quivered help-lessly in response as Devine tightened his hold on her. She felt his love like a magnet, pulling her closer and holding her in the circle of his protection and his love. Their kiss went on and on, and she never wanted it to stop. Would never tire of this deep and soul-searing affection.

"I love you too," she whispered into his mouth, loving the purr-like growl that told her his Dragon was happy.

Devine rolled her onto her back and slid between her thighs, filling her in a single thrust as he told her with his body how much he worshipped her. Plea-sure spiraled and soon, Sunny was out of control, bucking wildly against her mate, trusting him to bring her to and back down again from the heaven only he could bring.

Fuck, it was good. So good. And even if times got hard and emotional, Sunny was a fixer, and Devine was a warrior. They would never give up on each other. Knowing that, trusting in that gave them both a purpose that was greater than themselves.

Many hours later, Sunny was lying on top of Devine, resting her well-loved body in the cradle of his embrace. A smile played at the corner of her lips, and she felt their matebond wrap them up tightly like a security blanket.

"I chose you too," she murmured, giving him another chunk of her heart gladly.

"Es meus." His Dragon growled, and Sunny's Wolf howled inside her mind's eye.

He'd once told her he did not like surprises, but later Devine amended that statement.

"You're the Dragon's surprise, Sunny Daye. The best one this beast of a man has ever gotten."

T*he end.*

Did you enjoy this Paranormal Romance? Awesome! You

can read the other Falk Clan Tales here! Look for Nicholas' story in The Dragon's Dream.

&

You might have noticed mention of the Macconwood Wolf Pack in this story. You can read about the whole Pack by starting here.

Sign up for C.D. Gorri's newsletter today and never miss a sale or new release.
Thank you and happy reading! Xoxo

THE DRAGON'S DREAM

DREAM

A FALK CLAN TALE

USA TODAY BESTSELLING AUTHOR
C.D. GORRI
THE
DRAGON'S
DREAM
A FALK CLAN TALE

THE DRAGON'S DREAM
A FALK CLAN TALE

Dear readers,

After writing The Dragon's Treasure, I just knew Dev and

his brother Nick needed stories of their own. Devine got

his in The Dragon's Surprise, so now, it is Nick's turn.

I hope to enjoy it!

Del mare all stella,

C.D. Gorri

Don't forget to sign up for my newsletter here:
https://www.cdgorri.com/newsletter

BLURB

He's a hardcore realist until she dares him to dream.

Nicholas Graystone's Dragon is restless. He needs a mate—one who will overlook his gruff exterior. With something of his own to care for and protect, his angry beast might finally settle down.

But things in modern Maccon City are so very different from the life he was used to. Even after almost killing one of the legendary Falk Clan, those Dragon brothers generously invite him and his brother into the fold. How can he refuse?

Simple—he can't. Especially not now that his

brother is mated to a local Werewolf. Seeing Devine's happiness has sparked something inside Nicholas. His own desire to find a mate by any means. But can the *TopazDragon* be redeemed before it's too late?

Minerva Lykos is a Werewolf and renowned artist who needs a break. What better place to restore her creative energy than her old family beach house down in Maccon City?

Of course, the curvy she-Wolf isn't expecting to meet her muse in the gorgeous Dragon who lives next door. Can she convince the hunky shifter to pose for her?

Things get heated between the sculptor and the Dragon in this Falk Clan Tale.

PROLOGUE

The waves crashed, and thunder roared like monsters at war outside Castle Blackthorn. Nicholas waited for his brother to return from his latest assignment, nerves on edge.

Just recently Dragomir had started separating Nick and Devine when sending them to do his evil bidding. The Chief was often callous and cruel, and he cared nothing for the welfare of the Dragons in his care.

Nicholas wished he could rise against the false Alpha's rule, but too many supported his claim. Or did they? It was all up in the air at the moment. The rumblings of discontent had been sown by Dragomir's own hand.

Devine had been sent on this evil deed without Nick for backup, and that did not sit well with him. For the *first time in his long history, the TopazDragon had tried to fight against the Alpha command in the tyrant's voice. But Dragomir was slick and oily as an eel, giving his orders when Devine was not about.*

Nick's beast snarled and roared. He did not want to kill for Dragomir. The bastard had sentenced one of their own to death for the sin of simply having too much, and he'd chosen Nicholas as his blade.

He needed Devine to ground him before Nicholas was forced to carry out his duty. Obeying the Chief had been ingrained in his very blood, but he wanted to roar and burn down the whole damn island in protest.

Fuck Dragomir and his evil ways.

The Chieftain was full of poison and greed. He wielded the Graystone brothers like a warrior did his sword. The only reason Nicholas had not taken off to the skies was because of his brother. He'd been out on assignment for days, and that was, of course, the Chief's game.

Separate. Isolate. Make wholly dependent. Then control.

But Nicholas was more than just a monster doomed to do Dragomir's bidding. He had a heart. He had a soul. Devine and Nick both repeated those truths and often. They had to in order to survive.

His younger brother had been used by the tyrant as his

blade, and Nick had been his hammer. The last hundred years might as well have been a millennium, as far as Nicholas was concerned.

He mourned the loss of their innocence and bore the guilt like a cross on his back. Nicholas had failed his brother. But as the explosions started and the sound of dragons clashing began, he knew the time to leave had finally come.

Screams tore from Nick's throat as he tossed and turned in his bed, far away from the Isle of Pain. Images from the last days and the bloody battle that had raged on and on replayed themselves like some sick news broadcast again and again. He had fought to keep himself and his brother alive against the remaining Dragons who had hated them.

His old Clan had reason to. They blamed the Graystone brothers for being harbingers of torture and death to so many of their own, and they were right. Dragomir had turned them into that. There was much to repent for, and damn it, he was trying. But still the nightmares came.

Lightning crashed and thunder boomed along the stormy shores of the Atlantic. Nicholas woke up panting.

Fuck, he hated those dreams. Snow was falling

outside his trailer, creating small drifts across the gravel strewn ground. He sat up and gazed outside of the small window to the lot where he was building his next development. His brother and mate were tucked away safely in the home he and Devine had built a few minutes' drive away, and he was there, in the trailer.

Safe.

He co-founded *Graystone* Builders, a construction and real estate development company, with his brother, but this was his first solo project. Nicholas had needed something to keep his mind and beast occupied lately. The nightmares plaguing him were relentless, and it was all he could do to keep his beast sane.

Work was good for that. The business side provided a challenge for his brain, while the construction work allowed for him to blow off steam. He did not mind breaking ground and hefting materials about the lot while they waited for their permits to come through. Hiring all Shifter crews meant Nick did not have to hide his strength. None of them did.

His company was quickly gaining notice as being highly reliable. In a business where most dragged out contracts and failed to deliver, *Graystone Builders* were unique in that they worked hard and fast, providing safe, environmentally conscientious, reliable work delivered on time.

Of course, they had to pick and choose projects. It would not do for humans to get wind of the supernatural world, but there was plenty of work among their kind, and Nick preferred to develop his own properties.

The trailer was small and cramped, but it suited his needs just fine. Sure, it was Christmastime, and Sunny had complained she did not feel right about pushing him out, but truthfully, he could not stay at the beach house.

He did not tell her that, of course. Only a few weeks had passed since Devine and Sunny's mating, and Nick was happy to give them space. He sure as fuck could not stay in the house, knowing what those two lovebirds were doing on their side of the house despite the soundproofing.

No way. Giving the new couple time to enjoy their honeymoon phase was the least he could do. A thoughtful gift, if he said so himself. Technically, he could've gone home. His side of the mansion was separated and sound-proofed, but Nick did not want to crowd the newly mated pair. He liked his brother's mate. She was bright and happy—*the complete opposite of Devine.*

Sunny was exactly like her moniker. A local Werewolf from the Macconwood Pack, she was everything his brother needed. She and Dev deserved some space and privacy. They did not need his grumpy ass hanging around them all the time.

Memories of his nightmare crowded his brain and Nick walked naked to the mini fridge to grab a cold bottle of ale. The crisp apple taste was sweet and satisfying. That was the thing about New Jersey, plenty of local breweries, farms, and ranches abounded across the land, reminding him of days of old.

The click of the tab opening followed by a hiss of carbonization sounded loud to his sensitive ears and yet so satisfying. Nicholas downed it, breathing heavily as his keen gaze traversed the construction site. His night vision was excellent. The lot was secure, and his vision for the complex he intended to build was right there in his brain. A small series of townhouse like structures, but not for permanent residence. These would be rentals for supes needing a vacation spot or just some quiet time.

The Macconwood Pack Alpha had been onboard with the project, and Callius Falk, the Chief of his new Clan was, as well. This was going to be great, he thought, hoping the work would occupy his beast from the thing troubling him most as of late—*finding a mate.*

Nicholas' gaze roamed over the lot and across the sandy dunes to the empty old house sitting a couple of hundred feet from the building site. That place was the bane of his existence. He'd tried to gain rights to the property, wanted to buy it, but it had been impossible to find the owner.

It was blocking the development's access to the road, and he needed the owner's permission to connect his driveway to it. Better to just buy the whole thing, but it was proving difficult. He would not give up his pursuit, though.

Truthfully, the damn thing was an eyesore— worn wood shingles, sagging porch, broken windows on the ground floor, and a whole damn flock of seagulls nesting in the attic.

His Dragon growled softly, the enormous beast restless and ailing. The desire to find a mate to steady his creature had all but consumed him over the past few weeks. But dating apps and countless meaningless hours in bars and nightclubs had yielded nothing.

"Easy, old boy. We still have time," he told his Dragon.

Nick had so many regrets from his old life, and he desperately wanted the chance to right them. How many times had the sounds of his sins awakened him at night?

Too many.

CHAPTER I

Grrrrrrr.

Nick crushed the empty can of ale and cast it into the recycling bin. He should try to sleep, but as usual, rest eluded him. Thoughts of his past filled his head.

Devine might have been Dragomir's blade, but then Nicholas had been his hammer. Not as refined a swordsman as his brother, he'd used pure bulk and muscle to carry out the evil Chief's commands. His strength had always been his blessing and curse.

No Dragon on the Isle of Pain had bested him in a single challenge. It had gotten to where he'd been fighting almost nonstop. Even now, his beast could not rest, always waiting for the next throw down.

Nicholas craved a mate. His Dragon could not

settle without one. But the man was afraid. What if a mate was not enough to tame his powerful beast? After all, he'd been down this road before. Once upon a time, Nicholas thought he had found a suitable female in Constanza, but it was not meant to be. He'd come upon the maiden fair when scouring the eastern Italian coast for treasure to increase his horde.

It was there Nicholas had spied the buxom beauty and thought to claim. But a freak accident had him revealing his true self too soon, and she'd feared his Dragon right from the start. Constanza renounced her affections and ran away to wed a human farmer. It happened so many centuries ago, and yet the pain of her rejection still stung.

It would not be so bad, being alone, if everyone in his new Clan was not already mated. He was the last single Dragon, and honestly, it sucked. Especially during this festive season. There were parties and dinners he was compelled to attend, and there he stuck out like a sore thumb. So desperate for a female companion, Nicholas had even tried dating apps, but it was hopeless. Maybe the *TopazDragon* was just destined to be alone.

That brought up another point of contention

he'd been avoiding. Nicholas' Dragon was not responding as quickly as he used to.

"Don't grow cold on me yet," he muttered, rubbing his skin to mute the hollow ache above his heart.

His topaz rose was wilting. The magical marking was his to give to his one true and fated mate, but Nicholas was a realist. He was over six hundred years old, and he still had not found her.

Fucking hell. Would this be his end? Finally, he and his brother were free of Dragomir and the Isle of Pain, but what did he do with this newfound freedom?

Waste away. Go cold. Lose himself to the dark.

Lights flickered on over at the abandoned house, and Nicholas scowled, his attention diverted. Twice now he'd chased away squatters from the seaside home he'd been trying to purchase for months now.

Fucking humans, always taking what was not theirs and lacking the means to hold on to it. He snarled angrily and rolled his shoulders.

"Owwww! Dammit!"

His keen hearing picked up the sound of a shout as he dragged his jeans up his legs and Nick frowned. Whoever was yelling, the stranger sounded female—and she was seriously pissed. But the female was also crying.

"Fucking hell," he muttered, telling himself to mind his own business.

"Shit," he growled when he knew he wouldn't be able to resist investigating.

It was the crying that made him curious. Dressed in jeans, Nick was already out the door before he could second-guess himself. He didn't bother with shoes or a shirt before he strode out the door, feet pounding over snow-covered sand as he hauled ass to render aid.

"Sonovamotherfuckingwhorebitch!"

Nick faltered in his advance, eyebrows raised as more crashing and glass breaking reached him. His Dragon snorted. Whoever this female was, she was pissed as hell and cursing like a sailor. Usually, he found that sort of language off-putting in a female, but right then, he was more concerned with what caused her to curse and rage. He wanted to help, to make it right for some unknown reason. His Dragon agreed and was more than a little strange. Nick usually did not care for saucy females.

"Suck my balls, you two-timing, cheat! My lawyer is gonna rip you a new asshole by the time he gets through

with you, you lowlife. My money, my car, my condo. Just get out of my face, dipshit!"

He didn't even realize he was smirking until he caught his reflection in the cracked glass of the front door. Nicholas peeked in through the half-opened portal and his eyes bugged out of his head.

Inside was an angry, hysterical female, and she was yelling into her phone. Who was she? He did not recognize the weeping woman, but something was familiar about her, something tugging his beast forward.

Sniff. His inner beast growled. The female was all Wolf—not a human as he had previously thought. Nick paused, observing the miniscule creature. She was curvy in all the right places but stood at least a foot shorter than him. She cursed and hopped around on one foot, snarling at a rusted nail sticking up out of the carpeted floor.

Green shag—old, smelly, and hideous.

Go to her, the Dragon hissed.

Nicholas froze. This was not his concern, no matter what his scaly alter ego thought. He was about to walk away and leave her to it when he remembered where he was. He needed this property. Maybe he could get in good with the owners if he stopped her from doing, *er*, whatever she was doing there.

Keep her safe.

What? No. Shut up! Nick growled at his Dragon, pushing the enormous beast down.

Okay, the she-Wolf might be cute when she was upset. But neither that nor her injury gave her leave to break into the place he wanted to buy. The Dragon scratched and Nick wrestled with him until he was almost panting with the exertion.

Fucking hell.

The Dragon was already preparing to press forth again, and Nick had to think fast. *New plan—run with it.*

This was the perfect opportunity to nail two birds with one stone. He could satisfy his beast's need to see she was okay, and perhaps there was finally a reason for the owner to contact him.

"Excuse me, Miss?"

Keep it professional, simple, that was his motto. But the she-Wolf turned around, large, golden brown eyes wet with unshed tears, and his heart faltered inside his chest.

Fuck. She's beautiful.

"Eeeek! Christ, you scared me," she accused, hand over her heart. "What do you want? Can't you see I am having a lousy frigging night over here? Who even are you?"

The stranger turned to face him, standing on one foot, her golden eyes flashing at him beneath her dark lashes. She had a shapely body, revealed in tight leggings and a figure hugging sweater. A halo of glossy, dark ringlets circled her head, and her face —*fuck*, her face was perfect.

Even with smeared makeup and a slight hiccup in her voice, the strange she-Wolf was stunning. He'd noted the flashy red Camaro outside and the bags she'd dragged into the dusty home curiously.

"You can't be here, Miss, *uh*, I don't know your name," he said stupidly.

"That's because I didn't offer it. And you know what? I am tired of big dumb men telling me what to do!" she shouted. "You wanna know what I'm doing here? Fine. I'm here cause this is my house, pal. My grandmother left it to me, and since my entire family is gone for the holidays, and my winter show is indefinitely canceled, I came here to, to—I don't know!" she wailed, slumping to the floor in a sobbing mess of Werewolf.

What the fuck was Nick supposed to do now?

He scratched the back of his neck, rubbing his hand over his head and face while her sobs grew in volume. Her narrow shoulders shook, and he thought he heard her snort. This had to be that thing the females of his Clan had once described as an *ugly cry*.

Damn. They were right. It was ugly. But that did not stop his heart from wrenching inside his chest. Nick could not stand it another minute.

"Okay, come on," he grunted, plucking her off the floor. She weighed next to nothing, but he liked the feel of her plump curves snuggled against his chest.

"Stop that! I didn't say you could manhandle me," she growled, slapping at his hands.

Wasn't that cute? He could have stopped it, a Werewolf was simply no match for a Dragon, but Nick rather liked her feisty nature.

Odd. Very odd. He'd always preferred his females docile—wait, she wasn't his female. He growled and shook his head.

"Quiet, minx," Nick barked, sitting her down on the counter.

He ignored the electrical zing that had zipped through his fingertips when he lifted her off the floor. Now that contact was broken, his fingers buzzed with aftershocks, as if missing the feel of her.

Not good.

"Let's see your foot," he rumbled, pulling off her

cute furry boots none too gently and assessing the damage.

"Don't use the faucet water," she mumbled, observing him cautiously.

Nick grabbed the bottle of spring water she must have carried in with her from off the counter. Next, he wet a clean napkin she'd handed from a pile in her pocket. He snorted and shook his head.

Who the fuck kept twenty napkins in their sweater?

Females. Sweet smelling, soft to the touch females.

"It's already healing," he growled, patting her skin dry and stepping back quickly.

Touching her again was a terrible idea.

No, it's not, his Dragon growled.

When the fuck had his beast decided to come to the party so aggressively? Nick growled his frustration and turned to leave, even if his Dragon threatened to gut him if he did.

"Hey, *uh,* thank you," she mumbled after him.

"You're welcome," he replied, remembering her connection to the house, and wanting to get on her good side. "Uh, you know, I have been trying to find out who owned this place for a while now."

"Oh, really? Why?" she asked, putting her sock

back. Next, she checked the inside of her ruined boot, trying to assess the damage, he guessed.

"I was hoping to buy it."

"Ha," she cut him off with her barked laughter. "Why? Gotta wife and kids you think would love to live in a drafty old house down the shore?"

"Uh no," he growled. "No mate. No young. I just, *er*, actually, I want to knock it down."

The woman's eyes met his. She narrowed her gaze and heaved a sigh. Then she cocked her head and squinted at him.

"You said mate, so you are a Shifter. I just can't tell what kind," she replied.

"Is that so? Good," he rumbled.

"Ah, okay. Well, look *Mr. Need to Know Basis Pants*, if you're gonna barge in here and tell me you want to knock down my house, I figure you might as well make yourself useful. I have a couple of boxes in the trunk of that hot rod outside that I need for work, go get 'em and we can chat," she answered, tossing him the keys as she hopped off the counter.

Werewolves must be nuts, he mused as he watched the spunky little woman start dragging two enormous suitcases across the floor and over to what looked like a dangerous staircase. Nicholas caught the thrown key fob easily and scoffed.

Who did this tiny female think she was, ordering a mighty Dragon around? Strangely enough, though, he was already turning around to obey her dictate.

What the hell?

Nicholas was not the type to be bossed around. It angered and confused him, but even after considering the reasons, he sure as shit was not prepared for his Dragon's response to his rhetorical question.

Who is she? Easy.

Es meus.

CHAPTER 2

arlier that evening...

"It's not me. It's you, babe."

Roger's whiny voice annoyed the fuck out of Minnie. Always had, she thought as she watched a moue of distaste spread across the face she'd once thought boyishly handsome.

"You stupid fuck, that isn't even the saying,"

Minnie had raged at him.

This was why her folks said to never date a human. Roger Singer was a lousy lay, a terrible manager, and he'd been stealing from her for months. She snarled as she skimmed the list of lame ass descriptions he'd used to label his frivolous spending at her expense.

"It's not my fault—*you* hired *me*, Min," he whined

some more, using the nickname she fucking hated. "If you can't afford a manager of quality, then your art will suffer, babe," he began, his condescension almost enough to pull her Wolf forward.

We can gut the human. Leave him to wallow in his own putrid stench.

Minerva snorted. She sometimes wondered if her Wolf wasn't some straight up Ancient Greek warrior reincarnated or some shit. The she-Wolf was quick to temper and deadly with her sharp fangs and enormous claws.

Keeping her supernatural side secret from the normals she infrequently dated was always difficult, but she'd never felt comfortable sharing her Wolf with Roger. Now she knew why. Thank fuck.

Grrrrr.

"God, you're like so cold all the time," he said, mansplaining his infidelity. As if it mattered. "Pushing me away the last few weeks, I'm just human, Min. I have needs. But even though you couldn't meet them, I stuck around for *you*, Min. I'm hurt you think I would use you—"

"*Ohmyfuckinggawd.* You did use me, Roger. For fuck's sake, look at all this. Look at these so-called legitimate expenses. *Business appearance fee?* You charged $750 to a department store that only sells women clothes, and I know you didn't buy me anything from that store, you lying, cheating sack of shit," Minnie snarled and poked him in the chest with one, too long to be human claw.

Shit. She needed to keep her cool. She paced away from him, continuing to read down the list of ridiculous expenditures.

"It's not cheating, babe. You broke up with me."

"I broke up with you after I found this Roger *because* you were cheating. I kept you on as manager because I thought you were good at your job. But after finally looking at the books after the last two shows, I see you ripped me off for almost 30% of my earnings."

"I am entitled to make a living too, Min—"

"Yeah, you are. But not from mooching off me. What is this, Roger? *Manager vehicle service and maintenance-* you charged a $40,000 car to *me? Health & Wellness fee*—this is a massage parlor, you exploitative fucking pervert!"

"You know, if you keep calling me names, I am going to have to quit on the grounds of mental cruelty," Roger said, pouting at her from across the West Village art studio where she kept a tiny storage unit to house some of her sculptures.

Her favorite New York City art gallery, *Deirdre's*

Dungeon, had booked her for the whole month, and her opening night show had sold out. She should have been celebrating, but here she was, dealing with this bullshit.

There were a couple more weeks left till Christmas, and Minnie had a ton of work to do to get more pieces ready for the gallery. She had promised Deirdre more of her fantasy miniatures for the holidays, but how was she supposed to create when she was being robbed blind?

Minerva Lykos—celebrated sculptor, and Macconwood Pack Werewolf—was being taken for a chump by this baby-faced human and his tiny pencil dick. How humiliating!

What. The. Actual. Fuck. Was. Happening?

Minnie closed her eyes and counted to ten before turning to look at the revolting male, "Roger, you are fired. I've already called the bank and all the studios I deal with. You are cut off from all of my accounts and business relationships. You have one week to pay me back every single cent you stole, or you will regret it. Do you hear me, Roger?"

"A week? I don't know, Min. I mean, how am I supposed to pay you back? You know, maybe we can work something out—"

Next to the clueless little boy expression he often

preferred, Roger's wannabe smolder was on Minnie's *top ten worst facial expressions list of all time.*

So fucking gross. How the hell had she ever messed around with this cretin? Minnie pressed her thumb and index finger to the space between her eyes and rubbed. The migraine building there would be a whopper before her Werewolf's healing abilities kicked in.

"Come on, babe. How 'bout you get on your knees and give me a little head to help that headache—"

"*Ohmyfuckinggawd,*" she groaned. "Please, do not tell me you are propositioning me! And that's not even how that works, asshole. You should have offered to give *me* head, not the other way around. UGH! Roger, just hand me your keys."

"My keys?" he asked, scratching his head.

Poor Roger. Cursed with a small dick and a small brain. It was best to cut her losses now, but that didn't mean she had to pay for this idiot's departure. Not waiting for him to move, Minnie reached into his coat pocket, took his keys, and ignored his petulant stare.

So unattractive.

"But those are my keys!"

"Are they? You're lucky I like red," she muttered

and stalked over to the cherry red Camaro SS convertible parked outside.

"Min, you can't take my car!" he yelled, following her out the door.

"Motherfucker, you bought a car in *my* name, with *my* money, right? That makes it mine."

She opened the door, dropped her oversized bag in the passenger seat, and when Roger started running alongside the car, yelling and crying real fucking tears on the sidewalk beside her, Minnie had finally had enough.

"Come on, Min. Who else is gonna deal with your temper?" he yelled the question, stepping off the curb, arms wide.

That was it. The last straw. Going after her insecurities only pissed her off more. Minnie drove through a puddle of muddy slush, pointing the front of the car so the wheels churned up the guck and flicked it all over his nice new suit.

Prick.

Good riddance, snarled her Wolf.

He stood there gasping, spitting out slush and Minnie pressed the pedal to the metal on the *new to her* snazzy muscle car.

"Fuck you, Roger," she yelled and turned up the volume. With some classic rock blasting, she drove all the way to her hometown of Maccon City with the top down—*fuck the chill.*

Minnie never shed a tear throughout the entire drive. Her inner Wolf was too damn mad for that mushy nonsense. But now what? She owed the gallery big time, but there was no fucking way she was staying in the city or anywhere else near Roger.

Her Wolf was liable to tear the fucker's throat out. No. Minnie needed a reprieve. Her family had gone away for the holidays, thinking because Minnie had the hottest little gallery in the West Village hosting her art for the entire holiday season, she would not be around. They'd taken advantage of her absence and booked a trip to Tahiti.

Yay them.

Christmas used to be such fun, but it was hell on her now. Sure, she would have been busy and staying in the condo she still shared with that asshole Roger had she not intercepted a call from *Merlin Banking Solutions* asking for approval for a charge on a ten thousand dollar men's watch to her business account.

She wanted to ask if it was a digital watch, since there was no way that moron could tell time otherwise. But what did that say about her?

Minnie had been so desperate for a connection

she let some weak-willed human part her thighs for the last two years. Not that he did, with any regularity or success, to her undying disappointment. Good thing for batteries and adult toys.

When was the last time Minnie had orgasmed with Roger, or any other living person, for that matter? Far too fucking long. That loser was out of her life for good now, and she was glad. It was like having a weight off her shoulders, or as her Aunt Tanya once said about her ex-husband.

"Minnie, girl, leaving that man was like having a really gnarly hemorrhoid removed from my ass crack. Relief, girl. I felt nothing but relief."

"Relief, Aunt Tanya. I get it now," she murmured, but her words were lost in the wind as she raced down the parkway.

She had made one stop and packed up as much stuff as she could from her condo. Before she left, she'd tipped the doorman to box up all of Roger's shit and toss it in the alley, after allowing him to keep what he wanted first.

She'd paid for it all, so technically, it was hers. The doorman, Otto, was grateful, and being a fellow Werewolf, Minnie trusted him to do right by her. Her grandmother's beach house was about ninety minutes away at the speed she was driving.

Sure, it had seen better days. Okay, fine, it was a wreck. She wished her Werewolf night vision wasn't that good when she finally spied the property. Hot mess did not begin to describe it.

Damn. How had she let it go this long without repairs? She knew how. That motherfucker was supposed to pay to have the property maintained while she worked her ass off and tried to break into the art scene.

Minnie had meant to visit more, but she'd been working on her career, losing herself in her art, and trusting the wrong person to take care of her business.

"I'm sorry, Gran," she murmured as she got out of the car.

She grabbed a few heavy bags and started to walk up the stairs when her phone rang. Shit. Ten missed calls, and the jerk still did not get the hint. Sighing heavily, she clicked the little green button and made to answer, but Roger was screaming at her.

"GODDAMMIT, Minnie! You locked me out? Threw out my stuff—"

"Owwww! Dammit," she yelped, stepping on something cold and sharp as she tried to get a word in edge wise while Roger screamed like the whiny little bitch he was.

Ugh.

Minnie's eyes teared as she hopped inside. What the hell was that—a sword? She cursed, grabbing her foot, mind reeling. The jerk on the other end of the line was still raging. He even had the audacity to threaten her with a lawsuit.

Was he fucking kidding? Her foot felt like fire was shooting through it, and she hopped flamingo style across the room to what was once her favorite place in the entire world. Eyes round as she allowed her Wolf to enhance her vision, Minnie sucked in a sharp breath.

Her childhood happy place was a disaster. Kinda like her life. She needed a change, was desperate for it, but there was only so much a Wolf alone could do. Her family was gone. Her bestie was busy with a new mate and would be useless at the moment. If Minnie was going to fix her life, she needed to start now. This place might be the answer to her needs, but it was falling apart and smelled like mildew and cat piss.

Step one in the fixing my life plan—clean Gran's house.

CHAPTER 3

Minerva gasped, turning in a circle, mindful of her injured foot, as she took in the terrible state of her childhood summer home.

This place was once her haven. Her grandmother had loved having the children stay with her during those long summer days, and Minnie fondly remembered making iced tea with the older she-Wolf.

More memories came racing through her brain as her gaze roamed around the place—sitting on the porch swing with her cousins, watching the sunset after a long day of swimming, eating bowls of moussaka while binge-reading romance novels with Sunny in the tent Granny used to set up for them in the yard.

Her best friend had often been included in their

adventures, and all in all, it was a wonderful child-hood. How many years had passed since she'd been entrusted with this place? How long since she'd left it to rot?

Shit. Minnie had fucked up, big time. She'd let Gran down, and the guilt was so fucking thick it threatened to strangle her. Wiping her face, she concentrated, making a mental list of everything that needed fixing.

Outside, the stairs on the porch were sagging, the siding was cracked and falling off, and several windows were broken, not to mention a rather hilarious cartoon portrayal of a walking dick with enormous balls as his feet and a silly grin on his penile face adorned the front door. The graffiti artist had tagged some of the inside too, and Minnie wondered if he or she had left their signature.

She loved street art. In her not so humble opinion, graffiti was not vandalism. It was the voice of the people displayed in public venues for the enjoyment of all. Graffiti could be traced back to ancient Rome, and if they were doing it, well, it had to be important.

Didn't most of modern society base itself on what those crazy toga wearing dudes touted? That was an oversimplification, of course. But Minnie was fine with it. Her art history classes had taught her much, and even though she'd gone into sculpting for her career, Minnie loved all forms of artistic expression.

Whoever had drawn the image was good, if a little immature. Still, it did not mean Minnie wanted his or her work adorning the outside of her house. So, step one, remove the dick from her door. Or maybe that was step two since she'd only just removed a major dick in Roger from her life. Yeah. That made sense.

Step one—kick Roger to the curb—was complete.

Step two—remove door dick—was next.

Step three—fix house—but how?

Minnie heaved a sigh and turned in a circle, blatantly ignoring Roger, who was still yelling through the cell phone about how unfair she was to ruin his life like this.

As if.

Inside had fared little better. The wallpaper was falling down, and the carpets stunk like feral cat piss. Obvious signs of water damage darkened the ceiling in huge, unsightly spots that dripped down the corners of each room. There was a certain unmistakable mildewy presence in the air, amidst the cat urine and rodent droppings.

"*Sonovamotherfuckingwhorebitch*," she grumbled, spying what was obviously a rat's nest boldly sitting on the floor beside the refrigerator.

She wondered if the rats were still there, or if the cats had chased them away. Both presented quite the problem. Minnie might be a Werewolf, but she was not messing with rats.

Nuh uh. No way.

Roger sucked in a sharp breath, drawing her attention back to the phone dangling in her hand.

"What did you call me? This is why I had to look elsewhere for comfort, Min. You are just a mean person with a filthy mouth. I did right by you, and you took my car and my home, stole both of them. What kind of woman does that?"

Really? Minerva could not believe this asshole. Now he was claiming her perpetual potty mouth was why he cheated. Okay. She'd had it, and when Minnie had it, that meant all hell was about to break loose. She growled deep in her chest, careful not to let the moron hear her. Last thing she needed was him being in on her Wolfish secret.

"Suck my balls, you two-timing, cheat! My lawyer is gonna rip you a new asshole by the time he gets through with you, you lowlife. My money, my car, my condo. Just get out of my face, dipshit!"

The hair on the back of her neck started tingling, but she was so riled it took her a moment to catch up. Her Wolf was already taking notice—good little beastie always had her back. Still, Minnie was not dumb enough to act on her Shifter instincts.

Instead, she turned slowly and took in the six and a half foot giant standing in her doorway with one long glance. Christ, he was gorgeous. And he was *other*—like her.

Minnie pulled in a deep, long breath, and her Wolf perked up, interested. She smelled smoke and fire, and something else clinging to his deliciously bronzed skin. His hair was short and dark, but she could make out thick strands of silver at the tips.

The stranger was supernatural, and hot as fuck, but what the hell was he doing darkening her doorway? She'd hung up on Roger, and her puny ex-everything had all but left her head as she exchanged a few brief sentences with the man.

Before she knew it, he had her on the counter and was tending to her injury. Protective. Caring, though guarded, she could tell. Most supes were, and Minnie was not holding it against him as he bathed and cleaned her injury. He needn't have bothered, but she allowed it.

Minnie always was a sucker for beauty, and right

now, she could not stop staring at the striking figure he made in the decaying kitchen. If *Mr. Tall Dark and Sexy* wanted to, he could handle her feet all dang day.

His touch was gentle, efficient, and when his thumb stroked along her instep, certain ignored girl bits swelled and moistened, demanding attention. She licked her lips, an idea forming in her head.

"Where do you want these?" the stranger asked, returning from her car with the rest of her things.

"Just put them down there," she said, hopping off the counter.

"You really should not stay here tonight, Miss—"

"Minerva Lykos," she replied, and extended her hand. The giant took it, shaking slowly as he cocked one elegant eyebrow. "I can tell you're like me, not a Wolf, but something, so we have that in common—"

"I thought it was bad etiquette to ask after a person's nature?" he asked, a haughty, *and decidedly sexy*, expression in place.

"Maybe, but I'm not a fan of wasting time. I'm an artist, a sculptor, actually—I use various mediums like wood, stone, clay, glass, just about anything really—anyway, I think you and I can help each other."

"Help each other? How?" he asked, crossing his arms over his incredible pecs.

It was freezing out, but he only had on a pair of perfectly worn jeans, hanging off trim hips and showcasing that deliciously sexy v that led the way to heaven as far as she was concerned.

Minerva growled softly in appreciation. The strange Shifter was all smooth skin and curved muscles. He had dips and bulges in all the right places, including that very tempting spot between his muscular thighs.

Oh yeah, handsome. Come to mama.

This was just what she needed. Minerva smiled as she walked a circle around the male, her growl growing in volume as she noted his spectacular glutes.

Nice. Very nice.

"I'm starting to feel like a piece of meat, she-Wolf," he growled, eyes flashing at her. They were the most unique color, silver circled in a ring of fire. Gorgeous.

"If you were meat, you would be prime Olive Wagyu, handsome."

"I have no idea what you are talking about," he grunted, but she noticed his jeans seemed a tad bit tighter.

Awesomesauce.

"Well, since we don't have to work around secrets, I'll just come out and say it. I'm in a tight spot," she hedged, biting her lip. "That argument you overheard was with my former manager, ex-boyfriend, and general mistake—"

"Seems harsh, Minerva."

"Nah. Just facts. He's human and doesn't know about me. Thought I couldn't smell his lies, and well, I let him get away with it for far too long. I recently discovered he was stealing from me as well as cheating—"

"Want me to eat him?" he growled the question.

"Ha ha ha," she chuckled, tucking her hair behind her ears. "Oh, you're serious." Minnie stopped laughing abruptly, a ghost of a smile on her lips. Was it wrong she found his bloodthirsty ways sexy?

Probably.

Okay, fine—she had issues. Whatevah.

"Your animal must be fearsome. Bear? Tiger? Lion, maybe?" she asked, but she already knew the answer. Minnie did not smell fur on him.

"Nope. But you can keep guessing if you like, minx. So, eat him or not?"

"Um, not, thanks though. Does your kind usually eat humans?"

"Not recently, but we've been known to. Continue, please."

"Okayyyy," she replied and huffed out a breath before coming out with her proposal. "Look, I'm the family fuck up. The black sheep, *er*, Wolf. Everyone else is happily paired up or mated with kids, and here I am—thirty-three years old, totally alone, and I've just been made a fool by a freaking human."

"That sucks, but what does it have to do with me?"

"I am getting to that. I came back home to recoup and work on some stuff I owe this NYC gallery, but I'm tense, and my best friend has invited me to like half a dozen holiday get-togethers to show off her new mate—"

"Failing to see the connection, minx," he grumbled.

"Well, you're healthy, and a Shifter, and you are interested in my property, right?"

"Yes," he replied and nodded.

"Then I have a proposition for you. Be my plus one during the holidays and I will consider your bid on my house."

"What?"

"Look, I'm gonna be here all month, I need to straighten out this place—make it livable even if temporarily, so I will be living here for the next few weeks at least. My family is away, but I have friends —my best friend, actually, in town, and she's invited me to a ton of parties."

"So?"

"Well, I hate those things. Especially when I have to go alone. But if you are interested, and from the sizeable evidence you're rocking behind your fly there, pal—*congrats, by the way*—I would say you are very interested. That said, you can help me with this. Be my plus one, and we can work out each other's tension during this extremely busy and troublesome holiday season. After New Year's Day, I will consider selling this place to you."

The giant man cocked his head to the side, as if considering her offer. Minnie waited, holding her breath for his reply. A rolling growl-like purr started low in his belly and built up till it spilled from his thick, masculine lips. She had never heard anything like it, but her body reacted to it all the same.

Nipples hardened, sex warmed, and the butterflies in her stomach started flapping around excitedly. Even her Wolf was watching, waiting for him to respond to her blatant proposal. Minnie did not like to beat around the bush. She'd always been aggressive—a real go-getter with stuff she wanted, and yes, that included men, too.

"Let me get this straight," he said, his deep voice gritty with his beast, and fuck, she'd be lying if she said it didn't turn her on. "You are asking me, *a virtual stranger*, to be your holiday fuck buddy, no strings attached, just mutual carnal satiation and the occasional dinner party, and afterwards, we part ways, none the worse for wear. Afterwards, *maybe* you'll discuss selling this property to me?"

"Yeah, that about sums it up."

She waited a beat, hoping he would follow up with something other than the confused look on his face. Crap. Had she done this wrong? His nostrils flared, breathing in the air as if testing it for something. Whatever it was, his beast seemed satisfied. His gaze was full of silver and orange fire as he stalked across the room and placed his enormous hands on her waist. Then he pulled her in close.

Minnie hissed as her palms flattened against his chest. Her fingertips sizzled and so did the rest of her, pressed up against the naked skin of his torso with all those bulging bronzed muscles everywhere. Christ, he was even hotter than she'd thought. Potent, sexy, and the cocky bastard knew it if his crooked grin was anything to go by.

"What are you doing?" she asked.

"Seeing if we're compatible," he grumbled, dipping his head to steal a kiss.

She expected rough, but what he gave her was anything but. The giant was gentle as he sipped from her lips like he was tasting fine wine instead of making her wet with his soft, insistent kisses. The smoky spice fragrance she'd noted earlier flavored his kisses, and hell, she loved the taste, opened for him to devour even more of it.

On and on, the sexy stranger kissed Minnie, hands never straying from her waist. Without a word, the fucker broke away from her and turned around, leaving her to stare after him as he strode purposefully to the door.

"Well, come on, minx. I'll be damned if I'm taking my clothes off in this place," he said, and walked outside.

He was sending a message on his cell phone, but Minnie couldn't see what he was saying from where she stood. She was frozen with shock. Sex was not a big deal for her, but this, this felt heavier than that. Nerves threatened to disrupt her reserve.

What's the big deal? It's just sex.

He turned slightly, a questioning look in his eyes, and she swallowed down her doubts. This was her idea, after all. She'd be damned if he was going to take charge of this thing and follow him around like some brainless dolt. He grinned and turned, still texting as he took off behind the house.

"Damn my short, stubby legs," she grumbled as she locked the door to the house and raced after him across the sand dunes behind her property.

He was moving towards a trailer that was sitting in what looked like a construction lot, and Minnie frowned. When had they started building there?

She knew someone had bought the land bumping up against her inherited property a couple of years back, but they'd left it alone for so long, she'd forgotten all about it.

"Coming or not, minx?" he asked, standing in the doorway of his trailer, gorgeous body lit up from whatever was on behind him.

Minnie bit her tongue to keep from sighing. This was a purely pleasurable, no strings attached, fun smexy times kinda thing. Eyes narrowed, it was her turn to grin.

"If you can hold up your end of the bargain, handsome, I will be," she replied, and sauntered past him like she owned the place.

Hopefully more than once, she added silently.

CHAPTER 4

Blood thundered in his veins, roaring in his ears as Nicholas walked away, he could not be sure the little minx would follow, dominant as she was, but he sure as fuck hoped so.

It had been a long time since he'd met someone so interesting, too bad she was only looking for a temporary situation. Desperate as he was to settle his inner beast, Nicholas was a realist. No she-Wolf worth her salt would want someone as broken as he for a mate. He'd had this half-brained idea after Devine found his mate that he too could find happiness with a female.

Nicholas was wrong. Sure, he'd only spent a fortnight scouring bars and dating apps, but how long did a Dragon need to find his fated mate? No. If he was meant for a mate in this new world, he would have found her by now. It simply was not to be.

Besides, Minerva Lykos was not looking for a mate. Her indecent proposal had his Dragon—*and other parts of him*—more than a little bit curious. A holiday affair?

Hmmm. Yep. He could do that.

Nicholas had to admit this she-Wolf was unlike any he had ever met. She was pushy and loud-mouthed. Short really, but with curves in all the right places, corkscrew curly hair, and a pretty bow of a mouth, he would not mind getting to know better. She was cute as fuck, and yes, he would love to spend the evening between the sheets, finding out what noises she made when she came.

Nicholas growled softly, too low for even her werewolf hearing, as he watched the gorgeous little minx walk into his trailer like she'd done it a hundred times before. Confidence and sex appeal wafted from her, filling him with a sort of primal, sensual need he'd never experienced.

Minerva Lykos.

The name seemed familiar, but he could not place it at the moment. Of course, that could have everything to do with the fact half of his blood supply was tightening his jeans in a most uncomfortable predicament. The sexy she-Wolf was standing in the middle of the living room part of the trailer, her back to him as she looked around.

"You live here?"

"For the moment," he said, unashamed of the simplistic quarters.

"Nice bed," she said, pulling open the door where a platform held a king-sized mattress Nicholas had installed when he'd decided to give his newly mated brother some space.

"Thank you," he growled from directly behind her, nose pressed to the base of her throat.

He could not help it. She smelled of freshly fallen snow and the warm summer sun, like peppermints and cotton candy, and good red wine. Intoxicating, delicious, and Nicholas was ready to claim a taste for himself.

Minnie gasped as he ran his tongue from her earlobe to her shoulder. His hands were on his hips, but the female needed no more encouragement, she arched her back and rubbed her perfect heart-shaped bottom against his denim-covered cock, and fuck, he went cross-eyed.

"Name," she moaned.

"What?"

"Tell me your name, so I know what to cry out

when I start seeing stars," she replied saucily, turning around and shoving him against the wall *hard*.

His inner beast growled, the Dragon liked the woman was strong, powerful, and not easy to break. She was not like the humans he'd tried dating. No, Minerva was different. A beautifully seductive she-Wolf who knew her own mind.

Mate.

No. Fuck that thought.

"My name is Nicholas," he growled, cupping the back of her neck, and dragging her mouth to his even while she shrugged out of her clothes. He liked that she wasn't shy. Shifters rarely were.

"Nicky? Oooh, I like that."

"Not Nicky. Nicholas," he growled, voice even deeper with his beast.

Minnie raked her sharp nails down his chest to his abs, and lower. She flicked open the button of his jeans, taking him in her hand and grinning like the cat that got the canary.

"Oooh, Nicky, what have you been hiding from me? Let's see," she purred, if Werewolves could do such a thing, dropping to her knees as she pulled his jeans down to his ankles.

Fuck.

She looked so good, head between his legs as she

took his dick inside her mouth and sucked the tip. Minerva watched him with her whiskey eyes as she lapped at the slit, then sucked him in again, this time farther.

Fuck. Fuck. FUCK.

He was a Dragon, for fuck's sake, and prided himself on control. But this gorgeous little minx was rendering him stupid with slow long pulls of his cock with her mouth while her hands cupped and massaged his balls. Helpless to do otherwise, Nick bucked his hips in time with her swallows, growling loudly when she hummed her pleasure.

"That's enough. I'm not coming without you," he groaned, removing her lips from his dick, knowing his Dragon was gonna kick his ass for that later.

Too bad. Nicholas was a considerate lover. What-ever deal he'd made this night, he promised to ease the little she-Wolf's tension, and he knew exactly where to start.

"How do you want me?" she asked, licking her plump lips as if she could not help herself.

Good. Something primal inside of him liked that she enjoyed his taste. He could not wait for her mouth to be on him again. But first, he needed to make her come. It was like a biological imperative. He moved on instinct, going in for a deep, passionate kiss and pressing her back into the mattress. Minnie clung to him, no apparent reservations, as she spread her thighs and allowed him access to her most secret places.

She wore a tiny scrap of black lace over her mound, and no bra. Her dusky nipples were tight and puckered, begging for attention. Nicholas bent his head, sucking one into his mouth while his hands explored every hill and valley of her plentiful curves. He tugged on her panties, sliding them down her legs and skimming his fingertips along her smooth, impossibly soft skin.

Damn. She was beautiful, responsive to his touch as she arched and said his name in a breathy moan that made his dick grow even harder. Was he really doing this? Taking this she-Wolf to bed after only just meeting her.

Um. Fuck yeah, he was.

Nicholas was not dead yet, despite his Dragon's lonely state. If things went well, who knew what could happen? No. He had to stop that line of thought. Focus on the now. Soft hands cupped his face and Minnie pulled his mouth to hers, her Wolf strength moving him where no human could have.

"Stay with me, Nicky. Right here with me," she

murmured in a husky whisper that brushed against his senses like a lover's hands.

Nicholas growled, catching her bottom lip with his teeth as he pressed into her. He wanted those whisky eyes on him, and he was not disappointed when she met his stare.

Sexy wolf. Dominant female.

Good, because his Dragon could not stand it if a woman was cowed by him. It was damaging to his psyche, but he did not have to worry with Minerva. She met him thrust for thrust, raking her nails down his back, and urging him to move harder, faster, deeper all at once.

Bedding her was like tasting pure joy, and even as he drove her out of her mind, he found himself catching the same high energy wave of passion zipping through his veins like lightning.

"*OhfuckNickyI'mcoming.*," she screamed like it was one long, drawn out word. She squeezed him like a vise, and damn, he went right along with her, filling her up with his hot cum, and marking her with his scent.

Yes. Mark. Mate.

What? No. Shit.

"Oh gods, Nicky, that was, that was," she sighed, and smiled up at him, weak with satisfaction.

All Nick could do was stare. Holy fuck. This she-Wolf was his mate. His heart thundered as the truth of it hit home. She was his mate, and all she wanted was a fuck buddy for the holidays.

Es meus.

CHAPTER 5

Minnie woke up to the smell of coffee and cinnamon rolls, her favorite. She felt perfectly sore and sated. Smiling at the memory of the bedroom gymnastics, she stood and ambled over to the tiny bathroom.

Her Wolf hearing was good, but she could barely make out the murmurs of Nicholas talking on his phone as she hurried through a shower and rummaged through his closet for something to wear.

She chose a pair of compression leggings—the kind joggers wore in the cold—and a long-sleeved t-shirt, foregoing underthings which were not handy at the moment.

"Morning," she murmured, walking into the tiny

kitchen, and trying not to gawk at the picture he made in a pair of loose sweatpants.

He spun around, abs on point, and grinned at her, nodding over to where a plate of warm cinnamon buns sat with an extra-large coffee that smelled heavenly. Minnie growled in approval as she sipped. One cream, no sugar—how did he know?

Choosing to ignore his amazing sense of intuition, she bit into one of the glazed pecan cinnamon rolls and almost died on the spot. Was it possible to orgasm from pastry? Maybe not. But when her sexy AF lover ambled over and licked a glob of sugary goo from the corner of her mouth, stealing a kiss or two along the way, Minnie sure a shit almost came, and hard.

Fuuckk.

Nicky boy was one hunk of burning love in the AM, and she was all kinds of approving.

Keep it light, Minerva, she scolded herself, but it was no good. He was giving orders to someone—his foreman, maybe. Damn, he was sexy with those silver eyes gleaming in the December sun shining in from the RV's smallish kitchen windows.

"Rip it all out. I don't give a fuck, make it happen, River. Today," he snapped, ending the call with a huff as he dropped the phone back on the counter.

"River?" she asked, watching the big man's gaze focus on her with unerring efficiency. "River Daye?"

"You know him? Well, you would, I suppose, he is a Wolf—"

"Wow. So, what you think like all Wolves know each other?"

Minnie bit the inside of her cheek to keep from revealing the game too soon. The gruff mystery Shifter was too dang adorable, standing there with a look of abject horror on his sexy AF face.

Holy hotness was his cute, she thought with a growl in her throat as she approached. She did not know how he would dig himself out of his faux pas with words, but it was fun watching his face turn a ruddy color as he sucked in a breath.

"Look, of course I do not think that. I only meant—"

Too late. She cracked. Giggling, she touched his skin, helpless to do otherwise. He growled softly, nostrils flaring gently as she stepped right into his space.

"Shhh," she murmured.

Electricity sizzled between them, and Minnie pressed her mouth against his, stroking along the seam of his lips without her tongue until he allowed her entry. It was the best kind of high, being wrapped up in his arms and giving into her need to rub herself against his deliciously hard body. Fuck, this was going to be a problem. The man was addictive and so utterly masculine, he made her want to swoon.

Minnie was not the swooning type. A Werewolf rarely ever was, but there was something so heavy about him. Nicholas had a natural dominance that made her she-Wolf want to pant and rub her fur all over his body to bathe him in her scent.

Mmm. So good.

His face had paled so fast with her teasing, it would have been funny to drag it out, but something stopped her. It was ridiculous. Minerva was known for her ball-busting pranks, but she did not feel like yanking his chain. Right now, she wanted a little morning nooky, and maybe some cuddles afterwards, and this she-Wolf was not too proud to take them.

"What are you doing to me, minx?" he growled against her lips, cupping the back of her head as he pulled her in harder.

"Whatever you want me to," she replied, tugging his lower lip with her teeth and pushing him down into a nearby chair.

Minnie did not have any hangups over sex. She

was a physical being, and this was damn good fun if she ever saw it. A few shrugs and pulls, and she was astride him, burying his thick, long length all the way inside her soaked pussy. Even ready for him as she was, the man was so big, he stretched her to the limit.

"Feels so good," she moaned, arms wrapped around his neck as she rocked her hips, sucking him deep into her core.

After another shower and redressing in more borrowed clothes, the two of them took off for Minnie's house. She was surprised as they made their way across the sandy lot of his construction site, littered with clumps of snow, over to her house that there was a crew already hard at work.

"When did you do this?" she asked, shocked at what she was seeing.

A familiar face in the distance had her grinning and with no explanation, Minnie took off like a rocket, tackling a blast from her past into the compact sand and gravel driveway.

"Goddammit, Minnie!" River Daye yelled, groaning as he tried to pick himself up off the floor.

She was still giggling and had his legs tangled between hers. One move and he was on the ground again, spitting out a mouthful of rocks.

The sound of something angry and growling reached Minnie's ears, and she turned to see Nicholas baring down on them, eyes glowing a fantastic shade of orange as he hauled her off the ground and placed himself in front of her.

"What are you doing?" she asked, truly confused, but Nick was snarling at River, who was wisely averting his gaze from the huge man.

"Hey boss, that was all Minnie. I did not touch her—wait a second? You and her? You two? Oh shit. Sunny is gonna flip!" River exclaimed and clapped his hands.

"What the hell are you talking about? What are you even doing here, River?"

"Oh, well, I work for Graystone Builders now," he hedged, rubbing the back of his neck.

"Nick? How do you know Sunny? And stop all that damn growling. What the hell kind of Shifter are you?" she asked while the two men exchanged strange looks.

"How long till she can move in?" Nick asked, ignoring Minnie's questions.

"Tonight. I got a plumber fixing the pipes and the electricity and gas and water companies have all been alerted this place is going to be in use again," River said.

Well, that was nice. She hadn't expected Nicholas to put so much money into making the space livable for her. Biting her lip, she waited for the men to include her, but they were going on and on about some construction-y shit she could not follow.

"Will someone talk to me?" Minnie stomped her feet angrily, hands on her hips as she stared at the two big idiots.

Nick glanced at her, one perfectly sculpted eyebrow raised, and she barely contained her responding growl. The stupid, big, sexy man thought he could just ignore her, did he? He turned his head back to River and Minnie bent down and grabbed some dirty snow from the ground. She formed a ball and whacked him right upside his head.

Take that!

But the damn man merely wiped it off and kept right on talking to River. She growled and bent down again, making a bigger, sloppier snowball this time. When Minnie hurled it, Nicholas simply dodged his head. She didn't even shake his concentration with that one.

Grrrr.

"Give me a rundown, River," Nick said, crossing his arms and making the dark blue sweater he wore strain against his muscles.

Minnie exhaled sharply. She should not be so observant. Who cared if he was ripped? She was a Wolf, for fuck's sake. Most of the males she knew were devastatingly gorgeous and had muscles on their muscles.

But there was just something more about him. Nicholas was more than just six and a half feet of pure iron and sex appeal. He was sharp as a tack, funny, and powerful. Plus, he had damn near fucked her stupid and made her orgasm more in the last twelve hours than anyone else ever had.

"What about the rodents and cats?"

"Well, I took care of that, um, personally," River hedged, and the rapid rubbing of his neck increased.

"I see. Is that why it smells like Wolf piss?" Nicholas snarled.

"Well, Nick, sir, I mean, boss, *er—*"

The man's chest was getting all rumbly and, *damn*, Minnie felt that delicious purr zoom straight through to her core. Eek. He was jealous! But poor River, who was like a brother to her, should not bear the brunt of this surprising emotion.

"Thanks, Riv. Best way to get rid of unwanted pests, Nicky—Wolf piss." She affirmed with a nod of her head.

"See? She knows what I was doing." River's relief

was evident, but Nicholas still did not seem all that happy about it.

"Grrrrrrrrr," he stepped closer to the Wolf, eyes blazing and almost causing him to kneel under the pressure of his rage.

"Hey! I said he is right, Nicky. Now back off," she mumbled, pressing her hand to the man's impossibly buff chest.

Fuck. Did his muscles grow in the ten minutes since the last time she'd touched him? Lucky her.

Minnie huffed out a breath and stepped away, crossing her arms as she pretended interest in what the crew was doing. The other guys and one gal were not paying their odd little trio any mind.

Good.

She hated complications of any kind, and she also hated witnesses—and not necessarily in that order. Her reaction to seeing Nick's rage was definitely not easily explained. Protective instincts she did not even know she had rose immediately, and all she could think about was soothing him.

What the actual fuck?

She should not give two shits about Nicholas' feelings, or River's, for that matter. That Wolf was like the little brother she had never wanted, and Minnie already had some of those.

"Minerva, are you okay with muted colors for now?" Nicholas asked her, and she nodded absently.

Great. I finally found the perfect body to fuck me silly, and here I am getting caught up in the f word—feelings. Gross.

"Okay, muted it is, boss. So, we gutted the bedrooms first, and the studio. Installed all new flooring, put in two new toilets. The bones of this place were perfect. We had to take out some sheetrock, but it's all been replaced and primed. I know you said it needed to be livable immediately, so we sacrificed style for functionality, but anything she wants later can be added or changed."

"Good," Nick replied.

"Okay, Good. Uh, later Minnie, I gotta get back inside—" River ended abruptly and raced back to the crew.

"It's going to need a few hours before you can go in," Nick grumbled.

"What do we do until then?" she asked, eyebrow raised innocently.

Oh, the possibilities.

CHAPTER 6

"I thought you said this would be fun?" Nicholas growled as they walked to her ridiculously small car.

He had to admit, he liked the shape of the Camaro, but his bulk simply did not fit in the damn performance seats. He preferred his Dodge truck any day of the week.

"Don't you like shopping, Nicky?"

"No, and my name is Nicholas, or Nick. Not Nicky."

"Oh, come on, you didn't seem to mind when I called you that last night. Or this morning," she reminded him with a jaunty wink.

The she-Wolf was not wrong. When her curvy little body was wrapped around him anaconda style,

Nicholas did not care what she called him. Her body was a heaven he did not know he would find on this earth, and when he was with her that way, Nick was lucky if he even remembered his name.

Minerva Lykos was a dangerous woman. She commanded his attention like no other female in the universe. Even his beast seemed enthralled by the Werewolf. The fact she had not guessed what he was had become a sort of game that lasted through her shopping expedition. She'd spent the better part of the day tossing out the names of ridiculous species at him, and he feigned annoyed, but it was really amusing.

"Your excessive purchases will not fit in the trunk," he said, not knowing what to do with the things she'd insisted on buying.

"They are not excessive. Nothing in the house was useable. I need sheets and blankets and towels and dishes, Nicky," she said with an easy smile.

"Don't you have a friend who could have gone with you?"

"Aww, now I'm hurt. I thought we were friends," she replied with a naughty wink as she reversed the surprisingly powerful little car and raced out onto the highway.

Fucking hell. She was a speed demon, and

Nicholas could barely contain his growls as more of that awful Christmas music came blasting tinnily through the speakers. He'd never had cause to celebrate the holidays before, and though he had enjoyed the peppermint mocha latte, she'd thoughtfully purchased for him, Nick could do without all the damn wailing.

"Not a fan?" she asked, laughter in her voice as she spied him out of the corner of her eyes.

His lip curled, and he turned his head. Nick was grateful that, despite the chill, the sky was clear enough for her to take the top down. Convertibles in December might not work for humans, but the female was a Werewolf, and he hardly ever felt the cold. How could he when he had his own personal furnace inside of him?

The Dragon rumbled, and Nick realized that the monster inside him was content sitting beside her. Allowing her to drive, no need to wrest control or dominance—like the beast trusted her, or something. And wasn't that the most dangerous thing of all about the surprising she-Wolf?

"Turn here," he said, directing her to the house he had built with his brother.

"Oooh, are you taking me to your bat cave? Are

you a Bat Shifter?" she asked, clapping her hands down on the steering wheel.

"A what? Bat Shifter? No, I am not a Bat."

"Damn it, I was so hoping you flew. Oh well, back to the old drawing board," she murmured, driving down the private road that would take them to the private beachfront property owned by the Falk Clan brothers.

"*Ohmygawd.* Is that a castle?" she asked, gaping through the windshield.

"Yes. It belongs to the—"

"Falk brothers," she murmured. "I mean, I know about them, but I never met them. Are you guys friends or something?"

"Something," he muttered, standing up and grabbing the bag of purchases he had made while she'd been busy finding stuff to refurbish her house.

My house. That's the only reason I am doing this. For the property. Right?

"Wow! This is so cool. I wonder if I can make miniatures," she muttered, snapping some images of the castle.

"You should probably ask permission first."

"Oh, of course," she replied, jotting down some notes.

"Where are we going?" she asked, following behind him.

"To see if my brother is still home. Then over to the castle. I have to drop this off."

"Oh, but you didn't have to bring me along—"

"That's our deal, though. We be each other's plus ones," he replied easily.

This felt big. Important. And for some reason, Nicholas was simply not willing to go without her. the she-Wolf wanted easy, uncomplicated, but what she got was a Dragon looking for salvation.

Nicholas might not be a lot of things, but his beast was ready for a mate. He would make her a good one. He just had to show her they belonged together.

"Okayyy," she replied, dragging the word out.

"Don't pout, Minerva. You look like a sullen teenager," he teased, and the she-Wolf snapped her jaws at him.

"I'm not pouting, but I was hoping to get some work done this afternoon."

"You can do that, but let's give my crew some time to finish their jobs."

"They are working fast," she agreed, and he saw her glancing over the pics he'd had River send over.

Nicholas did not want the Wolf texting her

directly, he was not willing to look too closely at just yet. So, he'd had the male send him the photos, and he sent them on to her.

"How did you know this room was my old studio?" she asked, smirking as she ran her thumbnail over the image.

"Easy. I smelled clay and paint and fire in that room. I take it you started sculpting early?" he asked, holding the gate open for her to pass in front of him.

Christ, she smelled good. Wild like the wind that had flitted through her curls as she drove with no regard for the speed limit whatsoever. Sweet like the cookies they'd gobbled down in the food court. And savory like the deep throated kisses he'd given her against the car door in the parking lot when he could not let another minute go by without touching her.

She was warm and receptive to his need to touch and kiss her throughout the day. Nicholas had never been openly mushy, had always kept passionate interludes behind closed doors, but she was doing things to him he hardly recognized.

He was smiling more, taking time out of his day to do things like go shopping. He'd even picked up a game console and extra remotes so they could play together. Truth was, Nick found her company downright enjoyable, even with the sappy Christmas music she kept blasting just to annoy him.

"Okay, let's make another deal," she began, skipping ahead of him—*and yes*, he meant skipping.

She was carefree, and gorgeous, she bounded up the stairs, wiggling her sweet little butt in front of him, and fuck, if he did not want to lean over and take a nibble.

"Don't we already have a deal, minx?"

"Yes, and fun smexy times aside, I need a model."

"A what?" he barked the question, letting her enter the house he had built with his brother first.

"A model. I have a deadline and with only a few days to fill it, I'm gonna need some fodder for my creativity. The castle is good, and I can do more Wolves, easy peasy, but I want something else, and I am thinking you are it, Nicky boy., What do you say?"

"If I model for you, what do I get?"

"You get me," she replied quickly, and something primal inside of him went still. "I mean, you get me at your beck and call for things like this, without the proper heads up, mind you," she replied, squinting at him. "I mean, would it have killed you to let me know we were needed somewhere?"

"Why should you need a heads up?" he asked, cocking his head to the side, and looking her over.

She'd bought the cutest little skintight sweater dress at the mall that hit just above her knees. The soft fabric molded to her incredible body, and Nick had been sporting a boner the entire fucking time they'd been out. She'd paired the ensemble with brown knee high leather boots that made him think all manner of naughty thoughts.

"To get ready, of course. I mean, luckily, I got this dress and these boots, but I am still not wearing any underwear since they did not have the ones I like, and I left my clean clothes at the house—"

"Minerva," he growled, and faster than either of them could blink, he was on her.

No. Underwear. Fuucckk.

Pushing her against the wall, Nicholas bent his head and captured her lips in one of those soul-searing kisses he simply could not get enough of. His dick was hard and ready, and when he reached between her thighs, his fingers parted her silky wet folds. She was hot and needy, moaning as he shoved two fingers deep inside her heat.

"Fuck, that feels good," she moaned, and his beast snarled appreciatively.

In and out, he finger-fucked her in the middle of

the communal kitchen, aware that no one was home, or he'd never have started this with her. But once begun, he could hardly stop. Fuck that. Couldn't wasn't right. No, he *wouldn't* stop. Not until she fell apart in his arms.

"More," she breathed into his mouth, clinging to him as he bit her lower lip, moving down to her neck, and falling to the floor at her feet. He pushed the dress up, eyes fixed on her honey slit and the way she was rocking her hips against his hand.

"You are so beautiful like this, minx," he growled, leaning forward to lick that tiny, hooded nubbin that was peeking at him beneath her short-cropped curls.

Her heady flavor burst across his tongue. Cotton candy wine and peppermint wind, he growled and lapped at her, adding that deep vibration to the mix. And that was when she lost her mind. Gripping his free hand around one thick thigh, Nicholas lifted it over his shoulder, allowing himself better access. Minnie's fingers threaded through his hair as she pulled him closer, grinding against his hand and face with abandon, and fuck, she was glorious like this. He knew before this was going to be different That she was going to be different. But he had not under-stood just how different until right at this moment.

Nicholas had thought he was too damn damaged

to believe in happiness. He was too jaded for happy ever afters. At least, he had been until he met her. With one last lap, Minerva's back arched, her orgasm rushing over her.

He pulled his fingers out, turned her around, bent at the waist, palms flat against the wall, and had his cock buried deep inside her faster than she could scream his name. This was what perfection felt like. This was destiny.

"Fuck," he snarled, gripping her hips tightly as he withdrew and slammed back home, spurring on another release, larger than the last.

Momentous. Perfect. Hot and needy.

Minnie was everything he never knew he wanted. Her pussy squeezed him tightly. This was what he needed. A mate who could match him pound for pound, bite for bite, without coddling or pretense. Nick's orgasm blast through him like TNT, exploding throughout his body. Drawing it out as long as he could for both of them, he rocked into her, sliding his still hard dick inside her slick heat until they both sank to their knees.

Nicholas had been searching for a mate for most of his adult life, actively so over the past few weeks, but he never expected her to show up when he had just about given up hope. Minnie was raunchy and earthy. A dynamite female and he wanted to possess her. but at the same time he loved her independent spirit and her giving nature. She probably did not think that about herself, but Nick could tell she was one of those who gave more than she got in return.

No more though. Nick was determined to give her everything. To keep that sexy little smile of hers in place as long as he lived. He thanked the gods he'd found her when he did. Losing himself in her body was such sublime bliss but feeling the need to earn her heart was everything.

This was so much more than what she'd proposed. So much bigger than he ever dared to dream. This was real. This was now. This was theirs.

He just had to convince her.

Es meus.

CHAPTER 7

"Minnie!" Sunny yelled from inside the enormous sitting room at Castle Falk.

She gasped at the change in her best friend. Sunny had always had a disposition to match her name, but the brown eyed, braless, sometimes self-deprecating hippy she-Wolf she'd grown up with had been transformed into a gorgeous and positively glowing woman who exuded confidence and happiness.

"Sunny? OMG! You look radiant!" Minnie gasped, leaning in for a hug.

"Thanks," her bestie replied easily, eyes going wide when she saw the man standing behind her.

"Oh Sunny, this is Nick," she said, making introductions.

"No shit, it's Nick! I know Nick, Minnie," she replied, snorting her disbelief. "But how do you know Nick?"

"Hello, Sunny. I brought Minerva for the Outreach program party. Where is my brother?" Nicholas asked, and Minnie's eyes went wide.

"Wait a second? You know Sunny. And you are mated to his brother, and you told me you were mated to a Dr-Dragon? You're a fucking Dragon!" she screeched, drawing several pairs of eyes glancing their way.

"Yes. I am a Dragon. Is that alright?" he asked in a low voice, fiery eyes concerned.

Yessssss, her she-Wolf replied readily, which was odd cause she was usually blasé about Minnie's bedmates. And yet—Nicholas was more than that. Even though it pained her to admit it.

"Minnie," Sunny hissed, and her eyes went wide as she realized he was still staring at her, the original concern in his stare was now tinged with sadness. Fuck. He probably thought she was rejecting him.

"Fuck yes, it is alright. It's fucking outstanding," she said and bit her lip. "Will you show me later?" she whispered and could almost feel him relaxing by the second.

"Yes. My Dragon wants to meet you too. I will

show you later, *minx*," he growled and kissed her quickly.

Minerva spent the next half hour being introduced to the entire Falk Clan and their mates and children, along with greeting some high profile members of the Macconwood Pack. She was enjoying a glass of eggnog while she observed some of the art on display by the *Macconwood-Nighthawk Teen Outreach Program*.

"These are really good," she mused, looking over some small figurines that graced a table set up to look like a miniature of Maccon City.

"It's a *Maccon City Christmas*. My girlfriend Grace came up with it," a young man said, approaching her with a timid looking girl next to him. "Marty, and this is Grace," he said, offering his free hand.

"You're Minerva Lykos, the sculptor," Grace whispered, blue eyes wide as she stared at Minnie.

"Yeah, I am. You know me?"

"I know your work. My mom took me to the city to see one of your shows before she, um, that is—"

Minnie's heart squeezed inside her chest, and she reached out and clapped the girl gently on the shoulder. She smelled fur and pine needles and recognized the two as Werewolves without needing to be told. The reputation of the Outreach Program was known by everyone in the Pack. Minnie was proud to belong to a group of Shifters who were dedicated to helping those in need.

"Well, you are both very talented. Tell me which ones are yours," she said, turning her attention to the display.

The kids were clever, she would give them that. The tiny replicas of the town had been made using all recycled materials, and the attention to detail was uncanny. The inhabitants were where they'd really had some fun, she mused, looking at all the two-legged Wolves, Bears, Tigers, Lions, Jersey Devils, and Dragons walking about town. The result was whimsical and fun, fat snowflakes littered the ground, and a tall evergreen was lit up right in the center of town.

"This is great," a deep, familiar voice said from behind her, and Minnie turned so quickly she almost toppled over, but Nick's hand reached out to steady her.

His silver eyes were blazing, rimmed in orange flames, glowing bright with his beast, and something warm unfurled inside of her. Damn. He was sexy, and caring, and sweet. And she should not be having thoughts like that about a fuck buddy.

"Thanks Mr. Graystone!" Marty exclaimed, his

hand in Grace's, who was blushing furiously. "Well, Ms. Lykos, maybe you can come to our studio at the center someday and give us some tips," the precocious young Wolf said and winked before tugging Grace along with him to line up for cookies and hot cocoa.

"Talented kids," Nick muttered, not releasing her arm as he guided her towards a table heavily laden with all kinds of delicious little yummies.

He handed her a dish and started filling her plate with things, lifting the tongues and gesturing, mindful when she nodded, and when she scrunched her nose in a firm no.

"So, you like crab stuffed mushrooms, but not pimento cheese spread. That's a yes to the black olives, no to the green," he murmured, one hand on the small of her back as he offered more selections.

Minnie liked this game, and that was troubling since she'd never been the kind of girl who needed coddling from a man. But there was something about when he did it that felt different. Nick was not being condescending, he was taking care of her and that was as surprising as it was welcomed.

"You know, I would have guessed Dragon eventually," she said, biting the piece of battered and fried asparagus he held to her lips. "That's good!"

"It is, right? Noelle, Sander's mate, owns a catering company. It's how they met, actually," he told her as he made his own plate.

Minnie waited until they both held two plates overflowing with goodies, and laughing, they found a pair of empty seats at the long table in the formal dining room. There had to be a hundred people there, milling about the ornate halls of Castle Falk, but there was nothing pretentious about it.

"Look at all these children," Minnie commented with her eyes wide.

They were simply adorable and ranged in ages from toddlers to teens. A couple of older ones were reading Christmas stories and acting them out as they sat around one of the several large Christmas trees decorated throughout.

"Yes, it is a miracle, isn't it?" Nicholas replied, his silver-fire stare zeroing in on her. "I never thought I would live to see the day where so many supernaturals produced offspring so prolifically. Gives me hope."

She snorted her response, and Nick cocked his head to the side, watching her carefully.

"Explain that sound," he murmured, voice hushed as he waited for her answer.

"Well, you're right. I mean, Nick, I have never

seen so many happy young together either. It wasn't very long ago that Wolves had a terrible time of it. Just a few years, really. My parents," she said, hating the way her voice hitched.

She cleared her throat, closing her eyes at the way he brushed his fingers up her spine in a soothing touch. "My parents were beside themselves when they suffered a miscarriage after my birth. Then they had my brothers," she added with a sad smile.

"Brothers?"

"Oh yeah, I have brothers—well, let me back up. I have an older sister. Artemis was born first, then there is me, and then the twins. Damien is two years younger than me. His twin, Angel, never made it past that first day," she whispered, sadness at the loss damn near drowning her. "There was a complication. The midwife couldn't do anything, and the risk was too great for them to try again. My mother had to have an emergency hysterectomy a little while letter when the hemorrhaging got so bad."

"I am so sorry, Minerva. Devine and I are the only two surviving offspring of our sire and dame. Of her ten pregnancies, only five were viable, and three did not survive puberty. That was centuries ago, of course, but the memory of her pain and father's sorrow is still fresh in my mind. Apologies, sweet Wolf, I did not mean to make you sad."

"I know you didn't," she said, reassuring him with her words and a squeeze of her hand on his leg. "And it's okay, really. It was a long time ago. No one expects that kind of thing, of course, but the family has grieved about it and gone to counseling together, so we are good now. But thank you for your kindness," she told him, meaning every word.

"Kindness? Who me?" he asked, eyebrows disappearing into his hairline. "Woman, I am the gnarliest, grumpiest beast on the entire East coast."

"I call bullshit, Nicky. You have to be the softest-hearted, mushiest, touchy feely Dragon in the universe."

"Oh, am I? I'll show you how touchy feely I am," he growled playfully, then tickle-tortured her until she damn near peed herself.

"Nicholas? Is that you? And are you actually smiling?" a huge man with a booming voice said and clapped Nicholas on the shoulder.

"Hello, I'm Minnie," she said, grinning at the new addition to their group.

"Ah, the elusive Minerva. I have heard many tales of terror from your youthful exploits," the man stated mysteriously.

He looked very much like Nick except that he was taller, and not as wide. She liked him. He seemed friendly and genuinely surprised to see his brother having fun.

Interesting.

"I'm Devine Graystone, Sunny's mate."

"And that would explain the knowing about my bad kid days," she muttered.

"Indeed, it does. So, how do you know my brother, then? He is not the friendliest of beasts, and never strays from his routines, but here he is. At Castle Falk, mingling and laughing, and all without a decree from the Alpha, imagine that?"

"Dev," Nick warned, but Minnie was too curious to remain silent.

"Oh, well, that's easy. Nicholas hates bullshit, and well, I propositioned him to be fuck buddies for the holidays. That way we don't have to do any of these rapidly increasing—*and for some reason mandatory*—get togethers alone. So, we scratch each other's backs—*and other stuff*—and *bang*! Happy fucking Holidays, Devvy," she replied baldly.

Minnie batted her eyelashes, smiling brightly at the dozens of, *thankfully adult*, eyes that were now zeroed in on her and Nicholas. Devine gaped at her for a full ten seconds before he was laughing so hard, she thought he would bring down the whole damn house.

"Fucking hell," her grumpy Dragon grumbled while his brother continued to laugh so hard, the man was crying actual tears.

"Oh, Nick. Nick! She is perfect. Thank you, Minnie, I do believe you just gave me my first Christmas present of the year—"

"Hey, I thought I did that this morning?" Sunny asked, joining them with a grin and four glasses off spiked eggnog precariously balanced in her hands.

"My love, you are the only gift I will ever want or need," Devine replied, taking the glasses from her, and handing them out before dipping down to kiss her so thoroughly, Minnie had to look away.

Wow. Her best friend had definitely lucked out. The Dragon was so obviously in love with her, it was palpable. She swallowed a huge gulp of the frothy beverage, loving the way it burned going down.

"Are you alright?" Nicholas asked, seemingly unaffected by the way she'd introduced herself to his brother.

Shit. She did not deserve his ready forgiveness. Minnie had behaved badly. Anytime anyone tried to make her admit to feelings or put her in a tight spot, Minnie sabotaged herself by being a loudmouth. It was her coping mechanism, but for the first time, she felt guilty about it.

"Nick, I'm sorry if I embarrassed you—"

"Embarrassed me? When?"

"With your brother, you know, when I kinda said we were fuck buddies in front of everyone here," she said, cocking her head to the side.

He was there. It happened two seconds ago. Maybe the Dragon was crazy or something.

"Minerva, everyone here heard you. Supernaturals have that tendency, as I assume you well know, but my hide is not that thin as to have your harmless teasing hurt me—"

"No, I know. I mean, sometimes, my mouth runs away with me, but I did not mean to cause any hard feelings," she said, standing up and placing her dirty dish in a bin a passing server was carrying while Nick stood to do the same.

She started walking into the next room, but he caught her in the hallway. His cocky grin was her undoing, and Minnie allowed herself to be gently pushed into a dark corner, where Nick nipped her lip with his teeth before plunging his tongue into her mouth. He tasted like fire and eggnog and delicious man, and Minnie could not get enough.

"Little minx, the only hard thing between us is

this," he rumbled into her ear, leaning close enough so she could feel the steel rod in his pants press against her hip. "Stop worrying you offended me. Besides, even if you did, don't you know what Dragons do to naughty little minxes with sharp tongues?"

"What?" she asked, eyes dancing with mischief.

"We eat them," he snarled, and turned on his heel, leaving her to follow him.

Her sex tingled and heart pounded. The man was driving her nuts with his innuendos and constant touches. Hell, he'd gotten her off twice that day already, but by the time they left the party, she was a quivering, needy little mess.

But damn. What a way to go!

CHAPTER 8

"It looks great!" Minerva raced from room to room, her happiness so bright it was like a semi-visible little bubble of joy had enveloped the petite she-Wolf.

Nicholas watched her with equal parts want and need. Slow was not the norm for their kind, and yet, he seemed to be operating on a level faster than Minerva. His Dragon was done searching. She was the one for him.

His topaz rose. His chosen. His maiden fair. His mate. Es meus.

But why didn't she seem to know it? He exhaled slowly as he picked up the list River had left him. Things had progressed much faster than he'd expected of the young Wolf he had only recently hired to work for Graystone Builders. Sunny's brother had more than proven himself in the last few weeks. He was honorable, reliable, and he knew better than to leave his scent around the house of a Dragon's mate.

He'd damn near laughed aloud when Minerva had asked him if all the bleach had been necessary, and he'd replied with some noncommittal answer about mold.

Truth was, River had downed the exterior in commercial grade bleach to remove his Wolf's urine and had set up some normal, humane traps for the pests that had plagued the property in Minnie's absence. He scented nary a one now, and even better, the crew's lingering scents had also been cleared out of the dwelling.

Good. Very good.

Nicholas had yet to explain the change in his intentions to his mate. He would have to, of course. His Dragon was already pushing him to claim her sooner rather than later, and the beast would not wait long. His chest rumbled, anticipation building as he thought of what it was going to be like to finally have someone of his own.

"Don't use the upstairs shower yet," he called after her. "The caulking has to cure overnight."

"What? Okay, no shower," she said, running to the top floor landing.

"I'm glad we stopped at the laundromat and pre-washed all the bedding and linens. Come help me get this on," she yelled down to him.

Nicholas mounted the stairs, finding her in the master bedroom with no difficulty at all. This room had been in the best shape, and after a little paint and polish, he'd ordered a new mattress for the original four poster bed the crew had spent the better part of the afternoon refurbishing.

"This mattress," she said, and sighed as she tucked in her side of the pink rosebud patterned sheets she'd bought earlier that day.

"Smells good," he rumbled, liking the fresh spring clean scent of the detergent, and the fact it did not mask her own unique fragrance.

"Mmm. This is the only soap that does not interfere with my Wolf's senses," she told him, unfolding the large coverlet and shaking it out before they spread it over the top. Minnie heaved a happy sigh and lay down right on top of it.

"What color is she? Your Wolf," he qualified and settled down beside her.

Minnie rolled onto her side, and Nicholas did the same, taking a moment to memorize every centimeter of her pretty little face. Her eyes were dancing in that naughty little way she had, and he knew he would not get much of an answer.

"Oh, you teased me for a day about your animal and I'm supposed to just tell you everything about myself?"

"Sounds good to me, minx," he said and leaned over to catch her earlobe with his teeth.

Minnie giggled and struggled beneath him, and he allowed her to gain the upper hand, wrestling him onto his back. His hands cupped her ass, playing along the crack. She'd changed into a pair of light pajama pants and a tank top, and all her curves were on perfect display, tantalizing him with peaks of pert valleys and kissable mounds.

"You are so beautiful," he said when she settled her covered sex over his own hardened staff, throbbing need.

"Mmm, I bet you say that to all the maidens," she remarked and moved to kiss him, but Nicholas held her still.

"No, Minerva. Only you. No one else but you."

Then he was kissing her, and relentlessly so. Losing himself in the warm, intoxicating, and utterly sweet female who was claiming ownership of his Dragon's heart.

Her phone chirped, and damn, he wanted to crush the thing so it would just leave them alone, but she had work, was on a deadline, and so, he let her answer it even when she would have continued kissing him. He knew all about impatient mates, and demanding ones too. Had seen it happen repeatedly, and he wanted much more than a mad race to a mating that would burn them both.

Minerva was a she-Wolf, powerful and deadly in her own right. Yes, he wanted to put her in a bubble and protect her from the world, but that was not the right way to win her heart and get her to accept his claim. He had to show her he respected her as a person, as an artist, as a Wolf. Had to allow her room to grow and be content with knowing he would be there when she was finished, cheering her on from his seat beside her. That was what he wanted. A partner. A best friend. A lover who knocked his socks off. Minerva. He wanted Minerva.

"Deirdre? Yes, no, he is definitely fired. Do not give him access to shit," she snarled, and Nicholas grinned.

Was it wrong he got hard seeing her go all badass? Maybe. But he did not think so. His sexy sweet Minerva was about to carve someone a new asshole, and he had front row seats. As far as

Nicholas was concerned, this was just another facet of the incredible female the Fates, the man, and his Dragon had chosen to be his mate.

Es meus, the beast hissed inside his mind's eye.

Oh yes, Nicholas would content himself beside her, waiting while she handled her business. If she needed him, he was there, but he knew better than to interfere with her work stuffs.

His Dragon was in full agreement. He would wait till she was done, then he would tell her his plans, and if she refused now, well then, he would simply wait some more. For her, Nicholas would wait forever.

"That sonovabitch," she snarled into the phone. "I will be in first thing in the morning, until then, I am sending someone to watch the warehouse. Yeah. No. Okay," she muttered and clicked end on her call.

"What happened?" he asked, rubbing small circles on her lower back to ease some of her tension.

"Roger that douche canoe! He tricked the part-time manager of the gallery into allowing him access to the storeroom for my showing. The motherfucker broke three of the figurines that had already been set aside for a big buyer. He also took the cashbox that held payments for pieces that were bought. One of my customers only pays cash for his art."

"How much?"

"This time? Thirty-five thousand. The rest usually pay by check, and he took those too. These customers are my most loyal collectors. It doesn't look like Roger has cashed any of the checks yet, but the gallery owner is appalled by the idea of calling these people to tell them they need to cancel their checks and reissue. I agree with her. It's bad business. Fucking prick," she growled, rubbing the space between her eyes.

"I know you don't need it, Minerva, but if you would allow me, I would like to help you."

"Really? I mean, are you sure? Cause I really could use a hand. I have to remake the figures that sold like right now, so the customers have them in time," she muttered, her eyes blazing gold with her Wolf.

Fuck. Nicholas hated that she was hurt by this asshole, and he really wanted to help. But he was also shocked by how she was handling this mess. Instead of crying over what the stolen money meant to her, she was worried about upsetting her customers. Minerva was not pitching a fit over her broken art or whining about her lost work. She was more concerned for those who bought it would not have the pieces they'd wanted in time.

"Will you be able to replicate the pieces?" he asked, truly curious.

"Yes," she grinned. "I sort of have a photographic memory when it comes to my work. But even if I didn't, I catalog everything with sketches and pictures. I know these pieces well. I can redo them quickly."

"That's amazing."

"Well, the design takes the longest. Sometimes I can think on a subject for months and months before I ever try to create it with my hands. Once I have it perfectly arranged in my brain, then the execution comes fast. At least, for me it does," she explained.

Minerva's cheeks turned pink under his watchful stare. He liked her like this, talking about the things she loved doing best. Damn, she was beautiful.

"You're amazing," he murmured, touching her cheek with the back of his fingers. "Now, while you are busy creating, I will go see Roger. Do you have any idea where he is?"

"Actually, I know most of Roger's haunts. He just got his hands on a ton of my cash, so if I know him, that asshole is out stuffing twenties into every stripper's thong he can get his slimy paws on at this seedy club called *Wet Heat*."

"*Wet Heat?* Charming," Nick replied.

"It's this shady mobbed up club run by old timey gangsters. I went once and never again. I hated the way they treated the dancers there, and I told Roger how I felt, he told me he would never go again. Lies, of course," she said. "You know, I am so sorry to involve you. I mean, you're supposed to be this fun booty call guy, not my problem solver—"

"We can talk about that later," he replied. "So, my plan is to close out Roger's tab once and for all —good?"

"Yeah. I mean, I am not funding his ass any longer," she agreed. "But Nicky, he is human—"

"I get it. No flame-broiling his sorry ass. I'll just get the box back and make sure he knows not to mess with you again, okay?"

"Okay. Thanks. I, um, I never had anyone do this kind of thing for me before. My Pack is great, but it's so huge. I always distanced myself from the other Wolves, except for Sunny. My work in the art world means dealing with mostly humans, so I was just around them more, I guess. What I am trying to say, is thank you," Minerva said with a shaky laugh, blinking up at him with those gorgeous eyes of hers.

Nick stood up and kissed her hard and fast,

loving the way she immediately opened for him. He pinched her butt, grinning at her sharp squeal.

"Have everything you need to work on your art?"

"Yep. Brought it all the other day, and River fixed up my old studio, so I can get started as soon as you leave."

It was late, almost midnight, but his beast was wide awake and itching for vengeance, even if it was only a puny human who'd wronged her. No one fucked with Nicholas' mate. He caught a flash of flame-rimmed silver in the mirror and closed his eyes to wrangle his beast back under his control.

Above all, the Shifter secret was to be kept, but that did not mean Nick couldn't have a little fun with the bastard, did it?

"You'll call me when you're finished, right?" Minnie called.

"Yessss," he replied, his voice thick and guttural.

"Just get the box and make sure he knows this is over. Nothing crazy, right?" she asked, uncertainty in her big brown eyes.

"Whatever you say, minx."

"Okay, good."

Grrrrr.

CHAPTER 9

Minnie was waiting for the clay to finish baking in the kiln before she began painting the last of the three figurines that Roger had broken.

Of the three, this was the only one she had done in clay. The other two were a mix of wires and fabric string. That was the thing about sculpting, anything was her medium. Because of the holidays, she'd turned her attention to celestial beings like angels and constellations, bringing them to life with anything that took her fancy.

All day, though, she'd been dying to ask Nicholas for permission to use his form in her work. A hunk of stone Sunny had sent over to her sat in the corner of the room with a note identifying it as some kind of quartz. The silver, red, orange, and gold swirled through the beautiful specimen, reminding her of Nicholas' eyes.

Ever since she'd seen it, Minnie had associated the stone with Nick. The seed was already planted, she just needed to confirm her imaginings with actual visual representation of Nick's Dragon. Anticipation made her shiver, and she inhaled slowly, sipping tea as she tried to clear her mind.

He'd texted her an hour ago, stating he'd found Roger at the strip club and had everything handled, but Nicholas still had not returned. Her phone buzzed from its place on the worktable, and she turned to see a text coming in from Sunny.

SUNNY

Minnie? Nick texted Devine to run an errand with him hours ago, but he still isn't back. What is going on?

MINNIE

Sorry Sunny, I should have known he would call his brother. Nothing to worry about, they just went to get some things Roger took from me.

SUNNY

That creep stole from you again?

MINNIE

Yeah. Fucking asshole broke some of my sold pieces, too. I am finishing up new ones now.

SUNNY

OMG! I am so sorry, Min. That bites.

MINNIE

It's okay. I just don't want the customers to be disappointed.

SUNNY

I know how you are.

MINNIE

So, how's mated life?

SUNNY

OMG, Min. Devine is the best. I am soooo happy. And I can't wait to hear all about you and Nicholas. Has he claimed you yet? When are you going to tell your parents?

MINNIE

Whoa! Down girl. Not happening. We're just friends. Friends with benefits, Sunny.

SUNNY

I am calling you.

Minnie sighed and waited for the phone to ring. She put it on speaker so she could work with her hands while they chatted. Some folks needed peace and quiet to create, but Minnie was a little more chaotic than that. It was a quality some critics remarked was the only human thing about her work.

"Friends with benefits? Are you fucking kidding me? I saw the way you watched him at the party today, Min. I have never seen you like that. You looked happy, and at ease, and you were laughing, for fuck's sake—"

"Sunny, slow your roll," Minnie muttered into the phone.

"Slow my roll? Minnie, you love him. Admit it," her annoying BFF demanded.

"Okay, you're crazy. Multiple orgasms do not a love match make!" Minnie shouted, completely shocked by Sunny's declaration.

"There is more to life than sex, Min."

"Really, like what? Sunny, I love you and you are my best friend. Hell, you're more sister to me than Artemis, but you need to stop your crazy talk."

"Fine. Don't believe me. But Minnie, these Graystone brothers aren't like your other guys. These Dragons are tough to crack, but when they do, they stick for good," Sunny said softly.

Unease welled within Minnie as she bid Sunny

goodnight. This was not how things were supposed to go. Nicholas had busted into her life on a particularly chaotic night, and he'd seemed like the perfect distraction. She was a woman who prided herself on knowing what she wanted out of life.

Career as an artist? Done. Life outside the Pack? Have at it. Sex without strings? Yeppers.

Approaching Nicholas with her proposal might have been forward or even bizarre for a normal, but Minnie was a Wolf. Sex without emotional attachment was not new to her, but for some reason, thinking about Nick like that made her heart squeeze painfully. Sunny's words suddenly drifted through her brain—*you love him.*

"I do not!" she exclaimed aloud.

Only Minnie could hear her own lie within her words. Nicholas was so much more than a hot body to ride until New Year's Day. He was sexy and fun, and she loved teasing the grumpy man till he rewarded her with one of his thousand watt grins. They'd known each other for so short a time, but she'd already told him everything about herself. Including her humiliating experience with Roger the Creep.

When she'd told her brother about what

happened, he'd laughed at her, and Artemis had told Minnie it was her own fault.

"That's what you get messing with a human."

True, she'd always dated humans, but that was because of her close proximity with them for her work. People in that world were mostly all human, with a few rare exceptions.

She'd never been able to truly be herself around them, keeping the Shifter secret was of course one of the most important jobs of their kind. History had proven time and again that normals could not deal with the existence of supernaturals on a global level. Most of those previous incidents had been handled by the experts.

Humans and supes could fall in love, of course, but it had never happened for her. Maybe because Minnie was always holding back. Being with a Dragon sure had its perks. For one thing, Minerva did not have to hold back with Nicholas.

She could tell him anything, say anything about being a Shifter, and he was okay with it. Eating had always been an issue since she could never eat her full capacity in front of normal boyfriends, but with Nick, he not only anticipated her appetite when he'd piled food onto her plate, but he appreciated it as well if his purring growls and the bites of food he'd hand fed her were anything to go by. Then there was the sex.

Holy fucking cow. Sex was usually just icing on the cake in her not so humble opinion. But sex with Nicholas was beyond anything she'd ever experienced.

He was the perfect combination of rough and tender, insatiable and fulfilling. His carnal knowledge of her body made her tremble with memories of his sweet kisses, sizzling caresses, and incomparable body.

When she'd given herself to him, Minnie had done so with open eyes. Regret was not part of her vocabulary, and she did not for a moment think she'd made a mistake with him. But what if Sunny was right?

The wheels in her head began turning and panic took hold. Where was he? It had been hours and Nicholas hadn't called or returned. What if something had happened?

Her stomach turned with worry, and she paced. Was this love then? This feeling of going crazy, losing her mind with worry, and helplessness without a word from him. Is this anxiety ridden panic for another person really what love was about? If so, then Minnie did not want it.

Fuck. Fuck. FUCK.

The timer on the oven chimed, and she turned to remove it from the heat. Cool. Paint, Glaze, and then back inside. She spent the next few hours doing just that.

The clock chimed five by the time the front door opened, and Minnie had worked herself up into such a state she did something unforgivable when she met him at the door. Minerva Lykos covered her mouth with her hand, and she cried.

"Minerva, what's wrong?" Nicholas' eyes churned with worry as he dropped a bag on the floor inside the door. He was covered in snowflakes and his cheeks were ruddy with cold.

"This is your fault!" she yelled and stormed away.

"What are you talking about? Hold on a sec," he growled and took off after her.

But she was not about to stop. She couldn't. Minnie was having a full blown panic attack, and all because her no-strings attached policy was being blown to smithereens by a sexy Dragon.

"Minerva," Nicholas snarled when he came upon her in the bedroom.

She was grabbing some clean clothes and stuffing them into her bag. This was not right. She had to leave before she was permanently stuck on this man.

This big, beautiful man who had the power to hurt her more than anyone else.

"No. Nuh uh. No way. Not doing this," she muttered.

"What is going on? What changed?"

"Nothing. Everything. This was supposed to be no strings."

"Have I done something wrong, Minerva? I have made no demands," he said, and she slowed her movements.

Fuck. He was right. Nicholas had not asked her for a single thing. He had done everything she said, and more. And that was what hurt the worst.

"You did nothing wrong, Nick. I did."

"What are you saying?" he asked, eyes blazing silver as he looked at her.

"I fell in love with you," she confessed, allowing her tears to spill down her cheeks. "I didn't mean to. Sunny pointed it out, and I denied it, but then you didn't come home, and I worried. Me. I, I worried. I never worry, Nicky! Never ever. But I worried about you, and I feel all twisted up inside and I think I must be dying, or something, cause this sucks, and I know it is my fault, but I can't do casual with you. I just can't," she finished, slumping to the floor, and burying her face in her hands.

CHAPTER 10

Nick walked into *Wet Heat* with his brother Devine following closely. The place reeked of humans and something else in the darkness near the stage where females writhed on long metal poles in next to nothing.

He spied his prey front and center, waving around hundred-dollar bills that did not belong to him, and Nick's inner beast snarled angrily. He wanted nothing more than to take the human outside and burn him to ashes with a single shot of his flames, but Nicholas knew better,

"Not here," Devine whispered from beside him.

Movement to his right caught his attention, and soon two enormous men were blocking his path.

Devine grinned, his brother itching for a brawl, but Nicholas needed to keep his head.

"Boss asked us to bring you over," one male muttered.

"Make it quick. I have business here," Nick growled, motioning for the men to lead the way.

He was brought to a corner table where a beefy barrel-chested male sat smoking a cigar and watching the dancers. He smelled of fur and musk, a dank combination in the darkly lit establishment.

"Youse two coming into my territory unannounced, looking for trouble, that ain't good," the male stated.

"We are not looking for trouble, Mr.?"

"Call me Tiny."

"Well, Tiny, we are not here for trouble, but you see that human there?"

"Who, Roger? Yeah, I see him."

"He stole from my mate, but before I go any further, introductions perhaps?"

"Tiny DeGrassi, this is my club. That's Lou and that's Vino. We're part of the Gennaro family."

"Mafia?" Devine whispered.

"Silverbacks," Nicholas replied and grinned.

"That's right," Tiny said. "And you are?"

"Falk Clan."

The large man's eyebrows raised, and he nodded. Clearly, they had heard of the New World Dragon Clan, and Nicholas was glad. Silverbacks were a rare Shifter breed, and he would have hated to wage war on these men for interfering with his protecting Minerva.

"Glad to meet youse. So, what I know about that prick Roger is he came in today waving around money like he hit the lotto. I collected a debt he owed me and let him stay for the show. Is this money your mate's?" Tiny asked, shaking his head.

"Yes, I imagine it is," Nicholas replied. "You can keep your money, Tiny. I just need a word with Roger."

"Certainly. How about the back room?"

"Perfect," Nick replied and offered the Gorilla Shifter a small bow.

He followed Vino to the back with his brother, Devine, and ten minutes later, Roger was brought in. The human smelled like piss and fear, a combination that made Nicholas want to spit on the floor.

"Roger, is it?"

"Y-yeah, I'm Roger. Who the fuck are you, man?"

Nicholas did not tolerate rudeness from a lot of people, and Roger certainly was not one of them. He gritted his teeth and glared at the idiot male who was clutching a small metal box in one hand, like a child holding a lunch box, and trying to look tough doing it.

"Devine. Box."

His brother came out of the shadows and ripped the box from the human's weak grip. This was going to be easier than Nick thought.

How disappointing.

"Fuck, man! You came outta nowhere. Give that back. It's mine!"

"We both know better than that, Roger. And for the next five minutes I am going to show you exactly why you are not going to go near Minerva Lykos again," Nicholas growled, and his chest heated up dangerously with his Dragon's fire.

"What? OMG! What are you? Ahhhhhhhh!"

It seemed the weak-minded human had a fear of fire and physical altercations. Who knew?

Good thing for Nick that Roger's screams were covered up by the pulsating bass of the music coming from the club. By the time Nick was finished convincing the human not to utter a word about any of this and to leave Minnie alone, Tiny was waiting for them by the door.

"Thank you, Tiny, for the use of your backroom. I suggest not allowing Roger to build up any debt with you after this, since his well has officially run dry."

"Got it. Take care, fellas."

"Thank you. Good night."

He walked to the truck with Devine, placing the metal box in a grocery bag in the back seat. His Dragon was anxious and unhappy, the beast had truly wanted to finish the scumbag off, but he could not do that. Minnie had specifically asked him not to. As if he knew what the male needed, Devine snorted a challenge and Nicholas turned to face his brother.

"Want to do this here? Now?" Nicholas asked, already grinning.

"We can come back for the car, brother. What say you?"

"I say, get ready to lose!" he snarled, taking to the skies, and cloaking himself with his innate Dragon magic.

A race. Hurtling through the skies with his brother was exactly what he needed to expend his excess energy. He could not go back to Minerva amped up this way. His Dragon would demand he mark her with no explanation or consideration for her feelings and desires.

So, what is this really about, brother?

Hearing Devine's voice inside his head had been a typical occurrence back on the Isle of Pain when their job had been to circle their land and fight off demons from the Underworld who'd dared invade. But it had been a while and Nicholas almost allowed himself to be distracted for a moment.

You will not get the upper hand by employing tricks, Dev.

What tricks, you fool? I am asking my brother a serious question. Don't I have the right to know what you're feeling?

Um no, Mommy, you don't, Nicholas scoffed.

He beat his wings against the bitter cold air currents fighting against him. Their race would be to the bridge and back to the car again, and he was already in the lead. Devine might have a longer reach when they were in their skin, but his Dragon was not as fast and lithe as Nicholas', probably because of the hard spikes he carried with him, always on the ready for battle.

I just want to help, brother.

Fine. I am thinking of asking Minerva to be my mate.

Asking? What do you mean? Either she is or is not.

Not that simple. Mates might be fated to be together, but she is a person and has a choice in the matter.

But if your Dragon claims she is your mate, and she refuses, you could die, Nick.

I know. I am aware, Dev, but the thing is, I really love her. I care about her independence and her happiness. I will not bind her to me without her consent.

So, when will you ask her to be yours?

Fuck. I don't know. I had not thought that far ahead. Maybe a few weeks.

Weeks? Nick, you will deteriorate by then. Look at your Dragon tonight, for fuck's sake. You were two seconds away from lighting your car on fire and telling the whole fucking world that Dragon Shifters exist!

Fuck. You are right. I will need to move faster, but Dev —what if she says no?

The brothers slowed their pace and Nicholas looked at Devine for any hint of reassurance.

She would be a fool to turn you down, Nicholas, Even if you are doomed to second place in all of our races!

Nicholas snapped his jaws as Devine tapped the bridge with his tail and did an abrupt about face back towards the car. His brother had used Nick's own distraction to win their race.

Sneaky bastard.

Nicholas would have laughed if he could have, but Dragons do not go around chuckling loudly. His brother was a right devil at times, but he would never want anyone else for that position. Truth was, he had never seen him this happy before. That was because of Sunny and the Falk brothers.

Coming to Maccon City had been the turning point in both their lives. For a while, Nicholas had thought he was there solely for his brother to find a purpose. He'd felt alone and adrift, but now that he'd met Minerva, things were making sense.

His Dragon pushed harder, ignoring the fat, fluffy white flakes that started coming down from the whited-out sky. Christmas was not something he'd ever celebrated before, but he felt his spirit kindle at the thought of the holidays this year.

Finally, the TopazDragon had someone to share it with—*if she would have him, of course.*

His Dragon refused to believe the sexy little minx would turn him down, but there was always the possibility. Frowning, Nick swapped scales for skin and dressed under the cloak of his magic before he and Devine left for home.

After dropping his brother off at the beachfront mansion they had built together, Nicholas pulled into the sparsely graveled driveway and parked in front of the house he'd been hellbent on buying all year long with the express purpose of knocking it down—only, now, it felt different. *He* felt different.

Nicholas did not want to bulldoze the one place Minerva felt happy during her childhood.

It needed work, for sure, and much more than the small cosmetic changes they had made just so she could move in. Nicholas paused and looked at the small, beat up home, and inside his head he began to build castles. Two columns and a wrap-around porch, an in-ground pool, and a four-car garage.

They would need to add bedrooms for their young. *Fuck*, his heart thudded at the possibility that Minerva would want to carry his babes someday. Yes, it was no secret he wanted children, but for the first time, offspring were second in his desires to mate. He wanted Minerva, children or not, she was it for him. Having young would come later and it would be a choice they made together.

But if she said no kids, then that was fine. It was not a deal breaker. There was no such thing as far as he was concerned. He did not even understand the terminology humans tossed about so freely. No one should put a price tag on love, and wasn't that what deal breakers were?

Oh fuck, love?

Yes, love.

Nicholas exhaled a huff of air. Feelings were not

his comfort zone, but for Minerva, he would try. He mounted the steps, careful to avoid the sections his crew had cut out where the wood had rotted through.

Small piles of snow were forming as more and more flakes stuck to the ground and old porch, and he grinned, thinking how wonderful the future could be. They would live here, he had no doubts. And he would be sure to build her a rooftop studio first, so she had the best light for her work.

Nick was internally clicking off everything he would need to send in an email to the architect they'd hired as part of their firm. So caught up in his musings, Nicholas barely noticed the shift in energy when he unlocked the door and crossed the threshold.

His Dragon roared, the beast scratched at him from inside the metaphysical plane where he existed till called. Nick tried to keep up with what Minnie was saying, but the sexy little minx was a wreck, and his heart was breaking over it. She looked so damn cute in a pair of sweats and a tank top liberally splattered with paint and clay.

"What are you saying?" he finally found the nerve to ask, half afraid his voice would close permanently lest he get it out.

"I fell in love with you."

Whatever else she said, Nick was listening, but nothing meant as much to him as those six little words. Still, he stood and waited until she was finished, kneeling on the floor, and covering her face to quiet her sobs. That was the last straw.

Nicholas could not just stand there any longer. He crouched beside her, lifting her up and cradling her in his arms like she was something precious. And she was. The female was his whole heart, she just did not know it yet. An error he was going to correct right now.

"What are you doing?" she asked, her face buried against his chest.

"I'm taking you to bed, mate."

"Nicky, I can't. If I sleep with you, I'll just fall harder, and I know I said I wouldn't—wait, did you say *mate*?"

"That's right," he replied, placing her gently on the bed.

"B-but I'm not your m-mate," she stuttered between sobs.

"You are."

He removed his clothing first, then went to work on hers. A tug here, a pull there, and soon, they were both gloriously naked.

"Well, when did you know?"

"Almost from the start," he said, climbing over her body and nudging her thighs apart.

She opened for him, making room for him, and cradling him in the warmth of her thighs. Fuck, she was beautiful, and Nick had never felt so perfectly at home as right there with her. He leaned down, kissing her nose, her head, eyelids, and chin. All the while, he whispered the same thing over and over to her.

"I love you too, minx. My sweet mate. Pretty mate. Good Wolf."

"You love me?" she asked breathlessly.

"Of course. Didn't you know? Es meus."

Minerva's mouth opened. Her tongue was tangling with his and he deepened their kiss, swallowing her moans and sighs. She tasted like sunshine and winter winds, like all his hopes and dreams rolled into one perfect little package.

"My people have a tradition," he murmured against her mouth, taking her hand, and placing it on the mark of his rose he carried over his heart.

"What is it?" she asked, curiosity shining in her golden eyes.

"When Dragons choose a mate, we gift them with

part of our lifespan, our lifeblood, by marking them with our roses. I want you to have my topaz rose."

"Topaz rose," she repeated, tracing the pattern on his skin.

"Yes, love. Everything I am, everything I have, is for you. Will you take it?" he whispered urgently, their kisses growing more passionate with every thrust of their tongues and press of their lips.

Passion burned, and desire clawed at him like a living thing. She was right there, willing, waiting, writhing, but he needed her words first. He had to know she wanted this as much as him. His gums burned with the need to loose his fangs, and Nicholas' thick cock sat nestled right between her slick folds, but he did not press for entry—not until she answered one very important question.

"Can I keep you?"

CHAPTER 11

"Can I keep you?"

Minnie flexed her hips, trying to entice the sexy Dragon closer, but she stilled instantly when he asked that one simple question. Her heart damn near ran away with itself. It was all Minnie could do not to throw her head back, and howl at the moon—*er, sun, more likely since it was after five in the morning*—like some crazy banshee.

She cupped his face in her hands, her earlier tears dried now that he was here, and in her arms, professing love, and offering her the world. Her Wolf peered through her eyes, and she watched his Dragon rise to meet her. Minnie pulled him down, kissing him soundly as she nodded her head.

"Yes, you can keep me, Nicky. Especially if I get to keep you right back," she returned.

Electrical currents shot through every nerve ending she possessed, and Minnie felt her pulse taking off like a rollercoaster. Nick's heavy body crushed her into the mattress, but she loved it. Loved how he felt so close, but not yet a part of her.

Unable to control her movements, she arched her back and rocked her hips, needing, wanting more of him. He propped himself up on his arms, chiseled face hovering above hers as his flame-ringed silver stare held her captive. Nick adjusted himself till he was right where she needed him to be, and fuck, he felt good.

The room was quiet, but there was a storm roaring loudly inside her head, filling her ears as sure as he filled her channel with his long, thick erection.

"Es meus," he growled, slamming into her with one purposeful thrust that had Minnie seeing stars as she clawed at his back.

Nothing had ever felt as good, as real, as right, as Nicholas Graystone claiming her with his body, heart, and teeth. Yes. Teeth. Her Wolf howled appreciatively as his fangs scraped across her neck.

So good. So hot. So mine.

In and out, he thrust his hips, hitting her just right with every slow roll of his perfectly fine ass. He was made for her, built for this, for them. She was getting close, but suddenly she had a question of her own.

"Want to bite you too, Nicky. My Wolf demands it. Can I keep you?" she asked, throwing his question back at him.

"Fuck. Yes." he gritted, jaw clenched tight. "You honor me, minx. And I swear to honor you, my maiden fair, my topaz rose, my greatest treasure. Es meus," he snarled, driving into her with unerring focus.

She did not know how long they danced on that bed until the entire universe seemed to explode around her. All Minnie knew was all she could see, feel, breathe, and taste was him. Nicholas Graystone, her fierce Topaz Dragon, had burned himself into every inch of her body, mind, heart, and soul.

She moaned as another round of pleasure swelled over her as his teeth found purchase above her breast, and turning her head, she treated him to the same. Claiming him with her Wolf's fangs on his hard bicep for all the world to see.

Eons later, she fell back to earth, the steaming sizzle of her skin reminding her that this was not over. Minerva winced and Nicholas frowned, his eyes going right to where he'd bitten her.

"It is finished, love. Are you okay?"

"Okay? I am better than okay," she murmured, tears of joy welling in her eyes as she looked from his chest to hers.

Twin roses etched in silver with flecks of gold and orange throughout marked both their skins. The heat coming off of them was tangible, but it was the bond connecting them that was really spectacular.

"You have made me the luckiest Wolf in the world," she whispered, kissing him slowly and allowing him to tuck her into his side.

"And you have given me the greatest treasure I have ever known, sweet Wolf, You have taught me to dream again."

"Oh! Speaking of dreams," she said, smiling so brightly her cheeks hurt. "I made you."

"You made me?"

"Yeah. Sunny sent over this block of quartz, and I couldn't get this image of you out of my head, so I started chiseling away, and anyway, turned out I was revealing the Dragon within the stone. I know I have never seen your beast, so I know it is not exact, but I would love to show it to you."

"Really? Come on," Nick said, as excited as she to see her work.

This was huge. Minerva never shared early glimpses of things she was working on to anyone, but this felt right somehow. She led him to her studio and watched his face go blank as she showed him the twelve inch figure she'd carved.

"It is still rough. I have more to do. But what do you think?"

Nicholas' silence was troublesome, and she waited nervously for him to respond. Better than words, her man grabbed her and pulled her tight to him.

"It's beautiful, minx."

"Really? Thank you, maybe you can show me your Dragon and I can change it to match—"

"Do not change a thing. And yes, I will show him to you, after you finish though, this way you don't stifle your artistic creativity with reality."

"I guess you're right. I am glad you like it," she replied, feeling happier than she'd ever felt before.

"Come here, mate. Let's go to bed."

"Sounds perfect," she replied, and giggled when he swung her up and into his arms.

They slept till noon the next day, and after going over some plans for the house, Minnie made a quick trip into New York City to bring the cash box back to the gallery with every last check and all the cash that was logged inside. *Odd*, in her opinion, since Roger typically spent cash first.

Whatever. She was just happy to have the three pieces she'd needed to replace finished and had left with a promise for a dozen more to be delivered at the end of the week. Nicholas had stayed back to get some work done, and she was so over the moon in love with him she could not be any happier.

"Minnie! Come inside," Sunny said, dragging her into one of the enormous living rooms in Castle Falk. Nicholas had already texted he would be late, and she was fine as long as he showed up.

"I brought a gift," she said, holding one of her newest designs in a wrapped box.

"Awesome. Hey Fred, Minnie brought something for the castle," Sunny enthused. "Wait till you see her work, it's sublime," her bestie gushed as a tall, lithe she-Wolf came over.

"Thanks for coming tonight. You didn't have to do that," Fred said, then grabbed the box and squealed. "But I so love gifts!"

"Oh no, Minnie, bringing gifts is not safe around this one. Fred, behave yourself," Jozette admonished the older she-Wolf and giggled with a woman who had her hair in dark ringlets that sort of matched Minnie's own halo of curls.

"*OHMYGAWD!* This is gorgeous." Fred gasped and held the small metal Christmas tree Minerva had sculpted using her Wolf strength to bend and manipulate copper and steel wire.

The piece was almost two feet in height. Minnie had been very pleased with the final product, especially since, using her claws, she'd been able to scratch the thin wires in geometrical patterns, so as to resemble pine needles, catching the light, and making the sculpture appear to glow.

"Thank you so much. I can't believe we have a Minerva Lykos original now," the blonde she-Wolf exclaimed and grabbed Minnie in a tight hug. "You're claimed! Girls, she's claimed!"

"Minnie, you didn't call me," Sunny growled, and grabbed her in a tight hug while the others surrounded her and clapped her back and offered their cheers of welcome.

"*Congratulations!*"

"*Welcome to the Clan.*"

"*Yay!*"

"Wow, that was intense, Sunny. You could have warned me."

Minnie grabbed a large glass filled with ice and

soda, guzzling it down while the Clan kids ran amok across the room. They were wrapping gifts to donate to the hospital to be dropped off later that day for children, and adults alike, who would not be able to spend the holidays at home with their loved ones. It was sweet and thoughtful, and once again, Minnie was struck by the amount of community service her Pack, and now her Clan, was responsible for.

"I told you, you loved him," Sunny replied in a sing-song voice she found particularly annoying.

"Yes, I love him. You love Devine, but I'm not going crazy on you. Seriously, Sunny, why are you being weird?"

Sunny shrugged bumping shoulders with her while the two of them sat together filling out information on the gift tags so the hospital would know who to give the gifts too, for example, a set of coloring books and crayons from a popular TV show was appropriate for children aged 3-8, and so on. Minnie was a fan of making life easy for people, and this set up totally rocked.

"I don't know, I guess I am excited for you Minnie. You deserve happiness, but I admit, I never saw you settling down with one man, making a home, having kids—"

"Whoa. Kids? Um, Nicky and I have not discussed all that yet," she admitted nervously.

"Oh," Sunny replied, biting her own bottom lip. "It's just that Devine mentioned Nick wanting kids, as much as he does. It's like a biological imperative for their kind to propagate."

"You girls talking about a Dragon's need to make babies?" Jocelyn, Edric's mate, chimed in, dropping off a fresh pile of packages. "Better start investing in wipes and stretch pants now. I mean, you do want kids, right?" Jos asked, but her smile faltered as she read the sheer panic on Minnie's face correctly.

"Um, Minnie, uh, has her own ideas about family," Sunny explained as the room got really quiet.

Oh fuck. Oh fuck. Oh fuck.

Every single female there was a mother or pregnant or planning to be one super soon. She couldn't rightly express her concern over parenting, giving birth, or anything like it without insulting them, but the truth was Minnie was not ready for kids. Hell, she might never be, and that was something she had always considered to be a valid life choice. But what about Nicky? Was she taking something from him by not wanting kids right away?

"Um, I'm sorry, but I just remembered something," she muttered, and stood up, racing out of the castle despite the voices calling her back.

She couldn't do this. Claimed or not, Minerva had to break things off with Nicholas before she became any more bonded to him. It was the only way either of them could survive, but first she needed to run.

Minerva followed a path behind the castle and into the woods all the way to a cabin or hunting lodge. Sunny had told her about this place, and she smiled sadly as she pushed the door open and stripped out of her wintry ensemble so she could take to the woods in her fur.

Thick patches of snow covered the floor of the pine barrens, and more was coming down when she dashed through the door. Taking off like lightning, Minerva released her small brown-gray Wolf into the wild and let her run free. Her heart was squeezing her to death under all the weight of her guilt.

She'd told him about her parents' experience with her brother Angel. Nicholas had listened and responded kindly, offering support and comfort, but she had not told him the worst of it. That she'd been with her mother when the older she-Wolf had gone into labor. The memories of her mom screaming in pain, and the smell of iron as she bled and bled, waiting for the midwife to arrive and help her deliver the twin pups.

Birth was scary and messy most of the time, but for Werewolves there was a double dose of fear. The Curse of Natalis had rendered their species damn near helpless when it came to their Change and negotiating life with a Wolf inside of them. But it also made childbirth especially difficult. Yes, the curse had been broken, but that did not mean Minnie's fears had abated.

Fuck.

She should have discussed all of this with Nicholas first and given him the opportunity to make an informed decision about their relationship. How did she allow things to get here? No matter how many times she went over it, it made little sense.

He was supposed to be a no strings fuck buddy, not the love of her life. And why, oh why, did that make her feel any worse?

The woods blurred by as she raced and raced, her heart breaking with every step. Minerva never thought she would find her mate, and now that she had, it seemed cruel her greatest fears would be the thing to drive him away.

If only her parents and siblings hadn't all gone away for the holidays. Maybe then she could confront her fears and have a heart to heart with the people who were directly involved with the events that had changed her outlook on children.

Sure, she liked kids. Had enjoyed talking to the teens from the Outreach center about art, and she'd enjoyed playing with the Falk Clan's young, and cuddling Castor and Jozette's new baby. She did not dislike children, Minnie was just uncertain if she could be a mother.

It was a huge decision, but it was not hers alone. Nicholas had every right to expect to be a father. Didn't most men and women entering a relationship want that? Not knowing if she would ever be ready was something she had never really thought about. It was never anyone else's business.

Until now.

The wind grew colder, and she huddled into herself, thankful for her thick fur. The creek was frozen over, and she was getting thirsty now. Minnie knew she'd really messed up. There was no doubt about it. The sky was darkening, and she could not afford to dawdle in the cold any longer.

It was time to deliver the kill blow on Nicholas' dreams. Time to tell him she was not the right Wolf for him. He wanted a family, and she was not sure she could ever give him one. Not now anyway. Maybe never. Sadness dogged her every step, and before she reached the cabin Minnie turned her lupine head towards the big moon hanging low in the sky.

Can I keep you?

Her brain replayed Nicholas' sweet question over and over again, and if Wolves could cry, hers would be. She hoped he would keep her. Now and always.

Please don't hate me. Awoooooooooo.

CHAPTER 12

Nicholas took the steps to Castle Falk two at a time, barely stopping to greet Callius and his brothers in the foyer before setting off to greet his mate.

His mate. No matter how many times he thought about it, he always grinned like a madman. How did he get so lucky? Minerva Lykos was everything he ever wanted in a female.

She was feisty and fun, curvy and confident, brilliant, and surprisingly vulnerable when he least expected it. A goddess in the sheets, and a worthy adversary when playing video games. The game console was the next thing they'd set up that morning. He could not wait for a rematch of strip trivia and had been listening to a podcast featuring pop culture references just to brush up on his skills.

Afterwards, Nick reluctantly went down to the construction site to oversee the delivery of some important materials. He hated leaving her, but he knew better than to coddle his fearsome she-Wolf, besides, she'd had to run her finished artwork over to the gallery in Manhattan.

Fucking Roger. It had been so worth seeing that male piss his pants when Nicholas and Devine had cornered him in Tiny's backroom. The Gorilla Shifter had made sure the Dragons did nothing to reveal themselves, but there was more than one way to put the fear of the gods in a man. Especially a weakling like that rat bastard.

Stealing from a woman, Nick's woman. The lout was lucky he'd walked away on his own two feet. His Dragon had wanted him flayed and charred over Dragonfire. Not a bad idea, to be honest. But Devine had it right when he told Nick the loser was not worth getting in trouble with their Alpha. Callius Falk was one mean motherfucker when he had to be, and if it meant protecting his family and Clan, then he was downright scary.

But no. Nicholas did not need fangs and claws to get his message across. A well-placed snarl, and the threat of bodily harm seemed enough to have the man staining in his pants and handing over everything he had stolen, minus his payment to Tiny, which Nicholas had replaced.

He did not want the Silverback hurt by this affair, and besides, it was good to maintain friendships with other Shifter groups. Nick would not miss the money, having plenty himself. And he understood the gallery had yet to take their cut. Minnie had been livid for all of ten minutes, then he explained about his stock portfolio and Niko Falk's penchant for making money.

"I will pay you back," she'd said, but he'd tickled her until she relented.

"Don't want your money, minx. I want this," he'd said and buried his head between her thick thighs, his fingers tugging on the plump tips of her ripe breasts.

He readjusted his boner in his jeans and ignored the laughter and conversation going on around him. Where was his mate? He sniffed the air, catching her scent lingering in the room off the main parlor, but it was old by a few hours at least.

"Hey Nick," Sunny said, walking up to him with a worried expression on her face. He had never seen his brother's mate look so upset, and concern had him halting his forward progression.

"Is something wrong? Where is Devine?"

"he's fine, Nick, and so am I, but well, you see, I think there's been a misunderstanding—"

"She's right, Nicholas," Winifred Falk interrupted them, and Nicholas owed his head in reverence to the Alpha Dragon's mate.

"We upset Minnie by assuming she was ready for children. I am so sorry, and a little embarrassed that we came off as so pushy. I talked to the other mates, and they are all profoundly sorry for making Minerva uncomfortable—"

"I don't understand," Nicholas said, shaking his head. "Minerva got upset over talk of young?"

"Nick, her mother lost a pup during childbirth—"

"Her brother, Angel. Yes, I am aware, but what does that have to do with us?"

His heart was pounding, and his beast was snarling. Was Minnie alright? It was the only thing that mattered to him. He wanted to run out of the room to search for her, but listening to her friend might help, so he waited, and he listened.

"Well, she is afraid of childbirth and since I have known her, she has never mentioned wanting children—"

"That is her right to decide. I am sorry, I still do not understand the problem," Nick stated, rubbing his hand across his face.

The Dragon within him was snapping and scratching at his skin, demanding to be loosed to pursue his mate. Something had upset his sweet little minx, and Minerva had fled. He needed to find her, to let her know he would make right whatever had spooked her.

"It's just, well, look at everyone here," Sunny stated, pointing at Jozette coddling her newborn, and Noelle chasing a pair of twin boys around the tree. There were kids everywhere, and while he was thrilled to be part of a Clan with so many young, he was not in any way lacking for want of a babe.

"Look, we know how all you big Dragons crave young, so naturally we'd assumed she wanted babies—"

"Wait, does she think I only want her for young? Fucking hell," he murmured. "I have to go after her."

"Wait," Sunny said, flicking her gaze to Fred before stopping him with a hand raised. "Don't you want her for her ability to bear your young?"

"I have no idea what gave you that impression, Sunny Graystone, but I want Minerva because she is my topaz rose."

"But Devine said you both dreamed about fathering children for decades."

"I have a new dream now," he growled, voice barely human.

"She is mine. She is my dream. *Es meus. Est sominum meum.*"

Roooaaaarrrrr.

Nicholas was already shucking off his clothes by the time he reached the back of the castle. Pulling on his cloaking ability, he shot off into the dark skies and combed the woods for his mate. Her scent was faint, but he needed to find her, to let her know where she stood in his life—and that was above everything else.

Tugging on their new and fragile matebond, Nicholas hunted Minnie to the ends of the forest. Her sadness stabbed at him like a dagger, but she needed space. He realized that as he circled above. His mate was a smart, caring, and totally badass she-Wolf. But even so, she was entitled to time to work things out.

He returned to where her scent was strongest, to the cabin the Falk Clan used for changing and playing in the woods beside their castle. Inside, he hunted up a pair of sweats and waited impatiently for Minnie to come back to him. All the while, he kept the link to their bond open so she could find him when she was ready.

After a few hours, she came back. He knew the moment she stepped over the threshold. It was like he could breathe again, and Nicholas gave silent thanks to the universe for bringing her back.

Silently, he walked over to her, greeting her Wolf with gentle strokes along her snout and ears. He took a fluffy, clean towel from the shelf and started rubbing her dry. It was snowing, and she was cold and wet from her travels.

The she-Wolf sat back on her haunches, sadness welling in her gold eyes, and a whimper rose from her throat. It was killing him to see her so sad, but he needed her warm and dry and safely back in her human skin before he spoke. Nick did not have to wait long.

Thank fuck.

"Nicky," she murmured, tears flowing as he wrapped a second, larger towel around her shoulders. "I have to talk to you. I have to apologize—"

"About what, my love?" he asked, then nuzzled her helplessly. "Christ, I missed you. Come here," he murmured.

Nick busied himself wrapping her up in his arms and carrying her to the sofa in front of the fireplace.

He'd started a flame there a few hours ago, and the room was toasty warm—perfect now that she was in it.

"I'm sorry, I am so sorry," she began.

"For what, silly Wolf? I love you. Everything is alright."

"It's not," she replied, shaking her head. "I told you about my mom, but I never said I was afraid to have kids, and the truth is I don't know if I will ever not be afraid. It's just something I always took for granted. I never planned on finding a mate, so I never worried about it. I didn't know Dragons crave young to settle their beasts. Sunny told me, but if I knew, I would never have kept it from you. I understand if you want to leave me—"

"Minerva, my sweet mate. Are you quite finished, love? Now it's my turn. Yes, I had dreamed of being a father someday, but that was a secondary thing. My first dream was finding you."

"You don't have to say that—"

"And I wouldn't just say anything, my love, don't you know that by now? You are the only thing in this world I can't live without. You are my breath, my body, my soul, sweet Wolf. I need you, and only you, *my topaz rose.*"

Nicholas's forehead pressed against hers as he

confessed the depth of his feelings to his mate. She deserved so much out of life, so much from him, and damn it, he was going to spend his entire life trying to give it to her.

"You mean that?"

"Yes. I mean every word. I need you, Minerva. If you do not want young, we will not have them. We have dozens of nieces and nephews already to spoil between our combined Pack and Clan. Oh, and the females all apologized. They did not mean to hurt you or to appear insensitive—"

"They said that?"

"Yes, love. I swear it."

"And if I decide I want to try for a baby someday?" she whispered the question.

"Then we will try," he replied simply, cupping his hand over the back of her neck, and pressing his mouth to her head. "Silly woman. You and me—*we* are it for one another. I am yours forever, my love. Don't you know I cannot live without you?"

Minnie sighed and pressed herself firmly against him, placing kisses all over his face and neck. She straddled him then, and Nick's body reacted predictably, as it always would for her.

"There is one thing I must ask you to promise

me, mate," he growled as she pushed his sweats down and cupped his rigid staff with her hands.

"What? Anything," she replied, her golden gaze unafraid and full of feeling.

"No more running away. Don't ever be scared to talk to me. We can accomplish anything together, but I need you to trust I am here for you," he said, moaning as she stroked him lovingly, teasing a pearl of white from his slit.

"I swear it. I'll never run from you. I love you too, Nicky, more than I ever thought possible."

Then, his sexy little minx slid down his body and kneeled before him. Pushing him back into the cushions, Minerva covered Nick's head with her mouth, sucking it into her hot, wet cavern.

A slow, steady pressure built inside him, hot as Dragonfire and just as powerful. She was incredible. Sweet, sexy, powerful, beautiful mate. Nick held her curls away from her face so he could watch as she loved on him with her wickedly talented mouth and hands.

"Better stop now, minx. Fuck, I'm gonna come."

But she didn't stop. She increased her efforts, eyes flashing gold when he exploded into her mouth. His sweet Minnie swallowed down every drop of his climax, and damn, but it was the sexiest thing he'd ever seen. Nicholas could barely restrain himself. He tumbled them both onto the floor, sucking one ripe nipple into his mouth as he delved between her thighs with his thick fingers.

"Nick!" she yelled his name, bucking against his hand while he bit down on her tiny nubbin, curling his fingers to hit just the right angle.

Nick and Minnie stayed in the cabin for hours after, loving each other so thoroughly he did not think either of them were going to make it home. But after a while, he dressed them both in borrowed sweats, and took his mate back to their home.

"Are you still gonna knock this place down?" she asked as he carried her over the threshold.

"You kidding me? This is my dream house, minx. We're gonna turn it into a castle together," he said, nipping her lip playfully.

That night, as Nicholas watched Minnie sleep, draped across his chest, he relaxed for the first time in centuries. Everything he had ever wanted was right there in his arms.

Es meus.

EPILOGUE

"Whoever said dreaming was free had never wanted to own a Minerva Lykos original!" Winifred Falk joked as she and the other Dragon mates climbed out of the stretched limo they had taken together for Minnie's new show.

"You still outbid me, heifer," Noelle, Sander's mate, whispered, mock-glaring at the image of the tiny Dragon figurine the Alpha's mate had bought.

"Too bad, so sad," Fred said with a laugh. "So, when will they be delivered?" she asked.

"The gallery should have everything wrapped and shipped before the New Year," Minnie explained.

She was delighted that the entire Falk Clan, except for Castor and Jozette who stayed home to watch all the children, had come to her showing. The past two weeks had sped by in a blur of excitement, and Minnie could not be happier.

"I still can't believe you dedicated almost every piece to Dragons and Wolves. OMG! Look here, Artist Times says your showing was a raving success and Minerva Lykos' art is both profound and charming. The personification of fantasy with a touch of whimsy that makes it seem almost attainable—eeek! I am so proud of you!"

"Let me see that," Nick said, taking the cell phone from Fred and showing Minnie.

"Wow," she murmured.

That was a fantastic review, and from one of the tougher critics too. Minnie sighed, snuggling into Nick's embrace. They'd been on crazy schedules the last few weeks, with Nick putting his development on hold to oversee the construction of the house. He'd really been serious about making it into their own little castle.

Minnie wholeheartedly approved of everything he proposed when it came to refurnishing the place. The man had such good taste. She wondered where it all came from. He and his brother had what she and Sunny secretly called the three Cs—*compassion, caring,* and mega huge *cocks.* The last was Minnie's addition to the list.

What? She was still a Wolf. Even mated, she still craved a physical connection with her man, and often too. She'd produced three dozen unique pieces in the last few weeks, and the gallery had been thrilled. They'd sold out in the first two hours, all except for one piece.

The biggest of her offerings for this showing was the Dragon she had started in the piece of quartz Sunny had gifted her from her mate's own spikes. Nicholas seemed so proud of that piece. He called it his beast even though she'd never seen his Dragon. She had used an image from her own mind's eye to model it on. Still, he insisted it was perfect, and so she told the gallery manager that piece was not to be sold. It was her gift for Nick, and she'd had it packed into the back of the limo before they'd filed in.

The ride back was full of laughter and champagne, Christmas carols, and comradery as she basked in the glow of being part of his Clan. She was not the only Wolf, but there were humans and a Witch among them as well. The Falk Clan was small, but they were fiercely devoted to each other, and Minnie was honored to be one of them.

"Alright folks, see you tomorrow for Christmas

breakfast in our jammies," Fred called out before they piled out of the car.

Nicholas and Minnie were the last stop.

"One second," she said when Nick would have carried her inside. The man simply could not get enough of lifting her up whenever they came home. She secretly loved it, but she needed to get the statue first.

"What are you doing?" he asked, joining her by the trunk.

"This is for you, mate," she whispered, handing him the unwrapped statue.

"Merry Christmas, Nicky!"

"You little minx, I wondered why I couldn't find out who bought it," she scoffed, shaking his head. "I was going to buy it from them, but Deirdre wouldn't tell me a thing. Is it really for me?"

"Yes, of course. I mean, I know it's not perfect—"

"That is where you're wrong. Come on," he whispered, tugging her hand to mount the stairs. Once inside, he pulled her with him until they reached the new spiral staircase he'd had installed that led to her brand new art studio and a rooftop garden, only when they got there, it was more concrete courtyard.

"What is this?"

"A landing pad," he replied, grinning as he shucked off his clothing. "Hold this."

Minnie took the statue, watching him curiously as he stood before her, naked and gorgeous. The air around him hummed and shivered, and then her Nicky was gone. In his place was an enormous beast, thirty feet long at least with orange-rimmed silver scales on his back, and lighter flame-colored scales covered his chest and belly.

His Dragon was huge and stunning, and as tears pricked her eyes, she realized he looked exactly like her statue. Two horns spiraled from his head, and matching spines danced along his back and tail. He had wickedly sharp claws, and unforgettable wings, thin as gossamer but strong as steel. He was a warrior, a lover, and he was hers.

"Thank you, Nick. Your Dragon is incredible," she whispered, touching his snout, and giggling at the puff of heat he breathed at her.

A moment later and he was human again, lifting her in his arms, and spinning in circles. Minnie hugged him tight, smiling as she kissed his impossibly warm skin.

"See? I told you. S'perfect, mate," he growled, nipping her neck with his teeth.

"You're perfect."

"Not me, silly Wolf. *You.* You are the Dragon's dream. I am so lucky you're mine."

Minnie smiled, a face-splitting grin, and hugged him tighter. Nicholas might call her his dream, but he was the answer to hers in a million ways and then some. He often said she dared him to dream, and that was amazing. But even more amazing, Nicholas had taught her how to love.

"Merry Christmas, *somnium meum.*"

"Let's go inside," she said, wrapping her legs tight around his waist and kissing him with everything she had inside of her.

Minerva's life was so completely intertwined with her Dragon's, she could not imagine a day without him. For the first time, thoughts of having a family did not fill her with dread. Nick was her family. He was her mate. Her love. Her life.

"I love you, minx."

"I love you too," she replied, and gave in to the sweet release only he could deliver.

"Es meus," he growled, melting into her with a deep, guttural moan.

"Always yours. Whatever the future brings, mate," she replied, clinging to him.

Nick loved her with every inch of himself, giving as freely as he took, and bringing her more pleasure than she ever thought possible. It was more than simple sex. It was a communion of bodies, hearts, and souls she had never experienced until him. Intimacy used to be an outlet for Minnie, but with her mate, it was a soul changing event.

You are my dream come true, Nicholas' voice whispered into her mind as their lovemaking turned frenzied.

"And you're mine," she replied on a gasp, feeling their bond wrap tightly around them.

Nicholas and Minerva's love would forever bind them, and together they would continue to make their dreams realities until the end of time.

T*he end...*

Did you enjoy this Paranormal Romance? Awesome! You can read the other Falk Clan Tales here!

&

You might have noticed mention of the Macconwood Wolf

Pack in this story. You can read about the whole Pack by starting here.

Sign up for C.D. Gorri's newsletter today and never miss a sale or new release.
Thank you and happy reading! Xoxo

BEWARE... HERE BE EVEN MORE DRAGONS!

The Falk Clan Tales began as my stories surrounding four dragon Brothers and how they find their one true mates, but when a long lost brother arrives on the scene, followed by a few more Shifters…what can I say? The more the merrier!

Each Dragon's chest is marked with his rose, the magical link to his heart and his magic. They each have a matching gemstone to go with it.

She's given up on love. But he's just begun.

In *The Dragon's Valentine* we meet the eldest Falk brother, Callius. He is on a mission to find a Castle and his one true mate, one he can trust with his diamond rose....

His heart is frozen. Can she change his mind about love?

In *The Dragon's Christmas Gift* our attention shifts to Alexsander, the youngest brother of the four. He has resigned himself to a life alone, until he meets *her*.

Some wounds run deep. Can a Dragon's heart be unbroken?

The Dragon's Heart is the story of Edric Falk who has vowed never to love again, but that changes when he meets his feisty mate, Joselyn Curacao.

She just wants a little fun. He's looking for a lifetime.

We finally meet Nikolai Falk and his sexy Shifter mate in *The Dragon's Secret*.

Now available in a boxed set.

Guess what.... I've got more Dragons on the way!

Look for The Dragon's Treasure. Now available.

Coming in 2022 The Dragon's Dream and The Dragon's Surprise.

HAVE YOU MET MY BEARS?

Looking for a Paranormal Romance series that is loads of growly fun?

Meet the Barvale Clan first in the Bear Claw Tales! A complete shifter romance series about 4 brothers who discover and need to win their fated mates!

Followed by two more spin off series, the Barvale Clan Tales and the Barvale Holiday Tales!

No cliffhangers. Steamy PNR fun.
Go and read your next happily ever after today!

OTHER TITLES BY C.D. GORRI

Other Titles by C.D. Gorri

Paranormal Romance Books:

Macconwood Pack Novel Series:

Charley's Christmas Wolf: A Macconwood Pack Novel 1

Cat's Howl: A Macconwood Pack Novel 2

Code Wolf: A Macconwood Pack Novel 3

The Witch and The Werewolf: A Macconwood Pack Novel 4

To Claim a Wolf: A Macconwood Pack Novel 5

Conall's Mate: A Macconwood Pack Novel 6

Her Solstice Wolf: A Macconwood Pack Novel 7

Werewolf Fever: A Macconwood Pack Novel 8

Also available in 2 boxed sets:

The Macconwood Pack Volume 1

The Macconwood Pack Volume 2

Macconwood Pack Tales Series:

Wolf Bride: The Story of Ailis and Eoghan A

Macconwood Pack Tale 1

Summer Bite: A Macconwood Pack Tale 2

His Winter Mate: A Macconwood Pack Tale 3

Snow Angel: A Macconwood Pack Tale 4

Charley's Baby Surprise: A Macconwood Pack Tale 5

Home for the Howlidays: A Macconwood Pack Tale 6

A Silver Wedding: A Macconwood Pack Tale 7

Mine Furever: A Macconwood Pack Tale 8

A Furry Little Christmas: A Macconwood Pack Tale 9

Also available in two boxed sets:

The Macconwood Pack Tales Volume 1

Shifters Furever: The Macconwood Pack Tales Volume 2

<u>The Falk Clan Tales:</u>

The Dragon's Valentine: A Falk Clan Novel 1

The Dragon's Christmas Gift: A Falk Clan Novel 2

The Dragon's Heart: A Falk Clan Novel 3

The Dragon's Secret: A Falk Clan Novel 4

The Dragon's Treasure: A Falk Clan Novel 5

The Dragon's Surprise: A Falk Clan Novel 6

The Dragon's Dream: A Falk Clan Novel 7

Dragon Mates: The Falk Clan Series Boxed Set Books 1-4

<u>The Bear Claw Tales:</u>

Bearly Breathing: A Bear Claw Tale 1

Bearly There: A Bear Claw Tale 2

Bearly Tamed: A Bear Claw Tale 3

Bearly Mated: A Bear Claw Tale 4

Also available in a boxed set:

The Complete Bear Claw Tales (Books 1-4)

The Barvale Clan Tales:

Polar Opposites: The Barvale Clan Tales 1

Polar Outbreak: The Barvale Clan Tales 2

Polar Compound: A Barvale Clan Tale 3

Polar Curve: A Barvale Clan Tale 4

Also available in a boxed set:

The Barvale Clan Tales (Books 1-4)

Barvale Holiday Tales:

A Bear For Christmas

Hers To Bear

Thank You Beary Much

Bearing Gifts

Also available in a boxed set:

The Barvale Holiday Tales (Books 1-3)

Purely Paranormal Romance Books:

Marked by the Devil: Purely Paranormal Romance Books

Mated to the Dragon King: Purely Paranormal Romance Books

Claimed by the Demon: Purely Paranormal Romance Books

Christmas with a Devil, a Dragon King, & a Demon: Purely Paranormal Romance Books

Vampire Lover: Purely Paranormal Romance Books

Grizzly Lover: Purely Paranormal Romance Books

Christmas With Her Chupacabra: Purely Paranormal Romance Books

*Purely Paranormal Romance Books Anthology

The Wardens of Terra:

Bound by Air: The Wardens of Terra Book 1

Star Kissed: A Wardens of Terra Short

Waterlocked: The Wardens of Terra Book 2

Moon Kissed: A Wardens of Terra Short

*Now in a boxed set and in audio!

The Maverick Pride Tales:

Purrfectly Mated

Purrfectly Kissed

Purrfectly Trapped

Purrfectly Caught

Purrfectly Naughty

Purrfectly Bound

Dire Wolf Mates:

Shake That Sass

Breaking Sass

Pinch of Sass

Kickin' Sass

Wyvern Protection Unit:

Gift Wrapped Protector: WPU 1

Standalones:

The Enforcer

Blood Song: A Sanguinem Council Book

Spring Fling (co-written with P. Mattern)

EveL Worlds:

Chinchilla and the Devil: A FUCN'A Book

Sammi and the Jersey Bull: A FUCN'A Book

Mouse and the Ball: A FUCN'A Book

The Guardians of Chaos:

Wolf Shield: Guardians of Chaos Book 1

Dragon Shield: Guardians of Chaos Book 2

Stallion Shield: Guardians of Chaos Book 3

Panther Shield: Guardians of Chaos 4

Witch Shield: Guardians of Chaos 5

Vampire Shield: Guardians of Chaos 6

Howl's Romance

Mated to the Werewolf Next Door: A Howl's Romance

The Tiger King's Christmas Bride

Claiming His Virgin Mate: Howls Romance

Twice Mated Tales

Doubly Claimed

Doubly Bound

Doubly Tied

Hearts of Stone Series

Shifter Mountain: Hearts of Stone 1

Shifter City: Hearts of Stone 2

Shifter Village: Hearts of Stone 3

Accidentally Undead Series

Fangs For Nothin'

Moongate Island Tales

Moongate Island Mate

Moongate Island Christmas Claim

Mated in Hope Falls

Mated by Moonlight

Speed Dating with the Denizens of the Underworld

Ash: Speed Dating with the Denizens of Underworld

Arachne: Speed Dating with the Denizens of Underworld

Asterion: Speed Dating with the Denizens of Underworld

Hungry_Fur_Love

Hungry Like Her Wolf: Magic and Mayhem Universe

Hungry For Her Bear: Magic and Mayhem Universe

Shifters Unleashed Boxed Sets

Check out these amazing anthologies where you can find some of my books and the works of other awesome authors!

Midnight Magic Anthology (Water Witch)

Rituals & Runes Anthology (Air Witch)

Island Stripe Pride

Tiger Claimed

Tiger Denied

Tiger Rejected

NYC Shifter Tales

Cuff Linked

Sealed Fate

A Howlin' Good Fairytale Retelling

Sweet As Candy (single edition coming soon)

Coming Soon:

Hungry As Her Python: Magic and Mayhem Universe

If The Shoe Fits: A Howlin' Good Fairytale Retelling

Chickee and the Paparazzi: FUCN'A

The Wolf's Winter Wish: A Macconwood Pack Tale

The Hybrid Assassin

For Fangs Sake

Tempted By Her Protector: WPU 2

Alien Protector: WPU 3

Elvish Protector: WPU 4

Thrilled By Her Protector: WPU 5

<u>Young Adult Urban Fantasy Books:</u>

Wolf Moon: A Grazi Kelly Novel Book 1

Hunter Moon: A Grazi Kelly Novel Book 2

Rebel Moon: A Grazi Kelly Novel Book 3

Winter Moon: A Grazi Kelly Novel Book 4

Chasing The Moon: A Grazi Kelly Short 5

Blood Moon: A Grazi Kelly Novel 6

*Get all 6 books NOW AVAILABLE IN A BOXED SET:

The Complete Grazi Kelly Novel Series

Casting Magic: The Angela Tanner Files 1

Keeping Magic: The Angela Tanner Files 2

<u>G'Witches Magical Mysteries Series</u>

Co-written with P. Mattern

G'Witches

G'Witches 2: The Harpy Harbinger

G'Witches 3: Summoning Secrets

EXCERPT FROM WOLF SHIELD: GUARDIANS OF CHAOS

What a day! Fergie McAndrews headed towards the pick-up truck she'd borrowed from her roommate for work that morning.

Of course, the thirty-thousand dollar certified used luxury car she'd splurged on earlier in the year was in the shop. Again.

Just another in a long line of bad decisions. After leaving a perfectly good job for a startup company, she was laid off three weeks ago and had to borrow money from her parents to pay rent. Wasn't that humiliating?

"This is the last time, Ferg," her step-monster had said *after she'd Venmo'd the money to her.*

God forbid the mechanic call and tell her the car

was ready. She wouldn't be able to pick it up for another week. That was when she got her first paycheck from her newest gig at L-Corp. Not a startup, but an older company with new offices in Bayonne, which was only a half-hour commute.

But to commute, you needed a car. Fergie had no choice but to borrow the old pick-up from her best friend and roommate, Jessenia Banks. It wasn't like she needed the truck. She worked from home these days. Besides, Fergie promised to fill it up and have it washed.

She huffed out a breath. It'd been a really long day. A crappy one too. Fergie wanted to love her new job. Really, she did. But so far, it was the pits. If Fergie wanted to be a librarian, she would've been one.

Research was her jam. Well, when it was interesting. She had a knack for sniffing out information and compiling easy-to-read spreadsheets and time-lines. It wasn't the hard work that annoyed her. Her complaint was the content. The actual stuff her new boss had her looking up. It was beyond boring.

Why an enormous conglomerate like L-Corp needed old land surveys, cross-referenced with newspaper reports on accidents, crimes, etcetera.

She had no idea. She'd been at it for weeks now. So far, she'd researched six locations given via GPS coordinates across Hudson County. Her new boss wanted everything, every little insignificant piece of information she could dig up.

That was the easy part. It was the hassle of the actual job that really made her want to give up. Every day she had to drive to Bayonne to pick up her work laptop she'd dropped off the night before with all of that day's findings. Every single night they wiped her computer clean.

Like she was going to run away with the secrets of what happened on 2nd and Washington sixty-years ago. Can you say paranoid? Ugh.

Fergie had always looked forward to working for a huge global company. It was supposed to be her ticket out of the Garden State. Traveling the globe, seeing new things, visiting far-off places was always a secret dream of hers. Well, that, and having her own walk-in closet full of gorgeous designer shoes.

Best secret dream evah! In her opinion, anyway. What woman didn't love shoes? Fergie hummed as she daydreamed about rows and rows of Blahnik's, Jimmy Choo's, Garavani's, Ferragamo's, and her personal favorites, Louboutin's on every shelf!

Don't judge. Fergie wasn't shallow, she just liked pretty things. Haters gonna hate. But every time she ran across a thrift or second-chance store, she'd search high and low to see what they had. That was how she'd scored the pumps on her feet.

They made her feel good about herself. Being five-foot two-inches short with more curves than a racetrack, Fergie had had more than her fair share of self-esteem issues growing up. Alright, so she was chubby. She could admit that proudly now.

If everyone looked the same, the world would be one boring as hell place. Fergie liked herself perfectly fine these days, in spite of all the times her step-monster tried to make her diet growing up. So she liked food and shoes. Big deal.

She worked hard to feed and clothe herself, so as far as she was concerned, no one had a right to comment. So what if she wanted some excitement in her life? Fergie was aware she was better off than most, but what was wrong with having goals?

She'd spent a lot of time thinking about how a woman like her could have an adventure. Travelling was the only thing she could think of. Of course, she'd been hoping this job would be the answer to that. Even travelling for work was better than being stuck.

Sigh.

So far, her plans had fallen flat, but hey, at least she was earning a paycheck. Her new boss, Mr. Offner, might be a strange man, but he signed her checks, and that was enough for now. Fergie had never seen more than a glimpse of him. All of her instructions usually came via email.

Most of the time she was able to compile her research quickly, then she'd head back to the office to organize it into neat little spreadsheets, and finally, she'd hand it all in with her laptop. But not today.

Mr. Offner sent her an email detailing everything she could dig up on one of the oldest places on record in the county. Of course, land surveys that old, along with police reports, newspaper articles, deeds, and sales records were nowhere she could easily access them.

After wasting hours at both the court house and municipal building, Fergie had been directed to the *second* public library. Apparently anything over a hundred years old was filed away in the godforsaken place. She'd been shocked to find an entire room filled with musty old archives. And wouldn't you know it, there was no cell service and no internet access. Plus, their phone lines were down. She'd had to photograph each page using her cell. When she got home later, she would send those photos like a fax to her boss along with her spreadsheet. If she could manage that before collapsing into bed.

Grab your copy at https://www.cdgorri.com/books/wolf-shield

EXCERPT FROM PURRFECTLY MATED

How the fuck did I wind up here?

It was all Elissa could do not to slam her face down on the table as she pondered that question for the umpteenth time since leaving her cozy Hoboken apartment to go on this so called date.

"So, babe," the over-stuffed, heavily-cologned, and downright fugly man said.

Her date of the evening looked like something out of a bad sitcom as he tried to lean over the stained tablecloth of the rundown hotel buffet room, he'd driven two hours to get to. Waggling his caterpillar-like eyebrows, he gave her the once over and Elissa's skin crawled.

Oh, hell no.

"I got a room upstairs, you know, for *after*," he told her, nodding his head, and biting his lower lip in a manner she assumed he thought was provocative.

At best, it was nauseating.

FML.

How was this guy Elissa's date for the evening? What had she done to deserve this?

Little Gianni. Yup, that was how he'd introduced himself. And here she was. On a blind date with a guy who had the word 'little' in front of his name.

Well, what did she expect? Roses and champagne? In this economy? She didn't know where Cinder-fucking-ella got her prince, but it sure as fuck wasn't in Jersey.

Elissa could only blame herself for agreeing to go on this blind date. Initially, the whole Little Gianni fiasco had been intended for her roommate.

Wait a second. Scratch that thought.

It *was* all Gretchen's fault. That ungrateful cow!

She tried to play it off like she was some sweet little homegrown maiden. Oh, just wait till Elissa got home. Gretchen was never going to hear the end of it.

She owed Elissa. Big time. Like a whole month of

washing the dishes big time. The rat trap they shared in her hometown of Hoboken was all the two women could afford, and for the most part, they got along just fine.

In fact, they'd grown to be close friends over the three years they'd lived together. It was the only reason she'd ever agreed to this date from Hell.

Elissa sighed and looked over at Little Gianni. Maybe he wasn't all that bad?

"*BEEEELLLLLLLLCHHH!* 'Scuse me, doll. Better out, am I right?"

Gianni winked and Elissa wished for a black hole to open up and swallow her up right through the floor.

OMFG.

The man just burped out loud like he was in a frat boy belting contest, only those days passed him up about thirty years ago.

For fuck's sake. Gretchen, you so owe me.

Elissa cursed her roommate and tried not to groan. But Little Gianni wasn't quite done. The grown ass man lifted his leg and let one rip.

Right. Fucking. There.

Elissa was going to die before the end of the night.

Literally.

This is what you get when you do a friend a favor without asking for details! Idiota!

The voice of her Italian grandmother sounded in her brain. She tried to ignore it, willing herself not to wince at the man while he sucked air, and who knows what else, noisily through his coffee-stained teeth.

Ew. So gross.

That was the perfect word to describe it. The only word, in fact. The entire date was just so fucking gross. She still couldn't believe her sweet little roommate from Iowa, *Gretchen Kaepernick*, she of the wispy hair and baby blues, had set her up with this guy!

What the actual fuck was up with that?

Little Gianni was a slob. Actually, he looked just like her Uncle Nico, and that was not a good thing. Seriously, not good at all.

He wore his hair slicked back in a too tight ponytail that emphasized his rapidly receding hairline. As if that wasn't enough to put her off, he was sporting an enormous paunch. Now, being a curvy girl, Elissa appreciated food and was in no way against men showing the same appreciation.

She liked bigger men. Always had. But bigger did not mean you had to be sloppy. Little Gianni's stomach was literally hanging out from under a tight tan golf shirt that had definitely seen better days.

The man didn't even look like he had ever played a sport of any kind. With it, he wore brown polyester pants that were three inches above his ankles and unbuttoned at the waist.

He didn't look like he tried at all for this date. What kind of guy did that? His shirt collar was bent and wrinkled, and all three buttons were open to his chest, revealing a mat of oily, dark hair and pimples.

Somehow, he'd managed to tuck the back of the shirt in, but the front simply would not hold in that stomach. What worried her more were the tight brown pants.

As he sat back and stretched, she wondered if she should take cover. They looked like they were one bite from exploding off his body. Elissa shuddered at the image.

Please God, if You have an ounce of mercy, don't let that happen, she prayed.

"Hang on, doll, I gotta take this," he said, and turned to answer his cell phone.

It was ringing to the tune of '70s disco music she

hadn't heard since the last family reunion. Her eyes kept going to the huge stain on the front of his shirt. It was a little game she liked to call *what the hell is that*.

Coffee, she guessed.

"Up your ass, Bruno. I gotta have it by Monday," he cursed into the receiver.

Elissa winced at the spectacle he was making of them both. There were only a handful of people there, but still.

Deep breaths.

Ew. Maybe not.

She coughed as the strong body spray, that he'd obviously used a ton of in lieu of a shower, bad move in her opinion, invaded her lungs.

Oh, this was so bad.

Elissa was, by no means, a snob. But this guy looked like he'd stepped out of a bad 1980s mafia spoof film. What's worse, he kept smacking his lips together as he hung up the phone and looked her over from head to chest.

Thank fuck for the table, she thought, wishing she could hide her bosoms from his view.

"Ssssss," he hissed, like it was sexy or something.

She just grimaced. Elissa might be able to forgive a lot of quirks, but she hated mouth noises. Really hated them. It was a super pet peeve of hers. Never mind his totally inappropriate and unwelcomed leer.

She started counting the minutes, willing the date to be over already. Plenty of people would tell her she shouldn't be so choosy, but really? She was not this desperate.

Not yet anyway.

So, she was curvy and a little mouthy too. But was it wrong to want a man with good table manners? Even if men were thin on the ground for someone like her.

As a chef, she'd worked in a lot of restaurants and even as a personal cook for professional couples. She'd seen her fair share of unhappy couples and downright uncomfortable marriages. But as far as she was concerned, all relationships went downhill when good table manners were dismissed.

Good manners were merely a sign that a person was thoughtful and respectful. At least, that was what Nonna had told her. Gianni here had clearly missed that lesson as a child. Elissa had to work not to groan in disgust as he slurped a raw clam down his gullet.

Shudder.

Was there no end to his feeding? That's what it reminded her of. Feeding time at the zoo.

OMG. That was rude, she scolded herself. But it wasn't like she said it out loud.

All she wanted to do was go home. At least she was comfortable. *She'd* worn her softest pair of black leggings for this disaster date, paired with one of her favorite tunics on top.

It was dark green with tiny black buttons down the front and showed just the right amount of cleavage. She'd gone for neat and tidy as opposed to downright sexy.

Good call, in her opinion. Elissa looked perfectly fine for a nice *getting to know you* dinner, which is what she thought she was getting when her roommate asked her to step in for her on a blind date that one of her best client's had set up for her.

Elissa shuddered now, thinking how good old Gianni here would've reacted to the red dress and heels she'd contemplated before checking the weather report.

Gulp.

The lewd man was already salivating, and she was so not having it. Fending off his unwanted advances was not how she wanted to finish the night.

Ew again.

Elissa shivered, slightly chilled despite the fact

they were indoors. It was a cold, gloomy evening, and the forecast called for even more rain later that night. Not at all unusual for this time of year in the Garden State.

November was always chilly in the evenings, rainy too. Elissa tended to run warm, but she was glad she'd brought a jacket with her. Especially since her date refused to turn the heat on in the car.

When she'd asked, he'd looked offended and told her it wasted gas.

Um. Okay.

She checked her phone. It was only seven o'clock, but the two hour drive was still ahead of them. Maybe they could make it home before ten if they left soon.

Ugh. Did he just blow his nose?

"Allergies, doll. Say, you gonna eat that?" he asked before scooping a fry from her dish and swallowing it down.

Elissa was gonna kill her roomie. Gretchen was a hair and nail stylist. A lot of her clients were elderly, and they just loved her. They were always offering to set her up on blind dates with their nephews and grandsons.

Mostly, the sweet old ladies were kind. They swore they could find her curvy roommate the right man, assuming she was single because she was new to town. Well, when Elissa got home tonight, she was going to tell Gretchen she needed to fire the old lady who set this date up from being her client.

Like *ASAP*.

No one who liked Gretchen would've sent her out with this guy. Gianni reached over and touched her hand and Elissa pulled back, reaching for the napkin.

Gross.

"I sure hope you ain't a cold one, doll," he said, shaking his head.

"What?"

"Ain't gonna matter. I know just what you need, doll."

She was still wiping the greasy residue he'd transferred to her skin from the food he ate sans utensils. This was too much. Elissa was beyond uncomfortable with all the leering and bad attempts at innuendo.

Plus, she was starving. One look at the dump he'd taken her to, and she knew she could never eat there. The chef in her wouldn't allow it.

To think they drove two hours for this! She'd practically frozen to death in his maroon Cadillac, listening to a CD of the Rat Pack, while Gianni crooned loudly, and off key, to the music.

Normally, she was a fan of the famous group of legendary singers. Having grown up in Hoboken, she couldn't not be a Sinatra fan. Though, to be honest, Dean Martin had always been her favorite.

Still, Elissa was a firm believer that there were just some people you did not try to imitate. Especially not if you were Little Gianni. While he was belting his heart out, he'd been trying to get his right hand on her thigh. She'd asked him politely to stop.

Twice.

Then she'd been forced to try something a little more drastic. Like spilling her hot tea on the offending hand the third time he'd tried it. Finally, he'd removed his hand from her leg. Not making a fourth attempt, which she was grateful for.

Elissa should've taken that behavior as a sign and gotten out of the car. But no. She'd wanted to do Gretchen a solid. So, against her better judgement, she gave the creep another chance.

Idiota, her grandmother's voice echoed in her brain again.

The old woman had loved her. Elissa knew that without a doubt. She'd raised her after her own parents had passed on in a tragic automobile accident when Elissa was just twelve.

Her grandmother was a no-nonsense kind of lady who dished out priceless wisdom with brutally honest insights. It was the same way she dished out huge bowls of pasta with her amazing meatballs and homemade sauce. Not to mention a side order of back-breaking hugs that Elissa still missed.

Nonna cooked like that all the time. She made a huge pot of sauce every weekend, and she was happy to serve it to Elissa and her teammates and friends, especially after games and tournaments.

Soccer had been her sport of choice, and cooking had soon become her favorite hobby. Her grandmother had encouraged her in both pursuits. Guiding her in one and cheering her on in the other. Elissa still missed her terribly.

"Hey babe, ain't you gonna eat nothin'? You know they charge twenty dollars just to sit down," Little Gianni interrupted her train of thought.

Elissa was forced to turn her mind back to the present, which unfortunately included watching, *and hearing*, him as he sucked on his teeth and stuffed another breaded shrimp down his throat.

"I'm fine," she answered with a polite smile plastered on her face.

Just get home, Lissa. Just get him to take you home.

Elissa closed her eyes when he looked back down at his dish. Thank God for small favors, she mused. At least he was more interested in eating at the moment.

He'd taken her to the rattiest looking hotel and casino she'd ever seen in her life. And the buffet room?

Ew.

Seriously, the place had to be violating at least a dozen health codes. When Gianni had said Atlantic City, she'd thought at least the atmosphere would be exciting. But they were so far from the real glitz and entertainment, they might as well be anywhere else.

She sighed, looking at the plate she'd made for herself. Elissa couldn't even fake an interest in the food. As a chef, it was hard enough to dine out.

She was always judging the food, the service, the ingredients. How could she not? It was her business. And that was when the food was good!

This was not good. Not at all.

She'd been to hospitals that served better food. Old yellow lights buzzed and blinked around the buffet, giving it an abandoned kind of feel. The menu was made up of mostly frozen then fried or baked cuisine.

Reheated actually. It was like a giant TV dinner buffet where every item was previously frozen when already cooked and warmed up in an oven.

It was the kind of food sold cheap at restaurant supply stores in bulk. Yeah, this was much worse than hospital food, in her opinion.

There was a worn carpet on the floor, a handful of scattered tables in the dining room, elevator music on in the background, and the entire place smelled like canned soup.

Not to mention not one of the five people there besides them was under sixty years old.

"Gianni," she said, leaning forward so as not to hurt his feelings.

"I thought you mentioned something about seeing a show tonight. Is it here?"

Please don't be here.

If he was taking her somewhere else, she could beg off and hire a cab to take her home. There was no way she was sitting through anything else with this man. Not now. Not ever.

"Ah, I see, babe, you want some entertainment first, I get it," he snickered loudly, and she blanched.

Whatever he thought was going to happen wasn't. She needed to disabuse him of the notion, and fast.

"Alright, alright. Lemme finish this, babe. Then we'll go up to the room I got for us," he said.

Before she could make sense of the ludicrous statement, he slurped another fried shrimp, don't ask how. Then he grabbed her arm and yanked her from the seat before she could even react.

Elissa tugged on his hold, but the man was immovable. Tossing a five-dollar bill on the table, Little Gianni snatched a toothpick from the hostess stand before dragging her outside.

Great, he was a cheap tipper, too.

All she wanted was to go home. Figuring the best way to do that would probably be to get him to the car, she let him lead the way.

Once inside, she would ask him to drive back to Hoboken so she could wring Gretchen's neck. Fuming, she pulled her arm out of his hand and walked behind him.

The rain was really pouring, and the cheap bastard had refused valet. Elissa ducked her head so she wouldn't get so wet. Of course, the jacket she'd brought was light and had no hood.

Gianni had an umbrella, but he didn't offer to hold it for her, and honestly, she did not relish the idea of getting any closer to him than necessary.

Seriously, not happening.

Now all she had to do was break the news. She had no intention of watching a show or returning to the hotel with him.

What could go wrong?

Grab your copy at https://www.cdgorri.com/books/purrfectly-mated!

EXCERPT FROM BOUND BY AIR

Troy Waman looked down at his smartphone to the little red arrow blinking on his map app, indicating he had reached his destination. He frowned pensively before shaking his head.

"What a fucking shithole," he murmured to himself as he exited the nondescript black SUV his Station Master, Rex, had given him for the job.

"Try not to scratch it," the tough Bear shifter had said with a barely contained growl after their meeting the day before last. After a thousand years of waiting, The *Wardens of Terra* were being called to duty and this was Troy's first assignment.

It took him a day and a half to make his way to Shadowland, New York from the little suburb in Virginia Beach where his Station was located. There were dozens of them across the continental United States and even more overseas, though he'd rarely been out of the county himself.

Troy rolled his shoulders and exhaled. He was the first from his Station to be called to duty. A fact that left him both proud and humbled at the same time. He'd trained damn hard since he was a child waiting for such an opportunity. Now he had it, and it was almost too much to bear.

Fuck and damn. It's time Troy, get your ass in gear. That was all the sympathy he had for himself. Why the hell should he have any at all? Troy Waman was no tenderfoot normal. He was a Warden of Terra. He didn't need to remind himself of the honor and duty that went along with his position.

The *Wardens of Terra* were an ancient group of elite warriors. All of them Shifters. Identified in their youth and trained throughout their preternaturally long lives, they were guardians as well as fighters. *Station Masters* led teams of Wardens across the planet.

Though they'd been deactivated sometime in the last millennium, Wardens were born, chosen, and trained every day with the distinct knowledge that someday, they'd be called upon to defend the earth. That day was here.

Troy Waman had been trained as a Warden since before he learned how to spell the word. His heritage was a mix of Anglo and Native American. His father's blood was a mix of tribes including Algonquin, Lenape, Cherokee, and a few others. He hadn't stuck around long enough for anyone to learn the rest.

He supposed he could get a DNA test, but that might raise too many questions with the normals. Especially in this day of advanced technology in biogenetics.

Besides, it was quite common in today's world to find Native American peoples descended from multiple tribes. Troy Waman was uncommon for an entirely different reason. He was a Shifter, a special race of dual natured beings with one foot in the supernatural world and one in the human. Troy was a *Thunderbird Shifter* to be exact. Something unique even amongst Shifters.

He stretched his long, lithe body as he stepped away from the vehicle. It was already dark out despite it being fairly early in the evening. *Daylight savings my ass.* He sniffed the frigid air. The unusually high winds made the cold seem even more bitter. The street lamp stuttered on the corner, a rusty fence squeaked, and a black cat crossed the street, ducking under some parked cars. Troy's frown deepened.

It looked like the setting of a B-horror flick. All it needed was some half naked co-ed to run down the street with a masked bogeyman stalking behind her, traditional blood-coated knife in hand. *Oh yeah.* They might call it *Shadowland Nightmare* or something equally cheesy.

He stopped his musings and used his heightened senses to take in the downtrodden area around him. It would seem upstate New York wasn't all orchards and sprawling suburbs. He smirked as the "I love New York" song ran through his head. *Yeah, right.*

Apparently, parts of the Empire State were as fucked up as the street where he was born in Newark, New Jersey. He'd visited that shithole back when he was in his teens just out of curiosity. What a mistake that had been! He'd left almost as soon as he'd arrived. His extended family had been, shall we say, less than welcoming.

His gray-haired grandmother had screamed and crossed herself when he stepped over her threshold. He was what they called a *skin walker.* They feared and loathed him as something evil. Him evil? Like he was the motherfucker who knocked-up some unsuspecting normal and left her ass with a Shifter baby.

He was not evil, but he was something they did not understand. He'd been angry and ashamed that day. He'd crashed through his grandmother's kitchen to hitch a ride back down to his Station in Virginia Beach.

In his youth it was more like a military training camp, but it was all he knew of home. After all, it was where he'd lived his entire life. He'd made his peace and settled fully into his life there.

The incident with his grandmother had happened over a decade ago, when Troy had stolen his records out of Rex's office. Still, the memory remained fresh in his mind as if it were only yesterday. The fucked-up street where he was standing only brought back the painful reminder that he'd come from the same kind of squalor. *Fuck this,* he thought.

The pungent scent of despair washed over him. *Reminding him.* A young man with a hood pulled up over his head, eyed him from the street corner. *Drug dealer. Shadowland* indeed. It was an apt name for this shamble of a neighborhood.

The young man continued to stare until Troy allowed his beast to shine through. His golden eyes pinned the errant youth through the inky darkness of the night. Startled, the kid dropped the bag he was holding and ran down the alley.

Punk. Troy walked over and picked up what he had so hastily left behind. A couple of grams of crack cocaine and heroin, *probably cut with Fentanyl.* There were also various sized baggies full of what smelled like some below average marijuana and half-rotted psychedelic mushrooms.

Just your garden variety of illegal substances to be found on most street corners in neighborhoods like this one. *Fucking normals.* He frowned and dumped the still sealed contents down the closest storm drain. He sent a quick text to Rex earmarking the location.

Rex would make sure the local police department got an anonymous tip to retrieve the narcotics before someone got hurt. Recreational drug use, mainly the opioid epidemic, was wreaking havoc amongst the humans with more and more of them succumbing to their addictions.

It was troubling, but not Troy's problem. Shifters were extraordinarily hard to kill. Most human drugs had little to no effect on supernatural beings. *Normals,* he growled the thought, *such weak creatures.*

To be fair, Shifters had vices too. He just had little

experience with it. Cecil, a Station-mate of his, had an adrenaline addiction. He was always putting himself in dangerous situations, even during simple training exercises. Fernandez, a Jaguar Shifter, was always trying to get into some chick's pants. *Sex addict.* And he knew of others who channeled their energies into ways he considered to be mostly unproductive.

His opinion, for sure. He'd always been something of a loner by nature. There weren't many Thunderbird Shifters around. Hell, he was the only fucking one he knew of in this part of the world.

He didn't blame or judge his Station-mates for their proclivities. Most of the Shifters he knew had large appetites which included food, exercise, and sex.

Troy had certainly explored that part of him. He wasn't a man-whore or anything, but he'd had his share of women. None of them mattered to him. Just a means to satisfy the occasional itch.

Troy was determined to live his life as a Warden of Terra alone. He never expected to find anyone willing to share what was a potentially deadly existence.

Those who followed the Darkness and evil were always looking for ways to gain the upper hand and it was his job to stop them. The way he saw it, it was an honor and a duty to serve.

He shared this great responsibility with the entire organization. The core belief of the Wardens was based on one indisputable fact Shifters had walked the earth since the dawn of time, even before humankind; therefore, they were responsible for the well-being of the entire planet and all its inhabitants. Especially those who were inherently weaker. Mainly females and *normals*.

There were other supernaturals who believed humans, or normals as they referred to them, were a blight on the planet. Those creatures wished to destroy them and take over.

Demons, Dark Witches, and a whole plethora of evil beings sought the destruction of the normals and the world they lived in. *Idiots! Did they even realize if they destroyed the world, there would be nothing left? Where the fuck would they live?*

Of course, the supernatural world had many agencies that worked towards the common goal of saving the planet. The *Order of the Guardians*, for example, were responsible for policing the various factions of supernaturals.

Shifters generally tended to ally themselves with the Guardians. Sure, there were *bad* Shifters, but he'd never come across any willing to follow the Dark. Simply because most agreed the destruction of the world could not be allowed to happen.

Different Packs and Clans, etcetera, of course, had different ideas. Some wanted to remain secret, others wished to come out, and other still wanted to rule the weaker humans. It was a whole fucking thing, and they argued about regularly.

Troy didn't know from any of that. He spent little time in the human world. His efforts better spent making himself worthy of being a Warden. Training, exercise, and following orders. That's what Troy lived for, it was why he was chosen.

Thunderbird Shifters were very rare. *Special.* He scoffed at the stray thought. But no matter what way he looked at it, Troy was indeed unique. In more ways than one. He was born *marked* by the stars. A *Shifter of Terra.*

From infancy, he was told he carried the power of his sign within him. *Aquarius* ruled his destiny and it would aid him in the never-ending battle against the forces of darkness.

Every single Warden he knew was a Shifter like him. They were the fiercest warriors on the planet. Like many others throughout the last thousand years, Troy, *a Shifter child who was marked,* was taken from his parents and trained by his Station Master until the time when he would be called into use.

All that time, he thought, *and here I am.* He tried to ignore the pressure building inside of him. He felt anxious. His animal pressed against his psyche, comforting him with his presence.

The significance of the moment was not lost on him. The Wardens had waited a millennium to be called to act. *He* had been waiting his entire life.

"Do not fear the future, Troy," the Herald who had visited his Station said to him when he'd brought word that they had been activated, *"Your destiny awaits."*

Troy wondered if the old man referred to the Wardens finally being called to act, or if the elder spoke of yet another legend. Troy had been shocked to say the least when the Herald had entered their tidy little Station in Virginia Beach with his flowing white hair. After he told them the news, he turned to Troy and recited another old tale.

"Young Thunderbird, you are the first to return us to Terra. Do not doubt your worth. Your destiny has been written in the stars since before you were born, Troy Waman. Remember, a Warden discovers his true measure when his fated mate is thrust upon him."

Whatever the fuck that meant. Troy looked down at

his phone, then to the street sign on the corner, and finally, to the faded numbers painted on the mailbox in front of the ramble of a house his map app had brought him to.

Fuck, am I thinking? Fated mates are myths. Stories made up so orphaned Shifters would sleep through the night. He scoffed at the thought. Memories of tales the head nurse, Sr. Maria, had told him at the training camp he'd called home for years invaded his brain.

Memories were pesky things. Sometimes eternal, and always fucking portable. But he was no longer a child. *No more stories, Sister. Now, I act.*

"A thousand years we've waited, and I'm walking into a fucking scene from a bad episode of *Hoarders*," Troy shook his head and frowned at the decrepit house that sat a few hundred feet away from him.

It was cold as fuck outside and his leather jacket did little to warm him. Avian Shifters did not carry around the same bulk as other types of Shifters. He ran hotter than normals, but the single digit temperature froze him to the bone.

True, he wasn't beefy like some of his fellow Shifters, but he was just as incredibly strong, and he was wicked fast. Much stronger than any average male. He paused briefly gauging the atmosphere.

There was something off about the place. He scented *Magic* and something else. His Bird bristled beneath his skin. *Easy now.*

Lightning flashed in the darkened skies, allowing him to see the worn shingles, and cracked siding of the beaten-up colonial in greater detail. More than one window had been smashed and boarded up with cheap plywood.

If anything, it enhanced the creepy haunted house feel of the place. The porch sagged dangerously. He wondered how the place had managed to not be condemned by the town. One thing was certain, it was an ugly little turd of a house.

Who the hell put gray siding on their house anyway? Maybe it wasn't always that color. Maybe the owner liked gray. *Whatever.* He couldn't give two shits about the siding.

His only concern was the increased supernatural activity in the area over the past two weeks. Ever since the owner, a *Mrs. Renalda Curosi,* passed away. *A haunting?*

A creaking sound floated up to his ears and he stilled his movements. The sound developed into more of a *moaning* noise. An unearthly wail. It grew louder as the lightning continued to flash in the sky.

Troy had never seen a ghost. True, there were a

lot of things in the universe he had never seen nor heard of, but that didn't make them any less real.

If ghosts were real, and they made noises, he imagined that pitiful wail was damn close to what it would sound like.

No such thing as ghosts. Yeah, well, most people had never heard of Shifters either. And yet, there he stood.

His Thunderbird shifted once more beneath his skin, the beast flexing his senses as the lightning in the air drew him to the surface. *No.* He told his other half. His human needed to be in control now. He walked across the street, keeping to the shadows.

Something was indeed off about the creepy old house. He inched further to the black door. The knocker was in the shape of a face or mask. No discernible features, just a vague impression of eyes, nose, and mouth. *Shadowland indeed.*

He listened with his enhanced hearing and frowned. There was a distinct voice somewhere beneath the moaning and creaking. A *female* voice. His curiosity was piqued.

From what he'd seen in her file, Mrs. Curosi was ninety-seven when she passed. Her closest living relative was a half-sister, a *Magdelena Kristos,* and she lived over three hours away in New Jersey. The half-sister was cut from Mrs. Curosi's will recently. She'd bequeathed her entire estate, house, bank account, and all her earthly belongings, to someone named *A. Kristos. Another sister? Maybe.*

Troy hadn't given it much thought until now. A crash sounded from inside the house. He perked up as the feminine voice he'd thought he'd heard earlier screamed in pain. *Time to act.*

Grab your copy at https://www.cdgorri.com/books/bound-by-airbooks/bound-by-air!

ABOUT THE AUTHOR

C.D. Gorri is a USA Today Bestselling author of steamy paranormal romance and urban fantasy. She is the creator of the Grazi Kelly Universe.

Join her mailing list here: https://www.cdgorri.com/newsletter

An avid reader with a profound love for books and literature, when she is not writing or taking care of her family, she can usually be found with a book or tablet in hand. C.D. lives in her home state of New Jersey where many of her characters or stories are based. Her tales are fast paced yet detailed with satisfying conclusions.

If you enjoy powerful heroines and loyal heroes who face relatable problems in supernatural settings, journey into the Grazi Kelly Universe today. You will find sassy, curvy heroines and sexy, love-driven heroes who find their HEAs between the pages. Werewolves, Bears, Dragons, Tigers, Witches, Romani, Lynxes, Foxes, Thunderbirds, Vampires, and many more Shifters and supernatural creatures dwell within her worlds. The most important thing is every mate in this universe is fated, loyal, and true lovers always get their happily ever afters.

Want to know how it all began? Enter the Grazi Kelly Universe with Wolf Moon: A Grazi Kelly Novel or pick up Charley's Christmas Wolf and dive into the Macconwood Pack Novel Series today.

For a complete list of C.D. Gorri's books visit her website here:

https://www.cdgorri.com/complete-book-list/

Thank you and happy reading!

del mare alla stella,
    C.D. Gorri

Follow C.D. Gorri here:
    http://www.cdgorri.com
    https://www.facebook.com/Cdgorribooks

https://www.bookbub.com/authors/c-d-gorri

https://twitter.com/cgor22

https://instagram.com/cdgorri/

https://www.goodreads.com/cdgorri

https://www.tiktok.com/@cdgorriauthor